True Colours

ANTHEA SYROKOU

Anthea Syrokou
True Colours
ISBN-13: 978-0648157458

antheasyrokou.com

For Mum and Dad

CHAPTER ONE

It was a humid morning, the sort that marks a typical Sydney summer. Tess hastily pulled the letter from its delicate white envelope, which bore a stamp featuring a London cab. As she unfolded it, her heart raced with anticipation, and she felt the *joie de vivre* she always did when she received a letter from her dear friend, Cathy. She read the opening line and laughed. Back at school, so many years ago, she and Cathy were fond of reading the classics. They'd always imagined living back in the day where manners and conversation were as refined as the polished silver that graced the elaborately dressed tables in the dining halls of aristocratic manors. The letters they wrote captured the essence of such eras.

Tess read the letter with an exuberant heart.

Dear Tess,

I hope I find you well, and that life has been treating you with the utmost benevolence. Of course, I am almost certain you will rise above anything that vexes you, as it is a faculty of your nature to find it in your generous heart and good-natured disposition to do just that.

I was astonished to hear about the unbearable heat you have been having, and I shall inform you that in the city of London, nature has been most forgiving and kind, offering its surprising warmth to spread in abundance throughout the day, while the nights have not been as anywhere close to the harshness of last year's dreadful winter, which cast its mean spirit of vengeance upon us all. I was in a state of dysfunction through most of those long, dreary months, but it is with great pleasure that I write and inform you that this is no longer the case. Rather, my present state is quite the opposite.

I have been busy at work, keeping my spirits high, occupied in pleasant and heartfelt occupation, delighting many with my ability to style and cut hair to a most agreeable fashion. Many of the fine ladies, and even the gentlemen, are of amiable character and share their fondness of my work with great enthusiasm and with a generous heart. Servitude can be humanity's friend as the soul can become as restless as the wind, if one is not engaged in some means to otherwise satisfy their inner longings and need for action.

LOL!

Okay … enough of that for now. All the above is true. In simpler words, although I know you don't always do simple in these letters, unless you really need to talk, I can't believe I heard from your ex. He actually called me about how I find living in London, as he mentioned he might be transferring here soon. Sounds like Michael's fast becoming a man of great importance, so to speak, and that he has acquired a different situation, too! Isn't that weird? Although, I must say, I've had a few conversations with him lately. I hope you don't mind. I know you were once married to him, but we were all friends in high school, and I'd feel bad giving him the cold shoulder, or should I say, to treat him less agreeably.

I'm looking forward to visiting Sydney soon — I really miss all of you. I just found out that my mum has another tattoo on her arm. I can't believe she has more than me now. I might just have to get another one too. I'll send you a photo if I do. Oh, and my hair is now jet black — for the time being, anyway.

I can't wait to hear from you soon, as I hold you in the highest esteem. I hope the salon is going well, and I won't mention anything about any potential suitors. I remember the pact you made with Pamela — about not needing men in your lives. We'll see how that turns out, for at the age of six-and-twenty years, you are at a natural inclination to meet a suitor. I'll stop right there, shall I? :)

Lots of love,

Your "best" friend always,

Cathy xxx

Tess smiled as she folded the letter and placed it back in her bag. *Michael might be moving to London*, she thought, sighing with regret, her smile slowly fading. She didn't have time to process it all right then. She had to get back to her client, who was waiting to have her highlights done.

Tess began to mix the colour. She swirled the pale blue mixture around with the long-handled tint brush, creating lovely lines and ripples. The strong smell exuding from the dye and the lightener tore through the icy air-conditioned air, mounting a challenge against the 90s café-chill music that had created a mellow vibe all morning. Tess had found one of her mother's old CDs when she'd visited her parents in the country a few weekends ago. The music blended beautifully with the cool air in the salon and the lazy, sunny summer's day.

She hurried back towards her client, a woman in her early twenties named Briana who had long, lustrous, shiny brown hair. Briana sat patiently in the black leather chair, examining her youthful features in the mirror before her. Tess placed the rectangular-shaped pieces of aluminium foil onto the tray beside her one by one, admiring her nails as she worked. The deep hue — almost black — was her usual colour of choice, that or a rich burgundy red.

"I love the colour of your nails," Briana said as Tess skilfully separated strands of the young woman's hair with the pointed end of the tint brush, then brushed the lightener onto the narrow sections.

"Thanks!" Tess replied.

"I can't wait to have highlights!" Briana exclaimed, excited. "I've got another party on tomorrow night, for work."

"It won't be long now," Tess replied, catching sight of her next client in the polished mirror as she applied another piece of foil to Briana's hair. *Her colour's grown out,* Tess thought, sneaking another glance at the woman, who was sitting on the light brown leather lounge near the entrance to the salon, her eyes scanning analytically as she scrolled down the screen of her phone. In the past, her face would have been hidden behind a magazine, plucked from one of the piles neatly stacked on the small, glass coffee table next to the lounge. Now, she wondered why they even bothered with them. Everyone was on their phones these days, although some of their old school clients seemed to still peruse them occasionally.

In the reflection, Tess saw Helena, the florist across the street from the salon, gracefully place a fresh bouquet of flowers in a silver bucket out the front of her shop. The pink, burgundy and white petals, set amongst a spray of green, created beauty in the morning sunshine. Helena appeared to be deep in thought as she walked along the street, away from the shop, looking towards the cobalt sky, her eyes squinting in the glare of the hot sun. *Put them back inside. It's way too hot!* Tess thought. She smiled as Helena obviously came to the same conclusion, returning to the shop and taking the flowers back in.

"I can't believe this heat we're having. It's unbearable!" cried an older woman as she stepped briskly into the salon, fidgeting with the strap of her bag irritably and straightening her blouse, which seemed to be stuck to her with perspiration. She combed her hair with long fingers as she caught a glimpse of herself in the mirror.

"Hello, Mrs Sanders," Tess replied with a warm smile. "Don't worry. It's lovely in here with the air conditioning." She pushed her freshly-cut, rose-brown fringe to the side and adjusted her ponytail. Pamela, her friend and business partner, had given her a haircut earlier that morning, and she was still getting used to having a fringe.

"Hi Mrs Sanders," Pamela called out as she walked out of the back room, giving the older woman a warm smile. Her hair, cut into a short, chocolate brown bob, bounced with every move she made.

"Okay, I'll let the foils do their job," Tess said to Briana.

"Sure," Briana said, smiling at herself in the mirror. The pieces of foil formed a blunt, square shape around her face. "I look like Cleopatra!" she exclaimed. "Maybe that's what I should be for the dress-up party. It's on next Saturday."

Before Tess had the chance to ask if she wanted a magazine, Briana was on her mobile, happily sending a text message.

"Tess, if you have a few seconds, can you take the towels to the laundromat?" Pamela asked. "We're running short." She plugged the hair dryer into the outlet, then switched it on. She turned to Mrs Sanders and said, reassuringly, "I'll be with you in a minute."

"Yes, yes. You do what you have to do," Mrs Sanders said as she picked up one of the magazines. "What are they wearing these days? I'll never understand it. They call this fashion?" She studied the cover of the magazine carefully.

Tess smiled to herself. Mrs Sanders lived in a neighbourhood that was full of diverse types of people, and was a hub of creativity. It had changed immensely over the decades she had lived there. The older woman often feigned disdain for the younger generations and their trends, but Tess felt she secretly enjoyed living there. There was so much activity around her that she could never feel lonely.

"There are some pieces inspired by the Victorian era," Tess offered.

Mrs Sanders lifted her head up from the magazine, and contemplated Tess' outfit. "You dress really nicely," she said. "Your dress, with the gold buttons all the way to the neck — it looks really lovely. I don't know about the hair colour though, and the nails," she continued, eyeing her sceptically.

"Thought I'd try something different for a change. The dress is from the vintage shop a few shops down. I love the Georgian and the Victorian era — Jane Austen, the Bronte sisters, and all that," Tess said excitedly, remembering her plan to read *Jane Eyre* that night. She pictured a night seated in her cosy armchair with a pot of Earl Grey tea, some gourmet sandwiches from the deli, reading until way past midnight.

"You're quite the romantic, aren't you?" Mrs Sanders noted. She took off her glasses and studied Tess carefully.

"Why aren't you married? I've never heard of you dating anyone since I started coming here."

Tess flicked her fringe awkwardly, taken aback at the sudden digression. An image of Michael, her ex-husband, instantaneously flashed through her mind, and she instinctively looked at Pamela for support. Her friend already had her chance to field the very same question from Mrs Sanders in the past, and gave Tess a knowing smile.

"Um, I don't know … I'm busy with the salon … There's no time for that," Tess managed, feeling like Mrs Sanders' eyes were peering into her fragile soul. Her heart beat rapidly and her face felt warm. All eyes were on her. Even Briana sacrificed a second's glance away from her phone, and turned to look at her, eyeing her dress as well.

"Tess doesn't need a man. She's too independent," Briana declared. She examined her. "That dress is so romantic and vogue … you look so cool and alternative. My friends would love it. Besides, who needs *one* man when you can go out with a few." Her two cents added, Briana looked down at her phone again.

Tess was grateful for Briana's interposition, even if Mrs Sanders seemed to be completely flabbergasted by her comment. Tess' embarrassment quickly turned to surprise. She wasn't used to being called "cool". Alternative, perhaps. She was definitely different, but the word "cool" conjured up images of the athletic girls and boys back at school who hung out together all the time, seated at the back of the class with their effortless beauty and incomparable talents, who talked about … Her mind suddenly failed her. She didn't actually know what they used to talk about. To Tess, it had always looked like they had so much to say, including the cutting words of judgment that spilt through their plastered, almost sour smiles, as though they were on a cruise ship drinking margaritas, looking down on the mere deck crew. In fact, they only thing she remembered hearing them talking about of any significance was *her*. They'd snickered and giggled every time she'd passed them, muttering cruelties, as they did in the presence of most of their inferiors. Otherwise, the few times she'd accidentally eavesdropped on them, they'd seemed to be talking about nothing much at all. It was all just idle chit-chat, behind that veneer of looking like they had so much to say. The girls often looked interested yet staggered when talking to any of the boys in the group. Their mouths hung open in surprise; Tess would often wonder if they ever swallowed a fly or some other airborne creature. If they did they would never have noticed. Their focus on the boys was so intense that even a wasp hovering by their agape mouths, or even trying to make a nest in their hair, wouldn't distract them.

"What am I doing?" Tess suddenly cried, brought back from her reverie by the smell of peroxide. "I'd better go to the laundromat before it's time to wash Briana's hair," she said, eager to end Mrs Sanders' analysis.

"Now I know!" Mrs Sanders shrilled, her high-pitched voice sending shockwaves around the salon, and rippling through Tess' body. "Now I know."

"Sorry?" Tess asked, perplexed. "Now you know what?"

"Now I know who you look like! *The model on the cover of this magazine*. You have the same amber-coloured eyes, the same cheekbones. If your hair was a lighter brown colour, you would be identical."

"Oh … *do I?*" Tess queried, trying to discretely look at the magazine cover while desperately trying to hide the fact that she was flattered. As irritating as Mrs Sanders could be, she had the unique ability to make her feel special — glamorous, important even.

"Anyway, I'd better go," she called to Pamela over the whooshing sound of the hair dryer. "I won't be too long. Can you keep an eye on Briana's hair?"

Pamela nodded. "Sure thing. See you soon." Pamela's client, a slim blonde woman named Jessica, seemed to be deep in thought, and had been since she'd entered the salon. Tess had seen her there a few times before. *She must be in her early thirties*, Tess speculated, *just a few years older than me*. She seemed to be upset about something. Tess wondered what had her looking so melancholic.

As Tess stepped out of the busy salon and onto the narrow footpath, she felt like she'd just entered a sauna. Unbuttoning the top button of her pale pink, floral chiffon dress, she looked back through the shopfront window at the woman with the melancholic eyes. She then turned and saw Helena through the black French doors of her lovely flower shop. She waved to her from across the street. Tess loved seeing Helena working, carefully placing flowers in beautiful, delicate pink or purple tissue paper. A feeling of happiness would wash over her as she gazed at all the beautiful colours. Sometimes, Helena would use floral tissue paper to wrap the bouquets, reminding Tess of some of the beautiful books on her bookshelves at home, written in a time when etiquette was treated with the utmost importance. Tess always felt that she belonged in those eras — that she would have fit in perfectly.

Tess contemplated buying some flowers for her flat to accompany her planned reading night-in as she walked briskly along the street. She came to a sudden halt when she noticed some elegant perfume bottles in the window of the shop owned by her friend Millie. Millie's shop was a delight to visit, stocked with perfumes, lipsticks, and other makeup from Paris that was hard to find elsewhere in Sydney. Tess would often muse about the French city as she admired the products through the display window.

"Tess!" Millie appeared by her side. "How've you been? I must remember to stop by and make a hair appointment. I thought I'd try something different." She ran her hands through her light brown shoulder-length hair, looking at Tess as if waiting for her opinion.

"I'm fine," Tess responded. "You know, keeping busy. I'm off to the laundromat. Come by whenever you get a chance. So did those matte lipsticks come in yet … from Paris?" Tess' eyes widened. "They're so old Hollywood," she said, hugging the laundry bag in her arms.

"You're such a romantic. You're always in a world of your own … in a good way, that is. Speaking of romance, have you seen Silvio lately? He finished refurbishing the restaurant. It looks so old-world. It has a grand, romantic vibe now — right up your alley, I'd say," she said with a cheeky smile.

"Um, no, I haven't seen it."

"You should take a look. They even have a new barista. He makes the best coffee. It's divine. He's not that bad in the looks department either — although I don't think he holds a candle to Silvio," Millie continued in the same mischievous tone. "I'm sure Silvio will be happy to see you," Millie added, studying Tess' expression.

"Millie, you never give up. I don't need romance. Yes, I'm a romantic, but I'd rather find my romance in my books. That's all I need to keep me happy. It's a lot less complicated," Tess said, nodding at her friend as she turned and walked away, feeling Millie's smile lingering behind her.

Moments later, after leaving the towels at the laundromat, Tess crossed the street to take a look at Silvio's newly refurbished restaurant. She wanted to see the changes he'd made, without seeing the man himself, or him seeing her. As she gazed through the window adorned with fancy gold writing, she was left speechless. *It's so beautiful,* she thought. The smell of fresh coffee awakened her senses as she admired the decadent space. Silvio really had gone all out. The front bench had been replaced —now, it was no longer fashioned from contemporary, industrial-looking steel, but from brilliant gold sheet metal. The tables were festooned with black and white floral tablecloths. Crystal chandeliers hung from ornate ceilings, and the walls were bedecked with Calacatta gold and pink marble. Ancient-looking Roman sculptures perched in the corners added to the grandiosity.

As she peered around the gorgeous place, Tess noticed Silvio standing near the coffee machine. His longish dark brown wavy hair, covered part of his olive-skinned stubbled face. Another man stood beside him. She felt an odd, uneasy pain in her heart. She turned and quickly walked away, hurrying back to the salon.

"Sorry I took a while," Tess cried, closing the glass door behind her.

"That's okay. The colour has worked out great," Pamela explained. "Briana's already been shampooed and conditioned, and I also added the toner, so she's good to go."

"Have you seen what they've done to Silvio's?" Tess asked as she took the scissors and small comb from the tray and placed a strand of Briana's wet hair between her fingers, ready to begin the task of layering it. "The usual?" she confirmed.

Briana nodded, looking up from her phone. "Silvio? He's hot!"

Tess could see Pamela's grin reflected in the mirror. She would often tease Tess about him — practically the whole street knew he was smitten with her. Tess had to admit, he was handsome and charming, and a big flirt as well. But she was too busy for men; she had too much going on in her life. Plus, she had made that pact with Pamela … Neither of them needed men in their lives to be happy. They needed their independence, and they both had their sad stories of relationships that had become as stale as the breadsticks at Silvio's in the hot summer heat.

"But have you seen the new barista?" Briana exclaimed. "Now *that's* a sight you wouldn't wanna miss. He's the whole package. I've gotta tell my friends to go and hang out there."

Tess gave Pamela a knowing look. Her friend grinned back at her.

By now, the melancholic blonde woman had left the salon. Mrs Sanders was immersed in a magazine, her head covered in dye. Tess gave the woman still waiting on the lounge by the doors an apologetic look. "Won't be long," she said, politely.

She continued cutting the ends of Briana's hair in a slightly diagonal line to create the layers. She then smiled to herself, remembering her planned evening with Charlotte Bronte and a pot of Earl Grey tea. She would buy some flowers, she decided. She paused and turned to look at the flower shop. The melancholic blonde woman was there, looking at the bouquets. Tess watched as she walked inside the shop, before evidently changing her mind and retreating as Helena approached her. *Poor woman*, Tess thought. *She looks really lost.*

The same odd, uneasy feeling tugged at Tess' heart when she saw a confident, sophisticated woman dressed in a crisp white dress cross the street. She held two beautiful light green boxes and a bag. They were from Millie's shop. There was something about her that made Tess wary, but she wasn't sure why. She turned back to the job at hand, but before she brought the scissors to Briana's hair once more, she turned to look at the woman again. By now, she had become a speck of white in the distance. Tess recalibrated her thoughts, and thought of the smell of ink on cream paper. Her momentary break from pleasantness subsided, and was replaced once more with comfort and tranquillity.

CHAPTER TWO

After she had finished for the afternoon, Tess headed over the street with roses in mind. "Hi Helena," Tess greeted her friend, admiring her polished appearance. Helena's dark brunette hair was tied back neatly, and her red lipstick made her skin glow.

"That's the lipstick from Millie's, isn't it? She's getting the matte ones soon. I can't wait!" Tess suddenly noticed that Helena appeared disengaged. Usually she loved talking about the products in Millie's shop, but today she was distracted.

"Are you okay?" Tess asked, concerned. "You seem to be in bad spirits. Is anything wrong?"

"I'm sorry, Tess," Helena said, with a hint of a quiver in her husky voice. "I'm fine. *Bad spirits?* You've been reading your English classics again, haven't you? Next you'll say that I look *vexed.* I am a bit down today. It must be the heat. I'm not really one for summer. I like to feel comfortable in my clothes. It's just that … I don't know … something seems off lately. I feel like … I don't know, like someone's watching me. It's almost as if something is about to happen, but I don't know what. Do you know what I mean? I know I'm not making any sense. Maybe it's because I breathe these fragrant floral smells in and out all day."

Tess straightened her dress. She too had an uneasy feeling, like something strange was in the air. "I'm sure it's nothing. Maybe it's the extreme heat."

Helena nodded. "You could be right. Anyway, what can I get for you? I know you'll love these," she said, pointing at some pale pink roses. "I saw you beaming at them the moment you stepped inside. They're lovely, aren't they? And very romantic. Splendid choice, my dear!" She was back to her chirpy old self again.

Helena smiled warmly, although her eyes still hinted at a slight uneasiness. Tess watched as she expertly placed the roses in the floral tissue paper and gently wrapped them up. Tess handed her credit card over. She placed the fragrant flowers to her nose, and revelled in the sweet-scented air.

"Have a nice night, Tess. Thanks for stopping by."

"You too. Say hi to Carter for me," said Tess, referring to Helena's husband.

"Sure," Helena said, almost dismissively.

Tess stepped out onto the sun-drenched footpath, and walked proudly with her purchase in her hands. Her open-toed mules with a slight heel beat melodiously as she walked along, admiring the interesting boutique shops. A few doors down, the cupcake shop caught her attention. The colours of the magical rainbow sprinkles brought out the little girl in her. She then stopped in front of the small art gallery, where she admired the many creative and somewhat unorthodox paintings and sculptures. Tess instantly thought of her mother — she was so proud of her for opening her studio full of arts and crafts in Lorikeet Creek, the country town she grew up in, in the New South Wales Mid North Coast region. Her mother had come so far, yet throughout her childhood, Tess was teased for her parents' choices. Their artistic lifestyle had been a source of amusement for her schoolmates, whose families undertook more traditional occupations.

Tess coloured as she remembered the mockery. "What's that picture on your dress, Tessie? Are you wearing mummy's dressie? Tess is wearing her mum's dress everyone. Isn't she adorable?" The sharp, piercing voice echoed in her head. Tess recalled the humiliation as the popular girls doubled over in mocking laughter, obviously wanting Tess and everyone around them to hear and feel their condescension. She had endured a whole year of primary school with "Queen Desiree" — the most popular girl in school — and her gang of mean boys and girls. But then in high school the snickering only became worse as the small popular group expanded into a much larger popular group, as similarly cruel girls and boys migrated from the neighbouring school when it closed down. Then, there were even more of them to make her life hell.

Tess never understood why she was chosen as the target for that type of vindictiveness — for their entertainment. In the circles her parents ran in, they were admired. They were considered true artists. Her dad was a musician who toured with some of Australia's most renowned rock bands, and her mother was a talented painter and dressmaker, who also dabbled in different sorts of crafts. Her work was sought out by Australian and international boutiques alike, and her prints had been used to adorn cushion covers, wallpaper, rugs and even fine china.

Tess cringed as she remembered another incident. The popular group always made sure Tess was mocked for her skinny frame. She took after her mother, who was tall and slim, almost boyish in appearance.

"That outfit looks so hot on you, Tess," she recalled Desiree saying, "I mean, if you're going for the *flat as a pancake* look!" Desiree and the other girls had giggled loudly, making sure the boys in the group had heard the witticism.

"Hey, cool it," Stewart Haymes, one of the boys in the group, had said.

Desiree had looked disdainfully in his direction. "Well, I'm just stating the obvious. You gotta admit, she still looks like a little girl. Nothing up top. Not like us," she said, looking around at her friends. "I mean, we're all pretty hot, right? We've got all the curves in all the right places. I'd say, we've got it going on, wouldn't you, Stewy?" Desiree had tossed her hair and pushed her chest out, emphasising her assets.

"Yeah you're … what you said," he'd stammered. "But Tess is … Well, she's …" He'd nervously paused when he looked at Desiree's staggered, impatient expression.

"She's *what*, Stewart?"

Stewart had dared to look her straight in the eyes. Regaining his assertion, he blurted in a loud, confident voice: "She's gorgeous." He held the stare, while Desiree looked like she would collapse from shock.

"*What did you say?*" Desiree had challenged, almost gasping for air.

"You heard me," he said casually, lowering his voice. "I think she's gorgeous," he'd repeated, still looking straight into Desiree's wide eyes. "She could be a model." He grinned ever so slightly as Desiree lost all ability to construct a sentence and stood there, agape.

Tess' heart had beat madly. She couldn't believe someone had challenged Queen Desiree so boldly — right in front of *her*, Tess, the girl who was the star of all her jokes, without having ever auditioned for the part. What happened next practically restored her faith in humanity. Stewart walked over to her. She felt his blue-grey eyes peer into her soul as he uttered the words that left her feeling like she was in one of her romance novels: "Don't ever let anyone tell you any different, Tess."

Stewart Haymes had gone in to bat for her, and had risked his reputation in the in-group. Tess always felt she was somehow connected to him from then on, as if they shared their own private secret. To her, it was akin to the bond that developed when two people went through a life and death situation together, and in those intensely hormonal and melodramatic teenage years, that seemed a justifiable comparison.

Another similar incident came to Tess' mind, one that also highlighted this feeling she always felt, that she and Stewart had a connection. Tess recalled the time when she had done remarkably well in her English essay. Their teacher had decided to read it out to the rest of the class. Before she had announced that she would read it though, Tess had snuck a glance at Stewart who was sitting to the left of her in the front of the classroom, despite the fact that the popular group always sat at the back. He had looked at his essay with a tight jaw when the teacher handed it back to him. His eyes appeared vulnerable and teary. The letter "D" stood out in red ink as Tess discretely looked towards his desk. Upon hearing her name, he immediately sat up straight, and diverted his focus to the teacher standing in front of the classroom. Tess had noticed that his teary eyes had begun to shine with admiration. He listened to her essay with unwavering interest. When the teacher had finished reading it, he'd gazed over to Tess' desk. His eyes had looked searchingly into hers. He gave her an approving nod before looking back at his desk.

After gathering her belongings when class was over, Tess had walked towards the door. Stewart was waiting there.

"Congrats, Tess. You did really well. It was such a well-written essay. You must be really proud of yourself," he'd said with intent.

"Thanks ... Stewart. Um ... how did *you* go?" she'd asked him, sensing that he wanted to talk about it.

"Definitely not as good as you did." He had paused before continuing. "It doesn't matter. It's okay. I'm really glad for you," he had said with an affectionate, heartfelt smile.

Before she could respond, one of his friends from the football team had grabbed him by the arm.

"Hey Stewart, you gotta get changed. The coach won't wait for slackers."

All Tess could do was to look on with a fluttering heart as she quickly lost him to a sea of blue and black football jerseys.

It does matter, she had thought. *It matters to you ... and it matters to me.*

"Hello, pretty Tess. What can I get for you today?" Mr Papas' voice boomed out from behind the counter. Tess couldn't even remember stepping into the deli. She had been in her own world. *Pretty Tess,* she thought, grinning to herself. Mr Papas could be old-fashioned, but there was a sweetness beneath it all.

Her stomach growled as she eyed the gourmet ingredients laid out in the Bain Marie before her.

"Hi, Mr Papas," she said to the elderly man. "Everything smells so nice."

"I just made the best sandwiches, with the freshest ingredients. I think they're all winners," he said with pride.

"I'm sure they are," Tess replied, her eyes combing all the wonderful treats imported from different regions around Australia, New Zealand, and various parts of Europe and the UK. "I think I'll have a mixture of the salmon and herbed butter tea sandwiches with fresh dill, and also a few of the cucumber tea sandwiches."

"Okay. I see I can't keep you away from the traditional English flavours."

Tess smiled. "They *are* my favourites. Oh, and do you have the tea from Derbyshire you had last time?"

"Yes, as it happens, I have a few boxes left. I'm sure you appreciate the beautiful image of the landscape on the packet, from the English countryside."

Tess looked at the elegant box and the image of an old manor amidst rolling fields. She could practically imagine Heathcliff, from Emily Bronte's *Wuthering Heights*, stomping in with his wet boots from the moors, top hat, attitude and all.

"So, are you having company over?" Mr Papas asked, eyeing the pink roses resting on the counter.

"Oh no," Tess jumped in, frowning at the thought. The only company she wanted was Jane and Mr Rochester, and perhaps St John, depending on what page she got up to. "I don't need company. I've got my books. I get to see whoever I want, wherever they may be in the world." Her frown disappeared at the thought, and she smiled in anticipation of her relaxing night-in that would transport her to a different world.

"Well, as long as you're content," Mr Papas said. "I mean, as long as that pretty smile isn't hiding anything."

"What do you mean? I'm happy with my own company. I see people all day in the salon. It's my quiet time at home."

Mr Papas looked at her intently for a moment. "I believe you," he continued, "but know that sometimes the mouth might be smiling while the heart is frowning."

Tess paused and thought for a moment. "That's quite profound," she said as she handed her credit card over. "Like I said though, I'm perfectly fine."

"Sure, you don't need to convince me," he said, looking at her with scepticism. "So, to change the topic, have your parents visited you recently?"

"No, but I visited them a few weekends ago. My mum has just opened up a new studio to house all her paintings. Various companies have been using her work on homewares, wallpaper, and other things." Tess beamed with pride. "They might even use it for tea packets, who knows? Her work is in great demand. I'm so proud of her, and of my dad, for following their dreams." Her cheeks became hotter as she got carried away.

"You really are a wonderful daughter. My kids don't ever visit me, except if they need babysitting. They all have kids now."

A darkness descended upon the small shop for a few moments as something blocked out the sunshine that had poured in through the window moments before. Tess turned and caught sight of the confident blonde woman wearing the white dress passing by the shop again. She felt a tight pain in her chest.

"Are you okay?" Mr Papas asked, concerned.

"Yes, I'm fine." She gave him the biggest smile she could muster. The sunshine soon returned, once again illuminating the cosy shop. "I've got my supplies now," she said, picking up the tray with the sandwiches and tea, as well as the bouquet of pale pink roses. Her cheeks trembled from the blinding smile, but her heart soon began to slow, returning to its natural rhythm. She thought of Mr Papas' words. Was her heart frowning?

Out in the street, she hurried up the steep footpath and around the corner onto the narrow street that led to her apartment building. Ominous clouds had crept in from the distance, obscuring the blue sky like unwanted intruders. Tess unbuttoned another gold button on her chiffon dress, the heat still not having retired for the day.

She stepped into the landscaped front garden at the entrance of her art deco apartment building. She walked up the paved steps and admired the windowsills draped with overhanging orchids that stood out amongst the old rendered wall of the building. She thought about re-reading *Romeo and Juliet* as the romantic balcony scene in Juliet Capulet's garden came to mind.

As Tess entered through the black French cast-iron door, she glanced behind her once more at the menacing blanket of grey storm clouds moving closer. Strangely, it comforted her. A sort of mystery resonated from it, just like the familiar, yet comforting fear evoked by a dramatic, haunting novel. The eeriness and darkness of a novel of that nature would often bring with it romance and passion — a break from tranquillity. Endless sunshine created an uneasiness inside her, just as it always had. Her thoughts returned to school, to hot afternoons when she would find solace when the storm that finally followed the endless heat would splatter the windows. She remembered the noise on the tin roof of the shed where her mother spent countless hours making art, where Tess also did her homework and drank tea from old bone china passed down from her grandmother. Tess loved the drama created by the storm. The theatrical orchestral music of thunder and rain made her feel like life didn't always have to be ordinary. Things weren't always smiles and perfection.

Her stomach turned again, and her heart lost its rhythm. The memory of a conceited, perfect smile tormented her. *Why would I even think of them?* she thought, irritated by her mind's distraction. *I'm so far from the girl I used to be — the girl who cared about what they thought.* Now, Tess was free to be whoever she wanted to be. She thought of getting lost in *Jane Eyre* as she walked up the stairs of the hallway, which was painted a rich grey. She passed Pamela's flat, situated a few doors down and across from hers, and wondered when she would be home. When Tess had left the salon, Pamela had still been with a client, and had told her she would lock up shop.

When they'd first rented the salon, Pamela had suggested they both rent the fairly spacious apartment above the salon for the added convenience, but it was already taken. Tess was secretly glad, because as much as she loved Pamela's company, she would rather live alone. She needed her space. Knowing Pamela was across the hall from her was comforting, but personal space was something she'd always savoured. She loved to indulge in the freedom to explore and pursue her passions, those mostly being reading or catching up on classic films.

As she opened the door, letting herself into her sanctuary, the old-fashioned brass bell hooked on top of the door jingled. Tess thought it was the most romantic and marvellous sound, that little brass bell greeting her every day with its friendly tinkle. She had found it in one of the scrapyards she would sometimes visit with her mother. Tess loved rummaging through all the interesting things people had discarded that could be used for art or craftwork. Tess often imagined the bell belonged to one of the old English pubs in Sydney, dating back to a time long ago. Or perhaps it was from an old Parisian bistro, having somehow ended up in remote Lorikeet Creek. One day she would find out where it came from. Perhaps it was a rare antique.

Her mules clacked as she stepped onto the black and white tiled kitchen floor. She placed her bag, the box of sandwiches and the flowers onto the marble kitchen benchtop. She took her prized Austrian crystal vase from the antique white distressed kitchen cabinet her mother had restored, and filled it with water from the sink. She added the sachet of flower food that Helena put in every bouquet, and stirred it in using a long handled silver spoon. Then she arranged the stems so that the graceful pale pink roses sat happily in their new home. Everything had to be just right before she could truly relax. The air around her was soon blissfully scented with the melange of aromas of roses, fresh dill and cucumber.

Tess hurriedly turned the air conditioner on, adjusting the temperature and placing the fan on high so that cool air soon filled the apartment. She then headed for the bathroom to freshen up.

After a quick, cool shower, Tess slipped into her champagne-coloured silk nightie and matching short-sleeved robe. She loved feeling the luxurious silk amongst her skin as she read, as though she too lived in an English manor. After running a comb through her wet hair, she rummaged through her slightly messy bedroom to find her favourite flip-flops. She then rushed to the kitchen and carefully took out her favourite teapot, a beautiful piece made from fine china, in pale lime with gold trimmings. Tess smiled at the delicate clinking sound made by closing the lid. To her, the sound of china on china was elegant, lady-like and refined.

While the water boiled in the 50s-style kettle on the gas stove, she headed for the bookshelf and found *Jane Eyre* sitting ever-so gracefully next to *Wuthering Heights*. She felt euphoric at the sight of all her books. How she savoured these sacred moments of solitude; having time to ponder and appreciate the words on each page that kept her company and conversed with her soul.

She placed the book on the glass coffee table, then prepared the sandwiches, placing them on a French porcelain cake stand in high-tea fashion. Finding a perfect spot for them next to the novel, she then began to prepare the tea. She opened the packet, instantly releasing the exhilarating, citrusy, mild scent of bergamot. Her breathing became calm and steady. There was something so relaxing about the rituals of making tea, pouring boiling water into a small teapot and smelling the scent of it as the tea steeped. *It was how they would have done it back in the day*, she would often think.

Almost ready, she thought, running her fingers through her wet hair. She'd have to dry it before she could surrender wholeheartedly to Charlotte Bronte's brilliant mind.

Standing in the small, provincially-styled bathroom, a loud noise from outside interrupted the familiar and comforting sound of the hair dryer. She turned the dryer off to hear more clearly. The remnants of shuddering thunder and a gush of wind ushered in calm, and sunshine streamed through the bathroom window, creating branch shadows on the wall from the tall trees in the courtyard. Tess momentarily looked at her reflection in the mirror. Her hair was illuminated by the light, appearing almost halo-like. An uneasiness crept into her heart as she heard the branches moving in the wind, which seemed to intermittently make its presence. A cool change was on its way. She brushed the anxious feeling aside, and continued drying her hair. She wondered, not for the first time, if she should colour her hair a deeper auburn, a colour celebrated and admired on Victorian women.

The nervous feeling suddenly returned when she realised that even with her freshly-cut fringe, she had combed her hair exactly the same way for the last two years, following the ritual to the letter. A vision of herself as an older woman in the same bathroom, with the same tea set and the same routine invaded her mind. Determined to stop the negative feeling from consuming her, she unplugged the dryer and placed it and the comb into a drawer, slammed it closed, and headed for the lounge room, where she settled down into the chesterfield armchair.

Who cares if people think I'm lonely? I love my life, she thought as she reached for a cucumber sandwich. She poured some tea and smiled at how beautifully it streamed from the spout of the dainty teapot as a cloud of fragrant steam caressed her face. This is how she wanted things to be — calm and peaceful. She didn't need adventure; her adventures were reading. Besides, she had had her chance at romance. It wasn't what she'd imagined it to be.

Tess had only just read the first chapter when a loud roar of thunder rattled the windows. She stood up and walked over to look out. The street lamps were now lit as night began to descend upon the quaint street. She gazed at the view of the city skyscrapers in the distance that were enveloped in thick cloud. Although they were close geographically, they were also far away from the world in which she felt she was really living. The modern clean-looking buildings seemed cold, and distant.

From the street below came the sounds of car horns beeping and car doors slamming, of people scurrying with umbrellas and their chatter as they raced along the street, trying to avoid the first heavy drops of rain. As Tess walked back to her armchair, she heard footsteps outside the corridor and wondered if it was Pamela returning home. She tip-toed over to the door and gently opened it a crack. The brass bell jingled, and Tess' nose was greeted pleasantly by the smell of basil and garlic. It smelled just like Silvio's restaurant. Her suspicions were confirmed when she caught a glimpse of a paper bag with *Silvio's* written on it in Pamela's hand.

Tess opened her mouth to call to Pamela who had her headphones on, but quickly refrained, realising it would take away from her reading if she started up a conversation. She felt guilty and a bit strange that they lived across from each other yet still ate alone, but she enjoyed her own company too much. As she looked regretfully at the now closed door of her friend's apartment, the eerie feeling of imminent change that had been lingering in the air returned.

Tess was about to close the door when she saw a woman in a white dress, with long legs and lustrous, golden blonde tresses appear at the end of the hallway. One slender, toned arm led to a well-manicured hand holding a bag with the name of Millie's shop on it. The woman looked around the hallway, but not so far that she could see Tess' face peering through the crack in the door. She headed for the hallway window, which had a spectacular view of the city. Tess realised with surprise that it was the confident, preppy and stylish woman she'd seen earlier that day.

Tess closed the door before the woman had the chance to look in her direction. *Why would someone like her be in this building?* she thought. It didn't suit her. It was a lovely old building, but not fancy at all. It seemed odd for her to be here. Tess knew everyone who lived in the building, and had certainly never seen her before. Maybe she was visiting someone. She would probably live in one of those huge, contemporary penthouse apartments with views of Sydney Harbour, not in a cosy art-deco apartment. She walked over to the lounge, and sunk into it. The pink roses looked friendly in their crystal vase, and brought a smile to her face. She then recalled Mr Papas' words. *Could my heart be frowning, even if my mouth is smiling?* She thought of Pamela and their pact. *We don't need men in our lives.* Then she looked at the teapot and the half-eaten sandwiches, and thought of Pamela eating such a wonderfully romantic meal alone. She also thought of *Jane Eyre*, the heroine who had also insisted she didn't need any man in her life — who was determined to prove her independence.

Tess took a deep breath. She did have her independence financially in the salon. She was proud of herself, just like she was proud of her mother for pursuing her dreams. *My heart is smiling,* she thought, as she caressed a cushion her mother had given her, decorated in a geometric chartreuse print she had designed herself. But then, just as quickly, she thought of Desiree's piercing, wicked grin, and her heart frowned.

"You? Married? I can't even imagine you ever being able to keep a man," she remembered Desiree saying to her scornfully, one of many insults that had cut Tess deeply as a teenager. It struck Tess as odd that she'd been thinking about her

teenage years throughout the day. High school was so long ago. Why was it suddenly on her mind again? She got up and turned the air conditioner off, as she could feel that a cool change had definitely settled for the night. *How long will my private safety zone stay secure?* she wondered uneasily. *Nothing lasts forever. Not relationships, that's for sure.*

She took the novel in her hands again. Her books would keep her company and keep her safe. That was one thing she could always rely on — her books and her salon, the two places where she could create the world she wanted to live in, where she could change a mundane existence, or a dull appearance, and give it a romantic air. She would always have her independence. As lightning lit up the small room, she turned the page to the next chapter with trembling hands.

CHAPTER THREE

A small hint of sunlight partly illuminated the tiny kitchen table the next morning as Tess took a bite from her wholemeal toast, spread with a generous amount of butter and marmalade. She needed something warm and comforting that cooler Friday morning, to ease the uncertainty causing commotion in her chest. Since she was a child, the safety of her bedroom and the way she wanted to live life had always been under threat. Everyone and everything outside that world, her parents excluded, told her time and time again that the way she lived life was wrong. She always felt like forces were conspiring so that she would never be able to feel entirely comfortable in her own space, or happy with being on her own. She was supposed to suffer like many in her hometown — in a dreary, mundane existence, disguised by freshly manicured lawns and picket fences to make things look cheery when in fact they were drab. That's why she loved being with her parents and their circle of friends. They did things differently in their little corner of the town. Most people around them seemed to accept what was handed to them, but her parents sought out what they wanted in life. If life as it was didn't make them content, they would move, or change what they were doing.

"You only have one life, Tess," her father would often say. "Those kids at school know nothing about the big, wide world. They think they have everyone and everything figured out, but they'll soon find out what life's really about. Don't you let them bother you for a second! You're free to be whatever you want to be and whoever you want to be."

Tess remembered one terse afternoon, when she'd unfairly snapped at her mother. They were sitting on the front porch, on the old wooden bench that gave them a view of bushland and the mountains in the distance. "I hate it here. Why can't we leave? You always say that we can pick up whenever we want, like the gypsies do. Why do we have to stay in this stupid town?"

"Look Tess, I know what we said," her mother explained, "but look how we've managed to make this place shine. We'll keep doing the restoration on the cottage — it's old, but it's so lovely, and most of it has been restored and brought back to life. And they've just offered your father a permanent gig at the pub up the road, and he can keep teaching music on the side. It's always been my dream to have a garden with a pond, and to restore an old cottage like this one, and after all these years of fixing things here and there, the restoration is almost complete." Joy beamed from her mother's eyes.

Tess sighed. "But Dad loves touring with all those bands. Why would he just want a normal job? Are we going to just be like everyone else? You always tell me you need to love what you do. Are you just going to work and be depressed like most people?"

"Tess!" her mother had laughed. "There's nothing wrong with settling down, as long as you find things you love to do and create a life full of contentment."

"But from all the places to settle, you chose this one?" Tess had huffed. "A place where I don't fit in at all? I thought we'd be out of this place a long time ago. One year of primary school was long enough … to be with *those kids*! You could have settled anywhere! Since when do I belong in a school like this? They think we're weird. None of the popular kids in my school live like us. Their parents all have normal, boring jobs, and some have so much money they practically own the whole town! That's why they think they can talk to me like that. Why can't I go to art school in the city, like we used to talk about?"

Her mother had gone on. "You know your granddad always wanted us to restore the cottage. He loved the place, but he just couldn't look after it once he got older. It's something we really want to do, because he never got to do

27

it himself. Anyway, it'll only be a few more years until you'll be off to university, and you can have your city pad and just visit Lorikeet Creek on holidays. You're doing so well at school regardless of the pettiness of others. Your marks have improved so much. Besides, don't you love helping me make things in the shed? It really works so well as a workshop. Isn't it fun doing your homework in there while I work? And it's next to the pond, with the ducks. It's like …

"*Anne of Green Gables,*" Tess had finished, sighing. "Yes, it is nice here," Tess conceded. "Okay Mum," she managed, her reluctance causing her voice to tremble. "I'll try my best to fit in."

"Tess, that's not what I said. You go be whoever you want to be. No one can tell you how to dress or how to act. Why not have fun in life? Don't ever dim the light in your soul for anyone, you got that?"

She'd looked at her mother sceptically. She *had* been going well in school. That was because she spent many lunchtimes in the library studying or reading when her best friend Cathy joined the school band which often rehearsed at lunchtime. She had a few other friends, but they were always busy doing extra-curricular activities at lunch. Tess would sometimes join them, hanging out watching the school band rehearse as Cathy played drums for a while, and sometimes she'd help with the newspaper production team, and the student in charge of it all, Michael Peterson.

When Cathy had decided to audition for the school ballroom dancing group, Tess had decided to join her, not wanting to be stuck with the popular group snickering at her all alone, until it occurred to her one day — she loved her own company. *What's wrong with being alone anyway?* she'd often ask herself. Sometimes she felt more lonely having more friends at school, not less. Cathy had always been her saviour. Cathy also loved books, and loved accompanying Tess to book fairs and hanging out with her when Tess' parents held parties with their artistic friends. She was like the sister she never had. It felt good to have an ally, especially one who wasn't scared of Queen Desiree and her loyal followers. Cathy would always give Desiree a dirty look when she passed her. Desiree seemed to be freaked out by Cathy and would respond jumpily, just like a horse spooked by a snake.

Cathy's mother Mel was a hairdresser whose salon was cutting edge for a small town where the town hall served the purpose of hosting parties and dinners. Before Cathy's mother had opened the salon, everyone seemed to have the same hairstyle, as if all the women had held a meeting and decided they would all colour their hair the same colour and cut it in a certain style — a monochrome sea of ash-blonde bobs. That all changed when Cathy's mother opened the salon. She had a way of convincing the most conservative client to try something new, even if it was just to cut the length by a few inches, or try a slightly lighter or darker shade than the usual.

Tess loved visiting Mel's salon. Mel got along with her own mother — together, in their artiness, they were the rebels of the town. Tess admired their independence and nonconformist attitudes, but it didn't make her own life easier.

"Sure, Mum. Got it," she'd finally replied that day. Tess had looked into her mother's sparkling eyes, which shone with joy and hope. How could she dim that light, just because of Desiree and her ilk? And what about her granddad's dreams? Besides, her mother had been right. There were only a few more years before graduation. She'd decided not to mention her issues at school to her mother again. Her home life would become her safety zone — her cosy world where she fit in — and her parents and their friends would become her mentors and teachers in life.

Her father had joined them on the front porch. "You know Tess," he'd said, "school is important, but it's not life. It's not the real world and it's not permanent. The world is ever-changing, full of diverse people. It is a great place where possibilities are endless. Each person needs their own compass to find their way home, to create the life they want."

Tess remembered walking back to her room after the conversation, feeling that she had a responsibility to herself — to her parents, and to her granddad — to not allow anyone to spoil their dreams. She'd looked out her bedroom window at the pond, sighing contently. It *was* like *Anne of Green Gables*. Feeling inspired, she'd opened that very book, remembering all the times her mother had read it to her as a young girl. She opened the beautiful hard cover and escaped into a world where life had drama and passion, a world where she could go wherever she wanted to go, from a lovely country town to a fantasy world of her own, with interesting and diverse characters, where she could turn the page and everything would change.

The next day she had gone to school with a new attitude. She had suddenly wanted to rub it in their faces — that she didn't care what they thought, and that she wouldn't shy away from what she wanted in life. But it wasn't easy.

One day, to her dismay, their Year 11 English teacher had assigned them to read the novel *Tess of the D'Urbervilles*. Tess had heard snickering from the back of the classroom, which crept its way between the desks until her ears were met with an irritatingly familiar blend of condescending, low-pitched laughter. Halfway through the lesson, Desiree had suddenly become interested in all matters academia, and had apparently found it quite fascinating that the central character in the classic novel was from a poor background. She made a pointed note that the Tess of the book didn't quite fit in with "refined society".

The teacher had looked shocked to get any form of feedback from Desiree, who was usually more entertained by frivolous matters, such as which boy had the cutest smile, or who had done what on the weekend. She'd been seemingly relieved that the student who usually disrupted the class the most was partaking in intellectual conversation about literature. Tess hadn't believed the teacher's naivety. How could she not have had an inkling that Desiree was having a go at her?

"Mmm … *Tess*," Desiree had said disparagingly. "I mean, it's quite interesting that they chose a misfit with such a name, who doesn't belong in refined society," she had continued, her head slightly tilted towards her. Tess could see Desiree's cheeks trembling as she strenuously tried to stifle a snigger. "I mean, to wear such horrid, hideous clothes, she probably had her mother make them for her, unlike the other more refined characters, who must have had theirs sent from the finest boutiques in Paris or London. It's rather sad, isn't it? Poor, pitiful Tess." It was evident she was finding it nearly impossible to stifle a mocking smile.

The snickering from the rest of the group at the back of the class coursed through Tess' body.

"Yes," the teacher had continued, still oblivious to the fact that Desiree's comment was aimed at Tess, "there was a great class division in that era, perhaps even more than today. I don't know if her clothes were horrid, though. But you could be right, perhaps her clothes *were* at the low end."

Tess had felt so hot with rage and humiliation, not just at Desiree's words, but at the utter betrayal of her ignorant teacher. And of course, there was still *class division* — it was happening literally at that very moment, in their actual classroom. In fact, the town they lived in was entirely living proof of its existence.

Shaking with anger, Tess had decided she wouldn't react, and kept her eyes downcast. When the feelings of rage had subsided, she'd summoned the courage to look up from her books, and had caught Stewart looking at her in sympathy.

That afternoon, Tess had practice for the ballroom dancing competition. Her mother had helped out and made all the costumes. Tess had, however, accidentally placed her school uniform into Cathy's schoolbag instead of her own, who had by now run off to make the school bus. Tess had had to walk home in her dancing costume, a generously full crimson ball gown that fell straight to her ankles and flowed out with a generous amount of tulle underneath. She gasped for air as she took quick, long strides down the hill above the school oval, hoping no one would notice her.

She'd heard the voice from a distance. "Look everyone! It's Tess of the D'Urbervilles walking through the rolling hills!" Desiree's voice had ruined her concentration. She'd tripped on the long, flowing skirt and lost her balance. She'd awkwardly tumbled down the hill, landing at the feet of Queen Desiree and her loyal servants, her beautiful dress torn and muddied.

The laughter echoed throughout the wide open space. Tess could feel her whole body bruised, and hot from humiliation.

"*Tess!* You really *are* Tess of the D'Urbervilles. Look at you with your torn dress, all muddy like a peasant. What a sorry sight!" Desiree had cackled. Tess had thought in dismay, *She's the Wicked Witch of the West.*

Tess thought back to her father's words. Perhaps some people really would never belong to the world thrust upon them. They had to create their own world. That's how they survived. She couldn't keep running from herself. She had her world. Her apartment provided the safety she needed — full of romance, adventure and fantasy. Her precious books were windows to unknown worlds, just as the many lighteners, dyes and hair products in Mel's salon were like rays of hope, promising to transform anyone into whoever they wanted to be, highlighting their uniqueness. Tess could feel as safe as she felt in her mother's shed, creating beautiful things — changing the ordinary and making them extraordinary. This was her world — where she truly belonged. No one could take that away from her.

Instinctively, she stood up and headed for her bookshelf. It was adorned with incandescent, mini twinkle lights that lit up the beauty of what she often referred to as her "windows of hope". Her fingers ran across the book-binders on the bottom row of the classics section. They stopped at *Tess of the D'Urbervilles*. She had read it many times. She hadn't run from it because of the awful incident. She had embraced it as she embraced who she was as a person. Besides, she saw his face every time she read it. It was that day, covered in mud in a torn dress her mother had created for her, tailored to fit *only* her; that Stewart had reached for her hand. He'd scolded the others with a serious look before asking her, "Are you okay? Please, let me take you to the nurse's office." Tess hadn't cared what the others were thinking — only what those words did to her. It was the most romantic thing. He was her Mr Darcy. She would be Elizabeth though, not Tess of the D'Urbervilles. She would be rebellious and free — not a damsel in distress. A strong woman who knew who she was and wasn't afraid to speak her mind.

They couldn't hurt her anymore. The most humiliating thing had happened and she'd survived it, and Stewart had witnessed it and didn't join them in their filth. He had done the honourable thing. He was a decent human being.

As she gazed at him thoughtfully, she inwardly sighed. She and Stewart were from different worlds. She knew that in her heart. He would, no doubt, end up working at his father's car dealership. He would marry, Evie, his high school sweetheart, and Desiree's best friend. He didn't need to worry about money, and was used to getting things handed to him, but he was a decent person. Tess would never understand how he failed most of his exams, and cared so much about hanging out with that clueless and conceited group. To her, there was something deeper about him, something beneath what others saw on the surface. In that moment, he'd showed her that chivalry and standing up for yourself and others were to be applauded. His concern gave her the strength she'd needed. It wasn't her fault they were so cruel to her. That was their problem, and she would rescue herself from it by no longer caring what they thought of her.

After telling Stewart she would be okay, she walked out of the school slowly with her head held high, not like a helpless victim, but a woman who knew herself. She'd headed straight to Mel's salon, where Mel had coloured her hair a liberating pink, marking the start of a new era.

Tess had spent all her free moments over the next few months reading and listening to Kate Bush and other old records in her room. She had one of the best years of her life — not caring what anyone thought of her, dying her hair from pink to red to blue to green, and doing whatever she loved. She'd worn her mother's designs with pride — dresses and T-shirts with prints designed especially for her. She'd also spent plenty of time in Mel's salon, helping out with Cathy, until she was hired to work part-time after school. Cathy had eventually dropped out of school and headed to the city, where she'd worked in some of the most renowned hair salons before moving to London. She'd told Tess of her escapades and how accepting everyone was in the city, and Tess had planned to leave too, as soon as she finished school. Then, she would be part of that world.

Sighing with the memory, and deciding she wouldn't waste another minute thinking about negative people, Tess rinsed her plate in the small sink, and headed for the bathroom to retouch her make-up. As she opened the make-up case by the sink, she remembered the new lipsticks that would be in Millie's shop, and grew excited to take a look at them later that day. She walked back to the lounge room, and as she reached for her fan-shaped bamboo bag, she noticed the model on the magazine tucked in it — the model Mrs Sanders had said looked like her. Tess had snuck it into her bag when Pamela wasn't looking. She didn't want her to think the compliment had gone to her head, but Tess wanted the chance to take a closer look, to see the resemblance. The model had the same porcelain complexion. Her big, almond-shaped eyes had a magnificent amber hue. She then looked at her own reflection in the round antique mirror on the wall before her and saw the same colour reflected in her own eyes. She didn't have pink hair anymore, but the rose-golden brown tint still held hints of that hue. And she hadn't lost her romantic nostalgia from the past; it was reflected in her make-up — in her rosy cheeks, her defined brown eyebrows, and the shade of brown pencil around her eyes. She would alternate between old Hollywood, Parisian chic, and a more classic English look. She did have a unique-looking face, with high cheekbones, full lips, and a slightly aquiline nose and naturally long lashes. Her unusual features often attracted too much attention, and while others often paid her compliments, she didn't always like to stand out when she was a young girl, before she had decided to embrace her uniqueness.

Then she remembered *his* kind eyes. They had calm shades of blue and grey in them, but when they'd become serious, they reminded her of heavy grey clouds in an uncertain sky. Sometimes, she would notice confusion and hurt in them. Suddenly that day flashed back before her eyes, and she saw those eyes looking at her with the hint of storm clouds rising as she gasped for air, bruised and humiliated from the harsh, cold laughter and the tumble down the hill. It was the last time she would talk to him. He had vanished out of her life two weeks later, but his comforting words and kind eyes remained in her mind, and were etched permanently into her soul.

Tess couldn't help thinking that Stewart had left without getting the chance to tell her something. That feeling stemmed from the fact that she'd seen him on that last week, before he'd left, looking so lost and dejected. Evie was comforting him. As Tess passed them, she had felt his gaze on her back. Instinctively, she had turned around to look at him. Their eyes had locked. Stewart had opened his mouth to talk but Evie had begun to kiss him instead, her long, shiny chestnut brown hair, covering his face. Tess had abruptly looked away, her heart palpitating at the scene. She snuck another glance at him, as she continued walking. He wasn't looking at Evie. His sad eyes were gazing over at *her*. His jaw was tight, but then his face gave way to a sincere, warm smile. Tess managed to respond by giving him one of her own awkward smiles. Evie had then spun him around so that he would redirect all his attention back to *her*. Sadly, it was the last time she would look deep into those kind, gentle eyes.

She looked at the glossy magazine again and shook her head from side to side in disbelief. *I'm definitely a romantic*, she told herself. She left it on the coffee table, grabbed her handbag and headed for the door. The brass bell jingled.

Tess walked across the hallway and knocked on Pamela's door, wondering if she had already left for the salon. The hallway appeared darker than usual. The small glimmer of light had disappeared, and it looked different to how it usually did on a bright summer's morning. *Pamela must have left*, she thought, looking at the time on her vintage watch. She sported a rose-coloured, vintage visage knit that spoke old Hollywood, paired with long, wide-legged black pants that billowed slightly as she walked down the stairs. She felt that she was channelling Lauren Bacall in the 1940s. Her hair, swept to the side with light curls at the end added to the look, as did her pearl brooch. With the 40s on her mind, she thought of authors from the era, and made a mental note to read Betty Smith's *A Tree Grows in Brooklyn* when she next had the chance. *Perhaps it's time to change era for a while*, she thought, feeling excited.

As she walked along the downstairs corridor, she noticed the door of the apartment that was for lease was open. She peered in, and saw a cleaner in there, dusting the picture railings. It smelled like Millie's shop — of her musky room mists from Paris. She wondered who the new tenants might be. Perhaps the stylish blonde woman would be moving in.

Maybe Pamela knows, she thought as she stepped out into a new day.

Instantly feeling a chill in the air, Tess hugged her jacket, relishing the colder weather. She looked at the wet streets before her, ensured she had her umbrella in her bag, and, taking a deep, excited, breath, realised it was Friday, and that their planned girls' night out would take place that very evening. It had been a while since they'd had one. *Looks like my reading will take a back seat for a while*, she thought.

Every now and again, Millie insisted that she, Pamela, and Helena take off their 'shop girl' hats and become reacquainted with the bitter/sweet taste of margaritas and daiquiris. Tess was more of a wine girl herself, but the taste of dry liquor reminded her of old movies like *Casablanca* and films like *A French Affair*. Parting with her books for the evening was perfectly justifiable when you had rum married to live jazz.

Maybe it was exactly what she needed. The trace of anxious unknowingness lingering in the air mystified but also frightened her.

She stopped outside Millie's shop and wondered if the lipsticks had arrived. Pamela would have opened the salon early, but since her own client wouldn't be in until 9:30, Tess had time to wander. She stepped inside the shop, her eyes wide with anticipation as she approached the counter, which was adorned with a huge vase full of deep red roses.

"Wow!" Tess exclaimed. "How romantic are these roses? Are they from Hugh?" Millie looked up from the counter, where she was sorting lipstick holders in a neat row. Her natural light brown hair sat tousled on her shoulders. Her brown eyes only had a hint of make-up around them, but her full lips were traced with a bright matte red. *They've arrived!* Tess thought joyously. *All the way from Paris!* She looked happily at the small boxes sketched with drawings of the Eiffel Tower and chic-looking women draped in scarves. Tess eagerly reached out her hand, but Millie looked up at her and scratched her nose. "Um … Tess … I'm so sorry but they haven't … I mean, I don't have any left." Millie saw Tess' face fall. "Look … um … I'll order some more from the supplier. It shouldn't take that long for them to get here. I'll just finish sorting these and I'm onto it. Tess, I'll make it up to you. I promise."

Tess was perplexed. Her heart began to beat faster, and her face felt warm. The new batch of matte lipsticks *must* have arrived. Millie told her that her last red matte lipstick had run out and that she couldn't wait for the shipment, because it slid on so smoothly, much more so than any other lipstick she'd ever owned.

"But you're wearing one now, aren't you? That means they must have arrived …" She trailed off, looking at the scintillating lipstick holders intently. "I don't understand. I guess I can wait. It's just that I had my heart set on it."

Millie abruptly stopped what she was doing and looked Tess straight in the eyes. "Look, Tess. I had saved some for you and I saved one for me, too, which I had already used, but then she came in with her attitude, and I didn't know what to say. There was something about this woman. She ordered the whole batch. She said she loved them and didn't want to run out, that she would spread the word about my lovely shop; that she would definitely be back again. I just couldn't say no. The way she convinced me … It happened so fast. The next thing I knew I was handing her bags full of products, neatly packaged, with a few other purchases — room mists and perfumes. I mean, she was ready to buy the whole store." Millie played with the lipstick holders nervously. "She looked really polished and snooty. I couldn't get a word in. I'm so sorry. Can you ever forgive me, Tess?"

"I guess so," Tess managed.

"I don't think it'll take so long this time." Millie's eyes combed her outfit. "The red and the burgundy brown would have definitely looked glam with your look today. Rita Hayworth, right?"

"Close. I was going more for 1940s Lauren Bacall. Anyway, it's fine … about the lipsticks." She shook herself out of her disappointment. "Are we still on for tonight?"

"You can definitely count me in!" Millie replied. "A night out with my favourite 'shop girls' is exactly what I need right now." She sighed as she watched her crestfallen friend walk towards the door. "I'm really sorry, Tess. I know how excited you were …"

Tess turned back to look at her friend. "Millie, it's okay. You're right. I was really excited, but I know it wasn't your fault. Believe me, I know how demanding some clients can be. It's enough to make me want to dye their hair purple," she managed with an uneasy giggle.

"See you tonight," Millie called out. "And, yes, the roses are from Hugh. He is quite the romantic fiancé."

"Well, they're lovely. And he is *very* romantic," she said, forcing a smile as she stepped out into the wet street.

Tess felt glum as she took apprehensive steps around the small puddles that had formed in the crevices of the footpath. She waved to Helena, who was carrying flower pots back into her shop. "Hi Helena! See you tonight," she called over the noise of cars, buses and scooters in the quaint, narrow street, knowing that her enthusiasm was forced.

Helena nodded in agreement and looked sadly at the wilting flowers in the pot in her arms. The heat obviously didn't agree with some of the less sturdy ones, no matter how much Helena nurtured them. Tess found herself daydreaming as she watched her amongst her own little sanctuary of nature, which contrasted with the buildings and the noise of the traffic. As Tess looked on from across the street, she saw Helena and her flowers as a comfort. The black frame of the French doors looked like the frame of a painting — one that boasted within it vibrant and warm colours and a lovely lady amidst it all. From where Tess was standing, on the outside looking in, she couldn't shake the feeling that her friend didn't fit in with the cheerful colours today — not like she usually did. The sadness Tess sensed around her didn't seem to just be because of the wilted flowers.

"Hey, Tess," Pamela said. "Where were you?"

"Sorry," Tess said as she stepped into the salon, the smell of dye and shampoo enveloping her. She headed straight to the counter, and looked for her appointment book. She still insisted on using one. Even if she entered the information into the calendar on her phone, she loved the idea that all one's plans for the day were locked inside a beautiful little notebook, which in her case was housed in a most lovely gold and white floral print cover.

"You're still using that?" Pamela looked surprised.

"Well, I let you order those sterile-looking chairs. I need to have something that's 'me', don't I?"

"So the antique/vogue chandeliers you had us install — even though we had to get an occupational health inspector to declare if they were safe to hang up on the ceiling — that was whose idea?" Pamela teased.

Tess smiled. "Well, you obviously haven't seen Silvio's recently. Oh, what am I saying? You *have* seen it. He has definitely gone all grand, hasn't he? Maybe we should get a sculpture in here and place it in the centre, or even a fountain … You know, create some drama in here!" she speculated, eyeing the small space of the salon.

"Okay, enough thinking! We're a salon, not an art gallery. Speaking of Silvio," Pamela continued. "You seem to mention him quite a bit lately."

Tess looked up from her notebook and placed her handbag on the counter. "What do you mean?" she said, her eyes widening. "I just saw what he did to the place. Millie told me about it, so I thought I'd take a look."

"Okay, okay. You don't need to convince me."

"*Pamela!* What are you suggesting? First of all, you know I've sworn off men. Remember our pact? You know, the one where we both agreed that we'd spend a whole year without so much as a date?"

"I remember. I just thought you slightly deviated from the plan. The whole idea behind it was that we don't want to settle again, you know, both of us being so young and already divorced, but if you feel that it's more than that with someone like Silvio …"

"I definitely haven't deviated from our pact. Anyway, I haven't spoken to Silvio for days. I took a quick glance and hurried down the street. I didn't want him to see me, you know …" Tess trailed off awkwardly. She placed her appointment book in the drawer of the large counter. She looked up and caught Pamela looking at her. The speculation in her eyes was very clear. "Well, Millie won't stop having a go at me about him. I don't want anyone getting any ideas about the two of us, and I know he'd want to show me around. Millie even hinted that I was his muse — the way I'm such a nostalgic romantic," Tess said, grabbing her bag as she headed towards the back room, eager to escape Pamela's gaze.

"So, you've never contemplated the idea? He is quite the catch, you know."

Tess felt her whole body tense. The fact that everyone knew that Silvio had had a crush on her for years made her feel uneasy. She didn't like the attention. It's not that she didn't think he was attractive. He *was* brilliant — sweet, smart, and gorgeous — but there was no chemistry between them. Pamela was right. They had promised themselves they would not settle again, and live the life of boredom that represented. Being married for just a year when she was 22 was enough to make Tess realise her life needed drama and passion. She would find that elsewhere — not from a man. Things like that didn't happen in real life anyway, only in books. Tess often thought that her romantic expectations were too much for the real world. She knew they came from the fantasy and comfort of fictitious worlds, which were far removed from boring normality.

"I don't see him in a romantic way," she said, walking away from Pamela's inquisitive stare. "Anyway, what's with all the questions? You know my stance — our stance." A bout of fear washed over her again — the feeling that something was on the horizon. Pamela seemed different these days, like she made more of an effort with her appearance. "Anyway, didn't you see him yesterday?" she queried again. "I mean you *did* get dinner from there, didn't you? I could smell the garlic and basil from my apartment."

Pamela looked away and started to tidy the pile of magazines on the coffee table. "Well, I apologise for overpowering your lovely sandwiches and fragrant tea from Derbyshire, was it?"

"Yes, but that's ok, I didn't mind the smell. It was quite enticing. I'm not sure what the new tenant would think though. For some reason, I don't think she'd ever eat pasta. I mean she looked so toned, like she would spend a lot of time at the gym … if it's her that's moving in, that is."

"A new tenant? Is that what all that noise was this morning? I snuck out early to get my coffee fix and I heard all this murmuring from the empty apartment."

"You didn't notice who it was?"

"No." Pamela looked thoughtful. "I'll try and get a glimpse when I get back home." She looked down at Tess' long, broad pants. "Rita Hayworth?"

"Lauren Bacall, actually," Tess replied with a smile.

As Tess placed her bag in the back room, she thought of Michael, and one of their many arguments.

"Aren't we going out at all?" she'd exclaimed as she sat across from him at their small kitchen table. "We haven't had one lavish dinner since we got married."

"We have a mortgage to pay off. Besides, I'm happy eating here with you," he'd said, running his fingers through his hair to ensure every strand was neat and tidy.

"But a dinner out now and then won't have us on the streets. My parents always made sure they had a nice night out, even if it was just sitting outside, under the stars, having a dinner picnic with gourmet food, and we have more than they ever did when they were young."

"Don't you think this is romantic? Being young, saving to buy our first house in the suburbs?" he'd asked her defensively.

Tess had looked around their kitchen, at the vintage or, rather, half-falling apart furniture, and the view out the window of another wall right next to the concrete edifice that was their apartment complex. Yes, it was exciting living and working in the city, but everything was so expensive that they spent all their savings paying the steep rent. At what cost would they try to have the lifestyle they wanted?

Tess sighed. "Like I said, I'm happy to live in one of the older art deco apartments a bit further out. We don't have to live in such a fancy apartment in the middle of the city. Wouldn't it be better to live close by, able to travel easily into town, but still have fun in life?" As she'd looked up at him, she'd seen a man she no longer recognised — one whose pupils dilated at the sight of money. His job in an investment firm was consuming him. He wanted to have a lavish lifestyle so much that he was depriving both himself and her of even the simple pleasures in life. It was ironic really — he wanted all those lavish things so much, but would not allow himself even a taste of them. It was definitely not how she'd envisioned married life. He was losing perspective. She had begun to think that they had made a big mistake, rushing into marriage so young.

At that very moment, Michael's mobile had chimed. "Look, Tess, I've got to get this. It's an email from work. We'll talk later." He'd barely looked at her, his eyes focused on his phone.

"Sure," Tess had said, a numbness setting in again for yet another day. Anxiety flooded through her. The numbness was suffocating her with boredom. Was it going to be like this forever? She grew up learning to appreciate things — to use the fine crystal if you owned it, to sit on the precious antique dining room chair — to truly feel. The anxiety told

43

her that no matter how much money they both acquired, things with Michael would never change. They would never use the fine crystal — if they ever owned any. And if Michael's thirst for wealth was consuming him at such a young age, how would he be when he was older? The sudden thought of raising a family with him made her chest ache. It had only been ten months and their marriage had already become stale. She had to get out before she became so depleted and bitter that she accepted it all, and became scared to try and change things, before she forgot there was another way — a different way.

He'd smiled at her and loosened the tie around his neck — the one his mum had gifted to him when she'd heard the news that her married son had landed his first executive job "*in Sydney*," she would emphasise to her friends over and over again. Tess didn't know how her plan to follow Cathy to Sydney suddenly involved Michael — the studious boy she'd worked with on the school newspaper, who'd become the third party to their little group, hanging out in the library discussing politics, art, literature and poetry. They all shared a love of reading. Tess had seen something in Michael back then. She'd loved discussing so many different topics with him, Cathy and some of the other art students. Sometimes the chess club would even get involved in their library discussions. Michael had become one of her closest friends, and they'd hang out together, listening to music in her room and discussing plots, narrative arcs, and twists in books ranging from Dickens to Fitzgerald.

That all changed when they'd both packed their bags and headed to the city after finishing school. Tess had managed to get top grades but insisted on using all the skills she'd acquired from Mel's salon to become a professional hairdresser, just like Cathy had in Sydney at the time. Michael had also done well, and would be going to university to study economics. Armed with ambition and a sense of unbridled enthusiasm, they caught the express train to Sydney. It was just like the films from the golden years of

Hollywood, or a scene from a Jane Austen novel, where someone would leave their country manor and head for the bustling city.

In her mind, it was romantic. At the station, Michael had clumsily kissed her, his lips missing hers entirely at first before he settled on them wetly. He'd awkwardly grasped her hand into his as they sat nestled together in one of the seats as the train left the station and her bad memories of Queen Desiree and her crew behind with it. She was Tess of the D'Urbervilles no more.

She'd yelped as he'd kissed her again, nearly biting her lip off as the train bumped along the tracks, only to take the lead when she saw the hurt in his eyes. She would always have to take the lead, and create the romance she sought. But the romance hadn't lasted long. In fact, it had never actually begun. It existed only in her imagination.

After Michael had completed his degree, he'd undertaken an internship with a large investment company. Suddenly, he was part of the executive investments crowd, and his passion for literature and art became forced, while he became pretentious. He was fast becoming a poser — just like the popular group at school. The downside, of course, was that this *poser* didn't even want to suddenly spend a dime — not on books, not on art or the theatre, not even for a small dinner at their local Italian restaurant.

"We should update the front counter and make it gold, just like the one at Silvio's," Tess found herself saying, snapping out of her reminiscence. "It's so beautiful, what he's done with the place." Her face lit up at the thought of it.

She caught Pamela looking up from the front counter, studying her again, with the same speculative look. "Yeah, it's definitely beautiful."

Tess continued, wanting to shed the thought of her failed marriage from her memory. "Maybe we could also have books all around the walls — book*shelves*. I can just imagine it," she mused, looking at the bare, off-white walls.

Pamela laughed. She'd come out of her trance, and her shiny brown bob bounced vivaciously as she moved to the front door to greet her first client for the day. Tess thought that the orange/brown, shiny lipstick Pamela was wearing brought out her olive complexion and the deep brown colour of her eyes.

Tess then remembered the lipsticks at Millie's, and her stomach turned. She was baffled by her reaction. She couldn't help thinking that it was a sign of things to come. She hugged her jacket around her waist and looked out the window. The sky looked gloomier than it had for a long time. Sighing, she picked out a tube of dye, ready to mix the colour for her first client, a young woman who had just stepped into the salon. Tess smiled a forced, uneasy smile. "Hi Suzy. Take a seat. I'll be with you in a moment."

CHAPTER FOUR

Later that afternoon, the sound of the hair dryer blended with the sound of *Play That Funky Music* blaring from the speakers, and Pamela and Tess suddenly felt like doing the disco thing again. Lately, this had been a Friday reoccurrence. She and Tess would often dance in the back room as they mixed dye or drank coffee or pretended to look busy when they were, in fact, having the occasional sneaky "girl talk" — usually about not needing men in their lives, or which films they had recently watched. Tess would even encourage Pamela to read some of her books so that they could discuss them later. Her young client was looking at her hair disapprovingly in the mirror, and gave it a few sharp tugs. Tess smiled to herself. The teenage girl had been to the salon a few times before, and had confided in Tess about her problems at school. Tess felt for her.

"Okay, tell me," Tess asked. "What has you in such a state? You look like you wanna tear your hair out!"

"I hate it," the girl moaned. "I mean, look at the colour. Everyone teases me about it. None of the girls in my school have this colour — this horrible, thick, red hair."

"What? Your hair's beautiful. I love the colour. Auburn is so rich and warm. Most people who step into the salon want hair the very same colour as yours. It's unique. In the Victorian era, they celebrated it. Your colour was considered extremely beautiful — sacred even. Girls born with your hair colour were worshipped — adored by everyone."

"Well, maybe I should have lived in that era. I hate my school. I hate … I mean, I just want it to be another colour to fit in …" She trailed off, glancing over at her mother sitting on the lounge by the door, who occasionally looked over at her daughter. "What about *your* hair colour?" the girl asked Tess. "It's so nice. I'd love to dye it that colour. Then I'd stand out."

"I thought you wanted to fit in, not stand out."

"I wouldn't fit it — I'd rub it in their faces that I don't care what they think …" She trailed off again.

"But you can rub it in their faces and show them you don't care with the colour you already have," Tess pointed out, suddenly remembering she'd done the same thing all those years ago. She'd wanted to go all out and really prove her point — that she didn't care at all what they thought.

"I can't believe my mum won't let me colour my hair. She thinks my natural colour is *so nice*. But most of the other girls colour their hair. I'll be eighteen in a few years anyway," she mused. "And then I can do whatever I want."

An older, rather eccentric-looking woman sitting on one of the other salon chairs looked up from her magazine. "Colour can only hide so much," the woman said, sagely. "It can't hide the truth. The truth always prevails, no matter how much we try to hide it."

Pamela chipped in. "Yes, but we can hide it to some point, can't we Mrs Jones? That's what we're doing now with your hair — no one needs to know about the greys." She checked the woman's hair to see if it was time to rinse out the dye. "If they don't ever see them, they won't know that they exist."

"Yes, to a point they won't know," Mrs Jones continued, "but when something is really damaged, it can't be hidden. The pain and hurt seeps through into other parts, and the truth is always revealed. If you fix what's broken first — then only can you hide what nature changes. If you feel the need to hide it, that is."

Tess looked at the woman thoughtfully, then back to her client. "Anyway," she said to the young girl, "I'd better trim your hair. Your mother must be getting tired of waiting."

As she looked at her young client's reflection, she knew what the woman meant. *No colour* can *hide the truth, if the pain's so bad inside*, she contemplated as she turned around and saw the glass door opening. The song had changed, and *Born to be Alive* came on. The woman who entered was Jessica, who had been there the day before, looking despondently at the flowers across the street. She still looked listless and sad.

"Hi!" Tess greeted her. Jessica had hardly ever spoken to her before, and never responded with much enthusiasm when Tess had greeted her on other occasions. She'd nodded her head and muttered "hello", but that was as far as it got. Tess had, however, caught her looking at her on several occasions. This time, Jessica smiled at her, before walking to the counter.

Pamela spoke to Jessica as she guided Mrs Jones to the basins. "Do you need to make an appointment for Peter?" she asked her. Tess assumed Peter was her partner. She then noticed that Jessica was wearing makeup, which she usually didn't.

Mrs Jones looked at Jessica as she walked to the basins. "Yes, the truth can never be hidden, no matter how much we try to colour it," she repeated.

Tess saw Jessica flinch. She looked nervously at Mrs Jones, before clearing her throat and addressing Pamela, who was now behind the counter.

"Yes, my husband wanted me to make an appointment for him. I was passing by and I thought I'd do it personally. He's gone to visit his brother in the country for a while. We have some fancy birthday party next week for one of my relatives. He wants to look his best, especially now that he's not worki…" she trailed off, her cheeks colouring. "He's really proud."

Tess diverted her attention back to her young client. "You know, school isn't forever. It's just a part of life we all go through, but in the big scheme of things, it's minor. You'll be out in the workforce or at uni and realise that most people are accepting of your uniqueness. Don't let someone's small mind dim the light in your soul." She still found comfort in her mother's words from all those years ago.

Tess looked on as Pamela said goodbye to Jessica. A shiver coursed through her as a draft of cold air entered the salon as the door shut behind her.

"Like I said," Tess reiterated, "school isn't forever. Once you're out, you can leave it all behind. It's always with you, but it's all in the past." Though she had conviction in her words, her voice trembled slightly.

***

Dean Martin's smooth voice could be heard through the speakers. The dimly-lit room was full of conversation, vivacious laughter and sleepy nostalgia. Tess looked at all the old pictures on the walls — of Sinatra, Bogart, Bergman, and many more. Feeling her silver hair-comb move slightly, Tess moved it back into place, just above her ear.

Tess caught Helena looking at it. "I love that look," Helena said, sipping her martini. "What happened to all the Georgian and Victorian-inspired attire? You look so old Hollywood now. You really fit in with the atmosphere, amongst all these Hollywood photos. I hear they brought back the swing band as well, and a Frank Sinatra impersonator. We'll get to hear some Sinatra classics tonight."

"Well, I like to change between the decades, and the centuries, depending on what mood I'm in and what I plan on reading next." Tess smiled. She loved the venue. It reminded her of *Casablanca*. There were even photos from the actual film itself — Ingrid Bergman and Humphrey Bogart on set.

"You mean, you're giving up on Mr Darcy, or who was it? Who's the leading man in *Jane Eyre*?"

"That would be Mr Rochester," Millie said, proudly. "Oh, I remember, and St John."

"Yes, Mr Rochester, the master of Thornfield Hall," added Tess. She really needed this, to be out with her "shop girl" friends. She felt content, taking comfort in the knowledge that she could enjoy her girls' night out and be home early enough to finish reading her novel. She might even have time to start *A Tree Grows in Brooklyn*.

A piano began to play as Tess scanned the room. Clusters of people animated in conversation, looking either extremely mellow or enthused, filled the large yet cosy space. A tray full of champagne flutes passed her. The sight of the waiter carefully carrying them between the round, crowded, candlelit tables made Tess' heart flutter with excitement. She could almost see Bette Davis holding a crystal coupe glass filled with champagne, standing by the bar.

"You really are in your element, Tess," Millie said. "It's a shame you aren't wearing the lipstick I promised I would have for you. I'm really sorry, Tess, but she wouldn't let me get a word in."

"Millie, you've apologised profusely for the last hour," Tess said, smiling. "It's okay. Yes, I was disappointed, but I'm fine now. I was just overly excited."

"And I let you down." Millie raised her voice to be heard over the swing band that had just started playing, a chorus of trumpets, trombones and piano melodies — the works. "How can I make it up to you?"

"Millie. It's really okay. This way I have something to be excited about. You know me, I love my little purchases. It's fun waiting for something to arrive. I think that may be what I love — the anticipation that something special will happen, to brighten up the dull, mundane flow of routine."

Pamela sat down after freshening up in the ladies' room, smiling as she caught the tail end of the conversation. "That's our Tess. I mean, you can't get more sentimental than her. She still writes letters, and I caught her using her old-fashioned appointment book again today. She carries that thing everywhere," she teased with a friendly grin.

"It *is* romantic, receiving a letter," Millie commented. "Pray tell, who are the letters for?" she asked, attempting an English accent.

51

"It's nothing like that. They're for my best friend from school, Cathy, the one who works at one of the happening salons in London. We both loved reading the classics at school, so we thought it'd be fun to write letters to each other ... to do it differently. You know, write from the heart, as opposed to jotting down a few abbreviated words in a text message."

"That's nice," chimed in Helena. "So, no letters from a potential suitor then?" Helena gave her a mischievous look.

Tess looked at Helena. She *did* seem to be in good spirits that evening. She wondered if it was, in fact, due to all the good spirits Helena herself was consuming. Earlier, looking unusually sad in her world of nature, she hadn't been herself. Seemingly, the night was agreeing with her as well.

"What I think Helena is trying to ask," Millie said, "is if it's from someone like Silvio, maybe? I mean, he did refurbish the whole restaurant for you, Tess!"

"I'm not sure about that," Tess muttered, slightly embarrassed. She caught Pamela looking at her. "Anyway, I made a pact with Pamela, you know, that we don't need men in our lives."

Helena laughed. "Okay, give it a few months or maybe a few more weeks, and we'll see if we're sitting here talking about the new men in both your lives." Helena looked at Pamela and eyed the statement crystal necklace clasped around her neck. "That's nice," she said with an inquisitive look. "You never wear jewellery. In fact, you seem to have bought a whole new wardrobe. You seem to be wearing something new every time I see you."

"How's Hugh?" Pamela digressed, diverting the attention to Millie.

"I get it. You don't want me to pry, to see if there's a man in your life," Helena shot back with a smile.

"Hugh's fine," answered Millie. "We're planning our wedding. It will happen one day, but I don't want to rush things. I don't want the stress of planning a wedding to cloud who we are as a couple. People seem to forget what brought them together when they get obsessed with all that wedding stuff."

Tess thought of Michael and her wedding day as she took another sip of her margarita. Her mind went back to that stressful day — how she'd panicked at the realisation that her sacred "alone time" would be disturbed, at the anxiety that accompanied the frantic commotion to ensure everything was perfect, of not being sure what role she was to play once they were married. Michael had become very serious about the whole thing, thriving in his role as the responsible groom with many duties. He'd begun to stress about the seating arrangements months before the wedding. The night before he'd called her frantically during her third make-up rehearsal. Tess couldn't care less where people sat. She cared more about giving her wedding day a touch of romantic nostalgia. After seeing the tension between Michael and his parents about who wasn't talking to who, she and her family had handed them the reins on that matter. They weren't used to such trivialities.

By the end of the day Tess couldn't wait for it to be over. All day she'd been imagining reading her books and having a cup of tea as soon as the last guests went home. She'd held her tongue and hadn't said anything to Michael on their wedding night, but she couldn't believe that, instead of the pale pink roses she'd ordered, flowers that were half the price and not nearly as lovely were scattered clumsily in the church and the reception — without notifying her.

"You said that you didn't care about the wedding — that my family and I could take over," he'd said in his defence when she'd finally brought it up.

"I said you could take over *the table arrangements for your side*, not to cancel the one thing you knew meant so much to me! I even bought the less expensive dress just to have pink roses at our wedding."

That's when she'd realised he was changing. He'd replied. "We can't waste money on things like that, Tess. It's not wise. I mean, they're just flowers in the end. No one even noticed them."

"*I noticed them!*" she retorted, raising her voice. "I was so happy to have the church bedecked with them. That was the only thing I really cared about. The one thing that was important to me!"

"Tess, they're just flowers. I mean, what do they do anyway? They don't serve any purpose."

Tess couldn't believe her ears. He wanted to take away the things that gave her joy. It was bad enough that they'd had to postpone their honeymoon as he was being considered for an important role at work. They didn't even go to a hotel for the night. Tess had agreed, even knowing it might be the sign of things to come — the impending sacrifices. She bit her tongue, denying the truth because she didn't want to accept it. *Well, this is definitely the icing on the cake,* she'd thought. *And speaking of cake* … Their wedding cake was short a tier too. She'd had enough!

"They aren't *just flowers!* They're important to me and make me happy. How can you say that?"

"Tess, this isn't how the real world works," he'd said. "It's not a novel. We're married now. We need to act like it and be responsible for our choices in life." He looked at her, not like a man looking at a woman he loved, but like he was the older and wiser teacher and she was the naïve student.

She'd left their bed and walked over to her bookshelves. She'd then made herself a pot of tea and shut the door behind her. Tess had spent hours reading, losing herself in words.

Hours later he'd knocked on the door and finally uttered, "Tess, I'm sorry. I didn't know it would upset you."

She forgave him, even though she knew deep in her heart that their argument was not about flowers, even though she knew the man she'd married didn't really know her at all, and that she didn't really know him either. The eager, curious teenager who'd shared her passions was not who she had married. The man who had just pledged his vows to her was far from that. But she forgave him.

The incident had been the first hint that he would never be sorry because he refused to see her for who she was — and who she definitely wasn't.

"Planning a wedding can be stressful," Tess finally said, coming out of her reverie.

"It sure can," said Pamela, who knew all too well about getting married too young. Once the bells had chimed and the confetti had been thrown, reality had hit her hard. Pamela had married her high school sweetheart, and she'd thought they were happy until he realised that marriage wasn't really his thing. He hadn't discovered who he was without being in a relationship. He needed to travel the world — without her. It was because of their similar experiences that both she and Tess had made the pact.

The appetisers arrived — a mixture of different cheeses, green olives and some small, triangular quiches. Pamela turned her attention to Helena, who seemed pleasantly tipsy. "So, how's Carter?" Pamela asked her as she ordered a bottle of wine to go with the food.

"Oh!" Helena nearly spilled her drink. "He's okay," she said, scratching her nose with one beautifully manicured nail. Actually things have been okay lately. He just got me the most beautiful bracelet. In fact he's been getting me many things lately, small gifts here and there, mostly jewellery. Well, I guess there's no point getting me flowers."

They all laughed.

"*Things have been okay lately*?" Millie enquired. "You mean, they weren't before?"

"No, I just meant, we haven't really been seeing each other much. You know how busy couples can be," she said, trying to avoid the curious looks from around the table. "I just felt that things were strange for a while ... but this night is exactly what I needed. Oh, I love this piece!" Helena digressed, as Paul Desmond's *Take Five* filled the room with its seductive beat. "You do too, don't you Tess? My dad used to listen to this all the time."

Tess glanced at Helena. Her long brunette hair had been set free. Her rich plum lipstick reflected the candle's flame, and her face glowed in its amber light. As Tess looked around the table at her beautiful friends, she felt happy and comforted in their presence. But something still felt strange. Tess' mind momentarily went to Jessica, the sad woman in the salon. Maybe it was just her — who she caught looking at her now and then. Maybe that's why she felt like someone was watching her.

The band started up with the next song. *The Girl from Ipanema* made her heart sing. She sat back to allow it to soothe her, to serenade her.

"God, I feel so glamorous," Millie exclaimed as she took a small gold hand mirror from her purse with a stemmed rose etched onto it.

"Are you powdering your nose?" Pamela asked with a giggle. "Isn't that what they did back in the day?"

"Is that mirror new?" Tess asked, admiring the beautiful piece. She took out one of her own. "My mum gave me another vintage hand mirror when I visited recently, and she didn't find this in any garage sale or craft scrapyard. It was in the cottage they renovated. It must have belonged to my grandmother. Maybe my granddad gifted it to her. It does look really old. Or maybe it was from my great grandmother." Tess contemplated the mirror. She held it out for her friends to see. "Look! It has a picture of a woman and an elegant, tall cat," she exalted.

"Wow," enthused all three women.

"It's so old-world," said Helena. "You should have it appraised. What if all your mirrors are worth more than you think? In fact, a lot of the stuff in your flat should be appraised."

"Well, I have wanted to have the brass bell appraised, but I haven't gotten around to it. I hope it's from a Parisian bar or somewhere grand, that it has a story to tell."

People clapped as a suave male singer came out onto the small dance floor and took up a spot in front of the band, behind a microphone. The sound of his smooth, velvety voice soon filled the swanky space as he channelled Sinatra, and began to sing *My Kind of Town*.

Tess gazed at the lipstick holder Millie was now taking out of her purse, bedazzling her with its unapologetic shimmer. Tess instantly thought of the stylish woman, the one that might be moving into the apartment downstairs. *She must have purchased the lipsticks,* she speculated. Her heart sank slightly as she remembered the matte lipsticks, but she brushed the feeling away quickly. She didn't want to spoil the joy she felt in her heart. Being out with her friends was exactly what she needed to shake the uncertainty inside of her, and the feeling that she was too comfortable in her cosy world, that it needed to be shaken up a little — made more messy, more complicated. Her night out seemed to be putting those feelings to bed.

Sitting back comfortably in her chair, she looked at the band, and enjoyed the fact she was able to share comfortable silences with her friends. Around them, she always felt accepted, at ease. *This is how I want my life to be,* she told herself, *to have the occasional girls' night out, my salon, and my time to myself.* Tess sunk back into her chair and listened with whimsical joy. *This definitely is my world,* she thought with pride, as applause thundered around her.

CHAPTER FIVE

Tess and Millie walked home after what had been a very enjoyable night. Pamela had gone back to the salon, needing to check on a few things, and Helena had also retired for the night. She needed to wake up early to arrange flowers, as Saturdays were always busy. Tess and Pamela would also have a busy day at the salon as a few of their clients were attending the same wedding.

"I love this street," Millie sighed. "It's so charming, yet hip. It's rather quirky, don't you think?"

"It is lovely, and quirky," Tess replied as she stopped to peer into the window of a vintage clothing store, feeling mellow from the sweet liquor they'd had with dessert, the taste still lingering in her mouth. Her eyes widened as she took in all the interesting clothes. Some fashionable skirts caught her attention, as well as a Victorian-inspired dress she could imagine herself in.

"That dress is beautiful, isn't it?" said Millie, following her gaze. "I can see you in it. I wonder if it's a genuine vintage piece. So, are we reading another Bronte novel soon?"

"Sorry?" Tess looked at Millie, whose expression glowed in the lights of the shop window.

"You change your attire as you change the era of the books you read. You were saying that back at the bar." Millie smiled. "It was a great night. I haven't felt so glamorous for a while. Tonight was exactly what I needed."

"I know what you mean," Tess replied. "I needed it too. I've been feeling strange lately … like something isn't quite right. Even Helena sensed something in the air."

"Oh? How so?" Millie's eyes revealed her curiosity.

"I don't know. I can't really explain it."

"Well, the weather's sure changed the mood around here," Millie said. "How much longer could we have lasted in that heat? I like this change — for a while anyway. I've been worried that all my cosmetics would spoil as soon as I turned off the air-con. And poor Helena … Her flowers have seen better days. Anyway, Tess, are you okay to get home? I'm meeting Hugh for a late night coffee. I think it's good to make time for dates like we used to — to not get all tangled up in the wedding stuff. He's meeting me at the shop. Do you want us to walk you home?"

"No, I'll be fine," she said, her eyes still on the dress. "I might walk in and have a look in here for a bit before I head home." At that moment, Penny, the eccentric shop owner, appeared from behind a rack of jackets and waved. Penny was petite with platinum blonde hair cropped short. She wore black denim overalls over a tight red and white striped t-shirt. On her feet were wooden platform clogs and her wrists were bedecked with colourful bangles.

Both women waved back. Penny always kept her shop open until late. Her husband, Dante, worked with her. She would often joke that people spent more money after they'd had a bit to drink. Tess was feeling tipsy and was ready to peruse the many interesting clothes. A few of the other boutique shops were open as well — the local Independent book shop, the record shop and, of course, the many restaurants, wine bars, and cafés that fronted onto the long, narrow street.

Millie leaned over to hug her. "Bye Tess," she said, kissing her on both cheeks.

Tess reciprocated. "Bye Millie. Come over for a haircut when you can. I'll fit you in, just not tomorrow. There's a wedding on and you know how frantic everyone gets, even the guests."

"Don't I know it?" Millie said with a grin. "Tonight was fun. Maybe we should make it a weekly thing instead of monthly. Anyway, I'll let you know when those lipsticks arrive. I'm really sorry …"

"Millie, it's okay. You don't have to keep apologising. I understand about difficult customers. Anyway, you'd better get back to that handsome fiancé of yours."

"Okay, bye!" Millie said again, waving as she began to dance to Jimmy Hendrix's *Foxy Lady*, which was blaring from the record shop a few doors down.

Tess laughed. One minute they were mesmerised by the soothing voice of the Frank Sinatra impersonator, the next by …

Her thoughts were interrupted by Penny, who appeared next to her at the door. "Come in, Tess. I can see you're eyeing something. Did you have your monthly girls' get-together? Sorry I couldn't join you all. We've been flat out here."

"That's okay. You did miss out on a fun night, though. I have to admit, I'm not exactly a party animal, but drinks at Vinnie's leaves me feeling like I just stepped out of an old film. It's a different world in there."

"Yeah, Vinnie's is magical. Dante and I have some of our business meetings in there. Anyway, come and try it on. I'm sure it'll look great on you."

"Try what?"

"I saw you looking at it. It's a gorgeous dress. I know you Tess — you won't relax until you see yourself in it. I can give you the loyal customer discount if you like it."

"You don't have to do that," Tess said as she stepped into the shop, admiring the vintage lamps scattered around, their soft yellow light complementing the mellow, sleepy, tipsy feeling that had taken over her.

"Yes, I do. You're one of our best customers," Penny said, taking the olive green dress from the rack and handing it to Tess as she opened the lilac velvet curtains of the small dressing room. "Try it. It's not an original, though. It's one of my creations —inspired by the Victorian era. I thought you'd like it."

"It's amazing. You're really talented, just like my mum," Tess replied. "I don't mind if it's not an original. Sure, I'll try it. You don't have to convince me." She felt the delicate fabric between her fingers.

Moments later, she stepped out of the dressing room. "So, what do you think?" she asked, looking into a long, heavy, black-framed antique mirror.

Penny appraised her as Dante, a man of medium build and height in his thirties, stepped out of the back storeroom to have a look. He sported a ponytail and a tight-fitting, 70s-style shirt with jeans. "Wow," he exclaimed. "It's like it was made for you."

"It really is amazing!" Penny cried. "It looks wonderful on you."

Tess admired herself in the mirror. She did look great in it, and she knew it wasn't just the alcohol. It reminded her of when her mother made clothes just for her that sat perfectly, fitting like a glove. She did a little twirl, giggling. "Sorry, I think I may be a bit tipsy," she said to Dante and Penny, who were both smiling with her.

The three turned towards the door as another customer stepped into the shop. "That looks so amazing on you!" the woman exclaimed the moment she saw Tess. She then looked around the shop, enthused by everything she saw.

"Thanks!" Tess called after the woman. Turning back to Penny, she said, "I'll take it. It's so roman ... I mean ..."

"It *is* romantic, Tess. Relax! I'm not going to start asking you about ... What's his name?"

Tess looked at her with an awkward smile. Why did she always feel weird when people had romantic expectations of her and Silvio? Relationships scared her; she felt like she couldn't breathe at the thought of being in one. Silvio *was* the perfect guy — he was intelligent, philosophical, well-read, and he understood how she felt about owning her own business. He was also handsome, with cute dimples, green eyes, and brown slightly curly hair that hung just above his shoulders. He also looked after himself, even if he was passionate about food. Any woman would be lucky to have a meal cooked by him. He was also really kind. Yes, Silvio would definitely know how to make a woman feel special. And he was so different from Michael, who had also been passionate about reading, of conversing with her on different interesting topics, of having heartfelt moments. But the chemistry between them had only been in her imagination. Silvio was different — he had innate charisma, and she had to admit there was some form of chemistry. Yet, her heart didn't beat wildly at the thought of him. When she was around him, it wasn't wild horses — it felt more like a stroll in the garden, pleasant enough but too tranquil. Tess needed wild horses, the same way she needed storms to break days on end of sunshine.

"Tess?" Penny interrupted her thoughts.

"Oh, sorry Penny. What were we talking about?"

"Um, I know what I was talking about, but I'm not sure you were in the same conversation. You were miles away!" she said with a curious smile. "You know, you need to be careful. If you keep reading so many romantic books, you'll expect to run into a man on a horse with a top hat and an English accent."

Tess laughed awkwardly.

"Yes, he might reach out his hand and rescue you from this mundane existence — from the filth of modern living!" Dante exclaimed melodramatically, his hands raised and his expression fierce.

Tess laughed. "You can tell you used to work in the theatre with that performance!"

Dante smiled. "I did, but only as a set designer, where I met this wonderful woman here," he said, reaching out his hand like a distinguished gentleman and taking one of Penny's in his own. "If Penny hadn't designed all the costumes for that particular production of *Hair*, we wouldn't be together, working in this shop." He pulled his wife close to him and gave her a kiss on the lips.

Tess gazed wistfully at them as they shared their private moment. They were definitely in love. *It must be fun working together — sharing their passions with each other*, she thought. They seemed to be a couple who really understood each other — and what they needed and wanted in life. Dante would definitely want Penny to use the fine crystal if she wanted to — to have all the pale pink roses ...

"Sorry about that," Dante interrupted her thoughts. "I just can't help myself sometimes when I'm around my beautiful wife." He walked towards the counter to ring up a few items for the other customer in the shop, who was smiling at the public show of affection.

"Anyway, I'd better pay for this," Tess said. "I'm going to head home and do some reading." She felt her heart flutter. She looked at her watch. It was way past eleven, definitely time to head home. "Is it all right, if I pay for it like this, while it's still on me? It's so nice, I don't want to take it off." ,

"That's fine with me. I'll put your other clothes in a bag instead," Penny said, grabbing a white paper bag from under the counter.

Tess looked down at her dress with pride. It was as if she was in a strange and wonderful dream, being at Penny's shop so late, in her glorious new dress.

Her mind went back to a moment with her mother. "Stand still, Tess," she remembered her telling her as she placed one of many colourful pins on the end of the very same ball gown that would be ruined that day at school. "I'm almost there. Your gown will be ready before you know it. It fits perfectly on you. I'm happy with how all the costumes are turning out. Maybe I should add ballroom dresses to my resume!" She laughed.

Tess had kept still and quiet, observing how her mother worked so expertly. She loved that she was passionate and talented about everything she made, and admired her precision and attention to detail.

"Bye Dante, Penny," she called out as she walked out of the shop. The reflections from the street lights and moonlight danced on the footpath, giving the night a film-like quality. Her dress flowed around her in the breeze. The record shop was now playing Ella Fitzgerald. As she passed it, a fluorescent green door caught her attention. It fronted the indie bookshop. Tess hadn't noticed the colour change. It had been a dark sea blue a week ago. Before that, it had changed from black to red, and now this bright green hue. Tess noticed the timber underneath the paint hadn't been sanded back around the edges of the door. The colour didn't blend smoothly in those sections. She found herself mesmerised by the different colours seeping into one another. The door looked rough, but it was just natural wear and tear — it wasn't truly damaged underneath the surface. It also suited the feel of the street — the old amongst the new, where all were accepted, young or old, artistic, creative and bizarre, which Tess found so much more interesting than normality.

Tess looked at the many books in the window display. A few were classics she already owned, but had seen better days, so she stepped in and quickly grabbed them. She also picked up two contemporary reads from a local author. She paid for them and stepped outside, looking at the lovely rustic door again. She remembered what Penny had said to her — that she was a romantic —and thought of how Dante brought so much joy to Penny's life.

Slowly turning around, her mind instantaneously thought of the kind, noble, handsome and intelligent man that was interested in her. Why didn't she even dare consider the possibility — the possibility between her and Silv…

"*Oh, Silvio!* I didn't see you!" Tess cried, looking at the charming man who had suddenly appeared before her.

"*Signora,*" he said in his usual sweet, flirtatious way, still revealing a trace of an accent, even though he'd been living in Sydney since he was a teenager. "So nice to bump into you like this. I haven't seen you for a while. You found another Italian restaurant?" he asked in a playful, accusatory tone, as if she had been blasphemous. "Or have you realised that it's not so hard to cook some of my dishes at home?"

'None of the above, Silvio." She found herself matching his friendly tone. Tess studied his green, thoughtful eyes that shone with passion. "I must drop by soon. I don't think I can cook your *Scallops Caprice* the way you make them, or your *panna cotta* — no matter how much I try."

"Phew," he said. "I just wouldn't be able to live without seeing your pretty smile. Anyway, there's nothing like the present. Come over now," he said, his eyes illuminated by the streetlights above. "You haven't seen what I've done with the place. I know you'll love it. You were my inspiration — seeing some of the pieces in your salon, the way your eyes light up when you talk about your parents' restored cottage, the classics." He eyed the bag in her hand with the bookshop's logo. "You made me realise I need a touch of the old in my environment as well. It suits this street — how the new and old blend here."

"Oh …" Tess managed. She hadn't really believed Silvio had been inspired by her, thinking Millie was only teasing. Tess suddenly felt burdened with the responsibility to show her gratitude. She felt slightly overwhelmed to be placed on a pedestal. It took her out of her comfort zone. She so hoped Silvio didn't have any expectations regarding the two of them. She didn't want to have to reject him. Was it his way of saying he was serious about her — that it wasn't just innocent flirting, or just a crush?

"Come on. Come and see it. It's exactly what I wanted, and more," he exalted.

Tess looked at his sincere, excited expression, and felt bad to let him down. His eagerness reminded her of herself; it was as though she was looking in the mirror — the way she became excited about the past and anything that reflected it. "Sure," she finally said. "Why not?"

Part of her thought it was romantic and sweet — that she was his muse. If she gave herself permission to indulge in such things, and let herself enjoy it for what it was, instead of being scared of it, she would think it was touching.

They crossed the road together. Silvio gently pulled her back towards him as a horn sounded and a car passed them at high speed. There was no doubt about it — he cared about her safety. She could imagine him being her boyfriend right then — he would be protective and supportive. He would be wonderful, and yet she was scared of him ... of him wanting her. Her feelings confused her. *What do I want?* she asked herself.

"Tess, are you okay? You're always in your own world. I'd like to visit it one day," he said as his hand brushed hers.

Tess felt a slight shiver at the touch. "Sorry Silvio. I do tend to live in my mind a lot."

A broad smile crossed his face. "Don't apologise. It seems like a wonderful place to reside."

Even at this late hour, the street still buzzed with the noise of traffic and the voices of people enjoying the many cafés and wine bars. A pleasant aroma of tomato, garlic and basil enticed her senses, bringing out passion like good food always does.

She heard a female voice. "Hi Tess." She turned around and saw Millie and Hugh waving to her as they waited to cross the street a few cafés further down. She could see Millie's grin at the sight of her and Silvio together from a mile away. She waved back, a little embarrassed.

Tess turned and walked through the beautiful, low-lit entrance of the restaurant, where an old-fashioned counter stood, stacked with menus and a huge vase with a diverse array of flowers in rich, warm reds, with tall, green, full-leafed stems. Tess instantly noticed the massive white Roman statues on both sides of the entrance. Before them sat numerous round tables, dressed in provincial styled black and white floral tablecloths. The chairs resembled that of the finest hotels, rounded on their tall backs, hugging whoever sat on them with their velvet cushioned arms. The sight of the gorgeous gold bench at the bar still left her marvelling in awe. The smell of espresso danced with the other aromas lacing the air, blended together with the unique aroma of Italian cuisine. People were conversing — some animated, others more subdued, contently sipping their wine or coffee. Tess noticed a couple sitting on a small round table by the window, holding hands and staring into each other's eyes. Piano music embellished the gentle murmuring.

"So, what do you think?" he asked her.

Tess didn't want to reveal that she had already seen some of the restaurant's new interior, especially the gold bench, when she'd peered through the window. She looked into Silvio's sincere, kind eyes as he awaited her approval. "Silvio, it's like I'm in my own world — one with stars and magic, where …"

"Where dreams can come true?" he interrupted.

She blushed. "Yes, that too."

"So, is it similar to Vinnie's club? The feeling you get there? You went there tonight, didn't you?"

Tess nodded slowly, momentarily taken aback by the fact he knew she had been at Vinnie's. "Yes, it is a bit like that, although the marble and gold — not to mention the statues — give it an authentic Italian look, rather than old Hollywood," she smiled. "How did you know I was at Vinnie's?"

"Pamela came by in the morning to get a cup of coffee and told me. She said your girls' night out was long overdue, and that you would be having it tonight. She also stopped by for a late night coffee a few minutes ago."

"Oh," Tess said, surprised. *She must have stopped by when I was trying on the dress,* she speculated.

"Anyway, take a seat. You must be hungry. I know they only serve finger foods at Vinnie's. Here, we have hearty Italian cuisine."

"Oh no! It's a bit late for me. I've got to get home and …"

"And what? Read? I know you, Tess. You don't have to hide it from me. It's not like it's something you have to hide, right? I admire your love of reading. It's one of the things that I lo… I mean, it's something that's close to my heart too." He looked at her intently. "Surely you want something to drink. How about something warm? I'm sure you've had your share of alcoholic beverages already."

"Um …" Tess looked into his hopeful eyes, then around at the opulent, charming room. It was the perfect environment to sit and have something warm to end the night. She felt like there was magic in the air again. Her doubt and uncertainty had eased slightly, and she felt free and pretty in her new dress.

"Tea? I know you love that tea from Mr Papas' deli. I don't have those particular brands, but I think we have some great Earl Grey. I'll get you some, okay? I've got a few minutes to spare. I'll join you and we can discuss books and films." His eyes danced as he looked at her, before turning towards the bar to motion to one of the waiters. "By the way, you look really nice. That dress really suits you."

"Thanks, Silvio," she said, feeling guilty. *What's happening? Is this a date? It's so late at night, the time when feelings and romance usually run free — unencumbered. He wants to sit at a cosy table, and discuss films and books with me.* A sudden rush of panic coursed through her. *What should I do?*

It was too late to do anything. Silvio appeared by her side, guiding her to a small round table lit by candlelight in the most private part of the restaurant. "Speaking of films, it's Italian film week at the boutique cinema down the road," he said, helping her to her seat. "Now, as I was saying earlier, I must tell you that you really were my inspiration to refurbish this place, your love and respect for the old — for restoring and bringing things back to life and appreciating their beauty, even if they have many imperfections. That's who you are, Tess. You're truly one of a kind. Not many young women are like you. You're a rare gem."

"Thanks," she responded, adjusting her hair-comb slightly, trying to hide the tremor in her hand, in her voice. She picked up the teacup and held it with both her hands to ease her nervousness.

Silvio locked his eyes with hers as she lifted her head up after taking the first sip. "Tess, I don't want you to be uncomfortable around me. I want you to be yourself."

"I'm fine," she said, almost too quickly, setting down the cup. "It is really beautiful here. I'm glad I inspired you! It is definitely my cup of tea," she said, then giggled awkwardly. "Tea? I can't believe I said that ..."

Silvio looked at her intently. He placed his hand on one of hers. "Please, Tess. Tell me. Are you afraid of me?"

She laughed uncomfortably. "No, Silvio. I think I'm just a bit tipsy. Those margaritas ... you can have too many. And then we also shared a bottle of wine, and some type of sweet liquor. They even had a swing band. It was great!" she enthused, flustered. She knew she was talking too quickly. His eyes looked so beautiful, as the gentle flame from the candle illuminated their kindness. Why was she so afraid of the look in those eyes?

"Sounds like you had a great time," he said, smiling. "So, which book is it tonight?"

Tess instantly felt comforted at the thought of her books. "I need to finish *Jane Eyre*, and then I might move on to a book from the 40s."

"Jane Eyre?" he pondered sceptically. "The heroine who wanted to prove her independence, who didn't want a man in her life? Until her heart had other ideas." He shook his head. "It's a shame ..."

"What is?" Tess asked, unable to draw herself away from the intensity of his look.

"A life without romance. Without sharing intimacy, coffee and conversation, dates at the cinema, comfortable quiet moments. That's the essence of life for me, the garnish — the colour. It makes life complete, don't you think?"

Tess unlocked her eyes from his and played nervously with her spoon. She looked up at him again. He was still looking at her with the same serious, intense expression. *Comfortable quiet moments*, she thought, remembering how she'd felt with her friends earlier that evening. "Those *are* good," she said, avoiding eye contact.

"What is it you're looking for, Tess?"

"Looking for? I don't know what you mean."

"In the past? What is it that has you running there, away from the present?"

"I'm not running," she said, defensively.

"You know, recreating the past is fine. I mean, you were my muse for this place. I know how you get swept up in the romance, but it would be a shame if you miss the present because you're always looking back."

"Silvio, you're a great guy ..." she managed.

He looked down at his teacup as the piano upped the tempo. "Anyway, I was thinking we could see an Italian film together, or even an English classic. They might be playing *Persuasion* next week." He looked up at her again. He seemed to have digressed intentionally, so he didn't have to hear something that may shatter his hopes.

Tess began to feel weary. A wonderful, handsome man was asking her to see a film with him. He had refurbished his whole restaurant for her, and yet she was terrified. Her heart beat ferociously. Then there was the thought of Michael and their stale marriage. She was sure Silvio would give her all the roses she could ever want — that he would do anything for her. Was that the problem? Was it all too easy — too good to be true? Her heart was beating from fear, not wild passion. She looked at Silvio with regret. With her own heart melting, knowing that she was breaking his, she leaned over and kissed him on the cheek. "I think you're a wonderful guy ..."

Tess felt his finger on her lips.

"Please, don't say it, Tess. I can't hear it."

"Silvio," she said over the music and the murmuring, which seemed louder as her thoughts became more and more tangled. "I'm so grateful and honoured that you were inspired by me."

"Tess, you don't need to thank me. This place brings joy to me, the way seeing your pretty smile does. Where is that smile? The one that shines when you talk?" he asked in a lighter tone.

Tess smiled, slightly relieved that Silvio's sadness had been replaced with a glimmer of happiness again, even if the sudden change appeared forced. Her heart felt heavy with regret, from the burden of hurting someone so wonderful, of letting him go. Suddenly, she realised she had to leave before things became intense again. She hadn't planned to be swept up in such drama. She only ever wanted to read about it, had made a pact to avoid it, to avoid complications — to create and live in her own safe world. She stood up abruptly. In her haste to leave, she knocked over the teacup, and was shocked when the tea spilled all over her new dress. "Oh no!" she exclaimed.

"Tess, I'm so sorry. I'll get you another cup … or maybe some coffee? The new barista is exceptional."

Tess looked at her dress regretfully. A tea stain ran down the delicate, free- flowing chiffon skirt. "It's not your fault. I'm the clumsy one. It's really okay, Silvio. Don't worry. I'm friends with the dry-cleaner. She's one of my clients at the salon. I'm sure she'll be able to take out the stain. I really have to go though. It's getting so late."

As she walked towards the door, making her way between the elegant tables clustered with people, Silvio followed her. "Tess, I'm sorry," he said again. She turned to face him. His kind eyes looked at her searchingly.

"Silvio," she said, smiling as broadly as she could muster. "It's really fine. You've been great. You're great." *You're the whole package*, she said to herself. *But it's not enough.* "Bye, Silvio, thanks for everything."

"You know, Tess, Jane Austen, apart from being considered a literary genius, was also considered by many as one of the greatest romance writers, but she never married. That wasn't the norm in those days. Whether she ever fell in love isn't known, but many think her heart was closed to

71

many offers. Of course, one never knows what will make them happy, and only some really find true love. Others hope for it, search their whole lives for it, while others find it but disregard it."

"Yes I heard that too, about Jane Austen," she responded, puzzled by his comment. "You don't need to worry about me, though. I'm fine." She smiled again.

"I hope that's true, for your sake. You're a wonderful woman. Just know, though, that sometimes the ones with the biggest smiles have the biggest regrets in their hearts."

She looked at him searchingly. It echoed what Mr Papas had said, and what the eccentric Mrs Jones had said back in the salon — about what the eyes revealed. Tess looked at his smile — it added so much colour to his face, yet his eyes looked dim in the moment.

"Anyway, let me walk you home," offered Silvio. "It's getting late."

"That's okay. It's still pretty busy outside. I'll be fine. Bye Silvio," she said, the smile still on her face while her heart hurt with regret.

"Bye Tess," he said emphatically. He opened the door and a cold chill snuck into the opulent, warm space. She stepped out into the night air. His gesture was not enough for her, and she didn't even understand why it wasn't enough — enough to capitulate to his advances. She didn't know what would be enough for her. Maybe nothing would ever be enough. *Maybe nothing will ever match what I see in my imagination.*

CHAPTER SIX

Tess walked quickly, looking at her watch. It was late, and she had a big day at the salon the next day, so there would be no time for reading that night. In some ways, she'd been the protagonist in her own romance novel. There was something so final about Silvio's goodbye, as though he needed to know where she stood. As relieved as she was, she also felt uneasy. He was always there — waiting. Now there was no one in the horizon. But she did have to let him go. She couldn't make him wait forever. She took a deep sigh of regret, because she may never find another Silvio, even though she wasn't sure she wanted to.

She looked down at the tea stain on her dress. *What a shame*, she thought sadly. She admired the fabric and the embroidery. She hoped the dress could be salvaged — that it wasn't damaged and could serve its intended purpose. Suddenly, her heart beat with anticipation, thinking about all the books she owned in which women wore such similarly well-made, beautiful garments. Feeling hopeful again, she hugged the bag containing her new books. The smell of new and old books combined enlivened her senses.

She walked slowly, enjoying the feeling of the cool night air on her face. It had been a strange but pleasant evening, but she was glad to be heading home to her sanctuary. Her thoughts gave her the comfort and reassurance she needed to ease the guilt about Silvio, until she heard someone behind her — footsteps coming towards her. They seemed to be getting faster, louder. She took a quick, panicked glance behind her, and saw a shadow of a man. Her footsteps became more urgent. She resisted turning around again, knowing it would only slow her down.

Picking up the pace, she took each hurried step with great trepidation. *I should have turned around — gone back towards Silvio's*. The street was eerily quiet. Usually there would be at least a few cars and people, but tonight there was no one around — no one but her and the man behind her. Her head was spinning. The alcohol, the conversation she had with Silvio clouded her vision. Her heart rate was increasing with each step. She wasn't even supposed to be out so late. She should have gone with Pamela, or Millie, or Silvio. Her hand brushed the fabric of her dress — it was still damp from the spilled tea. Oh how she wished she was still sipping tea with Silvio; how she wished the man behind her was Silvio telling her she forgot something. *What am I going to do? Is it wise to have him see where I live? But where will I go if I don't go home?* She looked up at the street lamps as she strode past them. The light streaming through the branches of trees created shadows on the walls around her. She wished the branches were arms, hugging her and keeping her safe.

Her thoughts were becoming hysterical and her heart beat even faster as she neared her flat. *Should I scream?* she speculated. *That might scare him away.* There was no more time to think. It had been such a pleasant night, and for it to end like this … *I should have been at home reading.* She was practically running now, struggling in her high heels, which felt like they were about to break under the pressure. There was no mistaking it. The man was following her, and there was nowhere to go except home. She felt her hair-comb fall to the ground, making a soft clanking sound on one of the bins outside. The distraction made her instinctively pause. It slowed her down. The man's footsteps were now louder. *Why is this happening? It was only this morning that I was upset about the lipsticks at Millie's* … She couldn't think. *I'll have to bolt to the front entrance*, she thought as she tried to work out how she would open the door fast enough. *Where's my access card?* she thought desperately.

The footsteps became slightly softer. Maybe her imagination was getting the better of her. *I can't take any chances*, she told herself. She slowed to a fast walk as she rifled through her bag with trembling fingers, looking for the card. She began the climb up the wide paved steps to the front entrance of the art deco building. But she suddenly couldn't move. Her dress ... it was stuck. She felt dizzy with paralysing fear. She pulled at the hem, which had stuck on the gate on her way up. As she tried desperately to free herself, she heard the front door opening. *Someone's at the door.* Relief coursed through her. They could help her! She finally pulled the dress free, but miscalculated her steps and the heel of her shoe caught between concrete pavers. Before she knew it, she was rolling down the stairs. She felt the moist grass and dirt from the landscaped front garden on her legs, now revealed underneath the dress. She looked around and realised she'd landed right next to the bed of pink roses that grew outside, lovingly tended to by one of the building's residents.

"*Oh my God!*" a woman shrieked. The voice came from the front entrance, at the top of the stairs. It was a piercing, sharp voice that made her stomach turn.

Cemented firmly in the dirt, Tess anxiously looked towards the front entrance, catching a glimpse of her bag and her belongings scattered around her in the dirt and amongst the pink roses. The books she'd just purchased were lying on the wet grass. Her clothes were still in the paper bag. As she looked at the tea stain and dirt on her beautiful, ruined dress, she felt like everything dear to her — her safe little world — had been stained and crushed.

She pulled herself up onto her knees and instinctively turned around to see the woman at the door. It was the blonde woman she'd seen the other day. There was something about her ... She could feel a wild, hot rash start to spread across her skin at the realisation. It explained a lot, about why she'd been thinking of her past so much lately. Something had triggered it. Her heart began to beat intensely again. Tess felt like she couldn't breathe, like she was going to be sick. Was she in a dream? Did she hit her head? It was the same face, the one that had tormented her for so long, that had laughed at her expense. *Desiree* was standing at the front entrance! The front entrance of the cosy world she had created for herself. She was standing in her home!

"Tess? *Oh my God! It's you! I can't believe it!*" Desiree cried, as Tess looked up at her in shock, on her knees in the dirt in her once beautiful dress.

"Tess!" She felt a smooth, masculine hand on her arm. "Are you okay?" he asked gently as he reached for her hand. She looked up. It couldn't be, but it was. It was Stewart.

***

He gently helped her to her feet. She felt his hand on her face.

"We better get some ice on that," he said, looking at her forehead, which pounded. He looked into her eyes with concern.

Has the clock turned back? How could this be happening — again? Her thoughts ran rampant. For a moment it was like life had come full circle. He was looking into her eyes again. She felt no pain, even though she should with the fall she just took. He was back in her life again. *But why? How?* It didn't make sense. She struggled to find her voice in the sharp chill of the night air. It was as though she was in a dream, standing in front of her house with Stewart and … She could feel daggers behind her, eyes on her back. *But what is she even doing here — where I live?* Tess suddenly felt the pain in her leg and her forehead just as she felt Desiree's piercing eyes tear through her. She felt like she had been caught between the light in front of her, and the darkness behind her.

"Are you okay, Tess?" he enquired again.

She stumbled on her words. "Um … I'll be okay. Yes, I just need to put some ice on it. I'll be fine." The way he was looking at her wasn't making it any easier. He was so concerned, so handsome, so chivalrous. She noticed his full sensual lips, the slight beard tracing his strong jaw, his well-proportioned face. She saw the compassion and decency in his blue-grey eyes.

She felt dainty footsteps approaching their sacred moment, and her heart sunk.

"Tess, this is unbelievable!" Desiree exclaimed. "What are you doing here?"

She turned to face her. Tess could see her perfect little nose, her sun-streaked blonde hair. It *was* the woman she'd seen the day before, but it couldn't be the woman in the white dress — the one holding packages and a bag from Millie's, the one she'd guessed was *moving into her apartment building*. It couldn't be because that would mean that *Desiree* was moving — *into her building*! She struggled to steady her breathing. Suddenly she knew why she'd felt something strange was about to happen — something that would ruin her world. That *something* was standing right in front of her — adorned in designer clothes and her trademark conceited smile.

Dizziness made Tess unsteady.

"We'd better give her some water," she heard Stewart say to Desiree. "Let's take her upstairs to the flat."

Let's take her upstairs to the flat, she repeated in her mind. It was true — Desiree was the woman with the long, toned legs Tess had seen striding down the corridor the night before.

"Oh look at you! Poor Tess, you poor thing! And look at your dress, it's all muddied and stained. Stewart's right. We'll take you up to my apartment," Desiree offered with a burst of enthusiasm.

"*No!*" Tess blurted out, her vision returning to its proper state after hearing the familiar condescension. *Poor Tess,* the words rang in her ears. *Oh no you don't,* she thought to herself. She wasn't going to be called "poor Tess" by anyone — certainly not by *her.* "I don't need to go to *your* apartment. I live here. I've been living here for the last *three years,*" she managed between deep breaths.

"*Oh my God*! Really? What are the chances? This is so funny! Who would have thought that I'd be neighbours with *Tess* — of all people? We've just moved in. I must warn you

77

though, it's only temporary. We're only living here for a while — I thought it'd be cute to live in this humble little building for a few weeks. I thought I'd see how the other half lives. It's a nice change from living in a huge house, like a quaint little holiday. So, you live here, in this building, all alone?" she asked with obvious pity.

We're only living here for a while — *"we're"*, Tess speculated. Her breathing was restored temporarily at the realisation they wouldn't be living there too long. *But who's the "we" she keeps referring to? It can't be — surely, not her and Stewart, together?*

"Come on, Tess. Let's get you inside then." She felt Stewart's strong yet gentle hand on her shoulder.

Tess decided to take charge and somehow regain her composure. She began to limp towards the front entrance, feeling Stewart's hand on her shoulder. *How would she feel about that?* she thought. *How would Desiree feel about Stewart's hand touching my shoulder?*

"Watch your step," she heard him say.

"Oh, I have to get my bags, and my books," Tess cried when they reached the door.

"Don't worry. Desiree will get them for you," he said, glancing over at her.

"Um …" Desiree managed.

Tess saw the expression in Stewart's eyes as he met Desiree's glare at the very idea that she would collect all of Tess' things.

"Don't worry. I'll get them," Tess said, feeling uncomfortable about Desiree retrieving her beautiful bags with so many delicate and meaningful things inside — her clothes, and her newly-purchased books with their wonderful stories, being in the hands of someone so superficial, so shallow and rude.

"No, don't worry, Tess. You've been through enough for one night. It's no big deal. Desiree will get them."

"*Okay,*" she said with a quiver in her voice, as she saw Desiree apprehensively looking at her belongings amongst the roses scattered across the grass.

"Um, I *am* wearing my new designer heels though," Desiree said snarkily, "but sure, I'll go into the mud and get them for you. I mean, it's not something I usually do, especially in designer heels. It *was* such a heavy storm last night. Everything's still damp."

"You can walk on the paved path and reach them, unless you want to help Tess while I get them?" Stewart suggested.

Tess shuddered at the thought, and it seemed Desiree did too.

"No, I'll get them," Desiree said, much too quickly.

Tess noticed the serious expression on Stewart's face. He seemed to be embarrassed by Desiree's behaviour. But how could he be with *her* of all people? He was so considerate and kind. Tess also sensed he was intelligent — not that she ever had an in-depth conversation with him back at school. It was the way he looked at her, the way he looked at *them* — the whole group, when he'd scolded them back in high school. It was the way he carried himself. Tess knew there was a great deal of feeling and depth in his soul.

She heard Desiree's footsteps quieten, then some rustling behind her, then the footsteps growing louder again as she approached them, holding Tess' bags up in the air and away from her body as though they were covered in poison instead of a bit of dirt.

"There," she said, practically shoving the bags in Tess' face. Tess grabbed them and held them to her chest protectively. "See what I do for people? Not many would, in this outfit. It's from Paris, not that you would know about such … I mean, you don't own anything … um …" She trailed off, looking at Tess' dress. She then turned to Stewart, who was looking at her with a cold stare. "Anyway, let's get you all sorted, you *poor thing*. I mean, how many times do you trip over your dresses? It's just like old times, isn't it? You haven't changed at all, Tess. Even your hair has some pink in it …"

"It's rose golden-brown," Tess interrupted, annoyed. "It's really in style right now. Well, it is around here anyway, and in Paris and other parts of the world." She finished abruptly as anger took over her trembling body. She felt so childish and small for even justifying it. *I don't need her approval*, she thought in a burst of rage.

"Oh, is it? *In style*, that is? You follow the trends? I remember you would just wear clothes your mum made, didn't you?"

Tess struggled to find the words, to come up with a reply that would wipe the smirk off of Desiree's face. She tried to repress the feeling emerging from deep within —the feeling that used to consume her, back when she used to care what Desiree said to her.

"We can talk inside," Stewart interjected loudly.

"Sure, Stewy. Of course we can. It'll be fun to catch up with Tess — to reminisce, and all that. I mean, talk about coincidences. We should invite the whole gang from school, and really make it a reunion." She smiled at Tess as she walked past her, opening the door just enough to allow herself into the building, leaving it to close behind her. Stewart reached over Tess' head and managed to stop it just before it closed on her.

"After you, Tess," he said softly in a smooth, apologetic tone.

"Thanks," she said, looking at Desiree walking down the hallway so confidently, it was as if she'd lived there for years. Tess' face flushed with anger at her audacity to walk so boldly in her home.

"It is rather quaint and humble, this place," Desiree declared. "It's not what I'm used to. We have many investment properties with similarly sized apartments, and they might be okay for our tenants to live in on a long-term basis, but I think I would feel like pulling my hair out after a while. I need my space, and *my closet*, which is bigger than two of these flats put together." She laughed condescendingly.

"I think this building's warm, inviting, and full of character," Stewart said from where he stood next to Tess in the narrow hallway. Stewart examined the walls and the high ornate ceiling, his eyes then meeting Tess'. He held the stare.

Tess looked away, feeling slightly uncomfortable, helped along by the fact that Desiree's gaze was now focused on her hair. She could see her checking out each strand in the dim hallway, combing her hair with blades rather than delicate bristles. Tess couldn't handle having Desiree's eyes on her, so began to walk up the stairs. As soon as she took a step, she felt a sharp pain in her right leg. The pain was getting worse. "Ouch!" she cried.

"Careful, I've got you," said Stewart in his soft, kind voice.

She looked to see if Desiree had seen his hand on her shoulder again, but she was too busy inspecting her nails, no doubt for any minute specks of dirt that may have gotten on them after retrieving Tess' bags.

A few moments later, after Stewart had helped her up the stairs, with Desiree walking behind them both impatiently, Tess opened the door of her sanctuary. The brass bell greeted them with its sweet jingle. How she wished its greeting was for *her* only, welcoming her home before she planted herself on her chesterfield armchair with one of her books. But as she felt Stewart's tall presence beside her as she stepped inside, her heart couldn't help but flutter enthusiastically. It then beat heavier and with more difficulty when she processed what was actually happening — that Desiree was also there next to her, and would be in her life — *again,* the one person she wanted nothing to do with, the person who in many ways contributed to her decision to leave her parents' restored cottage and head to the city. Desiree had brought the past with her — and that same horrible feeling for Tess. She made her feel so small when she spoke to her — like she was an unhappy teenager again.

She heard Stewart's approving laughter, and noticed him admiring the brass bell on the door. "Wow!" he exclaimed. "I love the bell. Great idea! It looks really old."

"Yes, it is … well, I think it is. I plan on getting it appraised one day."

Stewart looked at her thoughtfully.

As she walked in, she was positive that Desiree was trying to stifle a giggle.

"Anyway, I think I'll be okay for now," Tess said, suddenly realising that the last person she wanted in her house was Desiree, and that she hadn't tidied up her flat, and that the boy she had thought of so many times since school was standing there beside her — now fully grown, athletic and manly. He was even handsomer than she remembered.

"That's okay, Tess," he said. "We'll help you. I still can't believe we ran into you like this. It's so weird."

"I'll say," Desiree said, scanning the apartment.

He held her arm and guided her to the lime-coloured suede sofa next to her chesterfield armchair. He then walked over to the kitchen. "Do you have any ice?"

"Just press the fridge … Actually, I'll get it," Tess said, trying to stand up, panic-stricken that her kitchen might be messy. She couldn't remember what state she'd left it in.

"How old's *this* thing?" Desiree asked as she looked at the armchair.

Tess instantly sat back in her seat. Just as she began to think of how she would manage to construct a sentence that could answer such an annoyingly rude question, she heard Desiree shrill, "*Wow*! She's *hot* … this model. She's so beautiful. That's the colour I want to make my hair. You think it would suit me?" she asked Stewart, her fingers twirling the ends of her long blonde locks.

Stewart was back by Tess' side with some ice in a sandwich bag. Tess realised the pantry where he'd found the sandwich bags had definitely not been tidied. *Oh well*, she thought, slightly embarrassed.

"*Stewart*, have a look at this model. Don't you think she's beautiful?"

Stewart made sure Tess was sitting comfortably before moving closer to Desiree to take a look at the magazine.

"Wow!" he exclaimed.

"Yeah, I know, she's beautiful isn't she? I was thinking of making my hair colour like ..."

"No, that's not what I meant," Stewart interjected. "I mean, she's definitely beautiful, but I can't believe how much she looks like Tess. You could be sisters." He looked at Tess searchingly. "There's something about her eyes, they're so deep ... just like yours." He gave Tess the most intense of looks.

Tess froze at his comment. She couldn't seem to look away from him, or to be able to construct a sentence.

"Yeah?" Desiree managed. "Actually, now that I look closely at her, I think her nose has a dent in it. Anyway, you should see one of my friends! She's so stunning and she's been chosen to be a model for something. She reckons that I should even try out, that I'd make a great model ..."

"I'm impressed," Stewart said.

Desiree tossed her hair with pride. "Yeah, I know, it's really impressive isn't ..."

Stewart interrupted. "These books are so impressive, Tess. How many do you have?" He marvelled at the bookshelves, his fingers scanning the binders delicately, as though they were silk.

Desiree walked over to the bookshelves, obviously offended by Stewart's response. "What are you looking at?" she asked irritably, as though she wasn't quite sure if the rectangular-shaped objects, bounded by beautiful covers that housed decades, or even centuries worth of stories and knowledge, were in fact books. "*These* are *impressive?* You're kidding me, right? You're beginning to sound like the kids at school." She looked scornfully at Tess. "You know what I mean, Tess? You hung out with them. Didn't you always

83

hang out at the library? You poor thing! You should have just hung out with us."

Tess' heart nearly stopped. She couldn't handle what was happening. Her heart palpitated. *Poor Tess … You should have hung out with us?* Was she in a dream? More appropriately, what planet was Desiree on? Why on earth would she hang out with her? Did she have amnesia?

Stewart looked away from the books, and gave Desiree a perplexed, serious look, obviously thinking the same thing. "I remember Tess having a wonderful time with her group. I remember passing them in the library one day, and I heard them having such a passionate and interesting discussion. I felt like joining in." He gave Tess another friendly look.

Tess felt like her heart was melting when she looked at him. She could feel it, the connection between them, and yet he was standing in her lounge room — *with Desiree.*

Steadying her breathing, she spoke. "*You* were in the library?"

Stewart laughed. "You don't think I ever went to the library? *Ouch!*" He placed his hand on his heart as though she'd insulted him.

"Relax, Tess. It was probably a one-off," Desiree stated. "As if Stewart ever read books! All he cared about was how well he was doing in the football team. Did you ever see him play? I don't think you ever attended a game. That's not very supportive of the school spirit, not to support the team, now, is it?"

Tess noticed Stewart's hurt and embarrassed look. He brushed a dark brown strand of hair away from his face, and gave Desiree another serious look. He then diverted his attention back to Tess.

Tess gave him an affectionate, knowing smile. *What on earth is he doing with her?* she thought again. She glanced at the old clock on the wall. It was way past midnight. Eager to rid her warm, cosy space of Desiree's coldness, she said, "Well, thanks for everything. You two probably have to get back downstairs to your *temporary* home. I'm sure you're both busy." As Tess looked at Stewart, a feeling of regret enveloped her. *If only she wasn't here. If only it was just the two of us and they weren't together."* Her heart beat rapidly again. What was she thinking? They obviously *were* together, and in any case, she didn't need a man in her life, even if it *was* Stewart. Anyway, the idea she had of him was just in her imagination. He was fiction, just like the leading men in her books. But she couldn't mistake what she had seen in him, because she could still see it in his eyes — the truth, the real person. A kind and compassionate man.

"I'd better go and get out of this dress … I mean, these dirty clothes," Tess stumbled. It had been a long and strange day.

"Oh, sure." Stewart said. Tess wasn't certain if she'd heard disappointment in his voice.

"Yes, well I've got a big day ahead of me," Desiree chipped in. "It's not easy having to manage so many properties. And I've got my man waiting for me downstairs. I'm sure he's got something romantic planned for our first night here."

"Yes, you'd better get going," Stewart said, practically kicking her out the door with the abruptness of his tone. "I'm sure you've got a great night ahead of you. Say hi to Keith for me, *if* he hasn't fallen asleep on the lounge again, that is." He gave Desiree an emphatic smile as she opened the front door of the apartment.

Desiree looked embarrassed at his comment. Tess felt he was trying to make a point, like he knew the truth behind her words.

They aren't together! Tess' thoughts were hysterical. *They aren't together*, she told herself, relief settling in her heart. *Stewart, he isn't with that shallow girl who ruined most of high school.* She awkwardly adjusted the cushions on the sofa as she watched him step back inside after sending Desiree on her way.

"There's no need to get up, Tess. I hope your leg isn't too painful, and your forehead. It was quite a day, running into you like this. I mean, what are the chances really?" With a nervous smile, he said, "You look great, by the way."

"Oh, thank you," Tess managed, surprised by her awkwardness. She looked down at her dress regretfully. It had been through a lot in the last few hours. "Well, I never planned on falling down the stairs and landing in the rose bushes tonight. I guess it's just like old times. I'm sure you remember when I fell down that hill. You must think I'm so clumsy." She tried to steady her heart rate as she began to process what was actually happening. She was in her lounge room with Stewart — and she was no longer in high school. But what were they doing here? In her building? In her world? And why was he here with Desiree if they weren't an item?

"I'm just glad you're okay," he said. "You are okay, aren't you? You look like you're shivering. Are you cold? It is strange … this weather."

"Yes, it definitely is strange. One minute we're in the most intense heatwave for fifty years, and now it feels like autumn."

She suddenly felt calm again. It was like the waves settled whenever he spoke, yet her heart beat so ferociously she may as well have been caught in a tsunami. His face, his eyes carried so much depth and feeling. At school he had been so different to Tess and her bookish friends, but deep down Tess always felt something had pushed him away from his studies — that he had great intellectual potential.

"Anyway, I'd better let you go," he said, heading for the door. He looked over his shoulder and said, "It really has been great seeing you again. It's just like old times …" He locked eyes with her as she gave him a searching look. "I mean, maybe not like old times. We didn't exactly hang out together back then, but here we are now."

"It's great to see you again too. You're right, it's surreal," she managed, suddenly feeling vulnerable. Feeling the intensity of his stare, she looked away, towards the door. She felt like she might cry if he didn't leave at that moment.

Stewart walked over to the door and looked at the brass bell. He pushed it gently to hear the jingle, and smiled. "It's sweet, the bell, it really is, and beautiful, and unique." He turned to face her. "Bye, Tess," he said, softly. "It's been wonderful seeing you."

"You too," Tess murmured as he opened the door. He gave her one last smile before slipping through it and closing it behind him.

In her chest the surging waves settled, and her heartbeat returned to normal. Tess allowed herself to repeat his words in her mind. *It's sweet ... it really is, and beautiful, and unique.* She chewed each word up slowly and savoured its sweetness. The fact that the little brass bell had made an impression on him made her happy. It was as though he understood what it meant to her — that it wasn't just a bell, but something much more. She'd always felt the little bell had a personality all of its own — it accepted everyone with its friendly jingle. Well, almost everyone.

She looked around her apartment, at the books *she* had ridiculed. She recalled her smirk when she referred to her as "*Poor Tess*", eyeing her furniture, her bookshelves — the secure world that she had created. That world would change forever, because chaos and uncertainty had returned to her life. The uneasiness she felt inside began to consume her as she realised that her world would never be the same again as long as Desiree was in it. But then an image of Stewart smiling and looking at her gently came to mind, and she couldn't help but feel he may be the change she needed.

She realised that even if the surging waves were messing with her peace, that as intimidating as those waves could be, they could also be magnificent, making anyone in their presence feel alive with their infectious strength and beauty, able to feel something bigger than themselves — something they never would have experienced if they hadn't ever felt their exhilarating presence.

At that moment, Tess realised those surging waves could add life to an otherwise peaceful landscape, and bring with them great beauty.

CHAPTER SEVEN

Tess woke in a cold sweat. She glanced at the clock on her bedside table. It was three o'clock in the morning. *It's just a dream*, she thought with relief. She'd been dreaming about standing out the front of her apartment building with Desiree — both of them wearing their school uniforms. She felt the bruise on her leg and the other on her forehead, and realised Desiree *was* back in her life. It wasn't a dream, but a nightmare! Her heart began to beat rapidly again and an anxious feeling emerged from deep within her. How was it even possible for her to be back in her life?

Then it occurred to her — what if she didn't see Stewart again? Was he just visiting Desiree? Did he live somewhere far away? She hadn't even managed to ask that vital question. How could she? She was in extreme shock — her thoughts had been a mess. The asphyxiating pain in her chest seemed to be getting worse. Why was this happening when her life was going so smoothly? It had been effortless for so long. The stillness of the night induced fear and uncertainty. Coping with any type of change was more daunting to Tess in the early hours of the morning. The surging waves now seemed threatening again, not as exhilarating as they had appeared before she had closed her eyes. This realisation was heightened by the fact that she only welcomed part of the change — the part which only included Stewart.

She freed her legs from the tight grasp of her bedsheets, which were curled up around her ankles as a result of tossing and turning all night. She lost her balance for a moment as she tried to get out of bed, and then stumbled her way to the bathroom. The moon cast its shadow on the wall next to the mirror above the sink. She could see the reflections of tree branches, intermittently buffeted by the wind. She then looked at herself in the mirror through blurry eyes. Her hair was a mess, and her face looked pale. After splashing some cold water onto her face, then wiping it with a small towel, she walked over to the narrow window and gazed out at the quiet, darkened street, hearing car horns and a train speeding on the tracks from a distance. The street lights highlighted the street's emptiness. It was eerily quiet. In a few hours, it would be busy, filled with people running their Saturday morning errands, having an early breakfast at the many coffee shops further along the street, or going to work like she and many of her fellow shop owners or employees would be doing.

"Ouch!" she cried as she bumped her bruised leg onto the side of the bathtub. She hobbled back to her bedroom and lay back in bed, wondering what on earth she was going to do tomorrow at work with her very sore leg. She reached over for the bottle of water on her bedside table and took a sip. Her mind wandered back to the past again.

"You? Married?" Desiree had sniggered all those years ago. "Tess, I really can't picture it. I don't even think you're interested in guys. I mean, the way you dress, it's almost like you *want* to frighten them away."

Tess had watched Desiree walk back to her best friend, Evie. Her uniform was skintight, as if glued to her. She could barely walk in it. It had reminded Tess of a penguin waddling back to the water, though she was sure that was not Desiree's intention. She'd obviously had her skirt adjusted way too much — it was definitely against school policy to be so short and tight — but Tess and her crew got away with everything. Their parents made huge contributions to the school every year, and in turn, the school would advertise their companies.

One night, there had been a special dinner for parents and students held at the town hall. Desiree's father, Mr Marsden, had even made a speech, being the CEO of a company that sold stationary supplies and electronics and contributed many supplies to the school. Mr Marsden had been loudly applauded.

Tess had walked past the Marsdens' table on her way to the bathroom after Mr Marsden had sat down and the applause had simmered. "Sit still," she'd heard him say to his daughter. "Try not to say too much, and smile, for God's sake! You look like you don't want to be here. Everyone knows who I am and respects me here." Tess had pretended not to hear as she stole a glance at Desiree, who was sitting quietly with a smile on her face, her hands clasped before her on the table.

Tess had walked back to where she was sitting with her family and Cathy's family. Michael and his family were sitting at the table next to them. In contrast to the quiet dictatorship of the Marsdens', their little corner of the town hall was full of vivacious laughter and heartfelt conversation.

Later that night, Mrs Marsden and Desiree had been standing near to Tess and her mother when Tess heard Desiree say something quietly in her mother's ear as she looked at Tess and her family. She was positive she'd heard her say, with a giggle, "That's that family I was talking about." Mrs Marsden then appraised Tess' mother from head to toe with a look of disdain. As Desiree and Mrs Marsden made their way past them, Tess looked at them for any sort of acknowledgment of her presence, or the realisation she had heard everything. But the pair had disregarded her like she didn't even exist.

Oh my God, Tess thought anxiously. *Why is she back in my life again?* She glanced at the clock again, then buried herself under the sheets. She had to try to get some sleep. She couldn't think of her anymore.

A few hours later, Tess was awoken by her alarm clock. She buried herself under the safety of her covers again, not yet ready to face the day. Her head ached and she knew she would have an excruciating migraine all day from lack of sleep, but she had to go into work. She couldn't let her clients down. As well as all the wedding guests, she had to fit Briana in for a shampoo, style and blow-dry for her dress-up party that evening. Briana had decided on going as Jane Eyre, as one of the guys she fancied at the party was into the classics. She wanted to resemble a woman from the Victorian era after seeing Tess' dress the last time she'd had her foils done. Tess was surprised at her choice, informing her that Jane Eyre was humble in her looks and quite modest. Briana had argued that it didn't matter, that no one would care if she wore a lot of make-up and glammed the character up a bit. The guy she was into would be impressed with her nevertheless. Her other choice was Cleopatra, but that would mean she would have to wear a wig, and wigs made her scalp itch. Besides, she knew that Tess was experienced at creating many of the styles from the Georgian and Victorian eras, as well as those of old Hollywood and the 50s and 60s. Tess had told her several times how, when she was younger, she had practised creating the styles on a mannequin her mother had found in one of the arts and crafts garage sales. She had managed to perfect the styles over the years.

Forcing herself out of bed, Tess headed for the shower. She caught a glimpse of herself in the mirror above the sink. *How on earth am I going to get rid of these bags under my eyes?* She hadn't had such a restless sleep since she was married to Michael. And it was all because of *her*.

She hobbled to the kitchen and placed two tablespoons in the freezer. She'd read that cold spoons could alleviate unwanted puffiness around the eyes. Her eye cream wouldn't be enough. Her chest began to feel a bit lighter when she looked around her apartment at all her treasured belongings. It was slightly messier than other days — not having had the time to tidy up the night before. Despite this, it looked beautiful, and shimmered with life.

Most of what she owned had something special to offer — it sparkled and fed the room with wisdom and character. Even her black and white kitchen tiles had been sourced from a French restaurant that had been remodelling. Her mother was always able to find old treasures and restore them, to find a new purpose with someone new to appreciate them. She loved the feeling that she'd somehow saved them and that they weren't discarded just because they had seen better days.

Her mind then went to Desiree again — her perfect smile, her perfect *everything* — then to her cold rudeness, and her colder eyes, which revealed nothing but meanness and hollowness. *It's not as though she's my roommate,* she reassured herself. *Who said she wants to see me again anyway? She's probably just as shocked as I am.*

Feeling more at ease that Desiree's resurgence in her life wouldn't impact her peace, she headed to her bedroom to work out what to wear. She needed to choose a colour that would hide the fact she hadn't slept well — although that might be impossible. As she looked in her bedroom vanity mirror, she realised she would need to devote a great deal of time to getting her hair to cooperate, to avoid looking like she had been caught in a wild storm. She would need to tidy up the place as well. It was Saturday after all, and since she was very young, Saturdays were left to clean all the mess that a week full of homework, arts, crafts, and music rehearsals had caused. It was her day to focus on doing mundane chores, and of course, dusting her beautiful treasures.

She opened her cupboard, feeling the bruise on her leg as she bumped it on the side of the bed. Ignoring the pain, she turned to look at the dress she'd left on her gold antique chair. It had gone through a lot. Looking at it brought back memories of sipping tea with Silvio, and then being stuck in the rose bush, covered in dirt, with Stewart gazing into her eyes. It was strange that the moment she'd rejected Silvio, another man had offered his hand — literally lifting her out of dirt again. *Poor Tess.* She remembered Desiree's patronising words as she looked at the dress, and she couldn't help but feel sorry for it. *No,* she decided. She refused to feel sorry for it. It would withstand anything that was thrown at it — it was resilient — and it, and she, would get through this. *It's only temporary. Things will be back to normal again.*

As she remembered Stewart's kind chivalry, she once again wondered if she wanted that to happen — for things to go back to normal. She looked at the dress again. She'd take it to the dry cleaners on her way to the salon. The hem might also need to be mended. She had an uneasy feeling the tea stain wouldn't come out — that it would remain *forever!*

Her thoughts were suddenly interrupted by a knock at the door. She jumped, startled, and felt pain shoot through her leg again. Grimacing, she was about to hobble to the door, but refrained when she caught a glimpse of herself in the mirror at the end of the narrow hallway. *Oh no! I can't let anyone see me like this ...* She tripped over her thoughts as she heard a familiar, female voice.

"Tess, are you awake?"

It was *her ...* and Tess looked like she had just stepped out of ... *Yes, the shower. I'll pretend I just stepped out of the shower.* She couldn't let Desiree see her in such a state. Tess looked around her apartment, at the clothes scattered on the lounge, the sun shining on her antique furniture, highlighting every speck of dust — as though the whole room was under a microscope. *I can't let her see me like this. I just can't.* This wasn't how it was supposed to be. She wasn't supposed to see her again — *ever,* and if there was the slightest, minuscule possibility that she did, she was supposed to be composed and looking fabulous. It was bad enough that she had landed in dirt the night before, with Her Royal Highness standing tall in her designer outfit, sniggering and looking down at her. She just wanted to go back to bed, lie under the covers and cry. But that wasn't an option. She would feel defeated, as though she was scared of her. She would face her, and she would have to try to look confident and unfettered.

Without thinking, scurrying around the room, her leg aching, Tess took off her pyjamas. She then froze under the pressure of not knowing what to do from there — she had to put *something* on. Her mind raced.

"Oh good! You're awake, Tess. It's me, Desiree." She had obviously heard all the commotion. Tess could hear movement and faint breathing from the other side of the door.

"Um ... I'm not dressed yet," she managed.

"That's okay. I'll only be a minute. It's okay. It's just me. It's not a stranger. I don't mind if you're still in your PJs. Honestly, it doesn't matter."

Tess pursed her lips and felt every muscle in her body tense. *I mind*, she thought angrily. *I mind! Of course you don't mind seeing me in the worst state possible — to have something else to tell the gang back home. Maybe you should call them all now, and have them knock at my door at 7.30 on a Saturday morning unannounced as well? Wouldn't that be grand! Like hell, you're not a stranger! Like you know anything about me. If you did, you would know that I don't have fake friends visit on a Saturday morning!*

Hastily, she ran to her bedroom and grabbed her champagne-coloured silk robe. She always felt beautiful in it, even if the rest of her had seen better days. She put it on over her trembling limbs, and clumsily managed to tie it around her waist, making sure it covered her. She then hurried frantically to the bathroom and splashed some water on her face and tied her hair up in a bun. She pressed her fingers under her eyes to try and alleviate at least some puffiness. She then grabbed the toothbrush and hastily squeezed out as much toothpaste as was humanly possible from the almost empty tube. "Damn!" she muttered.

Moments later, not having time to open the windows and air out the apartment, she sprayed some of her perfume in the air. *At least the apartment, and I, smell citrusy and fresh*, she thought as she walked towards the door. To her dismay, she realised her robe was practically slipping off and she wasn't wearing anything underneath. A scene from one of the English classics came to mind, where members of a family living in some English country estate scurry around the room in hysterics, tidying up themselves and everything around them upon hearing a knock on the door, only to pretend to be reading a book or needle-pointing when they finally let the unannounced guest in. The guest would say something like "forgive me" as they entered. But she would have a greater chance at winning a trip to the moon than have Desiree apologise for anything.

What do I care! she thought with vehemence. *I'm not going to become unhinged by her. That's what she wants to have happen. I refuse to allow her to make me feel like that!* As she placed her hand on the crystal doorknob, with false and volatile confidence, she suppressed the thought that she may already be letting that happen. *I'm being silly. It's not as though this is a scene from Pride and Prejudice. I mean, it's not like some handsome male suitor like Mr Darcy is at the door,* she told herself to ease another bout of anxiety that was, once again, emerging from deep within. It worked. She smiled to herself. Feeling that her moment of ease might be a transient one, she swung the door open. The little brass bell jingled just as she heard footsteps approaching, coming to a halt right outside her door. She heard Desiree say: "It's okay. She won't mind."

"Hi Desiree," Tess greeted her loudly as she opened the door, not wanting her to know she was bothered by her intrusion. Her heart felt like it would explode when she saw Desiree was standing next to someone, and that *someone* was *Stewart!* The footsteps were *his. He* was the recipient of the words: "It's okay, she won't mind."

Tess greeted him self-consciously. "Oh … hi, I mean …" Words instantly failed her. She couldn't even string a few words together to greet him, and as a long strand of damp hair fell out of her messy bun and onto her forehead, she realised she'd completely ruined her chances of looking regal and unfettered.

"Tess, look at you! *You poor thing* … always scurrying around or falling down."

"Sorry to bother you so early on a Saturday morning, Tess," Stewart said with concern in his voice. "Forgive us for intruding like this. I wasn't sure if I should come visit, but I was passing your building and noticed Desiree stepping out, so I thought …"

"Um … that's okay," she managed as she repeated his words in her mind. *Forgive us*. He *was* the perfect gentleman. He then looked at Desiree, who appeared to be smugly checking her out, as though she was adding another bonus point to her "Ways to Humiliate Tess" scoreboard. For some reason unbeknownst to Tess, Desiree's gaze landed on her chest, and she was obviously trying to stifle another snigger. Her pupils were practically dilated. She looked over at Stewart, who then too glanced at Tess' chest briefly before awkwardly looking away.

"Sorry," he said. "We've come at a bad time."

Tess quickly looked down at her robe, trying to be as discrete as she could, wondering why all eyes were on it. Horrified, she realised it had slipped right down, exposing far more skin than she wanted to. She instantaneously broke out into a rapid, wild blush and felt itchy all over. She hastily tightened her robe, ensuring everything that shouldn't be showing wasn't, before she awkwardly met his gaze halfway. Their eyes locked. Tess felt her cheeks getting warmer. It would have been a romantic moment if she didn't remember that her eyes were still puffy and she had no make-up on whatsoever, apart from some leftover mascara smudged around her eyes. And it would also have been so if she wasn't standing right in front of her nemesis.

Tess broke the stare. Her eyes rested on the lovely, dainty hair-comb he was now holding out to her in his strong, masculine hand. It was her hair-comb — the one that had fallen as she was running away from him, thinking someone sinister was following her.

"I forgot to give you your hair-comb last night," he said. "You lost it when you were walking home. You looked like you were late for something. I thought I might have frightened you. Of course, I didn't realise that it was you — in the dark, that is."

She took the hair-comb from him. His hand momentarily brushed hers. She shivered.

She could feel Desiree getting impatient, fidgeting with her bag. Of course, she was all dolled up, looking like she got up at the crack of dawn to fix her hair and apply her makeup. She wondered how she would have liked it if she knocked on her door before she was all showered and dressed, without any make-up. Surely she would never allow anyone to see her looking less than perfect.

"Anyway," Stewart continued, "I wanted to wait until later to give it to you, but Desiree insisted that you would be okay accepting visitors this early, so I thought I'd come over now. I wanted to find out if you were okay."

Tess was instantly touched by his gesture. She felt the warmth of his words protecting her from the coldness of the woman standing beside him. She could feel Desiree's impatience growing stronger, her mannerisms conveying her boredom. She was leaning against the doorframe, looking at her nails as if they were far more interesting than a conversation with her. She couldn't believe Desiree had told him it would be okay to visit so early, like she knew her so well. It was as though she wanted them both to see her at her worst. Tess knew how she operated all too well.

"Anyway," Desiree said, finally looking up from her nails. "You can see she's fine. Well, apart from the obvious, but she's fine. She walked to the door just fine, didn't she? Anyway, Tess we're both busy, that's why we're up and about already, whether it's Saturday or not. It's hard when you've got too much to do. I just read an article that said that people who have a lot of money are also the busiest. I can't even imagine sitting in front of a TV or just lounging around in my PJs and reading," she said, eyeing the bookshelves over Tess' shoulder. "Who even has time to read?" She rolled her eyes in disbelief.

Stewart cleared his throat. "Well, I think reading's great. It broadens the mind. Even the busiest people find time to read if they love it — if they're passionate about it. I often read," he said, looking at Tess.

"Do you? *Okay* …" Desiree said, scrunching up her face as though she was appalled by the idea. "If you include sports magazines as reading, well, I guess you do read. I'm talking about fiction — who's got the time? It's not easy managing properties — I mainly read about investing and things like that. So does Keith, my savvy husband."

Stewart looked at the ground awkwardly. It was as though he couldn't believe the absurdities that were coming out of her mouth. His jaw was tight. He looked back up at Tess apologetically. "Anyway, sorry again, for bothering you so early. I should have known better. It was obviously not a good time."

Tess tidied her hair self-consciously. *So, she's married to Keith*, she thought. She wondered what type of person would have married *her*, what type of person Keith was, and if he had any scruples at all. She could feel Desiree eyeing her hair again. She felt so uncomfortable standing there looking so dishevelled.

"Well, I'll let you both go," Tess said awkwardly. "Thanks for bringing my hair-comb, Stewart. It's a vintage-inspired piece." She tightened her robe and covered herself up to her neck, just in case there were any more accidents. Being messy and half-naked was definitely not how she'd envisioned seeing Stewart again.

As though reading her thoughts, Stewart said, "Yeah, I've got things to do too, as I'm sure you have, Tess. I'm going to look into some courses at the universities here. That's why I'm in Sydney." He sounded like he wanted to impress her.

Tess was positive Desiree looked shocked, like she hadn't known about his plans to study. "Um, yeah," she chipped in. "Stewart is looking into some university courses. Maybe Keith can help with that. He's so savvy with these things, you know, study types of things …" She trailed off, intertwining the ends of her hair between her long fingers.

"Oh, he can? With what type of things do you mean?" Stewart looked genuinely puzzled.

"You know … um, studying and all that …"

"Well, I'm looking into literature courses, so I'm not sure if he's into that," Stewart replied. "You did say that you're both too busy to read. I think maybe Tess might be able to help me."

"Oh, really?" Desiree said dismissively, planting her hand on her arm. "Anyway, we better get going. We've wasted enough time …"

"Sure, don't mind me. You can go," he replied. The shocked expression returned to Desiree's face. "You can go," he repeated emphatically, looking straight into Desiree's wide eyes.

"Fine," Desiree snapped. "I *will* go. See you, *Tess*," she snarled. Tess watched her walk defiantly down the narrow hallway towards the stairs like a spoilt child who didn't get her way.

"So, Tess, how about it? Can you help me with my course selection? I remember you were really good at English back at school."

"Oh, sure," she stammered, her heart racing. "We can arrange a time. How do you want to go about this?" *Stewart's asking me out to discuss books and literature?* she thought in bemusement.

"Yeah, that's what I'd like to do — set a time where we can meet and you can guide me, or be a mentor. You seemed to know what you were doing at school more than any of the group I hung out with ever did. I practically failed most of my exams. You probably thought I was such a slacker." He looked down at his shoes for a moment, before returning his gaze to her own.

"No, I never thought that. I would never think that about you," she replied softly. He looked so vulnerable for a second, like a child needing approval, as he peered deep into her eyes, and she into his. To Tess it felt like their souls were communicating through eye contact.

The front door to the building opened. Tess shivered and hugged her robe tighter as a draft shot through the apartment.

"I'd better let you go. I'll call you, if that's okay with you?"

"Sure," she said, feeling like she was in a dream. "Okay, bye!' she said, abruptly, feeling her upper lip tremble as it usually did when she was slightly nervous. Tess gave Stewart a half wave, stepped back and shut the door before he had time to say anything else. She leant back onto its smooth surface as the brass bell danced to its own melody. She needed time to process it all.

As she began to calm down, she realised she didn't even give him her number. She had, in fact, just shut the door in his face. She was acting like a teenager, all giddy and immature. She felt a gentle tremor on her back and a knock at the door. She turned around and opened it. Hugging her robe again, she gazed into his eyes. They were smiling.

"Um … you forgot to give me your number," he said playfully. "I don't want to make it a habit that I run into you like this — I might risk becoming a nuisance."

"It's fine. You're not a nuisance!" she reassured him. She gave him her number, her head spinning with all sorts of emotions. At the same time, she felt exposed and awkward. She felt a blush creep across her face again when his eyes briefly fluttered to the delicate piece of silk covering her bare chest. She met his eyes, which were now serious.

"Thanks," he said. "Now, I've taken up enough of your time, and you're cold. It's so strange that one minute we were in sweltering heat, and now you're standing there in your robe shivering, looking so …" He trailed off. "It really is great to see you again, Tess." He began to turn away, only to stop to glance once again at the little brass bell, which had witnessed the whole conversation. "It really is a sweet idea, to have a bell at your door, just like in an old pub, or restaurant, or bar back in the day." He smiled at her and walked away slowly, leaving her to bask in the warmth he'd left behind.

She closed the door again. The bell jingled. *Just like in an old pub, or restaurant* … She repeated the words in her mind. She hadn't even talked to him about it, yet he'd had the same idea. There was something about the way he looked at her … the way she felt when she looked into his eyes. "Looking so …" he'd said, then trailed off. *He was about to call me something. It must have been something good, the way he was looking at me, like he was mesmerised. But how, when I look like this?* She walked over to the mirror in the hallway. She touched the puffiness under her eyes softly, and looked at her hair tied in a bun with strands hanging out at the sides. Some of it was still damp. She looked into her eyes, and saw something she hadn't seen for a long while — a twinkle. She then looked at the time … *Oh no! It's almost eight o'clock, and I'm not at the salon*, she panicked. *The wedding!*

She heard Desiree's words, and her mocking laughter, in her mind. *"You? Married? I can't even imagine you keeping a man!"* She remembered the pact. *I haven't got time for men.* And *things like that don't happen in real life, only in fiction.* But why shouldn't she feel like that outside of the pages of a book? Why shouldn't she ever feel the adrenaline pumping in her veins as wild horses thundered past her? Why couldn't she be wild and free? Just because her marriage to Michael didn't work out. Didn't she deserve another shot at love? *Because you don't really want wild horses. You have a quiet, cosy life you've created for yourself, and apart from the occasional storm, you don't want any drama*, she advised herself. She walked over to her books, to her "windows of hope" — to adventure, passion and romance. She realised that as content as she felt after she read them, she always sighed as she closed the last page with a heavy heart, always wanting more. She realised why she sighed like that. *It's because I don't have it in my life. I don't have the things I crave.*

She remembered Michael's words. "They're just flowers, Tess. I mean, what do they really do anyway?" She wondered if he ever allowed himself to understand what they could really offer him. She remembered what Stewart had said to her about the bell. *He understands. He understands what flowers can do if we allow them in our lives.* She looked at herself in the mirror again. Her face was serious and thoughtful, but her heart felt light, as if it were smiling. As Tess headed to the bathroom to shower, she realised she hadn't known that, all this time, her heart hadn't been smiling.

CHAPTER EIGHT

The hairdryer masked the sounds of conversation later that Saturday afternoon. Pamela had saved her that morning, making sure her client was tended to. Tess had managed to get herself together, but was forty minutes later to work than she'd planned. *Considering the circumstances*, she thought, *my lateness was justifiable.* Complicated thoughts had occupied her mind so thoroughly on the walk to the salon that it was hard to focus on anything else, and she found herself stopping unexpectedly at the oddest of moments, accidentally tripping up another pedestrian here or there, caught up in a haze of speculation and daydreaming. She was glad to free herself from her thoughts for a few hours at the salon. The comforting flow of routine, familiar faces, familiar sounds, and the focus of occupation soothed her.

For a few hours, she felt content again. Too much energy had been exerted during her impromptu encounter. She now needed solitude and comfort, and the salon would have to be her sanctuary for the time being, now that her home had been taken over — *infested* — by the enemy. For now she would have to try to put it all out of her mind, but the cold air that blew in every time the door opened, and the brisk wind that was so out of character for that time of the year reminded her of Desiree's coldness, and she could not forget what had happened.

Tess gazed up at the chandeliers. The translucent crystals in the prisms and in each individual pendalogue made Tess think of Stewart's beautiful eyes — how they flickered in the light and looked teary when they were vulnerable, even if he carried an air of confidence and assertion. As she continued to gaze at the crystals, nestled among the black scrolls and arms of the chandeliers' central columns, she realised they did create drama in the salon. Tess sighed and looked away.

"That must be the tenth time today you've stared at the chandeliers with your mouth open and a strange smile on your face," Pamela quipped as she passed her on her way to the basin. She gave her a curious look as she began to apply shampoo to her client's hair.

"What? I haven't been doing anything," Tess said defensively. "I don't know what you're talking about." Suddenly she was appalled that she might be acting just like Desiree and her group back in the school cafeteria — rudely. "Well, maybe I have been a little bit," she continued, smiling at Pamela to show she wasn't upset at being caught out acting strangely.

Tess continued working, head down, needing to be free from Pamela's scrutiny. She'd have to tell her eventually about what had transpired since their girls' night out at Vinnie's. Tess knew Pamela would have a lot to say on the matter, especially about Stewart.

The flow of routine did help her immensely. She was positive that what happened that morning wouldn't happen again — being caught out, dishevelled, in just a robe in the early morning.

Tess smiled as the door opened and a familiar woman entered the salon. It was one of the clients for the wedding — her four o'clock appointment. Then Briana would be next, who she would excitedly transform into Jane Eyre. She would then head over to the deli again, and then treat herself to some cupcakes with plenty of sprinkles on top, although she was hesitant to pass Silvio's on her way. Millie had also sent her a message telling her the lipsticks would be in by Wednesday, and that she would call her as soon as they arrived. *Everything is the way it was before*, she reassured herself. There were no drastic changes in her life, just some minor deviations. *"Ouch,"* she cried, as she walked towards the door, suddenly feeling the pain in her leg flare up. It felt worse than it had before.

Pamela looked at her with concern. "Are you okay?" she enquired. The woman at the door looked at her as well, her eyes inquiring the same.

"I'm fine," Tess reassured them both. "I just fell down and bruised my leg. It's nothing serious. It'll go away." She pushed an image of Desiree from her mind and guided the woman to a chair near the window. "It's a long story," she said to Pamela, who by now had also noticed the slight bruise on her forehead poking out from behind a few strands of fringe. "I'll tell you all about it when we get a chance, over a cup of coffee."

Tess instinctively thought of what Silvio had said to her — about Pamela stopping by for a late night coffee. "So, did you get home okay?" she asked her friend as she walked by her, grabbing one of the black capes and a towel for her client from the shelves at the back of the salon.

"Yeah, sure," Pamela said.

"I ran into Silvio," Tess stated.

Pamela looked up from the basin. The smell of pear and papaya permeated the air, the scent of the new organic shampoo they had recently ordered.

Pamela looked down at the water spraying into the ceramic basin, making a loud gurgling sound. Pamela turned the tap, adjusting the temperature. "Is that too cold?" she asked her client, talking over the noise.

"It's fine," her client responded. "I'm just glad it isn't hot this week. The last thing I want is to attend a wedding in excruciating heat."

Pamela continued washing out the shampoo. "That's right! Your hair will look great in this weather. It should hold up just fine seeing as there's no humidity." Pamela then diverted her attention back to Tess. "Yeah, I did. I also dropped by Silvio's. I figured I could do with a coffee after all that alcohol. It was a great night, don't you think? Helena and Millie seemed to enjoy themselves too."

Tess made her way back to her client, feeling slightly uneasy.

Her client just needed a shampoo, trim, and a style, so she guided her over to the basins. Pamela gave Tess another smile as she towel-dried her client's hair, which Tess felt was rather forced.

"Hi Briana," Tess said as her next client stepped into the salon. Tess looked at the clock and realised she was twenty minutes early.

"I just wanted to see if you're free yet," said Briana.

"Ah, no I'm not, I'm afraid," Tess replied.

"That's okay! I'm gonna go hang out with my friend at Silvio's. We suddenly need a coffee." She stepped outside to where her friend was standing. They both began to giggle and kept walking, talking with their hands in the air in animated discussion.

Tess smiled to herself. "The barista must be a real hottie," she muttered softly.

Her client looked up at her from the basin. "He sure is," she said with a huge grin.

Tess turned the tap on and adjusted the temperature. As the water flowed over her client's hair, she looked up and out the window. Across the street she saw Helena stepping out of her shop carrying a bucket of flowers. She was talking to someone. It was her husband, Carter. Tess hadn't seen him for a while. He worked at the local real estate agency in a small adjoining street. Most people knew him as the agency leased a lot of the properties in the area for many of the businesses. He was a good-natured, handsome and gregarious young man, always greeting everyone and handing out fliers about the latest opportunities in the property market.

Helena seemed agitated. She practically threw the flowers around as she arranged them. Carter looked like he was trying to explain something to her. Helena shook her head from side to side, and walked back into the shop. Tess then watched as Carter crossed the road, heading for the salon. She looked down at the basin and felt the lukewarm water on her hands, then up as Carter opened the door. Jessica suddenly appeared behind him. It seemed she had just happened to be walking past the salon when the door had opened. Carter turned around when he noticed her, greeting her with a somewhat awkward smile, like he was caught off guard. Jessica gave him a quick smile and continued walking. *She looks really lovely,* Tess thought, *when she doesn't look so dejected.*

"Hi Carter," Tess greeted him as he stepped inside.

"Hi, Tess. Any chance you can fit me in for a haircut?" He gave her a hopeful look.

Tess thought of Briana and the dress-up party, and gazed at the clock on the wall.

Carter looked apologetic. "I have an important auction tomorrow. I know I should have booked earlier. Is it okay, Tess?"

"Um, sure," Tess said. *Mr Papas won't close that early,* she told herself. She would have her planned reading night tonight, and everything would be back to normal for a while. She thought of Stewart as she told herself this. She wondered what he would be doing on a Saturday night. She didn't want to imagine what Desiree was doing. *It'll be okay. She'll be gone soon. She'll be gone, and Stewart will stay and go to uni.* She smiled at that thought.

As she looked up from the basin and reached for the towel, she saw Carter looking at Jessica again, who was now on the other side of the street, walking past his wife's shop. He had a concerned look on his face.

Her leg throbbed in pain as Briana and her friend giggled their way into the salon, their cheeks rosy and grins satisfied.

"I can't wait to look like Jane Eyre. She was a badass. She's like Tess. She never wanted to settle for just any man. I also don't plan on settling for one," she laughed, suddenly noticing Carter sitting on the lounge. "Although, I do intend on going out with plenty of them. It's great to not be restricted," she said in the same rambunctious voice, tossing her hair flirtatiously as Carter acknowledged her with a friendly smile before looking at his phone. *She's obviously taken by his good looks, as a lot of women are*, Tess observed. She also couldn't help but smile at her comment. Briana was definitely enthusiastic about men. *She may be confusing the character of Jane Eyre quite a bit though*, Tess thought.

"Jane Eyre didn't need men, just like Tess doesn't." Briana turned to look at Tess. "You never put up with crap either, isn't that right, Tess?"

Tess nervously smiled and nodded at Briana's comment. Her client also smiled at Briana as she looked up from her phone.

Tess looked at her reflection in the mirror, and thought of what Mrs Jones had said. *No colour can hide the truth*, she thought. Although she'd nodded in agreement with Briana's comment, her heart had reservations, and now beat uneasily. She wondered why she felt like she was letting Briana and her friend down. Perhaps she was letting herself down. She thought of the bout of anxiety that had emerged from deep within her when she'd let Silvio go, and the same feeling that had occurred when she thought about seeing Desiree again. Then, she recalled the way her heart had beat wildly as Stewart's eyes had looked into hers.

CHAPTER NINE

Later that afternoon, Tess stepped out of the salon, feeling free from responsibility until Tuesday, when she would be back at work again. She had two full days to herself. The weather seemed milder — the cold change was still with them, but if wasn't as severe as it had been. It felt like a spring day, not like the middle of summer. She felt so beautiful in her choice of outfit, having decided on a pair of beautiful satin pastel pink pants, and a short-sleeved, soft cream cardigan. She had thrown on a long necklace to add some sparkle, a pair of pearl stud earrings, and a ring with a huge faux pearl on it. She'd needed some colour to offset the paleness in her complexion. She'd felt like making an effort that morning to make up for the fact she had slept so poorly.

She took slow, casual strides towards Mr Papas' deli. She could already smell the delightful aromas. There was something so comforting about them. It was like she was going on a food safari. As she excitedly stepped inside, she looked towards the counter to greet Mr Papas. Her heart sank. It couldn't be — but it was. The room lost its warmth in an instant. Desiree was pointing at something on one of the shelves. She was laughing with Mr Papas, now enquiring about some packages of tea at the front counter. Strands of her blonde hair whipped through the air as she turned and faced Tess, her deep red lips etched in an exaggerated smile. It was as though she was sacrificing that smile for Tess — as though it was an honour to be met with it, to even be in its aura.

"Oh Tess! Oh my God! Fancy seeing you here! I've just met the *sweetest* man. Let me introduce you to him!"

"Um … excuse me?" Tess managed, knowing she looked like a deer caught in headlights.

"Come and have a look at all these products. I've shopped at some of the best boutique shops, and I must say, I'm impressed with the range in here. In fact, I can't believe how many *cute* shops there are in this street alone."

"You have?" Tess asked, finding it hard to regain her composure. Hesitantly, she walked towards the counter.

"Hello, pretty Tess. What can I get for you today?" Mr Papas asked.

Desiree looked at Tess, eyes wide, as she studied her face and her clothes. It was the first time she'd seen her without mud on her face or looking like she had just woken up.

"Hi, Mr Papas," said Tess. "I'll just have …"

"You should try some of this tea," Desiree interrupted. "Mr Papas and I just had a huge conversation about it. The packages are so beautiful and they come from Derbysear… or something like that …"

"Derbyshire, they come from Derbyshire," Tess snapped, her anger giving her much-needed confidence. "I already bought a few packages. Mr Papas always lets me know when they're coming in."

"Oh … yes, that's the one. Debby … what *you* said."

"Desiree, here, loves the tea as well. Now I have two pretty ladies visiting my shop," Mr Papas said with pride.

"Oh, you know each other?" she enquired, giving Tess a pitiful look, as though Tess could not possibly be pretty.

Tess glared. It was clear she had been here before, many times. Obviously Desiree's mission was to dismiss anything she had to say.

"Anyway." Desiree diverted her attention back to Mr Papas. "*Mr Papas*! Me? *Pretty*?" she gasped in faux embarrassment. "Please, Mr Papas, stop it, you're making me blush!" Desiree placed her hand on Mr Papas' shoulder. Her heavy jewellery made a loud clanking noise, while her long, French-manicured fingernails threatened to rend his shirt apart.

"Well, you must love reading as well," Mr Papas smiled. "Tess imagines she's in the English countryside as she reads and drinks tea."

"Yes, I love reading too. I used to love contributing to discussions at school. We both did, didn't we Tess? Yes, believe it or not, Tess and I went to the same school. I know, it's hard to imagine it."

Tess looked at her angrily. *It's hard to imagine.* What did she mean by that? She couldn't believe what she was hearing, that she loved reading; that she contributed to class discussions? The only class discussion she remembered Desiree contributing to was the one about Tess of the D'Urbervilles, when she had ridiculed her. Determined not to allow her to make her feel small in the shop she adored, Tess found her voice. "I never knew you loved reading fiction. Didn't you say you only liked reading about investment properties and things like that?"

"Um ... yes I do, Tess. I read books from all gen... gen... um ... types. Don't you remember our English teacher was so impressed with my contribution on one of the books we studied? Of course I read about investment properties *now*. I have to so I can keep up with managing all of ours. It's hard to be as successful as Keith and I are. So many people ask us for advice, all the time! I was telling Keith the other day that he could be a motivational speaker. I'd love to be able to sit in my PJs and read all day, but I can't afford to slacken off. I don't have time like you do, unfortunately, to spend on myself."

Tess looked pointedly at Desiree's nails and fake tan, but she didn't seem to notice.

Mr Papas smiled, unaware of the tension bubbling around him. "Well, I have two pretty and smart customers who love my products. I'll let you know when the new products come in as well, like I do for Tess," he said to Desiree.

"Oh, would you?" Desiree exclaimed. "Thanks so much, Mr Papas. You're not only handsome, but a kind man as well."

Tess stood there in shock, fighting back the feeling she was invisible. Mr Papas suddenly seemed to have metamorphosed into her naïve English teacher. Both had unwittingly betrayed her by not recognising Desiree's cruelty.

Mr Papas looked at Tess directly. "I'm surprised to see you this time of the afternoon, on a Saturday. You were working, Tess?"

She nodded. "One of my clients has a dress-up party tonight."

"Oh, is that where you're going now?" Desiree asked, looking at her from head to toe with the same pitiful look. "I thought so … with that outfit!"

"You're always so busy, Tess. I guess you can relax now. She works at the …" Mr Papas began, looking at Desiree.

"Can I also have a box of that? That looks gorgeous," Desiree exalted loudly, completely ignoring anything Mr Papas had to say about the salon. It was clear Desiree didn't want to hear about it — that she didn't want to admit anything remotely positive about Tess, just like she didn't back at school.

Tess was completely flabbergasted about the comment regarding her outfit. *Dress-up party! The nerve of her!* She'd managed to insult her again with such ease, sneaking in the insult with a lovely smile on her face, as though it was actually a compliment. Tess stood there, words once again failing her. She began to fuss with her bag, her hair, not knowing what else to do. Then she gazed at Desiree. She looked so confident in herself — her shoulders straight, standing tall and proud. Every word she uttered was with an air of confidence and authority.

Briana's words to her friend came to mind. "Tess doesn't take crap from anyone, isn't that right, Tess?" She also remembered what she'd said to the young girl at the salon with the gorgeous auburn hair. She'd told her to stand proud, just as Tess herself had finally done back in high school. Why, then, was she allowing Desiree to make her feel so small now — in *her* world — with people who were always there for her, like a second family? Why was she letting someone she didn't respect treat her with so little respect? *Get it together, Tess.* She squared her shoulders and straightened her back. She cleared her throat as Desiree gathered her purchases together with a smile as big and strong as the Sydney Harbour Bridge — beautiful from afar yet cold and steely close up.

"Bye, Tess. Wish I could stand around talking to you but I've got things to do. I'm meeting Keith after he finishes work for a late dinner. Poor thing, had to work on a Saturday. He always wants to look out for me though. It's fun being in a relationship — being married. You'll see what I mean, when you hear about it from other people you know, or maybe when you read about it … in one of your books? Anyway, *au revoir!*" She bounded to the front door, her hair, purchases and curves swaying along with her every step, a strong whiff of musky perfume enveloping her and everything around her. Tess didn't know whether she should laugh or cry as she looked on. In fact, she didn't know how to feel. She had to get it together. She wouldn't let her rattle her. That's what she was trying to do — to watch her fade away while she became louder and more colourful. Well, Tess wouldn't fade away — she would stand tall, be vibrant, reflect light and thrive.

"So what can I get for you, Tess?" Mr Papas asked her with a smile.

Tess had the impression his smile wasn't as sincere as usual. It was as though he'd exerted too much energy with Desiree, and that all he could manage for her was half-hearted. She felt like she was getting scraps.

"I think I'll have some of the dill and cucumber sandwiches today," she said, a bit too enthusiastically, trying to find her light again, but she knew it was forced.

"Oh, sorry Tess. I just gave the last dill and cucumber to Desiree. She was really taken with them, with everything in here, in fact." He then smiled to himself, pausing as though he was processing what had transpired during his encounter with Desiree, as though he was under some spell.

A sinking feeling gnawed at the pit of her stomach. Her eyes suddenly became teary. *No, I won't let her do that. This is my street — where I work, where I live. I won't let her ruin my confidence.*

She caught Mr Papas looking at the clock. He began to pack up a few things on the counter. He was clearly eager to close the shop. Her presence was preventing him from enjoying the rest of his Saturday.

Tess felt so pathetic, like she was waiting for Mr Papas to give her back the confidence she'd just lost. She usually had that confidence inside of her. She never needed someone else to give it her, to have power over her like that. She hadn't felt like that for years. She'd even left Michael so she wouldn't have to feel like that — like she wasn't worth it, like her feelings didn't matter, like she didn't exist.

"Cheer up, Tess," Mr Papas said. "I'll make some more for you."

Tess met the older man's eyes. He looked like he wanted to make her happy, like time suddenly didn't matter. He genuinely wanted to make her the sandwiches. *See, I'm being silly,* she thought to herself. *Mr Papas still respects me. I just need to respect myself.* She snapped out of her mood and smiled at him, waiting patiently behind the counter. It was funny how the moment she started believing in herself, Mr Papas appeared friendly and kind again. And why wouldn't he? He knew her well — everyone did in the street. All the shop-owners looked out for each other. It was her world. Desiree was just a passerby.

"Thanks Mr Papas, but that's ok." She eyed the other sandwiches. There were so many to choose from. It didn't matter. They were all delicious. There was so much love and beauty left for her. She was being silly. She'd had a momentary lapse in judgment, but she would be okay.

As she said goodbye to Mr Papas, she held onto that thought. She breathed freely again, knowing that it was just

115

her mind causing her to doubt herself — not Desiree. *I won't give her that power.*

She picked up the pace when she remembered the cupcakes she'd planned on buying. Extra care would need to be taken in case she ran into Silvio. Her afternoon had gotten off to an uncomfortable start already. She would deal with that another time — not that afternoon.

Tess smiled when she saw the cupcakes in the shop window. Their colourful sprinkles filled her heart with joy. It was as though they'd been sprinkled with love from a rainbow, right after the rain had gone.

A soft hand on her shoulder startled her.

"They look great, don't they? You can do it though — it's mind over matter. That's what my personal trainer says. Just look at them, smell them, and walk away. I promise you — you won't look back and think, 'I should have eaten that', even though you're still flat as … um … really thin. You should come to the gym with me. I know the owner — the one down the street from here." Desiree ended her judgment and condescension with her signature self-satisfied smile.

Tess stood there with her mouth agape. She was dumbfounded. "I was just looking at them. I wasn't going to buy any. It's fascinating how beautiful they look — they're like works of art," she managed, feeling like a guilty little girl caught with her hand in the cookie jar, blanketed in guilt as a righteous adult looked down at her — one with tremendous willpower who watched her own fail her. She suddenly felt like Elizabeth Bennet in Jane Austen's *Pride and Prejudice*, having to justify her choices to the antagonistic Caroline Bingley. How she wished she could morph into Elizabeth Bennet — to have the confidence and grace that she had and really tell Desiree what she could do with the cupcakes and her unwanted advice, in a beautifully crafted sentence that did great justice to the English language. *Of course, Desiree would probably require a dictionary to understand it,* she thought slyly.

"Sure," Desiree said, eyeing her from head to toe. "Anyway, I'd better go. Busy, busy, busy. Let me know about joining me at the gym — get some curves happening. Anyway, have fun at the dress-up party. Your outfit will really get you noticed!" she cried as she sped off like one of her daddy's many fancy Italian sports cars.

Tess snapped out of her state of shock and looked at the cupcakes. Suddenly she didn't feel like eating any of them. They didn't look appealing and their colour looked dull and artificial. She carried herself despondently towards her flat. Every corner she turned, Desiree was there. She thought she wouldn't run into her; that Desiree would avoid her, but she seemed to want to be in her life — to finish what she started at school. As she kept walking, she felt like she was crushing her heart with every step she took, because she was giving Desiree permission to let her words crush her dreams — to crush her soul.

CHAPTER TEN

Tess' father's words entered her mind as she walked. She thought back to an incident that had occurred when she was fifteen.

She'd been sitting on the front porch of their cottage one hot Saturday afternoon. Her mother had just made iced tea for all of them, and had placed a huge canvas on the floor of the verandah. She'd mixed paint while Tess had daydreamed. She always loved to watch her mother work. Tess had looked on as her mother had rinsed the brushes in jars full of water. Her dad had his guitar on his lap and tuned it, before playing a song by one of the bands he'd toured with.

Tess had sighed.

"What's on your mind, honey?" her mother had asked her.

"I don't know," she'd said, not knowing how to describe what she was feeling.

Her mother had given her a curious stare.

"It's just that ..." Tess had continued, "I don't know. Do you ever want something that's out of your reach, like you want to feel adrenaline in your heart, in your veins, like wild horses thundering past you?"

Her mother had smiled at her, like she understood, but didn't answer. Instead, she'd begun painting something, like she'd just had an idea. Tess had always found it interesting to see how she worked when she was inspired by something. That was the look she'd had then. Tess realised that her mother created her own excitement, and could satisfy that intense need — that yearning for something more, through her art.

"Oh no!" her mother had suddenly cried. "The cupcakes! I hope they're not burnt!" She'd run into the big kitchen of the cottage in a panic.

Tess had peered at the pond nearby, deep in thought.

"What are you thinking about?" her father had asked her.

"It really is nice here," she'd said, sighing contently. "If only …"

"If only what?"

"If only everyone was nice as well. It would be the perfect place to live in. We're near the pond. There are so many lovely ducks and all sorts of birdlife. The grass is so lush and green, even in the winter, and the place has a poetic vibe. I just think it really does look like the perfect setting, just like I've read about in books."

"You've got lots of friends — Cathy and Michael, and all your other friends from the art classes," her dad had reminded her. "They're great."

"I know I do, but so many of the kids at school have parents who have a lot of power and influence in this town. It's almost like they think they also have the same influence as their parents do. It's like they're exploiting their power just because a lot of people work for their parents."

"Well, *we* certainly don't. They can't control *you*, and I think you've analysed your own comment. They *think* they have the same influence — but don't equate the word "think" with "do". People treat you how you let them treat you, Tess. If you allow them to have influence over you, then they will, unfortunately."

Tess had looked at her father as he'd continued playing his guitar, wearing a T-shirt with the band's name on it. He had looked so relaxed, confident and happy as he'd strummed the instrument. He never seemed to mind what people thought of him. He and her mother just did what they believed to be right for them. His longish brown hair had been tied in a ponytail, and one long strand had fallen on his forehead. He had flicked it back as he played. Tess had admired his quiet confidence and rebellious outlook.

Sunlight had drenched the porch, illuminating her mother's painting and her dad's guitar. It was as though the sun had highlighted what was important — what meant something.

119

"Tess, come and help me with the cupcakes," her mother had called.

Tess had walked into the air-conditioned kitchen, where her mother was scooping some frosting from the side of the bowl with a big wooden spoon. The kitchen was old, but some new appliances had been added, and the shelves had been restored. Her mother had kept the old gas stove as it added character. Tess had always loved eating breakfast at the huge table in the centre of the kitchen, as the sunlight stroked the table while she'd gazed out at the pond, hearing kookaburras laughing in the eucalyptus.

Tess had begun spreading the frosting carefully on each cupcake with her mother. Their cat, Winston, had looked on, anticipation revealed in his huge whiskered grin. He'd meowed as they worked.

"They don't have these funny shaped sprinkles on the packet," she'd told her mum. "We were supposed to get the plain ones and match the colours the way they do in the picture. They look so beautiful on the box."

Her mother had given her a puzzled grin. "Tess, if I looked at what each packet depicted and what the instructions said to the letter, my paintings would be perfect pretty pictures of sunsets and nothing else. Use whatever sprinkles you want, enjoy the sunshine, but enjoy the storm as well, because it might gift you a rainbow." She'd dabbed some frosting on Tess' nose. "Do you understand? Don't run from the rain …"

"Sing and dance in it?" Tess had finished.

"Yes — now you understand. You can have whichever sprinkles you want, and the more unusual, the better." Her mother had turned back to look at the trays of cupcakes on the bench, only to see Winston licking the frosting from most of the cupcakes. Tess had looked at her mum. She couldn't believe she had a smile on her face. Other mothers at her school would have screamed at the sight … for all their wasted effort. "Looks like Winston can have as many sprinkles as he wants as well. I think he agreed with me —

and I think he *really* understood me," she'd laughed. "Oh well, I'll just put the kettle on. A cup of tea makes everything better. Always remember that," she'd told her as she waltzed back over to the stove. Tess had looked at Winston, his black and white coat covered in frosting, the sunlight showering him with light, and she too had laughed as she heard the melodic and soothing sound of the acoustic guitar coming from the front porch.

Tess heard a car beeping in the narrow street, bringing her out of her thoughts. She stopped abruptly, feeling light in her shoes again. She headed back to the cupcake shop. She would buy some for dessert, and she would savour each delectable, sweet bite as she sipped her tea.

Moments later she was at her flat, a box of cupcakes under one arm. It was now five o'clock in the afternoon. Realising she hadn't had time to tidy up, she rushed to the hallway closet and took out the vacuum cleaner.

Twenty minutes later, she'd vacuumed most of the high-traffic areas in the apartment. She then dusted many of her prized treasures, including her many purse mirrors, and cleaned her large antique mirror and one inspired by Hollywood dressing rooms, as well as the glass coffee table in the lounge room. The roses were still looking fresh, thanks to Helena giving her a sachet of flower nourishment to place in the water. She then sprayed the room with a lavender room mist from Millie's shop, from Provence, France. She breathed in the scent of the fragrance, and then hurried to the bathroom to freshen up.

The kettle whistled on the stove, announcing that that the water was ready. Tess smiled at the familiar high-pitched, soothing sound. She stepped into her slippers, and threw on a pair of floral, cotton pyjamas. She tied her hair in a bun with a vintage oriental hair stick that held it together firmly. She even applied a face mask, feeling like her skin needed exfoliating.

After making the tea, she placed the cupcakes on the top tier of the cake stand, and spread the cut sandwiches out onto the bottom tier. After a quick dash to the bookshelf to grab *A Tree Grows in Brooklyn*, she was ready.

Chapter Six already! she thought as she closed the book. She stretched her arms out and then leaned over to grab a cupcake, placing it on one of the generous-sized, thick white serviettes. Just as she was about to take a bite, a feeling of guilt crept up on her. She looked around her apartment. She then heard her words: "It's willpower, Tess. Just look at them, smell them and walk away." Tess shifted uncomfortably.

She could hear footsteps outside, the scurry of people grooming themselves for Saturday night outings — dinners, parties and drinks out. She could hear the family down the hall from her, closer to Pamela. They had two pre-teen boys. The boys were giggling while their mother fussed over their outfits.

"You'll get your new shirts dirty if you eat those sticky lollies," she fretted.

Tess could also hear a trumpet playing from upstairs. *The music teacher must have returned from visiting his family in Hungary.*

Tess then wondered if Pamela was staying in. She was always out lately. Her stomach turned when she remembered that she had stopped over at Silvio's that night. She liked the way things were and didn't want any other change to interrupt the flow of things. Then her mother's words came to her mind. *If she'd followed the instructions to the letter, she would have painted pretty sunsets and nothing else*, Tess thought. *Do I just have pretty sunsets?*

The smell of garlic and basil snuck into the apartment and answered her question concerning Pamela. *She must be eating alone again.* She was surprised she was having Italian again, but Silvio's was the best restaurant around, so it made sense. Suddenly Tess craved Italian too, but she didn't want to face him. In any case, the sandwiches were delectable and complemented the tea and her book. *Maybe I would enjoy the sprinkles more with someone sitting next to me*, she then thought. *At least occasionally.* She was being silly. She took a defiant bite of the cupcake. *I'm not going to allow her to make me doubt myself*, she thought as the sweet vanilla flavour swirled in her mouth. But she didn't savour it — she felt ashamed. She *let* her make her feel ashamed.

Her mouth was still covered in frosting and sprinkles when her mobile interrupted her thoughts. She jumped at the intrusion. *Who could that be now?* she panicked. *Maybe it's one of my clients.* She had given her number to a few of her regulars. She walked over to her bag and took her phone out with anxious curiosity.

Her heart skipped more than just a beat. It felt like it had stopped beating altogether. It was *him*. He wanted to stop by her flat … *in a few minutes* … to talk about his courses. *Oh no! He can't see me like this … not again!* Her thoughts became a tangled mess. *Okay, breathe,* she told herself, taking a deep breath. *Tea … Tea always makes things better.* She took a sip. It was cold. She poured it down the sink and then poured some more from the teapot, which was still relatively warm. It calmed her for a moment. What would her mum do? Remembering Winston and the frosting, she knew her mother would laugh at the timing — at the irony. Yet she wasn't laughing. She felt like crying. And what really dawned upon her as she looked around her too comfortable apartment, at the sandwiches she'd had for dinner almost every night that week, she knew that she was far from the woman her mother was — her mother sung and danced in the rain, laughed at mess and things not being too comfortable. "Enjoy the storm as well, because it might gift you a rainbow." Was this the storm? Would a rainbow appear at the end of it? She *did* like storms, but lately she wanted them to pass before she felt their ferocity. She ran from them. She ran for her life. She had become an imposter in her own body.

Tess had to think and move quickly. She caught a glimpse of herself in the mirror — her hair was tied in a bun, she had her pyjamas on, and a face mask that matched the frosting all over her mouth! She breathed deeply as she paced around the room. She then looked at the message again. He was *asking* her if he could come over soon, not *stating* it. She would take control back this time, and she would look her best. She would simply tell him to come over in thirty minutes. *But what if he can't make it because he has to be somewhere?* It was Saturday night after all. Surely he had somewhere else to go. More importantly, she had to look like she was busy, like she had been out somewhere, doing something important, not looking like she just lay around in her PJs reading all day. That was how Desiree had portrayed her in front of him. It bothered her because she'd made it seem shameful and appalling. But it wasn't shameful. Reading was always her first love. She could rely on it. And for that she was proud.

Suddenly confident, she texted him back, asking if he could come over in about thirty minutes. If he couldn't make it, they could arrange another time. Her heart fluttered again at the thought of him. She rushed to her bedroom with her phone on hand.

He quickly responded. It was okay. He could make it.

"*Oh my God!* What should I wear?" she asked an empty room. *Thank God I tidied up.* Her eyes scanned the clothes on the bed she'd been wearing that day. How dare Desiree say she looked like she was going to a dress-up party while wearing them! She scoffed. *Who cares! Obviously she just wants pretty sunsets — nothing original, nothing out of the ordinary. Plain sprinkles and boring old sunsets.*

Tess rushed to the bathroom and rinsed the face mask off at the basin. As she dried her face, she saw her skin looked radiant. She quickly began to apply make-up, thinking of what she should wear. Feeling empowered from the memory of her parents' words, she made a decision to be herself and wear whatever made her feel at ease in her own skin.

The doorbell rang thirty minutes later. Tess looked at herself in the mirror. She couldn't believe how striking she looked. The Victorian-inspired, short-sleeved, brown blazer with gold buttons right to the top and exaggerated, slightly puffy sleeves worked so well with the flared matching pants — it gave the blazer a feminine touch, and the peach-coloured collar of her top contrasted nicely with the brown. Together, the colours brought out the amber in her eyes. Her rose pink lipstick made her lips look full and luscious, and her hair was swept to the side, held securely by a hair-comb on the opposite side — the same hair-comb he had rescued from the cold. She took a deep breath and glanced at her reflection again.

Thinking of her parents' nurturing words, she headed towards the door.

Tess placed her hand on the vintage glass doorknob, admiring her faux pearl ring as it glistened, catching the light of the crystal. The little brass bell jingled as she met his eyes, which locked onto hers instantly, before combing the features of her face and then her outfit. Tess patted her hair awkwardly until he met her eyes again. He looked serious, until he reached over and touched the hair-comb and smiled.

"Tess!" His voice was hoarse.

"Yes?" she managed, her heart pounding ferociously.

"You look *amazing!*" he said, as though he couldn't continue without letting her know.

She didn't know what to say. There was so much feeling and communication between them that words would only confuse things — they would only bring her back down from the clouds she seemed to be floating amongst.

Feeling like she would collapse from the smoothness of his touch as his hand accidentally brushed hers, she invited him into her home.

After he paused and smiled at the brass bell, Tess watched him step inside. "It's almost like the bell waits for you and greets you every time you step inside," he said with a smile that looked as warm as her face felt.

"Yes, it is I guess," she replied. "Although I haven't said 'hello' to it yet and I don't talk to it or anything like that," she waffled as her nerves took hold. Her brain began to process what was actually transpiring, not having had a chance during the expeditious task of getting dressed and groomed. She had imagined him in her mind all these years, yet never did she think he would not only reappear back in her life, but actually be in her home again. She closed the door behind her, her hand holding tight onto the crystal doorknob like it would give her strength. Her legs trembled. *Get a hold of yourself!*

Taking nervous, wobbly steps, she led him towards the lounge room. She caught him looking at her leg.

"You're not still hurt from the fall?" he asked, concerned.

"Oh, no. Why would you think that?" she blurted out.

"Just the way you were walking, kind of like you were limping a bit."

Tess had to get it together. Her nerves were making her look like she had never had a male visitor or dated ever in her life. Well, she really hadn't over the last year or so, but that was her own choosing. She was obviously out of practice, and it did take time to recover from the fact that she had just turned twenty-six, and she already had one failed marriage under her belt. Now that she thought of it, she hardly invited anyone into her apartment.

"No, my leg's okay now. It was just a bruise," she replied, surprised that her voice sounded normal. He then walked slowly towards her desk that sat under a large window in the lounge room. His eyes widened. "You write letters?" He looked, transfixed, at the papers scattered on the desk, playing with his slight beard as a strand of dark brown hair fell onto his forehead. "It's beautiful," he said, admiring the gold letter opener. "Who do you write to?"

"Mainly Cathy. You know, from school," she replied, slightly embarrassed at the thought of appearing a tad nerdy.

He gave her a warm smile. "I remember Cathy. She was quite a rebel. Between you and me though, I think a lot of the girls I hung out with were scared of her. Her mother shook up the town a bit, which we needed. I certainly welcomed the change. I admired people who had their own identity, like Cathy's family, and your family. You know, I envied you all from afar."

"Really?" Tess tried not to look shocked. She couldn't hide her elation at realising that she had been right about him — that he didn't belong with them. "Well, I thought you were so popular and …"

He suddenly looked up at her again — his eyes shining with child-like vulnerability. "Popular?" he asked. "I never felt popular. In fact, I didn't know what to feel for a while. I mean sure, I had a lot of people around me, but sometimes you need to share things with people, you know, more than just small talk. It's true what they say — sometimes you feel more lonely with a lot of people around you, if they're not the right people for you."

Tess found herself nodding. She completely understood what he meant. He smiled, somewhat nervously, Tess thought. "I've been lost for a few years actually. You know, I always respected you, back then. Since running into you again, I thought you might be able to help me find my way." He smiled again. "Can you do that for me? Help me find my way, with my career, that is?" There was a slight tremor in his voice.

His nervousness made Tess feel comfortable with her own awkwardness, like it was acceptable and quite appropriate under such intense circumstances, and that's what it was — intense. She felt like her heart would burst at any moment from the feelings emerging from deep within her, as his eyes alluded to a vulnerability — pathos and intense need.

"Sure, I'll help you," she said, her eyes locking with his again. She managed a smile, knowing that if her cheeks became any warmer, he might think she was coming down with a fever.

He interrupted her thoughts, breaking the stare like he wanted to put her at ease again. "You always seemed to know what you were doing at school — like you knew who you were as a person. And academically, too. The people I hung out with weren't exactly good role models for studying."

Tess was baffled. "I did?"

"Anyway, I thought we might grab something to eat and discuss some of my course options, if you're free, but I can see that you already ate," he said, eyeing the sandwiches and tea. Tess couldn't believe that she didn't pack the sandwiches away, or the fairly big box of cupcakes for that matter.

Stewart walked around the small space with his hands in his pockets, looking at the artwork, the chandeliers, the old mirrors, and even her prized collection of vintage and oriental hand fans, and jewellery boxes that she had collected over the years, along with her many purse mirrors.

"Very interesting artwork," he said, looking at the walls again.

"My mother painted that one," she said, pride taking over her.

He caught her in her moment. He studied her face before he spoke. "You seem really proud of her," he said. "And you should be. Your mother is really talented. I can't believe she made all the outfits for the ballroom dancing competition at school. I remember they announced it at the school assembly."

"You remember?" Tess felt like her heart was melting.

"Yes. I remember you looked so proud," he said, studying her again. "Like you do now." He placed his smooth hand on her hair. Tess felt her knees tremble. Her nose caught a subtle whiff of his musky cologne. He carefully took

128

something out of her hair, and his hand brushed her face as he showed her what it was. "You have pink sprinkles in your hair," he said, smiling.

"Oh! I didn't realise." She instantly remembered Desiree making her feel like a slob for even looking at the cupcakes. The way he was looking at her made her feel like she was a dainty ballerina.

"They suit you," he said, still smiling. "Pink always suited you."

Tess laughed, shaking her hair to make sure there weren't any more sprinkles in it. "You're talking about the pink hair I had at school just before you left? Well, you missed the time I dyed it green. You'd already left by then …" She trailed off. She never knew why he had left — the full story. She only remembered that Evie, who had dated him for a while, was heartbroken. She didn't know how serious they were, but Evie was devastated. She remembered walking past Evie and Desiree one day as they sat at one of the benches in the playground. Desiree was comforting Evie between sobs. "It's okay. You can visit him. He hasn't gone that far." Tess was surprised that Desiree cared so much about her friend. She felt that there may be some compassion inside of her after all — even if it was just reserved for her closest friends.

Tess remembered Desiree's kind words to her friend. "I'm so sorry, Evie. I never wanted him to leave like this. I'll miss him too. Maybe my dad can talk to his parents and …" She had trailed off, noticing she and Cathy were nearby. Tess had been surprised Desiree didn't make a smart comment to them. Instead she just looked at them with teary eyes, then abruptly back at Evie. She remembered asking herself why Desiree would be sorry. *It wasn't her fault that Stewart left,* she had thought.

Tess noticed that Stewart also looked uncomfortable at the mention of him leaving — like he wasn't ready to talk about it. His jaw tightened, and his shoulders were raised. He began to walk around the room again taking small, slow footsteps with his hands in his pockets. As he continued his musing, he became more relaxed again. She followed him as he inspected everything like he was in a museum.

"Everything's so beautiful and sweet in here, but also strong and resilient — just like the bell on your door." He glanced back at her, meeting her eyes again. "It's true what they say — they don't make things the way they used to." He headed towards a corner of the room that obviously caught his attention. "Anyway, I thought it would be great to …" he began, before turning to face her. "You look really great, Tess. I mean, that outfit … You look …" His eyes searched her face. "It's been surreal running into you like this."

Tess ran trembling fingers through her hair. She somehow managed to walk over to the tea set, even though her knees felt weak. "Would you like some tea?" she asked with a quiver in her voice, trying to hide the elation she felt at his comment, as well as how nervous it made her feel. The promise of him connecting with her unnerved her and lulled her at the same time.

She'd made some fresh tea before he'd arrived, and had placed two clean teacups on the tray. She'd always imagined pouring tea from her elegant teapot for a gentleman in her lounge room, dressed in beautiful clothes like they did in the classics, but hadn't anticipated her hands trembling like they were at that very moment, feeling his eyes intently observing her. Why was she feeling like this? Like she had a fever? Like she was a teenager again — feeling and acting nervous as she talked to an attractive man? It was all new to her — this "having a man over" thing. But this was Stewart, who she'd thought about for all these years. She felt so much pressure to make things right with him. She didn't want to tarnish the image she had of him. Too much was at stake.

She quickly placed the hot teapot down, remembering the scenario at Silvio's, when she had set him free.

"Tess, I need to know, are you afraid of me?" Stewart asked in a gentle voice as he walked over to her. "I mean, is this making you uncomfortable — being alone with me in your apartment? I know I didn't talk to you or hang out with you much in high school, but I felt that I knew you, even if we didn't really talk to each other that often."

Tess was taken aback by his sudden candour. She knew exactly what he meant. "I did too," she said quickly. "I mean, *of course* I'm not scared of you, Stewart." She laughed much too loudly, trying to convince him. "I know you're not a stranger."

"Thank God! That's a relief. I mean, it didn't even occur to me that being here might be inappropriate. You were practically running the other night. I figured later that you thought I might be some bad guy or something. I hope some guy hasn't frightened you. I would hate that. You're such a sweet and positive person — one who appreciates and accepts everything. Just looking around me, I can see that."

His words hit her hard. She felt exposed. Why *was* she running away from the thought of being in a relationship? Why was she afraid at the thought of being with a man? Was she afraid that they would never live up to her expectations, like Michael?

Tess decided to lighten the mood, suddenly feeling more relaxed. He had seen her in a vulnerable state and made her feel that it was okay, that she wasn't weird. Every time she felt she looked awful or acted less than composed, he didn't judge her — in fact, he admired her for it. Maybe he was sick of the posers.

He walked over to the bookshelves. Tess felt empowered as she saw him standing there, ready to converse with her about all the wonderful books. She was in her element again.

"I have to come over and look at these properly some time. I love anything to do with books. I would sneak into my father's office as a child and sit on the floor next to the huge desk and read when my parents were entertaining guests."

"Oh! Why didn't you just borrow some of the books and just read them in your room?" she enquired, her shoulders suddenly relaxing as she neared the bookshelves. "I used to love reading in my room. My room was my own world — my sanctuary full of books and everything I loved and adored."

Stewart turned around and gave her a warm smile. He seemed to be mesmerised whenever she spoke. "It must have been great, to have parents into the arts. My parents weren't really into art or literature. The bookshelves were just decor. Books and art wouldn't lead to money — to anything substantial — but then again, not many have talent like your mother. Still, it would've been nice if they talked about something other than the family business, or about training me to take over ..." He trailed off. Perhaps he had said too much. "Your family must have been so much fun."

"Yes, it was great ... and fun, I guess. I thought it was anyway. I know a lot didn't," she said, looking at her pearl ring, her eyes tearing. Standing there talking to him brought back the past — how vulnerable she'd felt at times, being ridiculed. "I mean, lots of people thought I was *weird* ..." Tears welled in her eyes.

"I didn't. I never thought you were weird," he said in a confident voice that needed to be heard. "Many were just narrow-minded, set in their own ways."

"I know you didn't." She felt like she might burst into tears in the presence of such deep compassion. "That's why living here is so wonderful. Most people are into art, or music, or acting, or studying. It's a hub of art and culture. This street alone has so many interesting shops, and there's even a boutique theatre that holds an Italian film week every few months," Tess said, remembering Silvio, and successfully stifling a stream of tears that had threatened to escape.

"Yeah, I actually heard about that," he said with raised eyebrows. "I might go there one day." He turned from her to look at the record collection, and the old retro record player sitting on top of another small bookshelf, which housed many memoirs and stories from old Hollywood.

"Wow!" he exalted. "I love the record player! That's quite a record collection you have. I could spend hours in your apartment. There's something interesting in every corner. Frank Sinatra, Dean Martin … I'm impressed."

Tess stood near him, looking on proudly with her hands behind her back. She loved talking about books, music, and all her finds and treasures. He then looked at some old Australian rock albums — some from as early as the 60s like The Easybeats and The Masters Apprentices. He kept gazing at the records in awe. Tess felt so comfortable standing there next to him. "I remember your dad toured with so many bands. *Wow!* Kate Bush!" he exclaimed. "I love Kate Bush."

"So do I … well, obviously," she said, light filling her eyes and her heart. "I would listen to that particular record for hours," she added, feeling mellow and comfortable.

"I love the song, *Moving*," she said. "It's so beautiful and …"

"Moving?" he asked with a laugh.

"Yes! I guess it is that too." She matched his laugh.

Stewart looked at her and sighed. "All this wasted time," he said. "I could have spent hours talking to you about all these things, and who knows what could have …" He cleared his throat. "It would have been a refreshing change." He looked down at the record in his hands, and stared at it for a while.

Tess began to feel protective of him. His heart was obviously burdened with regret. She also sensed that he really wanted her guidance, and she felt like she really wanted to help him as he stood there with the old record in his hands, looking like a lost boy. Her nerves had settled and she was now becoming comfortable having him in her world — letting him in.

She watched as he placed the record back, his eyes widening as he noticed all the memoirs. "Okay," he said, suddenly looking serious, "I definitely have to hang out here more often."

"Not a problem," Tess found herself saying. "I mean, I would love having you … Um, I mean, I would love having you *here* … in my home," she corrected.

Stewart instantly looked at her again, deep in thought, with a half-smile on his lips. His eyes were also smiling. He searched her face for a moment before turning away. His phone chimed with a message. She walked over to the lounge to sit for a while as he read it and replied.

"Well, looks like I have to get going. I hate having to cut the evening short. It's been great talking to you. I really needed this. We'll need to plan a time to talk about those courses then, if you're still up for it?"

'Yes, definitely. I'd love to help. Call me to organise a time," she said, suddenly feeling disappointed. Her heart sank slightly. Who had the message been from? What if he was seeing someone? What if he had a date?"

"It's the restaurant," he said, holding up his phone. "I'd better get going." He rushed over to her as he grabbed his keys he'd left on the coffee table.

Restaurant? Tess thought. *Who is he going to a restaurant with?*

He leaned towards her and touched her shoulder affectionately, then the bruise on her forehead. He caressed it gently. "It really has been great, seeing you again," he said, holding her hand firmly into his, as his full, soft lips quickly met the skin of her cheek. He then walked towards the door. She followed. The brass bell jingled.

He must be meeting friends — it can't be another woman. The way he touched me, kissed me. He had to have felt something … I definitely felt something.

"Bye! I'll call you soon," he called as he headed down the narrow corridor. He then turned around and gave her one final smile before he walked down the stairs and out into the night.

Tess stood at the door with her hand on her cheek for a while, the gentle jingle making her feel warm and content.

She could still smell his subtle cologne on her skin. She smiled to herself, shut her door, and walked over to her armchair. She sunk into it, needing to process what had just happened. She would recall everything in her mind again — to ensure she didn't miss anything, just like she would reread a wonderful book. She had to remember each word he uttered, and interpret its meaning. She didn't care about any pact for the moment. Her heart was galloping wildly and freely.

CHAPTER ELEVEN

When Tess stepped out of her apartment building that glorious Sunday morning, the sun was out, beautifying the street, even though it was still unusually cool for that time of year. Tess had decided to have her coffee out, suddenly feeling the need to be amongst the noise and activity. She wondered if Pamela was having coffee at Silvio's, as she often did lately. A boost of confidence had shot through her after Stewart had left the night before. She felt like singing, like being amongst friends, sharing her joy with the world. But she didn't want to get carried away, or reveal anything to anyone yet. Stewart needed her guidance, but it didn't mean anything. They were just friends. *It's his company that makes me crave conversation and intimacy with people*, she told herself. Besides, Pamela kept giving her curious stares whenever she asked her about men, especially about Silvio. She hadn't even told her what had happened that night in his restaurant.

Lately, Tess got the impression that each of them was waiting for the other to cave in first, that they felt comforted by each other's quest for singledom — like they had something in common, and could be there for each other. *But then what?* she often thought. *Is that what we both really want? Especially if that special person does appear in our lives? Do we push them away without even considering the possibility? Do we remain fearful of taking another chance, just because of a failed marriage at such a young age?* Yes, it was just a silly pact, made from panic and fear, not any common sense really, but even so, it seemed to have more power than either of them ever anticipated. Certainly for Tess it seemed to set boundaries and limitations when she tried to open her heart to anything more. Tess was slowly realising that they had agreed to something that was inviting the fear to remain — and not leave room for anything else.

She walked towards the restaurant. Everyone seemed to be raving about the coffee and the new barista, and she couldn't avoid Silvio forever. If Pamela was still there, they could have an overdue heartfelt talk between friends. Feeling relaxed in her straight girlfriend jeans, and a black, short-sleeved blazer with signature puffy sleeves, she was channelling a part Victorian, part 90s look. She took a deep breath, drinking in the positive vibes of the street, enjoying its overt creativity in its art supply shops and studios, the boutique cinema, craft shops, coffee shops boasting an array of modern and rustic cuisine, the many bookshops, vintage shops ...

"Tess! Come join us." A familiar voice interrupted her thoughts. Tess instantly turned and came face to face with Penny. She and Dante were sitting at one of the outside tables at an organic coffee shop.

"It's a gorgeous day, isn't it? I think the heat's slowly returning. It's been a weird couple of days — weather-wise that is, don't you think, Tess? Oh wait ... before you answer that, do we take credit for that? The blazer you're wearing? It's fab!" she continued in the same jovial tone.

Tess opened her mouth to speak, but was suddenly distracted.

"Tess, are you alright? Is it something I said? I won't mind if it's not from our shop! I know you don't just shop at our ..."

"Oh? Oh, sorry, Penny. I was just shocked because I saw someone I didn't expect to see," she managed, looking over Penny's shoulder and using it as a shield at the same time. Tess leaned down slightly as she watched the athletic figure stop at one of the shops further down the street. Watching her as she continued walking away from them, Tess decided to take Penny up on her offer, especially since Silvio's was in the direction Desiree was heading. She didn't want to take any chances of running into her on her day off. "Sure, Penny. I'd love to join you. I decided to have my coffee out today since it's a glorious day. And of course I'm not upset with anything you said." She kept crouching slightly so Desiree wouldn't notice her as she stopped to look at another shop window. She then watched her as she continued walking down the long narrow street. The coast was clear.

"Jeez Louise," Penny exclaimed. "Whoever you're hiding from, you definitely don't want him or her to see you."

Tess greeted Dante with a relieved smile as she sat on one of the chairs that circled the small round table. "*Jeez Louise?*" Tess teased. "Do people still say that?"

"Well, I don't care if they do or don't — that's one of the perks of owning a vintage shop — I can use the slang and terms from each era. So I'm always hip and on trend," Penny said with a smile.

"Good point," Tess said. "Yes, and whenever I get to wear many of those mentioned outfits, I too can match the era they came from with my choice of words. I am all astonishment," she said, laughing at her own attempt at acting like Caroline Bingley, from Jane Austen's *Pride and Prejudice*. "Oh actually, that was the Georgian society era — and this blazer is more Victorian? What do you think?"

"Those sleeves were also popular in the Georgian era," Dante commented.

Tess noticed a man sitting at the next table with short, light brown hair and chubby cheeks, dressed in a suit that looked a tad too tight for him around the stomach. He was evidently pretending he wasn't listening in on their conversation as he looked at his phone. He seemed to be perspiring heavily in his shirt with the collar too tight around the neck. He reminded Tess of the stuffy, uninspiring men in the Town Hall functions in Lorikeet Creek who hung around with Desiree's dad — their circle of friends. Tess assumed he worked for a real estate company like Helena's husband, for him to be dressed so formally on a Sunday, although Helena's husband wore a suit with great ease and style, which complemented his athletic frame and handsome features.

A whiff of musky perfume suddenly made Tess' stomach turn, its familiarity causing her whole skin to itch uncomfortably. The perfume was strong, confident and beautiful, but it made her sick to the core.

"Tess! Fancy seeing you here." Desiree's sharp, piercing voice nearly made her eardrum burst.

Tess struggled to turn around. She couldn't believe her luck. Running into her was becoming a habit — an *excruciatingly bad* habit. But how did she appear just like that — when she was heading in the opposite direction? Was she stalking her? "Um ... hi Desiree," she managed, feeling her cheeks colouring. Her only consolation was that she was sitting with Penny and Dante, which meant Desiree would just say hello and let her be.

"Talk about a coincidence," she said. "Hi honey!" Desiree then said to the sweaty man sitting at the next table.

Honey? Why would she call that man "honey"? she speculated. *It couldn't be!* Tess turned around, eager to see if her suspicions were right. Desiree was kissing him, or rather, pecking him on the lips. The man seemed to squirm the minute her lips touched his, obviously not used to the public display of affection.

"Yeah ... hi love," he managed, just barely. He then adjusted his collar, as the perspiration seemed to have gotten worse. A wild blush made his face look like an overripe tomato.

"Keith, sweetie," she continued, loosening his tie, as though she was rescuing him from asphyxiation. Tess felt like she was choking just looking at him. "There ... that's better." She then looked down at his suit pants, and two white tennis socks revealing themselves beneath the hems. Desiree quickly said something in his ear, and then the man who was obviously her husband sat up straight and hid his shoes under the small table.

"Anyway, as I was saying, I don't think he's working today. I just stopped by to say hi but he must have a day off, or he's starting later," she said to Keith. "I sent him a text to meet us here anyway since it's such a nice day today. He should be here soon but I can't believe that I ran into Tess again. She's the one I was telling you about … We were together in high school, remember?" she asked, and then turned to face Tess again. She moved her seat back, bumping right into Tess' seat, nearly squashing Tess' delicate fan-shaped bamboo bag she'd hung over the backrest of her chair. Tess caught Desiree eyeing it, seemingly impressed.

Keith witnessed the chair situation and decided to intervene. "Why don't we move these two tables together, since you know each other?" he offered. "We can have more space for the food. I ordered the jumbo-sized veggie burger, since there's no meat in it. Less fat, you know? So I guess I'll need more space anyway," he finished, as though he was checking with his wife for her approval, obviously being the one inclined towards fitness in the marriage.

"Oh …" Desiree said. "It's barely 9:30 though. I'm surprised they're serving them already."

"They're not. I put in a special order," he said with pride on his face.

"*Oh … Keith!*" she exclaimed, as she looked at him with a forced smile and a painfully awkward giggle. "He's used to getting what he wants — he knows how to be assertive, you know, being in the property industry," she explained to Tess, scratching her nose as each word in her sentence became more pathetic and less credible as she spoke.

Tess suddenly remembered her words to her the other day: *Just look at them, and then look away. It's all about willpower,* she had told her, as she'd gazed at the lovely cupcakes. Tess wondered if she used that line on Keith.

Dante had already stood up and both men had somehow come to the conclusion that the two females who knew each other from high school had agreed on this sudden plan — to unite and become one. To Tess' *astonishment,* Desiree also didn't seem as taken with the plan. She watched her sit back in her seat defensively, flicking her hair back from her face, and smiling a forced smile at her husband, her worked-out, toned arms placed in an awkward fashion on the table, revealing clenched fists.

"Well, yes, um she's the girl from high school, Keith … You remember me telling you, *don't* you, *honey*?" she asked, as though reminding him of an important fact he'd forgotten about, which could influence and alter his plan to reunite them.

Keith looked at her, completely unaware of what she was trying to tell him. "Yeah … I know. You two were friends from high school," he said, continuing to shuffle some spare chairs around, completely missing what Tess sensed Desiree was trying to hint — that they weren't friends at all. Quite the opposite.

Desiree sat back in her seat with her arms folded, looking defeated.

Tess too sat uncomfortably in her seat. This was not how she'd envisioned her glorious Sunday morning turning out. She'd have to have her coffee in again from now on — although her apartment had been invaded by Desiree now, as well.

"Oh, you two know each other?" enquired Penny, giving Tess a knowing smile. She obviously knew this was the person Tess was trying to avoid just a few minutes ago.

"Yes, we know each other," Desiree said, giving her husband a look that was only for *his* eyes. Her dissatisfaction with the turn of events was becoming increasingly evident. Tess wondered why the sudden change of heart. She had seemed to like bumping into her on other occasions, when Tess was unprepared, that is. The way she was eyeing her husband left Tess thinking that perhaps she was the one embarrassed this time — by him. He was obviously not wearing his best suit or the right socks, and he didn't look like the hot-shot entrepreneur she'd described him as on Friday night, when she had caught Tess in the rose bush, looking like an utter idiot — much to her delight! He was definitely not the type of guy she would date back in high school. He definitely wasn't the athletic, popular type.

After some more small talk, Keith's jumbo-sized veggie burger arrived, and he had a huge grin on his face. Without waiting for the others to receive their food, he dug in, taking huge bites, not at all bothered by the fact that his mouth was covered with sauce. Desiree looked on as her husband divulged the burger. Her eyes were trying to communicate with him again. She turned to the side, trying to hide her face behind her hair. Tess could see Desiree's mouth moving like she was telling him something. Keith kept taking huge bites, and then Desiree discretely placed her hands on her own mouth, obviously pointing to the section that she wanted him to wipe.

After a few more attempts at relaying the information, she gave up altogether, and practically threw a serviette on his plate. "You have sauce all over your mouth," she finally said, the sight of him eating rendering her incapable of forcing a smile on her face. The expression on it looked as broken as the burger on her husband's plate. She had momentarily given up on her attempt to make her husband look like the passionate, suave go-getter she had described. It was a most pointless and challenging task — a tall feat for even someone as fake as her, a person who was usually an expert at embellishing facts to make herself look better.

Just then, Keith decided to reacquaint himself with some manners, and wiped his mouth clean with several serviettes, which was just enough to make him look presentable again.

"It's Simon, from the office. He's the boss' son," Tess heard him say to Desiree. She watched Desiree adjust his tie before combing her hair with her long French-manicured fingers, and adjusting her blouse, making sure it was neat and tidy. With one huge smile, she became sweet and lovely again as she stood up to greet the man named Simon, and another man dressed in smart, casual clothes. Both men seemed to be in their late twenties, or perhaps their early thirties, Tess speculated. She wondered why Desiree and

Keith would care so much about looking presentable on a Sunday morning.

"So glad to see you both again," Desiree took the lead, giving them a warm smile, and making room for them at the tables. "Won't you join us for a coffee?"

"Yes, please, join us," Keith said, suddenly all formal. He began to move some seats from the empty table next to them.

Both men grabbed the seats and sat down, summoning the waiter and ordering two coffees. They made some small talk about their work before the man named Simon looked over at Tess, Dante and Penny. "So sorry. I didn't get your names," he said. Tess smiled at the men as she greeted both of them with a handshake. Just as she sat back in her seat, she saw Desiree's face fall. "Don't say much. Leave the talking up to me," she heard her husband whisper to her, as the two men conversed with Penny and Dante about their shop. They seemed really interested in all matters business. Tess wondered why they would run into work colleagues. That would mean that Keith worked nearby. Why would Desiree say that they weren't staying in her building for long? An anxious feeling emerged from within her chest. She quickly suppressed it, knowing it would be too painful to contemplate.

"So, Simon, we'll need to set up a meeting to see the latest sales' figures," said Keith. "I have a meeting today as well, with a client. He couldn't make it on another day, so I'm going into the office today — on a Sunday." His face beamed with pride. Tess sensed he really wanted to impress the boss' son.

"Yeah, sure. Don't worry about it, Keith. I'll just let the big boss know ... Well, my dad," Simon said with a cheesy grin. "About the meeting, that is," he added when he saw Keith's crestfallen look. "I'll make sure to let him know you're going into the office today — *on a Sunday.*"

Tess observed Desiree's mannerisms as her husband got into an in-depth conversation with his colleagues regarding their work. She noticed that Desiree sipped her coffee like an obedient young girl — it was almost like Keith was her father and she was the child that knew nothing of adult matters. An image of Michael talking down to her during their short-lived marriage entered her mind for a moment and she felt liberated to not be in such a stuffy and degrading relationship. It seemed like Desiree's personality had been momentarily suppressed, in case she misbehaved and ruined things for Keith. An image of Desiree sitting as a teenager at the local town hall also entered her mind — Desiree's father sitting next to his daughter, telling her to be quiet and smile.

Desiree was now smiling a radiant yet forced smile. Her eyes looked dull and timid, like a lost child's. Tess' heart suddenly warmed to her. She couldn't help but feel some form of pity, or even some compassion towards her. That compassion subsided quickly when Desiree gave her an icy stare, as if she was blaming her for her sudden feelings of inferiority — to be told to shut up so the adults can talk. Desiree's behaviour stirred something inside her — it always had. Apart from the obvious insults and the negative effect they'd had on her as a teenager, sometimes Tess didn't know if Desiree made her feel uncomfortable because she saw something inside of her that she saw in herself. She couldn't pinpoint it exactly. She did find her whole disposition irksome; her smile was never heartfelt — nor were her actions, even if she did reveal an ounce of compassion now and then, like the time she'd held back Evie's hair as she cried, reassuring her that she would be okay after Stewart had left.

As Tess sat comfortably back in her chair, she took a sip of her coffee with ease and confidence, smiling at Dante and Penny, who were talking with the other man about vintage shops making a comeback. She enjoyed the blanket of sunlight that covered her. Taking another sip, she realised she felt comfortable in her own skin, even with Desiree's negative aura threatening the tranquillity of the mild summer's day.

Her eye was caught by Desiree flicking her hair nervously, but was soon diverted to the other man at the table, who said, "I don't believe I caught your name."

"Oh, I'm Tess," she said with a smile. Her confidence surprised her. It was the opposite to how she usually felt and acted in Desiree's presence. As she looked at him, she realised he was rather handsome, and his eyes looked friendly and warm. His olive-skinned arms were toned and his dark brown hair was slightly long and wavy. He was obviously the less conservative of the two.

"Sorry, I didn't catch your name either," Tess said, her smile finding its natural form. The young man gave her one of his own genuine smiles that made his whole face and eyes glow with positivity, enhancing the handsomeness of his chiselled features.

She heard Desiree shift slightly in her seat. She had sat quietly without so much as a word for the last ten minutes or so, being on her best behaviour. Tess moved with ease in her seat and tossed her hair playfully. The young man answered, the smile on his face making his hazel eyes look as warm as a gentle flame. "My name's Jacob." He then picked up his coffee cup and took a sip, seemingly mesmerised by being in Tess' presence. As he placed the cup on the saucer, his eyes became fixated on the book poking out of her handbag. "*A Tree Grows in Brooklyn*?" he asked with raised eyebrows. "I remember reading that for school. You're into reading?"

"Yes, I am. I read every day," Tess answered confidently. Ever since she had revealed her sacred world to Stewart, she didn't feel shy about discussing her passion. It was as though he had liberated her — allowed her to be herself. It wasn't a passion to be ashamed of. In fact, it was brilliant and fascinating.

"Wow ... not only are you *gorgeous*, but you share one of my passions as well," he said, giving her another warm smile. "I make it a habit to read as much as I can."

Tess looked down at her coffee cup, slightly embarrassed but also flattered. She felt alive and carefree. This "flirting" thing was more fun than she remembered.

"I remember reading that book too," Keith suddenly said.

"You did?" Desiree blurted out, the shock evident in her eyes.

"Yes, I did. I loved that book. In fact I've always loved reading as well," he said, his eyes becoming brighter and more child-like. His clothes looked like they fit him more comfortably now, and he sat less rigidly in his seat as he looked at the book that Tess took out to show the rest of the table. It was as though he was able to breathe again.

Desiree scoffed, "I never see you reading! You read a lot of the investments section in the newspaper and online, and a lot of the investment magazines." Desiree looked at the two men as if they would award her some type of medal for her contribution. "Yes, Keith reads everything about the investments property market, like, all the time."

Keith nudged her in the elbow and gave her a questioning look, as if she had overstepped her mark. To Tess it looked like Desiree had broken some unwritten rule in front of his colleagues. Keith clearly shunned her interference, which made him look more desperate to please than smart and suave. The two men looked at her as though they were either fascinated or shocked by her naivety.

Keith cleared his throat. "I do read. I've always loved reading," he said sharply, no longer able to keep his cool and appear like the decent couple he had planned on acting like they were. His wife had rendered him nothing short of a liar, instead of making him look good in front of his colleagues. "It's because you never let me have any books anywhere. Our living space is so sterile. I'll have to get myself one of those digital reader thingies ..."

Tess noticed Keith looked like he couldn't breathe again. Desiree looked down at her coffee cup. The way she was looking at it with steely eyes … It was a miracle the warm beverage didn't turn into iced-coffee.

Jacob reached out to have a look at the book. His hand brushed Tess' as she passed it to him. He looked straight into her eyes and gave her another flirtatious, warm smile.

Tess pushed her fringe away from her face. She knew it was a flirtatious thing to do, but she found herself not caring. It had been a while since she flirted without worrying if she was breaking the pact, or without fearing that it would mean walking down the aisle and marrying a man who would change as quickly as the flowers arrangements would — in her case, roses, pale pink in colour. It was long overdue. She realised that she couldn't let all the characters she read about have all the fun.

"I've never seen this cover before. Where did you …"

"The indie book shop just a few doors down," Tess explained excitedly. "There are a few further down the street as well, but this one stocks everything from the classics to new up-and-coming authors. Some are even locals. You know the Italian restaurant, Silvio's? That really grand-looking restaurant that's recently been refurbished? Well, it's across from there."

"Yeah I know Silvio's. They make great coffee there."

Tess heard movement from Desiree's chair as she shifted nervously in it, once again fidgeting with her bag and jewellery. "They make better coffee here," Desiree blurted out in a voice much too loud. "I love the coffee here. You don't want to be going to Silvio's when you've got exceptional coffee here."

Everyone around her looked at her like they'd forgotten she was even there. Her voice seemed foreign and hostile amongst the flow and ease of the conversation. It was out of place, like a chorus in a song appearing much too early, or a saxophone not tuned properly playing against the natural flow and rhythm of well-timed and well-strung violins.

Tess had to admit, she thought the young men would be looking at Desiree with her athletic frame, perfect nose, and her preppy, designer clothes. Tess was surprised that they hadn't paid her any attention at all.

"It's nice here as well," Tess managed, quickly trying to clear the air from the sudden awkwardness. Everyone's wide eyes revealed they were baffled at the interruption, with most on the table looking down at their coffee or plates, wanting to have nothing to do with the bizarre comment. Finding her outburst very odd, Tess felt it was her duty to rescue Desiree from the humiliation, even if she didn't deserve her help. She wanted to do it for herself as well. She felt embarrassed for her and she hated how it made her feel. God knows Desiree deserved to feel humiliated. *Her odd comment was a way of trying to be included in the conversation, but it didn't work,* Tess thought. *Why else would she object so strenuously about having coffee at Silvio's?* It was like her husband barely tolerated her when she uttered more than one word, and she was just trying to be part of something she couldn't keep up with.

Tess then switched her attention to Jacob again, feeling that she had given all the help she should offer her, without feeling naïve or stupid. She smiled at Jacob. "In fact, the bookshop I was talking about isn't too far from Penny and Dante's shop."

"Yeah," Simon interposed. "Dante and Penny have been telling me all about their interesting shop. A lot of these retro-style businesses are making a comeback, I've been telling them."

"Well, that's music to my ears," Dante said as he placed his hand on Penny's shoulder affectionately. "I wanna work with my lovely and creative wife for as long as we can." He planted a kiss on his wife's cheek.

Keith seemed to be slightly embarrassed at their display of affection and looked at them like a child watching a couple kissing for the first time. Jacob, on the contrary, looked on appreciatively, nodding his head. He then looked at Tess intently. She broke the stare, and looked away only to lock eyes with another pair that were friendly and beautiful. Her heart began to beat wildly again when she realised they were Stewart's.

CHAPTER TWELVE

Tess' heart rate slowed to its natural rhythm again. It seemed like an eternity before he finally spoke. "Hi everyone," Stewart said, still looking at Tess. He sat down on the vacant seat. He scanned around the table and his gaze rested on Jacob, who he eyed suspiciously.

"Oh, Stewy!" Desiree exalted. "So glad you could make it. I wasn't sure if you got my text message!" The relief was evident in her smile — relief that someone who usually tolerated her superficial banter was now joining them. Tess watched her as she stood up, walked over to him and placed her hand affectionately on his shoulder, like he had saved her from falling into a social abyss — something she obviously wasn't used to. Her voice had become slightly more cheerful and less shaky.

Tess found herself adjusting her posture, sitting straighter in her seat and combing her fingers through her hair. Penny gave her a mischievous smile and Dante winked at her in a playful way like he knew something was going on. Stewart, ever the gentleman, gave Desiree a warm smile and touched her shoulder as though acknowledging her pain and her need to be rescued by him. He obviously knew Desiree's limitations — he had witnessed many of her loquacious conversations about nothing.

Tess found herself smiling at this gesture. He was a decent human being who tolerated people, no matter how infuriatingly intolerable they were. His eyes then met hers again and a smile appeared on his slightly stubbled face.

"Hi Tess," he said with a voice like silk.

Her skin broke into goosebumps, first on her arms, then, like a domino effect, spreading across her body. Her smile formed naturally again — genuinely and truthfully — and she knew that it made her face glow. She had seen this type of smile in her flat — catching it as she passed one of her antique mirrors. She had noticed that its rawness illuminated her complexion and made her amber eyes shine like polished gold.

Tess caught both men looking at her intensely with their mouths agape, as though they had fire in their souls. She thought their expressions conveyed their thoughts, those left to roam wild and free amongst jungles of raw natural instincts and desires. Tess tried to curb her imagination as she looked at the two young men. Her skin seemed to be acquainted with her own natural desires — it, too, felt fiery. Flirting was one thing, but she had two alpha males suddenly rallying for her attention — a bit too much for a casual Sunday morning.

"Yes, businesses are hard to manage. You need a lot of time on your hands," Desiree offered the group as though she had just come up with the smartest thing ever put forward. Now that Stewart was there, it was as though she had another lease of life. She looked over at him. "We were talking about all the interesting shops around here, Stewart. Dante and Penny over there have the most charming vintage clothes shop. I must visit it one day." She said it as though she knew them intimately.

Tess decided to ask Keith what he actually did — to ascertain if he yielded any power in the company. Why would he care so much about impressing his colleagues if he did?

"So, what exactly do you do, Keith?" Tess asked.

"I work for a property management company not too far away. I just started working in the …"

Desiree quickly interposed. "As I was saying, there are so many interesting shops here. The salon on the corner looks so charming and stylish too. I might go and get my hair done there. It looks really on-trend and unique, as does the cute flower shop across the street from it — so cute, the whole street is quite interesting. Of course Keith and I are used to living in more upmarket areas."

Tess couldn't believe her rudeness. She had completely interrupted Keith's explanation, as though she didn't want him to reveal something. And she couldn't believe she had mentioned her salon — *that she had to get her hair done there!* First her home, then Mr Papas' shop, now *the salon*? She opened her mouth to tell her that the *charming and stylish* salon in fact belonged to her and Pamela, but quickly refrained. Why should she know where she works? The less she knew about her, the better, even though she would've loved to rub it in her face. She was glad Penny and Dante were preoccupied with their own conversation when she had mentioned the salon.

Keith moved nervously in his seat. "This place is pretty upmarket, that's why we came to live here." He was evidently conscious not to offend anyone.

"You're right about that," Simon said. "The house prices have sky-rocketed in these areas. People love the café lifestyle."

Desiree cleared her throat as she looked at Tess. "Well, yes we're living here, for a while."

"We're residing here, to be near the office. I don't want to have to travel far …" Keith began.

"Oh my goodness! Keith, we really should get going!" Desiree suddenly said.

"I haven't finished my second coffee yet, and my dessert!" Keith wailed, staying cemented to his seat.

Desiree stood there with her bag over her shoulder, looking silly as she waited for her husband to follow suit. He stayed put, and she sheepishly sat back down.

Tess's stomach turned. *He just got the job!* She was positive that's what he was about to say. He was working at the company nearby. That's why he wanted to impress his colleagues — he was a new employee. Why would Desiree say they were just staying there temporarily? Fear began to consume again. What if she was in her life indefinitely? In her home? In her suburb? She took a deep breath to steady herself. She looked wildly around the table until she met Jacob's eyes. He looked concerned.

"Are you okay?" Jacob enquired.

"Yes, I am," she answered, looking now from Jacob to Stewart. She caught him looking at Jacob again, as though he was surveying the competition. Tess tossed her hair instinctively, not realising this would invite more attention from Jacob, and Stewart who was suddenly looking at her with deep emotion.

"So what other books have you read?" Jacob asked her.

Desiree chipped in. "Do you remember we had to read that book? What was it … *Tess of the Derby* …"

"*Tess of the D'Urbervilles*," Stewart assisted, giving Desiree a cautious look. He sat up straight as though he had to be alert — not knowing where the conversation was heading.

Tess's heart rate increased. She couldn't believe she would bring that up again — she knew she was desperate to please and sound intellectual, and it was becoming more evident that it was probably the only book she knew. Tess also knew how desperate she was to humiliate her any chance she got. That had evidently hadn't changed either.

"Yes, that's the one. *God*, how I miss English!" she said. "Remember when poor Tess fell down that hill?" she said to Stewart, who looked back at her, steely-eyed. Then she turned to Tess. "You were dressed in that funny ball gown your mum made. It was so weird looking! I felt so sorry for you seeing you in the mud, with the dress all torn — everyone saw it. Poor Tess! I was really concerned that you broke your leg or something. We were all concerned for you," she ended, her face awash with false sympathy.

Tess looked down at her plate. She then looked up and caught Stewart looking at her.

"*Poor Tess?*" Jacob enquired, as he gave Desiree a puzzled look. He diverted his attention to the subject of the discussion. "Somehow I imagine you had a lot of young men helping you to your feet. Although, I don't think you look like the type that needs rescuing. You look like you can stand on your own two feet just fine." Jacob gave her another one of his warm, sexy smiles.

"You're right about that," Stewart chipped in. "Tess is strong and confident. I thought it back then and I still do now. She could have been anything she wanted to be. Her parents raised her right — they taught her to be real."

Tess suddenly feared she would burst into tears at their kind words. Jacob looked at Stewart and gave him an approving nod. He suddenly backed down, sinking further into his chair, as though he was sensing that he was interrupting something profound.

Penny and Dante also exchanged knowing glances at Stewart's powerful and heartfelt words.

Desiree looked like she was about to throw her coffee over the two men, furious that they were fussing over her enemy. It was obviously not the intended result of her recalling one of Tess' most humiliating moments in front of everyone.

"*Weird-looking dress?*" Penny fumed. "Tess' mother is so talented. I don't think her designs and the word "weird" go together. Far from it! Original, perhaps. She's won awards for her designs and her prints have been chosen to make rugs and pillows …"

"Speaking of dresses," Desiree interrupted loudly, "would you believe Tess fell over again when we ran into her the other night in another weird … you know, one of those type of dresses … on Friday night!" Her vindictiveness had become increasingly more evident in her desperate, flustered face. She was clinging onto anything she might use to humiliate her.

"Friday night?" Dante looked sceptical as he looked at Tess. "Friday night … You bought that dress, the one that fit you so well," he said to Tess. He then turned to look at Desiree. "That other *weird dress* as you call it, was from *our shop* — our *charming* vintage shop — that you want so much to visit? Tess was wearing one of *our* dresses. Actually it was a dress that Penny made!"

154

"That's right," Penny added, giving Desiree a less than friendly look.

"No I didn't mean it was weird. Tess just looked weird … I mean …"

Stewart sat up straight in his chair. His jaw was tight and he became serious. "I thought she looked beautiful." He'd evidently had enough of standing up for Desiree —when she was being cruel, he just couldn't.

Desiree looked shocked and hurt. She opened her mouth, but words failed her. Instead, she began to cosy up to Dante and Penny, needing to do damage control. "Your shop really does sound wonderful. I'll definitely be visiting it soon," she said as she looked at both of them, with an exaggerated giggle. They looked down at their plates, not taking the bait.

Stewart wasn't having any of it. "As I was saying, Tess, I thought it was such a beautiful sight, seeing you there with pink roses in your hair. I just feel bad that fell, and that you hurt yourself. I was so lucky to see you again — to have you back in my life." He refused to look away from her, slightly embarrassed as she was. It was as though he sensed her uneasiness and was coaxing her to come out of the hole she was climbing into. He didn't want Desiree to get to her — just as he didn't back then.

"Well, we'd better get going," Keith said, appearing suddenly eager to stop his wife's words from creating more damage.

"I've gotta get going as well. I don't wanna be late for—" Stewart began.

"Walk with us, Stewart!" Desiree hastily said, cutting him off. "I want to show you a lovely shop I just passed by." She grabbed hold of his arm, pulling him away. Tess felt like Desiree was stopping him from saying something she obviously didn't want her to hear. And she also seemed to want to have Stewart to herself, to have him dote over her instead. She obviously didn't get that from her husband. He definitely was no Stewart.

"We'll organise a time, Tess. I'll call you to discuss the courses?" Stewart queried.

"Come on, Stewy," Desiree interrupted again. "You don't want to be late."

He grabbed his jacket from the back of the chair. As he leaned down to do so, Tess heard Jacob say to him, softly, "Don't let her go, man. Tess — she's the real thing." Jacob accepted his defeat gracefully, even though he had been a strong contender. Tess didn't know if Jacob wanted her to hear his comment, but she was leaning towards thinking he *did* want her to hear it, even if he was pretending to be discrete.

Stewart smiled at him. "Sure man. It was nice to meet you. It's been ... well, it's been interesting," he said, scratching his forehead, with a grin.

He then turned his attention to Tess as she stood up to say goodbye. "Bye Tess." He held her hand tight and pulled her close. "See you soon. Just be careful. If you get too charming, you might just break another guy's heart," he said with a warm smile, obviously referring to Jacob.

"Bye Stewart. I'll wait for your call ... for the courses that you need help with," she stumbled, matching his smile.

"That would be great," he said, touching her cheek affectionately. Desiree, standing next to him, was left to wait again.

"Bye all." He waved to the rest of the group before walking away with Desiree and Keith.

Desiree suddenly turned around and looked at Tess with menacing eyes. The steely glance felt like a warning.

After some more lively conversation around tables laden with breakfast offerings — pastries and other gourmet organic savoury treats — breakfast had become lunch, and suddenly everyone realised they had somewhere to be. Jacob shook her hand firmly and gave her a regretful smile. Simon also shook her hand, but not so intimately. Both men bade their farewells. Tess then walked off with Dante and Penny, who would open the shop soon. Tess planned to wander around the shops before heading home as she felt tipsy from too much sun, conversation, and plenty of male attention.

"The nerve of her!" Penny cried. "No wonder you didn't want to see her. She's impossible. I don't know how Stewart puts up with her … or Keith, for that matter."

Tess was about to contribute her own comments about Desiree but refrained, feeling, for some odd reason, slightly protective of her — like she had already succeeded at making herself look pathetic and didn't need any more salt rubbed into the wound. Part of her didn't understand this feeling of needing to protect her enemy. She then remembered the way Stewart had defended her again, and her heart beat with elation. Surely she wasn't imagining the intense look in his eye. *Stop!* she told herself. It was just some innocent flirting — and Stewart just needed her guidance and he had to defend her because he was a decent human being. Plus, there was the pact … She suddenly thought of Pamela. She felt like they had to have a heart to heart soon. Too much was changing and she felt like she had to let her friend in on her world!

Then she remembered the look Desiree had given her. She turned around to take a final glance, and saw the coffee table where they had all sat. The waiter was already parting the two tables. They were no longer united. She saw Desiree's steely look in her mind's eye, giving her that final glance.

The waiter hadn't placed the tables back to their original position, but on the opposite side. A shiver washed over her, and her chest felt tight as she witnessed the waiter working, stirring fear in her that things would change even more, like the storm had only settled for a while and hadn't yet inflicted its destruction.

"Hey Tess!" Penny brought her out of her thoughts. "Are you daydreaming about some romantic novel again? The way those two men were flirting with you, I don't blame you!"

"Yes, it was just my imagination again — just some silly thoughts," she said with an uneasy smile as she continued to walk with them in the gentle sunlight.

"No, I don't think they're so silly," Dante said. "It might be love! You know, that thing that makes everyone look like they're dreaming, uneasy and happy at the same time, euphoric even. Perhaps that's what it is?" He looked at her with a sparkle in his eyes.

"Perhaps," Tess said with an uncertain smile, as a mélange of emotions surged inside her. *Perhaps*.

CHAPTER THIRTEEN

Tess felt different when she stepped into the salon on Tuesday morning. It was as though she was seeing and hearing things more clearly, things she hadn't noticed before, like the bird call at the crack of dawn from her bedroom window, the street-sweeper cleaning the roads early in the morning. She noticed happy couples strolling past her as she walked to work, and that the grass appeared greener after the heavy rain had fallen. Tess also noticed how polished the shopfront windows all looked at the start of a new day. She even felt taller, like she had grown an inch. She stood up straight, carrying herself with a confident posture, breathing in and out slowly, allowing the air in her lungs to move more freely. She looked up and admired the chandeliers. She loved their melodramatic presence.

Pamela gave her a curious look.

"Like I said the other day," Tess said, catching the glance, "we should really think about adding some bookshelves in this place. It'd be a great idea!"

"Hi to you too. How was your break?" Pamela asked sarcastically.

"Oh hi, Pamela. Sorry, *wherever are my manners?*" she asked, playfully attempting an English accent.

Pamela just looked up from sorting out some tubes of dye and lighteners with raised eyebrows. "Okay …" she replied, most likely sensing that Tess was "in the clouds again", as she often called it.

"Seriously. It would be a great idea. I mean, some clients stay here for hours. It makes sense."

"And then what?" Pamela enquired. "When they don't finish their books, they continue them the next time they get their hair done?"

Tess processed what she'd said. Her eyes grew wider. "No! They wouldn't need to come back to finish it. They could borrow it!"

"Borrow it? What are we, a library?" Pamela asked with an added dose of sarcasm. She smiled to herself, but then looked at Tess, who was serious.

"Yes! Yes!" she cried. "Like a library! We could put a system in place where they borrow books. And they return them, we could have cards as well. Oh my God! Why didn't I think of it before?"

"Why would they borrow books from us when there are so many book shops around?"

"Yes, but they're shops, where they would have to pay for the books. They could borrow from us though … Think of how many people don't have time to read these days. They've probably forgotten that reading is the thing missing from their lives. We could remind them, and reacquaint them with the magic of books. They get their hair done and they have some adventure or romance as well. It makes sense."

"So, tell me … Would we also have a sign that says "Quiet, please"? Would we have to tone down the music or completely turn it off? And would the other clients who don't feel like reading have to keep their mouths shut? Perhaps we would have to wait for them to finish their chapter before we could even turn on the taps or the hairdryer …"

"Okay, okay, I get it!" Tess said, quickly feeling like Pamela had taken the air out from under her wings. Pamela might have a point. She hadn't thought it out. Still, she didn't have to be so sarcastic about it.

Tess felt offended that Pamela had completely shot the idea down. Now that she thought about it, she often did that, like the coffee machine idea she'd had a few months ago. She'd even struggled to convince Pamela to install the chandeliers without it becoming a major production. It made her feel like they weren't equals in their business relationship. A vision of Michael talking down to her, telling her they had to be responsible came to her mind. Then she thought of how Desiree was told to be quiet, to not speak her mind, by Keith, and her father. Tess suddenly felt awful for her, to be made to feel like that — to have her light dimmed. But then she remembered the look Desiree had given her, and the anxiety it stirred inside her superseded any pity or empathy. It was definitely a warning not to mess with her — that she would pay for it if she were to do so.

She looked over at Pamela working. Her face looked unusually serious. To Tess, it felt like she was distancing herself emotionally. That Pamela had so quickly dismissed her idea bothered Tess more than she wanted to admit to herself. Usually when Pamela questioned her she would also laugh if she thought her ideas were farfetched, and would also give her credit when it turned out to be one of her better suggestions. It was different this time. She was almost spiteful.

"Maybe you're right. I didn't think it through," Tess acquiesced. "It would need a bit of tweaking. Anyway, I didn't say we would do it straight away. It was just an idea." She felt herself retreat from the conversation. "Anyway, I was going to go to Silvio's yesterday, to have my coffee. I thought since you do — and everyone has been raving about the new barista lately."

This comment instantly got Pamela's attention. "Oh?" she said in a clipped tone, looking up from her work. "Why would you want to do that? You never have your coffee out."

"Yes, I know, but I thought maybe I should. You know, maybe I've been living too cautiously, following the whole routine to the letter — never changing it up at all. I mean, some people would never believe that I'm my mother's daughter, or my dad's for that matter. I need to stop running from the rain … I need more colour …" Tess backed down when Pamela looked at her like she was from another planet. There was an awkward pause. Tess wasn't used to such things with Pamela or any of her friends — only comfortable silences. She continued, hoping to break the tension. "I need more of the unusual-coloured sprinkles — not just sunsets and pretty pictures …" She trailed off again when Pamela's expression didn't change. "Not that coffee doesn't paint a pretty picture. I mean, everything seems better with coffee … and tea," she waffled awkwardly, feeling uncomfortable. The way Pamela was looking at her unnerved her. It wasn't like her. Her words had tangled under her watchful eye. It was as though she was analysing every movement, and what every word meant.

Tess decided she'd had enough of her friend's scrutiny, and walked to the counter to examine her appointment book. She felt Pamela's judgmental eyes on her as she scanned her gold and white appointment book. She'd had enough with her judgment. She wasn't going to be told who to be or how to live by anyone — not even her closest friend. She often wondered if Pamela thought she was too caught in the past, too into nostalgia and romance.

"So, you're going to be going there all the time now? At Silvio's for coffee?"

Tess looked up abruptly, taken aback by her question. "Um … no, not all the time. I just thought since you go there. I thought I might see you and we can have a chat."

"A chat?" she asked in the same suspicious tone.

Tess was dumbfounded. Why was she being so inquisitive about where she had her coffee? First Desiree, now *Pamela?* She had a suspicion Pamela was worried about her moving on from the pact, but this was about where she had coffee, not men or relationships. Did Pamela think she was interested in Silvio? That perhaps his refurbishing the restaurant meant that she was now interested in something more, because of his gesture? That had to be it. Pamela was scared because she didn't confide in her — she felt like she was moving on without her and had not even included her as she did so, like a good friend would. Her tone deeply saddened her. And at some level it also angered her, if she were to be honest with herself.

"So, would the chat have something to do with the talk you had with Silvio?" Pamela queried. "You know, that Friday night after Vinnie's? You've been acting rather mysteriously lately — ever since that night."

"Yes, actually, it had. I wanted to tell you about everything. Wait a minute, how did you know about that?" *Could Silvio have told her? Why would he tell her about something so private?* The thought of them talking about her made her feel slightly betrayed.

Pamela backed down from her somewhat confrontational stance. Avoiding eye contact, she continued sorting out the colours, arranging them in rows and placing them in their little cubicles on the wall shelf. "I just happened to see him on Saturday after work, when I got my coffee. He looked upset. So I asked him. He wouldn't tell me at first, but he really looked like he wanted to talk. You know, since I work with you and we're *friends?*" She looked up as she said this.

Tess felt a sudden pain in the pit of her stomach. She knew she should have told her earlier. Pamela probably felt that she didn't consider her someone worthy of confiding in. They weren't just business partners, they *were* also friends.

Pamela continued. "Anyway, I think he wanted to know if you were certain of your feelings about him. He knew that night that you definitely were. Even his gesture to refurbish the restaurant because of your love affair with nostalgia hadn't wooed you. So I guess I was surprised that you wanted to have coffee there again. You might give him mixed signals." Her tone had lightened, but she still appeared guarded.

"I should have told you!" Tess cried. "Things just got in the way. All these things have happened since then. It just skipped my mind."

"*Skipped your mind?*" Pamela seemed irritated at this reply. "So, having a kind, intelligent, sexy young man reveal his soul to you, a man who refurbished his whole restaurant because you were his muse, who pours his heart out to you — that took a backseat? You had more pressing issues? I mean, is it every day that that happens? This isn't Michael, your ex. This is an extremely handsome, extremely kind and considerate man!"

"Yes, I know he is." Tess couldn't move. What had gotten into Pamela? "Of course I know he's all that *and more* … He *is* attractive, and smart, and kind, and a great chef as well. I mean, I'd imagine he'd even be a magician in the bedroom."

Tess looked around in case any clients had sneaked in the salon and witnessed the unexpected tirade. Pamela seemed to colour at this, which wasn't like her. She seemed embarrassed by what Tess said, but also angered by it.

"So, you *do* like him. You *are* interested. I mean, it's clear you've fantasised about him. I think you're being completely unfair to him. You have no romantic notions, yet you've imagined him in bed? You've practically called him a god and you say you're not interested in him? Maybe you're in denial because with that description …"

"I just repeated most of the words *you* used to describe him," she retaliated.

Pamela fixed her hair awkwardly.

"Jeez Louise," Tess said, echoing Penny. "What's gotten into you?"

Pamela sighed. "I just don't want him to get hurt. He looked really upset. And then you told me about having coffee there, so soon. I thought you'd changed your mind, and that maybe you don't really know what you want. Maybe you like having him waiting in the background in case … I don't know, in case you suddenly *do* want a man in your life, or you think some other man may not be good enough. Michael wasn't good enough, so …"

Tess shot her a fervent look. "Michael?" she practically yelled. "Michael is *nothing* like Silvio. You said it yourself!"

"Calm down!" Pamela exclaimed. "You asked me what's gotten into me? What's gotten into *you*? That would be a better question, I think."

"*What!* I just come into the salon, and you come at me like, like ... like a tsunami! It was totally unexpected, and uncalled for, mind you. You're acting like I'm some diva who doesn't care at all if she breaks a man's heart. I didn't *ask* him to refurbish his restaurant for me. I thought Millie was joking!" Tess suddenly felt so sad and hurt by her accusations.

Pamela remained quiet for a moment. "Look, I didn't mean to accuse you like that. I know you wouldn't do anything intentionally to hurt anyone, but maybe you're slightly in denial about your feelings? Do you think ... even just a little?"

"Where is this really coming from, Pamela? Am I supposed to avoid him forever? I always used to go and get takeaway from there. Lately, I've been going to the deli when I don't feel like cooking. I didn't know I had to justify going to get coffee — you're the second person who's had an issue with that."

Pamela gave her a perplexed look. "Why would someone else have an issue with that? And I never said you can't go and have coffee there ... I was just surprised. I know how you usually are. You know, you've been avoiding things like that for a while. I found it odd that you would confront him so soon."

"How I *usually* am? How am I, exactly?"

"Well ... you know ... You sort of don't like drama in your life, even though you like reading about it. You want everything to be pretty and nice, not too difficult, lest you live ... I mean, stress out at all," she said, suddenly avoiding eye contact with her. "Anyway, so you *don't* have feelings for him. Good, because he was pretty certain you don't. If you give him the slightest indication that proves otherwise, well you might crush his heart irrevocably."

"*Irrevocably?*" she queried. "Don't you think that's a bit melodramatic? Anyway, I will *always* like Silvio, and yeah, I did feel bad to let him go. I have to admit, I was afraid that I may never find another Silvio. He is really great boyfriend material."

"It sure sounds to me like you're not sure, that you might change your mind …"

"I didn't say that, but he *has* liked me for years now, and I just felt a bit sad that it might change how we interact with each other. It was all so final."

"Well, is it better to leave him waiting? Hoping that there might be something between you? This isn't one of your classic novels — this is real life Tess," she said patronisingly.

"Like I don't know that!" Tess scoffed. "Look, if you're worried about our pact, I'm *not* moving on, and I would tell you if I was."

Pamela shook her head from side to side, in disbelief. "Is that what you think? It's not as if our pact is cast in stone. I know life can change all that — but I know we both are through with settling in relationships. We want the real thing."

"Yes we do, and Silvio isn't the real thing for me!" Tess retorted.

"Fine," Pamela said after a long pause. "It's just that you either like him or you don't. It *can* be that simple. Anyway, sorry. Are we all good?"

"Sure," she said with a nervous smile as the door opened behind her.

Tess went to greet the client.

"*Jeez Louise?*" she heard Pamela repeat in a lighter tone again as she headed towards the door.

Tess was left shaken by Pamela's words. She had felt positive about herself after seeing Stewart again, and had even planned on telling Pamela about him, and about Silvio. She also wanted to tell her about Desiree, but she suddenly didn't want to confide in her at all. Even if she wouldn't admit it, she knew that she might feel sad about being left

166

behind, but for her to react like that … Was Silvio that upset about the whole thing? She didn't think she'd broken his heart. He must have been more devastated than she thought, for Pamela to react that way.

Tess smiled at her client. "I won't be long," she reassured her as she walked to the back room to get a glass of water. She passed Pamela. She didn't really want to look at her. Things had become too intense for her liking. They'd had little arguments over the years, but they both held their tongues before things got personal. *I should have told her. Maybe she wouldn't have reacted this way had I confided in her before Silvio did,* she thought with a heavy heart. She met Pamela's eyes. Her friend gave her a half-hearted smile. Tess thought it still looked a bit guarded, cautious — like she had more to say to her.

She gave her the best smile she could muster. They worked together. There was no room for holding grudges. She had to let it go — but she felt so hurt by her words.

Tess walked back to her client after sipping some water. She dug deep and found the strength to carry on with the day.

"So how are you today, Sally?" she asked the young woman.

CHAPTER FOURTEEN

The following afternoon, Tess went for a walk to clear her head and to buy some fresh flowers for the salon — to inspire her and put her at ease. She also needed an excuse to step out. She'd been feeling like she was suffocating whenever she thought of her argument with Pamela. She'd been feeling slightly uncomfortable around her since then. Tess sensed that Pamela felt the same. There was no dancing in the back room, or joking about men, or gossip about pretentious and rude clients. The irony was that even if her keeping things from Pamela may have contributed to the misunderstanding, it made her want to not disclose anything about Stewart and Desiree as well. She had obviously offended Pamela, not confiding in her — like she didn't consider her a close, trustworthy friend.

It was bad enough she couldn't get the look Desiree had given her out of her mind. She hadn't seen her for a few days, but instead of rejoicing, she felt uneasy — like this was the calm before the storm. She'd passed her in the hallway one day, and Desiree gave her a friendly smile, which was odd after Desiree had evidently felt so out of place at the Sunday breakfast. It was strange for her not to retaliate. Tess just prayed she wasn't lying about them not living there permanently — even if Keith worked nearby. She hoped they still planned on moving regardless. From what she had told her, they could afford to move anywhere they wanted — at least to another apartment. *From all the apartments in Sydney ... how did she end up here?* Anyway, she'd said the building wasn't "sterile" enough for her, or spacious enough, so no doubt they *would* be moving on, if Desiree had anything to say about it.

Tess found herself thinking of Stewart, and even how wonderful Jacob had made her feel. She needed to feel positive again after Pamela had made her sound so heartless.

Of course she felt for Silvio. The truth was, she really didn't have time to think of what had transpired because that night not only brought a change in weather — it had brought Desiree back, and Stewart back with her.

Still, she didn't like holding any animosity towards her friend. *I'll make amends*, she told herself as she crossed the street and headed to the flower shop.

"Hi Helena," she greeted her friend as she stepped inside.

"Hi Tess," she said, turning briefly from her conversation with some customers. "I'll be with you in a few moments."

"Sure," Tess replied. She looked around the beautiful space. A spray of bright yellow roses with red tips caught her eye.

"They're Konfetti Sunset roses," Helena called out as her customers continued to peruse the flowers, "and the ones next to them with the coral and red petals are Ambiance roses. They're all so lovely, aren't they?"

"They're so elegant, and poetic," Tess enthused. "They'd look wonderful in the salon, and in my apartment."

Tess then looked at the cheerful painted daisies and admired their vibrant, bold colours. Her eyes then feasted on the lovely pale pink roses, and the pure white ones.

She finally decided on the Konfetti Sunset roses, knowing they would create some much needed beauty and kindness in the salon, to help clear the tension that had cast darkness and gloom in the air.

Tess watched as Helena served the customers, before she made her purchase.

"So, your hubby visited the salon the other day. He's looking very debonair," Tess said with a smile.

Helena looked down at the flowers. Her disposition had completely changed at the mention of Carter. She paused before replying. "Yes, I can't fault him on that," she finally said. "He always looks smart. He knows he has the ability to turn a few heads as he strides by. I even had one of my customers gushing over him, before she realised that I was his wife."

"He's a kind and attractive guy. You're both lucky to have each other. It's wonderful if two people connect — it's hard to find someone who truly knows your heart, who understands you — your soulmate," Tess said, looking at the roses, dreamily lost in thought.

Helena laughed. "Okay then. Who has you talking like that? Could a man have appeared in your life?"

"What?" Tess replied, much too quickly. "No … I was just …"

"Referring to one of your romance books, or you really *did* meet someone that has you singing a different tune? Well, if you have, I applaud you. You're right, it *is* hard to find someone you can truly connect with. If you *do* find them, hold on to them for dear life. They may be your only shot at real love — otherwise you can dream about it while you read your books." She handed her the flowers.

Tess looked at her with questioning eyes. "Helena? Are you and Carter okay? I mean, you're happy with him, aren't you? It's just that at Vinnie's you were saying that things are going better — that he's showering you with gifts …"

Helena looked straight into Tess' eyes. Tess thought they looked fragile and teary, like hurt lingered in them.

"Tess, it's just hard sometimes. Marriage can be tricky. You don't just find the guy and that's it — end of story. The book continues, and you have to find a way to make it work. It doesn't write itself — a person's story, a couple's story. Do you know what I mean?" Her cheeks trembled slightly, as if feelings she never knew existed were coming out into awareness and being set free.

"Don't I know it!" Tess replied, recalling the tight pain she'd felt in her chest when she'd lain awake so many nights, hearing Michael's heavy breathing, wondering what had happened to the man she had once felt so close and comfortable with. "But you said he's been so romantic lately?"

"Well, that's because he feels guilty. He's never around — well not for me, he isn't anyway."

"What are you implying? Not that he's seeing someone else?"

"No ... I mean, I hardly see him, but I don't think he would do *that*. He has a good heart — too good sometimes. He empathises with everyone — tries to help people. Even at work he's taken on more than usual. He's always there for his boss, the other agents, the clients. It may be a great thing to do, but where does that leave me? I just feel lonely sometimes, even when I'm with him. He's mind isn't with me lately — I don't think his heart is either. It's somewhere else. I'm worried that he's drifting ..." Sadness showed in her eyes.

Tess could feel Helena's loneliness — her isolation. She had her beautiful flowers around her to keep her company, giving her hope and strength, but a deep sadness still enveloped her. She was right — she did look out of place lately in the beautiful garden she had created around her, that reflected her hopes and dreams — the life she craved. Tess could relate. She had done the same.

Tess gave Helena a warm embrace as she left the salon, telling her that they should plan a girl's night out sooner than planned. *We all need to talk*, she thought, thinking of Pamela. She also told Helena to call her any time she needed a friend.

Tess walked back to the salon feeling like she wanted a fresh start. She breathed in the freshness and sweet fragrance from the roses as she pondered. Everything was becoming slightly messy and strange — they needed to fix things. She would start at that moment by healing her relationship with Pamela, and then she would have the strength to help Helena.

She opened the glass door of the salon confidently, with hope in her heart. But then she caught sight of *her* — *Desiree!* She was laughing with Pamela. It looked like they couldn't control their laughter. *Why on earth is she at the salon?* Of course! She had talked about their salon at breakfast — that she thought it looked charming. Maybe she should have told

171

her she worked there — but maybe it wouldn't have deterred her from entering yet another of Tess' worlds.

Tess cleared her throat. Neither had noticed she'd stepped inside. She purposefully made a loud noise with the vase on the counter to get their attention.

"Oh, hi Tess! You're back," Pamela said. "I didn't see you there. Desiree here was telling me such a funny story about someone she had run into … How this woman fell in the mud — with a long, ancient-looking dress. The way she said it sounded so hilarious!" Pamela exclaimed, trying to stifle another bout of laughter.

Tess' cheeks felt as warm as the edges of the Konfetti Sunset roses.

"*Oh my God!* This is just too weird," Desiree turned to meet Tess' wide eyes. "I can't believe I've run into you *again*, Tess!" she cried as her hair swept through the air and settled around her shocked face as though she was in a hair commercial. "Whatever are you doing here? Are you delivering some flowers?"

"I work here," Tess replied.

"What! You're kidding me, right? You work here? I had no idea. What do you do? Do you help sweep up and wash …"

Tess's anger was reaching boiling point. "I'm the part-owner of this business — Pamela and I own it, and I am also a hairdresser here," she said loudly. "This place you said looked so hip and stylish and charming. I own it with Pamela."

"Oh! Did I say that? I was talking about one of the other salons on the street," she said, as if it was such a farfetched idea. "But this one is charming too," she said, looking at Pamela, obviously not wanting to offend *that* particular part-owner.

"Well, there aren't any other salons nearby, and you did say it was around the corner. I do believe this is on a corner," Tess said, her spite growing as she began to arrange the roses in the tall vase.

"Oh well, it doesn't matter. There was also another one nearby. I'm fairly certain, but who care's anyway! *Potato patata*!" she said, dismissing the whole topic. "I hope you don't mind me telling Pamela what happened to you. I hope I don't sound insensitive, but you have to admit, it was hilarious," she said, with a high-pitched giggle. "I don't even know how we ended up talking about that …" She suddenly looked at Pamela for assistance, like they were best friends laughing together. "One minute we were talking about being clumsy … Oh that's right, it was when Pamela dropped the comb and nearly tripped on the cord …"

"Yes, my leg throbbing all night *and* the next day … that was *hilarious* for me too," Tess said, through gritted teeth.

"Oh, Tess, you've always been funny!" Desiree managed.

Tess caught Pamela looking at her curiously. "So, how do you two know each other?"

"Oh!" Desiree exclaimed. "Would you believe that dear Tess and I used to go to high school together?"

"Oh! *You did?* And so Tess was the woman that fell at the apartment. *She's* the one you were talking about … The woman you ran into a few days ago, on Friday night?"

"Yes, she's the one. Poor thing, always falls over," Desiree added. "You've got to be more careful, Tess. I worry about you," she said in a sisterly, caring voice.

"Well, that's weird. It's the first I'm hearing about it," Pamela said, giving Tess a questioning gaze.

Desiree laughed. "Anyway, it's been fun talking to you. I'm glad you could fit me in for an appointment. I'll see you then? It's always lovely making new friends when you just move in to a new place. I'll be coming here more often. I haven't laughed like that in ages," she said holding her chest as though she was in pain from all the laughing. "I'm sure you're a hoot with all your friends!"

"It's been nice meeting you too. You do know how to tell a story," Pamela said. "No offence of course, Tess," she added, barely shooting her a glance.

173

"None taken — of course," Tess managed. Her stomach felt like it was twisting into knots. This can't be happening. Pamela and Desiree? Friends? Did she hear Desiree correctly?

Desiree picked up several bags and walked towards the door. Tess noticed the bags were from Penny and Dante's shop. Why on earth would she shop there? She would mistake it for a costume shop. She felt like she was in some strange dream — where the past creeps up on you, to torment you, just like the dream she had with her and Desiree in their uniforms, standing outside her apartment building.

"By the way," Desiree said, turning and stopping briefly on her way to the door.

"That club further down. My husband was asking about it the other day. Is it any good?" Another tight knot formed in Tess' stomach.

"Yeah it is!" Pamela replied. "Tess and I, and some of the other shop girls — we all go there."

Just then, Desiree's phone rang. "Hold that thought," she said, holding up one French-manicured finger. "I've got to get this. It's my husband. Could be about business."

Tess almost laughed at her comment. *Yes, judging by the way your suave Keith told you to behave while the big boys talked — he would really need some of your business acumen!*

Tess then walked over to Pamela. "That's the girl from high school — Desiree, the one I was telling you about ... *remember?*" she said discretely.

Desiree hung up the phone and sighed dramatically. "Right. I've got to go. It never ends. Sometimes I tell myself I'd be happier if I had no money!" She gave Pamela a sorrowful look.

Tess couldn't believe Pamela was laughing at the comment. "Well, you do sound busy. Try to breathe. You need to have fun as well!"

"So, you think that Vinnie's is okay?"

"It's more than okay. Like I said, Tess and I and the rest of the "shop girls" always have our monthly get-together there." Pamela then noticed the bag Desiree was holding. "Even Penny from the vintage shop ... she joins us sometimes."

"Oh Penny. She's so hip and sweet. I just saw her and Dante. They were so thrilled with my purchases. I nearly bought the whole store. Like I said, it's great to make new friends. Isn't that right, Tess?" she asked with a huge smile on her face.

Tess managed a half-grin, but it was challenging. She noticed that Desiree's mouth was smiling but her eyes were looking at her pointedly. Tess remembered the steely gaze she'd given her on Sunday morning as she'd left with Keith and Stewart. She shivered at the thought.

"You know what? Why don't you join us next time, since you know Tess?" Pamela asked. She then looked at Tess. "What do you think, Tess? Why don't we plan a night out for next Friday? Who cares if we just had one! Penny might be able to join us this time," she suggested with pride, as though it was the most genius idea ever.

"I'd love to!" Desiree exclaimed. "That sounds great! Well, you've got my number. Call me any time. See you soon!" With one final wave and her signature fake smile, she was gone.

Tess walked over to the counter and looked at the flowers.

"They're so lovely," Pamela acknowledged.

"Yes, they are," Tess said, barely looking at her. "She's the girl I told you about ... the one that laughed at me and called me Tess of the D'Urbervilles. That's Desiree. The one that made my high school days a living hell."

Pamela looked up as though she was deep in thought. "Desiree ..." she speculated. "What! No, you're kidding! That's the same one? I can't believe it! I didn't even suspect that it was her for a second, that she was *the Desiree*. She was so nice, and funny. I think she means well about your fall. She just meant that it looked funny, now that she knows you're okay, of course. I think it was one of those laughing *with you* things — not *at you*."

"I wasn't laughing, though."

"You're not offended, are you? She's harmless. She makes me laugh — she doesn't take herself too seriously," Pamela finished. "Plus, we want her coming to our salon. She said she always has treatments, colour — the works."

She doesn't take herself too seriously? What did she mean by that? Tess sighed and changed the topic, not wanting to spend another second thinking about her nemesis. "Are you still upset about the whole Silvio thing?"

"No, I've already forgotten about it," Pamela said, slightly scratching her face, a bit too close to her nose. "Anyway, maybe you misinterpreted her motives back then. Maybe she was just being funny, and you thought she was having a go at you? Is that a possibility? I only say that because she's so down to earth … well, with me anyway. Do you think you may have made her feel intimidated? You know, with your literature and philosophical conversations — like you and Michael used to have before he let his work control him?"

Tess couldn't believe the words coming out of Pamela's mouth. "*No!* It's not a possibility. I didn't misinterpret anything. There is *no* doubt in my mind …" She trailed off, shaking all over as a client entered the salon. "Well then, maybe she's different now. People change," Pamela said casually as she went to greet the client.

Tess looked at the roses. Her heart felt like it was breaking piece by piece and that her world was collapsing — *irrevocably* changing before her eyes, and that there was nothing she could do about it!

CHAPTER FIFTEEN

Tess awoke on Thursday morning feeling weary. She had hardly slept all night. It felt like she was on a ride she didn't want to be on. She wished she could leave at the next exit, or better yet, that Desiree could leave at the next exit since she was the one who was supposedly just on a pit stop. Tess, however, had a sinking feeling — that it wasn't just a pit stop; that she was beginning to make herself right at home.

Uncertainty clouded her vision. Nothing felt sacred anymore — like it belonged to her. How she craved her solitude, her space. Her thoughts immediately went to Stewart. The way he made her feel encouraged her to contemplate the idea that her solitude, although much needed, would be more enjoyable knowing that he was also in her world — even if it was just on the sidelines, like music in the background as she read, comforting her and complementing the peace, but also stirring within her intense mixed emotions.

Pamela used to be another person who had always encouraged her. *Have I been neglecting her friendship?* Tess pondered as she looked towards her front door, thinking of the little, loyal brass bell which resided at the front of it. The corridor and the two apartment doors separated them both, yet behind Pamela's door lived a woman who had needs and wants, and perhaps craved companionship. Had they distanced themselves from one another just as they distanced themselves from the possibility of having men in their lives — a partner, a possible soulmate? Silvio's words plagued her. It was true — it *was* sad to go through life without a special someone to complement you, to share meaningful moments with and feel reciprocal love. The thought of Silvio made her chest tighten and her stomach turn, and the thought of Pamela attacking her hurt her to the core.

She decided to go and shower and spend some time on her make-up. She needed to feel and look her best. She wouldn't let Desiree make her feel small. Besides, adding a touch of colour to her face, her nails and hair always gave her hope — it made her happy, like it always did growing up with tubes and jars of paint all around the house.

"The lipsticks should be arriving today!" she exclaimed to an empty room in realisation. A glimmer of hope filled her heart — the anticipation of receiving something new, something wonderful. She quickly went to the kitchen to make a coffee, needing to wake up and start the day. She passed the desk and looked at the letter that she had begun writing to Cathy.

She recalled the conversation in the salon. *No colour can hide the truth, if the pain's so bad inside.* She caught her reflection in the antique mirror in the hallway, and looked deep into her fragile eyes. She brushed the thought aside, and regained the momentum to get ready for work.

Her heart had other ideas. Without thinking, she walked over to the desk and picked up the beautifully crafted pen. She wanted to tell Cathy everything — her fears, her hopes, about Desiree being back in her life, and the turmoil she was stirring inside her again. And she wanted to tell her about Stewart. Tess couldn't stop writing. One paragraph became four, and four quickly became ten. She had chosen to write in contemporary English, considering the intensity of her feelings and the subject, but couldn't resist ending the letter with:

I am sure you are astonished with my revelations concerning the insufferable acquaintance that I wish to not to be acquainted with in the slightest, as she is still of the most disagreeable character. My dear amiable confidante and esteemed friend, I await your thoughts with unwavering anticipation as I too engage in heartfelt occupation at the salon — at my station.

Faithfully yours,

Tess stifled a giggle as she placed the gold pen down, even if her heart beat uneasily. By the time she had finished, she realised that half an hour had passed. She didn't care about the time. She had to clear her mind, and she felt better writing down how she felt. She placed the letter in an envelope and threw it into her bag in her bedroom. If Pamela didn't understand how she felt, she knew Cathy would. She would believe her. She had seen firsthand the damage that Desiree's words could inflict on those around her.

As she walked out into the street, her heart felt lighter at the thought of Cathy — a friend she knew she could rely on.

Tess had let her client know she'd be a few minutes late. Her client had some shopping to do, so it wasn't an issue. Seeing she had some free time on her hands, Tess lingered around the shops to think. Passing her spare time at the salon with Pamela suddenly didn't seem so appealing.

She passed Dante and Penny's shop. Her heart felt heavy again. Everything dear to her had been stained since Desiree had re-entered her life — just like her poor dress. Tess peered through the window.

She heard Penny call out from inside the shop. "Hey Tess! Come in. I've got some new velvet jackets if you want to have a look."

Tess stepped into the shop robotically. "Hi Penny," she managed.

"Hey … are you okay? You don't seem yourself." Penny gave her a concerned look. "Is it because of the dress? The one that was practically ruined?" Tess looked into Penny's concerned eyes. "Ruined by tea and dirt," she sighed. "Do you believe the audacity of Desiree?" she added, recalling her telling Pamela about her fall, making it seem so tragic, sordid, and at the same time, comical. "I can't believe she told Pamela about my fall. I found her in the salon, making an appointment of all things. I felt so bad and embarrassed when she criticised the dress in front of you and Dante at the coffee shop."

"So she *did* end up going to the salon."

Tess' eyes narrowed. "What? What do you mean, she *ended up* going to the salon?"

"Oh, she was here at the shop, and she was going on about how she needed a haircut and the salon on the corner looked really stylish and lovely. I told her you work there — you and Pamela own it together. That was okay, wasn't it?"

"What? She knew I worked there?"

"Yes, I told her you worked there with Pamela, and that you two are also good friends."

"You did?" Tess asked, slightly irritated.

"Yes. She was sweet, and said she felt so embarrassed about the dress incident. She ended up buying so many clothes. I think she wanted to show how much she regretted her comment about calling the dress weird, and she loved so many things in here — especially the vintage designer brands."

Tess saw stars form before her eyes. The lilac-coloured walls warped, and purple patterns shimmered everywhere around her. The room around her began to close in on her; the walls, the funky curtains and the groovy lamps felt like they would crush her under their weight.

"Tess, I hope you don't mind. I know she was completely impossible on Sunday at the coffee shop, and that you didn't want to see her, but you seemed to be okay with her later. Plus, I think she's trying to make amends. Anyway, I was proud to tell her it's your salon since she was raving about it so much ... you know, to show her how successful you've become in your own right. Why hide it, right?"

Tess regained her cool. The walls became less blurry. The last time she was overcome with a visual migraine like this was when she'd left her home town with Michael, and had said goodbye to all her memories involving Desiree. The tension caused by the feeling of sheer desperate relief had been so intense it had made her dizzy. The realisation that liberty was in her grasp had been too much for her to process. It felt almost too good to be true.

Tess thought about it. Yes, it was good Desiree knew it was her salon, but at the same time, it appeared that the more Desiree knew about her, the worse her life became. Not only had she now cosied up to Penny and Dante, she was also making waves with Pamela when things were already volatile between them. Tess shivered as she remembered the look Desiree had given her on Sunday. It could only mean one thing — that she would seek revenge. Tess suspected she had an agenda. The fact she'd lied to her about not knowing she worked at the salon with Pamela was definitely suspicious. A heavy feeling of anxiety settled in her chest.

Tess decided she would not tell Penny that Desiree had criticised the dress *again*, straight after she'd apologised for doing so. She was beginning to feel like her friends would think she was whining — that perhaps *she* was the instigator of the problems between them. Desiree seemed to be charming everyone. The tactics she was using had, up until now, been deployed in an underhand way, starting with the "innocent" reminders about Tess' past humiliations, but who knew when Desiree would bring her A game, and permanently destroy her world? Was that her mission?

"I have to go," Tess said, suddenly wanting to be alone.

"Sure, see you soon," Penny said, oblivious to Tess' pain, as she raced out of the shop and back out onto the street.

That afternoon, Tess was glad to be heading home after dropping her letter to Cathy off at the post office. She was eager to stop at Millie's, not having had time to visit her during the day. It had been a busy day at the salon, and she'd made it through the day without conversing with Pamela much. It wasn't as awkward as it had been, and they'd remained amicable — but it wasn't the same. Everything had changed between them.

"Hi Millie," she greeted her friend, who was sorting some perfume bottles.

Millie turned around, and tidied her hair with a tremor in her smile. "Hi Tess … Um …"

Tess looked at the counter. It was full of invoices and some shipping receipts. Tess' heart began to sink.

Millie sighed. "It's the lipsticks. They aren't here yet. Apparently they haven't even left the warehouse. I'm so sorry, Tess. They reassured me they'll definitely arrive by the end of next week. Tess, I …"

"It's okay," Tess said, quickly trying to hide her disappointment. She felt silly. She was clinging onto the lipsticks as though they would save her from the fear that was consuming her. She was holding onto the idea that colour would brighten her day, and that everything would be okay. But she was fooling herself.

She began to walk out of the shop.

"Tess …"

Tess turned around and gave her best performance. "It's really okay, Millie. They're just lipsticks, after all."

"Okay," Millie said, her voice quivering.

Tess felt Millie's concern as she stepped out. *They're just lipsticks. They're just flowers. No one will notice them. I will … I'll notice them.* She felt like she was sinking into herself, hiding from the beauty she craved — from the sprinkles, the sunsets, the wild horses, the rain. She wasn't sure if Millie was convinced, but she had to try to convince herself that the lipsticks didn't really matter before she could convince anyone else. Perhaps the lipsticks didn't matter because she knew in her heart they wouldn't give her what she wanted. She needed colour in her life from a different source, something that would last and fulfil her heart and her soul. She wanted her heart to smile — then, she would really live, without trepidation, without guilt, and without building walls around her.

She walked into her apartment. Solemnly, she looked around at her beautiful objects. *That's what they really are,* she told herself. *Just objects.* She realised she was deceiving herself, painting a romantic picture in her mind, imagining those objects had more to offer than they really did.

As she sat back in her armchair, feeling like she had no real purpose, her heart ached from all the negative thoughts. She felt like she did when she was a teenager, before her rebellion took hold. She was letting Desiree do this to her, giving her permission to treat her terribly. The confidence she'd had that Sunday morning had waned again, and her thoughts went back to a time when she came home from school heartbroken because Stewart had left.

Tears had streamed down her face, blurring her vision, just as the pouring rain had that stormy afternoon. Tess hadn't known why she'd felt that way. She'd been angry as well — at Evie crying over him. It had evoked deep feelings she'd never known existed. She'd run home, passing the pond, mud all over her shoes. "Mum … are you home?" she'd called out when she saw no one in the main house. She'd headed to the shed, her clothes sticking onto her from the pelting rain. As she'd reached the door of the shed the heavy raindrops felt less like glass on her skin, and more soothing, like healing rosehip oil. It was as though it was a different world inside the shed. Peace had blanketed her the moment she'd stepped inside. The rain on the roof had created beautiful sounds that had complemented the colours on the canvasses that filled the space, swirling in all directions in a messy, beautiful way, like they were dancing to the chaotic but comforting rhythm.

Her mother had handed her a cup of warm tea. "Are you okay, honey?"

"I'm fine, Mum. At least, I am now."

Tess had looked at the objects around her and her mother's paintings. They hadn't been just objects. They'd had the means to create a mood — to evoke and invoke.

They'd had dents, and imperfections. They'd witnessed a lot of joy and heartache. They'd lived.

Tess resolved she would not let Desiree get to her. Her life was messy at the moment, but everything would be okay. She headed to the kitchen to make a cup of tea before looking at her phone again. He hadn't called yet, but the hope that he would, comforted her, because she realised he was one person with whom she could truly feel.

***

The rest of the week passed by quickly, and soon it was Sunday, another mild summer's day. Tess hadn't run into Desiree for a few days, and Stewart still hadn't called. She'd been tempted to call him, but something had held her back. *I'm happy to wait*, she thought. It had been a week since she saw him. She found herself immersed in her books, but her concentration still failed her and she would read a sentence a few times before comprehending it. She was pre-occupied with how her life had changed, how her friendships had changed, and why he wasn't calling her. Her peace had been replaced with confusion. But that didn't stop her wanting him to call. She would go over all their conversations — how he stood admiring her desk, the brass bell, her collection of books, her records, when he had kissed her goodbye. She also thought of how wonderful she'd felt that Sunday morning at the coffee shop, how beautiful his smile was — and then she thought of the menacing look in Desiree's eyes as they parted ways.

Tess decided to cast her mind to other things. It had been a while since she'd cooked a decent meal, so she headed to the grocery store. Italian pasta infused with garlic and Napolitano sauce lingered in the air from across the street. She glanced over at Silvio's, and her heart ached with regret and anger. She had a right to miss Silvio. No one could tell her how to feel, not even her friends. She also had a right to go to his restaurant. *Pamela isn't my keeper*, she thought in annoyance.

As she walked towards the grocery store, she saw Helena waving frantically at her from outside her shop.

She hurried across the street. Helena motioned her to come in, placing her arm around Tess' shoulder. She was shaking all over.

"What is it, Helena? Is it Carter?"

"Yes, it's him! Your suspicions were right! He's seeing someone," she said, closing the black French doors behind them as they entered the colourful, flourishing space.

"What? Are you sure?" Tess could feel Helena's desperation. Her face looked pasty, and her eyes were shiny with tears. Helena reached for a tissue with trembling hands.

"I know … because of *this!*" Helena pulled something out of a linen bag. "Lipstick on his shirt! How clichéd is that? Could he have been more obvious? It all makes sense though — the gifts, the sudden attention. Just enough for him to think he had buttered me up. Now he's back to hardly being around again. I had a feeling that something was up, that something weird was happening — a change on the horizon."

Tess tried to gather her thoughts. How could Carter do this to Helena? Why was everything changing? It was as though they had both lost control of their lives.

"Look, there has to be an explanation," Tess said, realising she had to try to be the voice of reason. "Let's not jump to conclusions. Lipstick on a white shirt *is* really clichéd, and obvious. Why would he not try to hide the evidence? He's a smart guy. He wouldn't be so careless. And I think he's one of the good guys, that he isn't capable of doing something like that. He's a real man, who would probably own up if he did anything like that to you." Tess saw her words were slowly sinking in. Helena had stopped sobbing and a calmness washed over her tear-stained face.

"Do you think? Am I'm jumping to conclusions? You're right, he *would* have hidden the evidence, wouldn't he? He knows I take his shirts to the dry cleaners." Helena paced around the shop in deep concentration. Her expression occasionally relaxed when she seemed to find some solace, but then her brow quickly furrowed again. "Or maybe this is his way of telling me?" Helena muttered. "Maybe he wanted to get caught, so he won't have to have that conversation, so he wouldn't have to explain that he's cheating on me. Yes, I read somewhere that there are no accidents, that the subconscious mind ensures the truth comes out. I was meant to see the lipstick. Carter *wanted* me to see it, even if he didn't know that's what he was doing!"

Tess sighed. "Helena, you have to give him the benefit of the doubt. Just have a talk with him tonight, when he gets back home."

"I have to keep a close eye on him, in case he covers his steps," Helena mused. "If I reveal my suspicions, and he doesn't really want to get caught, then he'll make an excuse, and cover himself. I need to monitor his actions, and try to catch him in the act. Can you help me, Tess? Keep an eye and an ear out? Please — I've felt uneasy these last few weeks."

Tess nodded. After hugging her friend and reassuring her she'd help her, she stepped out of the shop, leaving Helena and her sadness amongst the beautiful flowers. She felt dejected as she carried her own heavy load of worries towards the grocery store, walking unsteadily as her posture became slightly crouched, and her steps wobbly and uneven.

After leaving the grocery store a while later, she speculated about Helena's plight. Her friend was right. Everything *had* changed. Both of them had to remain strong in the face of adversity. She started to walk more steadily again, feeling her resolve strengthen. But then she remembered Stewart hadn't yet called, and felt despondent once more. She was suddenly appalled that she was relying on a man to dig her out of her misery. This wasn't how she planned on living her life. And who said he was interested in her anyway? He might have been charmed by her, as she was definitely different to the other women he'd dated. Perhaps to him she was like a book from an unfamiliar genre. Even if he acknowledged and admired the book's uniqueness, he might not want to read that type of book forever.

She looked at the contents of her shopping bag. She'd bought ingredients to make fresh pesto with penne, and rocket for a salad. As she neared her apartment building, she remembered that dark and dreary night when she had felt free and floaty in her dress. She had heard the footsteps and seen the shadow behind her, coming closer and closer as she ran in fear. She'd thought it would be the end for her until she saw his face — his kind, sexy eyes, his chiselled, stubbled jaw, and his toned, tall body towering over her as he lifted her up from the dirt.

As she reached the top of the front stairs and looked along the corridor, her breath caught. "Stewart?" she exclaimed. He was standing outside Desiree's door, looking like he'd just left.

"Tess! You're finally here," he said, the smoothness of his voice making her heart melt. It was then she realised that if he were *her* book, she definitely wanted to keep reading. It was a story she'd happily read over and over again. She didn't want it to end — the feeling she had inside. He was there when she needed him *again*. She needed him more than she realised.

"I swung by to drop off something for Keith and Desiree, and thought I'd see if you were home," he said. "I hope you don't mind me just dropping by." A warm smile added light to his eyes.

"Mind? No, I don't mind," she said as her breathing began to ease, comforted by the warmth he radiated. He seemed to always know how to make her feel better — just like a cup of tea or a good book, or strokes of colour on canvas, or sprinkles on cupcakes, but also like wild horses, or roaring thunder, igniting passion and providing comfort at the same time. "I don't mind at all."

CHAPTER SIXTEEN

They held the stare for a while. His eyes revealed a certain vulnerability. Tess couldn't seem to move or look away. Her deep emotions caused her to freeze. Her legs trembled and her skin shivered all over.

He cleared his throat before he finally spoke. "I thought we'd organise a time to meet."

"Oh, sure," Tess said.

Stewart peered into the shopping bag. "Looks like you're about to get started on dinner. What are you cooking?"

"Italian," she replied.

"Have you tried the Italian restaurant, Silvio's, down the street? It's really good. I actually ..."

As if on cue, a brisk coldness emitted from Desiree's apartment as she opened the door and peered at Tess through slitted eyes before closing it behind her.

Looking at Stewart, Desiree chipped in. "There are some other nice Italian restaurants on the other side of the street as well. Keith and I have tried some of them." She turned to face Tess. "Oh, hi Tess! Fancy seeing you here." She laughed and turned back to Stewart. "You obviously can't keep away from me," she said, tossing her hair. "I am married, remember?"

Stewart managed a half-laugh.

"Oh stop, Stewart! I'm not that funny. Well, maybe I am. So you're still here?"

"Yes. I'm just organising dinner with Tess," he said.

Tess' mind worked frantically. *Oh Stewart! Why did you have to tell her that? You're so kind and ... Dinner?* He wanted to have *dinner* with her? He did seem regretful last time when he'd seen the half-eaten sandwiches and tea.

"*Dinner?* Why would you organise dinner?" Desiree interjected. "I thought you just needed some assistance with university courses?" She looked at him like it was the weirdest idea ever presented.

"Because I'd love to have dinner with Tess. You make it sound like it's so shocking," he challenged her. "We can also catch up, as well as discuss my studies.

Tess was relieved he'd seen through Desiree's mockery.

Stewart turned his attention back to Tess. "I was thinking perhaps at your apartment. Is that too presumptuous of me? You have so many interesting finds. Like I told you last time, I could stay there all day perusing *everything* in it," he said, emphatically. He studied her reaction.

Tess felt goosebumps appear at the way he had said "everything". She found herself looking at him intently, like she was exposing her heart to him. "Or, if you prefer, at a restaurant?" he asked, his embarrassment making him look even more appealing.

She finally snapped out of her trance when she caught Desiree studying her with a furrowed brow. Tess raised her shoulders, straightening her posture. She was nervous under Desiree's microscopic stare. "Um … sure. The apartment is fine. It's a great idea," she managed, her voice almost sounding like it belonged to someone else.

"Great! I don't expect you to cook or anything. I can pick up some takeaway from Silvio's — bring the restaurant to us, so to speak. I can do that after my …"

"Tess, I can't believe you were married to Michael," Desiree suddenly interrupted. "Was it one of those whirlwind romances?" She turned to face Stewart, and giggled. "Isn't it funny, Stewart? It reveals a lot, doesn't it? We all thought that certain types stick together. I guess that's why Tess never hung out with us. You know, if she hung out with Michael and fell in love with someone like him, she obviously doesn't value certain things in a relationship like … I don't know … passion, romance perhaps? No offence, but I can't imagine Michael being in the slightest bit passionate when it comes to the L word.

189

You know, *love*," she whispered, as if it were a foreign language to someone like Tess.

Tess froze. She was speechless. How had Desiree found out she'd been married to Michael?

Tess felt herself becoming teary. She was vulnerable and exposed. It was obvious that Desiree was bent on humiliating her.

"Poor thing! Isn't it so sad, Stewart? I mean, it must have been hard to accept that someone like Michael, who didn't have a romantic bone in his body, left her?" She turned to face Tess again. "I told you back then. I was trying to warn you like a friend would — that relationships require both partners to make it work. You have to keep it interesting, or they leave. I feel so sorry for you that even someone as studious as Michael lost interest."

Tess felt every insult like a dagger to the heart. *You? Married? I can't even imagine you keeping a man!* Tess remembered Desiree's words all those years ago. She tried to fight back the tears, but the repressed emotions were coming to the surface. Everything began to overwhelm her, like the shock that her life had turned backwards, that those feelings of inferiority from high school were back. Even Pamela had sided with Desiree. Suddenly the guilt about breaking Silvio's heart flooded back, along with the fear she may never find someone like him. Next came a sudden rush of anxiety about Stewart, and the effect he had on her.

Stewart coughed loudly, breaking Tess' trance. She looked towards him. He caught her gaze and held it calmly and gently. "I can't imagine anyone losing interest in Tess," he said in a loud, confident voice. "If I was Michael, I'd sure regret that things hadn't worked out. I would never …" He trailed off, capturing the expression in Tess' wide, shocked eyes. It was as if they were communicating without words. For a moment, she forgot Desiree was even there, until a strangled sound caught her attention. Tess turned to see Desiree's mouth agape. The strangled sound seemed to be escaping from her throat. Desiree looked to be in shock, just as she had been back in high school when Stewart had also stood up for Tess.

Stewart continued. "I remember Michael being a fun, intelligent guy. I had a few interesting debates with him. I actually heard he's become really successful." He gave Desiree an intense, questioning look. "He's in investments now," he said emphatically, holding Desiree's shocked stare. "He was a great guy. Maybe he just wasn't the one for Tess."

The strangled sound evolved into words. "You think?" Desiree barked. "You might be right, she was probably too much for him. Too weird." She met Tess' eyes again. "You've always been weird. You and your parents were always different from everyone else. You probably didn't suit Michael's stylish friends and business associates. You have to understand that world, like I do with Keith. He needs someone that he can count on to attend all the business dinners and parties with him, I've plenty of experience, growing up in a family like mine. My dad practically owned the town. You remember how influential he was ..."

Tess caught sight of Stewart's expression. His jaw had become tight and his face red at Desiree's comment. Tess could tell he could no longer bite his tongue.

"Yes, Keith is a *great catch!*" Stewart finally snapped. "You two make a *wonderful* couple. I'm sure he's very well-versed with things like *passion*, and as you say, the *L word*. I'm sure that you're very *satisfied* in your relationship."

Tess was taken aback. Gathering strength from Stewart's comments, she regained her composure.

"*I* left him," she finally said, looking at Desiree straight on.

"What?" Desiree gulped.

"I left Michael. I ended our marriage," she said confidently.

Desiree looked aghast. "Why would *you* leave *him?*"

"Because he wasn't passionate enough for me — about the things I care about, about the things that mean something to me."

She could feel Stewart's gentle gaze, like an afternoon breeze on an excruciatingly hot summer's day. She looked at him again.

A half-smile formed on his handsome features. "I get it," he said. "I can see that you need passion in your life."

The stare between them grew ever more intense. Energy surged through her body, causing her to shiver all over. She felt warm but cold at the same time. She didn't even care that Desiree was witnessing their undeniably potent chemistry. And that's what it was — Tess couldn't deny it any longer. It had to be. She had read about it often enough. She could describe it word for word if she had a pen and paper before her.

They finally broke the stare. Tess felt like she would collapse.

She then met Desiree's steely eyes. She definitely did not look happy that her scheme to ridicule her had had the opposite effect — again.

"Come on, Stewart." Desiree grabbed him by the arm. "I'll walk with you. I have to go somewhere anyway."

"Sure," he said, wresting his arm back. "In a minute." He stepped closer to Tess. "Enjoy your dinner. I'm sure you're a great cook, amongst other things." He gave her a flirtatious smile. "Would next Friday night be okay? Around seven?"

"It would be perfect," she said, feeling dazzled by his sex appeal.

"I wish it could be sooner, but I have to go away for a while," Stewart explained. "I have to visit my mum. She lives in the city."

"Oh? She does? Your mum ... and your dad?" Tess queried.

"Just my mum," he said. "They're divorced. It's a long story ... I'll tell you about it someday. I was flat out this week. I had to visit my dad. Now that they're not together, I have to make time for both. That's why I didn't get the chance to call you. It's been a while since I saw him … and he made sure he let me know how he felt about it. Our relationship … well, let's just say it's complicated. I had to make sure he was okay, but I haven't stopped thinking of seeing you … to make plans …"

She heard Desiree fidgeting with her bag behind her. She cleared her throat, as though alerting them both that she was waiting. Stewart leant in close to Tess, and gave her a kiss on the cheek.

"See you on Friday," he said, stroking her hair behind her ear, and observing her every feature. He whispered in her ear: 'Don't let her get to you, Tess. She's okay, deep down. You're stronger than her — it's she who is intimidated by you."

CHAPTER SEVENTEEN

The following week, unfortunately, the tension between Pamela and Tess hadn't subsided. It lingered in the air of the salon along with the strong scents of the dye.

"I'll take the towels to the laundromat," Tess announced to Pamela that Wednesday morning.

"You don't have to. It's my turn," Pamela offered. Tess sensed that they were both walking on eggshells.

"No, I'll do it," Tess insisted, needing some air to clear her head.

Just then, Millie stepped into the salon. "I have good news!" she practically sang, smiling directly at Tess. "The lipsticks will definitely be here next week — Thursday to be exact — *and* you'll get a free lipstick holder, *and* the ruby red colour has just come out as well. So, it's good that you missed out the first time in a way."

Tess gave her a warm smile. "I guess it is! *Wow!* You know I love my lipstick holders, and the ruby red does sound grand."

Millie nodded happily. "In the meantime, you should look at the new range of lipsticks I just got in. They have the most unique colours. They're glossy though — not so old Hollywood — but look at these colours, especially this grape one. I think we're bringing back the 80s with that."

"They are unusual," Tess said as she examined the lipsticks.

"And the best part is that they're a hit, which means they're selling fast. Can I leave some samples at the counter, and I'll leave some more of your shampoos and business cards in my shop? How does that sound?" She looked from Tess to Pamela.

"Sure, it's fine with us, right?" Pamela replied, turning to look at Tess.

"Sure, fine by me, also. So, you say they're a hit?" Tess asked, taking the grape-coloured sample and trying it on the back of her hand. "Yes, it does have a retro vibe about it, 80s for sure, but there is still a bit of old Hollywood as well in some of the shades." There was something about the colour. It reminded her of something.

"Tess, are you okay?" Millie asked.

"Yeah, why are you suddenly so tense?" Pamela remarked.

"They just remind me of something — this grape colour in particular," she said. "It's nothing. Don't worry."

Millie looked concerned, but seeing Tess regain her usual composure, she continued. "Anyway, I'm sure you're excited about the red matte lipsticks coming in. Just don't camp out in the street until I open. I'll definitely save some for you, no matter who asks for them."

"I'll try to restrain myself," Tess said with a laugh.

"Oh, I'm sure you'll need it for the new man in your life," Millie called out as she headed for the door. "Penny told me *all* about him."

Pamela instantly looked up from the counter where she was arranging the lipstick samples and business cards.

Tess couldn't believe what was happening. She looked like she was keeping yet another secret from Pamela. She brushed her fringe from her eyes as her lip began to tremble slightly.

"Man?" Tess asked, trying to look perplexed.

"Yes, and I know it's not Silvio," Millie continued. "It's a guy you went to high school with, right? Oh, and she also told me about that Jacob guy flirting with you. Looks like you're turning a few male heads, not just Silvio's. Oh well, not all of us are tying the knot. Have fun with it!" She waved and walked out into the street.

"Bye Millie!" Tess called out, feeling Pamela's inquisitive stare. She turned to look at her. "Pamela, I've been meaning to tell you. Nothing has happened yet. I mean, I don't know if it will, to tell you the truth. It all happened so fast, and although I wasn't even interested in Silvio, he's not someone you can let go of easily."

Pamela didn't seem to take her reply well. "What are you saying? You regret letting Silvio go? My, my, we have changed, haven't we? From not being interested in any guy, to having three to choose from …"

"Three? I don't even know Jacob. He's a big flirt, probably with a lot of women, I'd imagine. And yeah, I feel a bit sad about letting go of someone special like Silvio. And I was going to tell you about …" Tess trailed off as Pamela raised her hands in disbelief. Tess was growing tired of having to defend herself. If she didn't know Pamela well enough, she'd think she was jealous of her getting all this male attention. There was something about her manner that made Tess waffle on like an idiot, stumbling over her words every time she questioned her. For now, she was done with trying to explain herself, so she turned on her heel and took the towels to the laundromat instead.

That afternoon, as Tess blow-dried her client's hair, she gazed over at the counter at the lipstick samples. The colour … She couldn't pinpoint what it was about it.

The glass doors opened, and Jessica, the woman with the sad eyes, stepped inside. Pamela greeted her. She wondered why she was getting her hair done so often lately. She looked like she had started to take more care with her wardrobe, and her face was glowing more than usual. The lipstick really suited her. It was a grape type of colour …. "Oh, what a coincidence!" Tess blurted out.

"What's a coincidence?" Pamela enquired.

"Sorry. I just thought that Jessica was wearing the lipsticks that Millie just showed us. It looks like the grape one, you know, from the new range?"

Jessica chipped in. "Yes, it's from Millie's shop. She has such great products. You can't find them anywhere else. It is the grape," she added. "I'm afraid they're a bit on the expensive side, but every woman needs to feel special now and then, I guess." Her tone had changed. She didn't look as sad as she usually did. "Tess, right?"

"Yes, that's right. How are you, Jessica?"

"I'm fine, thanks for asking," she said, smiling broadly as she sat down and looked at her reflection in the mirror.

Later that afternoon, Tess stepped out of the salon and began to make her way home after another long day. Suddenly she stopped in her tracks. *The grape colour ...* she thought. *Grape! The same lipstick shade on Carter's shirt!* Tess frantically stepped back into the salon and picked up one of the grape-coloured samples from the counter. She placed it in her handbag.

Pamela looked at her, perplexed. "What on earth are you doing? Tess, you know they're just samples, right? You're not supposed to use them."

"Yes, I know. I'll explain later. I have to go," she said, hurrying towards the glass door. She continued walking in a daze of speculation. *Could it be? Could the lipstick stain belong to Jessica? She seemed happier today. Could it be because of him — because of Carter?* It made sense — the way she looked at Helena's shop, almost obsessively. Was she sussing out her competition? She was sad, and lost for a while — was the guilt getting to her? Maybe it all changed because Carter promised her a future with him? Tess remembered Jessica saying her husband was out of town. It had to be! It made perfect sense! Helena felt like she was being watched. It was *her*. Tess remembered vividly how Carter had smiled at Jessica when he'd crossed the road, on his way across to the salon. It was so discrete, yet had some hidden meaning.

Pamela looked hurt when she didn't explain. "Sure, sure. I understand."

"I'm sorry, I can't tell you right now. I would if I could ..." Tess trailed off, realising Pamela wasn't buying it.

"You don't need to explain. I get it," she said.

"No, you really don't!" Tess cried. "I'll explain everything to you eventually! Now I've got to go before Helena closes her shop," she called out as she closed the door behind her before realising she shouldn't have said that last part in front of Jessica. Luckily, Jessica was absorbed in something on her phone. She was smiling, and definitely looked more energetic and more optimistic all of a sudden.

Tess saw Pamela peer out at her as she scurried across the road. She looked confused.

The French doors were closed. It was too late. Helena had left for the day. Tess decided to pass by the real estate agency. She walked further down the street and turned into the adjoining side street. She crept up to the shop window and peered surreptitiously through the glass. Carter was at his desk. Tess's heart began to beat ferociously. He was on his mobile phone — smiling as he read a message. Could he be talking to her? To Jessica? She couldn't be sure — it was all circumstantial at the moment. Her mind was frantic, trying to add together the reasons why Jessica could be having an affair with Helena's husband.

At that moment, a blonde woman appeared next to his desk. He wasn't looking at his phone anymore, but was talking to the woman instead. He was smiling a lot. He looked really sophisticated with his navy blue, slim-fitting suit and pale blue shirt. Both he and the woman had both stood up, and he was giving her an affectionate, rather sympathetic smile. She shook his hand and began to walk towards the door. Tess was suddenly shocked with the realisation that the woman sitting across from him was someone she knew. It was her, *again*.

Tess backed away, and walked quickly towards her apartment building. She was walking so fast, she was practically jogging. She would not run into her again. She was fed up of seeing her wherever she went.

Exhausted, taking deep breaths, she opened the front door. She climbed the stairs with haste. The little brass bell welcomed her with a louder-than-usual jingle from the force of the door being shut. Tess pressed her back to the door and tried to restore her breathing as the jingle of the bell calmed her heartbeat with its familiar melody.

Tess felt like she was in a nightmare that wouldn't end. It seemed that the more she avoided her, the more she ran into her. She sank into the lounge, throwing her bag next to her. She stared at the painting on the wall — her mother's painting. Abstract colours stared back at her, encouraging her mind to find its natural balance. *Why would Carter smile at her like that? Give her such a sympathetic look?* She did tend to charm people. Well, she had charmed Pamela, and even Penny. She was very successful at being able to weasel her way into people's good graces.

"That's it!" she said aloud. *She's renting the apartment from the agency. Or maybe she's looking into moving — buying in another area, perhaps?* She could only hope.

Tess looked around her apartment. *Oh no!* she thought. It was a mess. Stewart would be coming over for dinner *tomorrow*! When would she get the chance to give the place a thorough cleaning? She would be working all day at the salon tomorrow, so she had to do the majority of the chores that afternoon and evening. She couldn't think about Desiree, or Carter's supposed extramarital affair at that moment. She would visit Helena tomorrow and see if the lipstick matched.

As she stood up, she imagined his smile, and remembered how he'd been so gentle and kind at their last encounter. She'd been shocked that his parents had divorced, and wondered why he was pursuing another career. It then occurred to her that he hadn't mentioned his father's company. She had been certain back at school that he would be working in the family business. She remembered his tight jaw, and how teary his eyes had looked at the mention of his parents. She hoped he would trust her enough to confide in her. Tess sensed a sadness inside of him — a fragility. The way he told her she knew what she was doing, that he'd been lost. Her heart hurt at the thought of his sadness. She cared about him so much, and she wanted him so much — to have his arms around her, to nestle her head on his shoulder, and listen to her records with him. She imagined how the evening could progress. Her skin shivered at the thought of smelling his cologne, his warm breath on her.

Tomorrow, she said to herself, *I'll be with him again.* The pain in her heart now felt beautiful. It hurt but it danced at the same time. She could feel her heart smiling as she caught sight of her reflection in the mirror. There was no doubt about it — she was glowing. The feeling was new to her. She'd only ever read about it. She craved to be near him, to breathe him in. She felt like he could see her own pain, and what she desired. She knew if he looked deep in her eyes in the moment, he would see that she desired him.

Hours later, she looked around the apartment and sighed at how lovely and fresh it looked. She had dusted, vacuumed and mopped, cleaned the kitchen and the bathroom, polished mirrors and tables, and even cleaned the windows. He would be there tomorrow evening. She waltzed over to the kitchen and put the kettle on the stove.

Moments later, she sank into her chesterfield armchair, and enjoyed sipping her tea in her immaculately clean, enchanting space. She imagined him walking into the hallway as she opened the front door, greeting the bell with a dimpled smile. Walking over to the bookshelf, she took out a romance novel from a new author. Suddenly she was in the mood for all things romantic.

CHAPTER EIGHTEEN

It was Friday morning. Tess closed the door of her apartment gently, her fingers crossed against running into Pamela or Desiree. As she tiptoed past Pamela's door, it occurred to her that Desiree might not know that Pamela also lived in the building. Had they even run into each other yet — as they were entering or leaving the building? That was the last thing she needed — to have them become *besties*. She was extra quiet as she walked along the downstairs corridor, the floor on which Desiree and Keith lived. She would never have pictured Desiree living on the ground floor of any building — not having a view, or living in the penthouse.

Tess walked out into the street, making sure the lipstick sample was in her bag, vowing that she wouldn't let anyone ruin her mood. She was both nervous and excited; drunk with anticipation to see him later that evening. As she strode casually down the street, she heard laughter behind her — two female voices. Their laughter sounded familiar. She took a quick, discrete glance behind her. It was Pamela *and Desiree*. They were laughing together, oblivious to anyone around them. Tess instinctively turned into a narrow side street and into a trendy coffee shop. Conga drums beat loudly from the speakers inside. She bumped into a tall, male waiter, then pushed past him to blend in with the crowd of customers waiting for their coffee at the counter. Through the large windows, she saw the back of Pamela's denim shirt, floating freely like a cape, revealing long skinny legs in slim-fitting black leggings. Desiree's toned legs were also lycra-clad, and she walked confidently alongside her new friend, holding a yoga mat, obviously heading to the gym. To her dismay, she realised Pamela was also holding a yoga mat. *They're yoga buddies?* Tess thought uncomfortably.

The conga drums seemed to beat louder. The smell of freshly ground coffee beans woke her from her trance. She wiped away a tear and headed out the door. *I don't care*, she told herself as she walked with discretion behind them. She had to see Helena. At least she trusted her with her problems. Desiree hadn't cast her spell on her. *Yet*, she thought worriedly.

It was late afternoon. Tess avoided Pamela as best she could, even though she desperately wanted to ease the tension between them. She felt comforted by the fact that she had a beautiful secret all to herself, safe from judgment or scrutiny — something she'd become accustomed to lately. She caught herself smiling throughout the day. Even one of her clients asked her what had her smiling so much. Tess had blushed and brushed the comment aside. Her eyes often wandered, every so often, over to Helena's flower shop, to see if Jessica was there. Both women had agreed the lipstick shade had matched, and Helena felt gratified she'd been correct in thinking someone had been watching her. She even remembered a young woman looking at the flowers and retreating when she had approached her. Helena trembled at the thought that the woman had been sussing her out, like a python measuring its prey.

Organising dyes at the back of the salon, Tess' thoughts swung wildly from excitement at her imminent evening with Stewart to her worries for Helena. She glanced around the room, looking for something to ground her. She caught sight of Pamela's expression in one of the mirrors. She was running her fingers through a client's hair, contemplating the colour. To Tess' surprise, Pamela looked unusually dreamy-eyed.

"You look really happy today," Pamela's client commented. "Who's the lucky guy?"

"Lucky guy? Hardly!" Pamela managed.

"Really? I heard another client say the same thing to you, and you were rather eager to change the subject. In my experience, that look means you're in love. I remember that feeling — the dreamy eyes, smiling for no reason."

"Rebecca, I honestly don't know what you're talking about."

Tess observed the scene. She was positive Pamela's cheeks had grown rosy at her client's observation.

"I'm just thinking of something funny my friend said this morning."

My friend? Tess' heart sank. *This morning?* She was talking about Desiree.

"Your *friend?*" the woman asked playfully. "I think that smile reveals something more. That glow only means one thing. So, have you known him long?"

"Rebecca! There's no man," Pamela insisted, only to see her client wasn't convinced. "Okay okay … You found me out," she said with a smile of defeat. "It *is* a man who has me beaming like this."

"See, I was right!" her client exclaimed. "So who is he? Come on, I've known you for a long time. You know more about me than my family does. Who is he? I won't tell a soul."

Pamela paused. "Okay," she finally said. "Well, it's actually … Okay, why should I hide it? It's the barista. You know, the one who works at Silvio's," she said, lowering her voice to a half-whisper. "We're just dating though, so don't say anything. We're not exclusive or anything. He already has a queue of girls lined up. It's nothing serious at the moment."

Though Pamela kept her voice low, Tess could hear every word from the back of the salon. It was as if Pamela had forgotten she existed. Her avoidance had certainly been effective.

"The barista?" Rebecca exclaimed, unable to hide her excitement. "You're going out with the barista? He's hot, and he makes the best coffee!"

"Shh," Pamela pleaded. "I don't want anyone to know yet. It's all new. We're taking it slow for the moment, keeping it hush hush."

Tess was dumbfounded. *I shouldn't be surprised,* she thought. It explained why she was at Silvio's all the time. Of course! It all made sense. She'd started having her morning coffee out when the barista had just started working there, and she'd been making a greater effort with her appearance. Tess felt heartbroken that her friend didn't confide in her. What if she'd told Desiree everything about the barista instead? She had a sinking feeling things would never get back to normal. She felt betrayed by Pamela, who had sided with Desiree even after knowing she'd made her life hell at school. It meant she couldn't confide in her about Stewart, either.

Tess only got through the day by repressing uncertain thoughts about Pamela and Desiree. All she wanted to think of was seeing Stewart. She had so much to do before he came over.

As she packed up her things, eager to escape without any questions, Pamela stopped her in her tracks.

"So, are you doing anything tonight?" she asked Tess. "You look like you're in a hurry. I didn't get to talk to you much today. Talk about being flat out!"

"Yes, I have something on. I've got to go," she said, half closing the door. "I hope you're all right to close shop. I promise, I'll do it next time."

"Yeah, sure. Just go," said Pamela, and continued packing away some things on the counter.

Tess paused and looked back, momentarily wanting to explain everything, but then remembered the last minute tidying up, and continued walking.

She ran over to Helena's to see if she'd found out anything. Helena told her nothing had changed. Tess bought a bouquet of Konfetti Sunset roses to brighten up the kitchen, and after giving Helena a supportive hug, headed home.

As she stepped out of the flower shop, she saw Pamela across the street closing the salon. She met her eyes, and gave her an awkward wave. Pamela waved back without smiling, and closed the salon door. Tess was grateful Pamela walked in the opposite direction to home, relieved they didn't have to walk together. She would tell her everything later. Everything was far too rushed and awkward right now.

Back home, later that evening, Tess had just applied a fresh colour of teak rose lipstick. She was happy with the outfit she'd chosen, and her hair had cooperated and looked elegant and sexy, falling freely to the side. The room freshener created such a lovely atmosphere. She felt like she was walking through fields of lavender in Provence.

She sat on the lounge for a minute to regroup. Her black silk pleated skirt worked well with her flat mules, which were adorned with a pearlescent buckle in the centre of each shoe. Self-doubt told her she'd made too much of an effort. She walked over to the long, heavy antique mirror again, and checked herself out. *So what?* she told herself. *That's what he likes about you — that you are who you are.*

She sat back on the lounge feeling at ease again, until her phone, which she'd left on the desk, chimed with a message. Anxious at the thought it might be Pamela, she took nervous steps towards the desk. It was from Stewart. In the midst of showering and tidying up, she hadn't heard the phone ring, so he'd sent a message instead.

He couldn't make it. Something had come up he couldn't avoid. He was deeply sorry — he would make it up to her. He'd added a sad face emoji for effect, and a rose as well — like that could take away the sadness that had just engulfed her. With a despondent heart, she walked over to the kitchen, feeling safe in the small space amongst her many teacups and array of teas, and the vase with the roses. She looked down at the shiny black and white floor tiles, and watched a tear drop down onto them. She walked over to her bag, grabbed it and shut the door behind her. She didn't care if Pamela heard, or Desiree for that matter. She walked out of the building not knowing where she was heading. She couldn't be there — not after all the hope she'd had for the evening.

Millie was closing up her shop. Tess was surprised she was still there.

"Tess. I'm so glad I ran into you. I can't make it tonight. Can you let Pamela know? Hugh and I have to try wedding cakes. We're so far behind with our plans. I'll be there later for a drink, though. I might get Hugh to come as well, if that's okay? I'm sure we can do another girls' night some other time."

"What? I don't understand," Tess said.

"I can't make it to Vinnie's. That's where you're heading, aren't you, all dressed up? Pamela sent me a message saying it was short notice …"

"Oh yeah, Vinnie's. Pamela was about to tell … I mean, I know all about it," she managed. She began to walk away, calling out behind her, "I'm sorry, I've got to go. I'm running late. She's probably waiting."

Her mules clacked all the way down the street, straight to Vinnie's. Her thoughts went back to the salon, and she realised that Pamela was just about to ask her to come out with them when she'd cut her off, saying she was busy.

She stepped into the dim, spacious room with its swanky atmosphere. A woman was singing *Dream a Little Dream of Me* in French. She saw Humphrey Bogart on the wall, then Ingrid Bergman, Frank Sinatra, and his daughters, Nancy and Tina, followed by Hepburn, Bacall, James Dean … And then she saw them, on a huge round table with a crisp white tablecloth. It was decked with flutes of champagne, with nibbles and appetisers in the centre. Pamela was smiling. So was Penny, and even Dante. Next to Pamela, sitting ever-so-comfortably was Desiree, and beside her was Evie — Desiree's best friend from high school. *What on earth is she doing here?* Tess thought, perplexed. Evie had her delicate small hand on his shoulder as she laughed. On Stewart's shoulder.

She met Desiree's eyes. She was smiling at *her* now — at "Poor Tess". He was involved in an intense conversation with Evie. He didn't even notice she was there. But Pamela did. Their eyes met. Tess couldn't breathe. In need of air, she ran out of the club and down the street, the *clack, clack, clack* of the mules on the footpath echoing her pain and heartache. She was ridiculous to have thought she could have the love she'd only read about. As if she would ever be allowed to feel that passion!

"Tess ... *sweetheart* ... are you alright?" He touched her shoulder and pulled her close. She nestled her head into its warmth. She could feel his masculine smooth hands — Silvio's smooth hands on her back, stroking her silk blouse. "It's okay. It'll be alright," he told her, soothing the ache she felt inside.

She lifted her head up and met his kind, beautiful green eyes. His beard had grown slightly, and his hair was neatly tied in a ponytail. He was so very handsome. As she wiped away her tears, she noticed a woman looking at her. It was Pamela, staring at the whole scene from across the street.

Tess heard thunder in the distance. It subsided momentarily before there came another roar, louder this time. It was getting closer. She released herself from Silvio, and ran away from him and from Pamela, whose eyes seemed to reflect the anger the thunder was unleashing on the narrow, quaint street.

"Tess, you shouldn't be alone!" he called out to her, but she ran on.

Tess felt like Pamela's eyes were glass, cutting into her skin, as the drops of heavy rain melted the smooth makeup she'd applied so carefully.

"Yes ... I should be," she muttered to herself as she ran. "I should be alone. I was a fool to think otherwise."

***

The unapologetic rain settled into a heavy rhythm. Not knowing where else to go, Tess found the key of the salon in her bag and entered what was once her precious second home. She gazed up at the chandeliers bewilderedly. They represented the freedom and extravagance she yearned for. Then she looked at her damp hair in the mirror. The colour had faded — there were no longer hints of rose or gold. Now, it was just a soft caramel. Without thinking, she walked over to the dyes. Colours ... They had helped her feel like she could do anything and be anything, and not give a damn what they thought.

As she looked into her tear-stained eyes, she realised the pain would still be there. No colour would erase it if the pain hadn't healed.

She stepped out of the salon and back onto the street. The rain was heavier now. Tears ran down her face as it all came flooding back to her. She remembered the day she'd run home from school, feeling sharp drops of rain like sandpaper on her skin. Her heart had broken at the realisation she wouldn't see Stewart again.

She opened her apartment door. She could feel her mascara bleed down her cheeks. Desiree had infiltrated her life slowly, insidiously, like roots from a tree strangling and destroying everything below the ground's surface. On the outside she was like the tree's friendly branches, providing shade and comfort, but you couldn't tell what destruction the roots were unleashing slowly and unexpectedly until it was too late. That was what had happened to Tess' world — it had been strangled by Desiree's noxious roots. She'd already taken so much of her youth, and had now somehow invaded her adulthood. The world Tess had created just wasn't strong enough.

She had left her hometown to escape her, but she'd brought the past and all its pain back to her, delivered to her doorstep with a fake smile.

Tess remembered her mother's expression that stormy night when Stewart had left. She'd felt her mother's warmth as she watched her painting, the wonderful colours creating something beautiful that had soothed her pain.

Tess stepped into her kitchen, bringing the dampness from the wet streets in with her. She looked at the teapot, and the colourful canvas on the wall above the lounge, illuminated by the lamps which were still lit, and which had promised light and hope that evening. With a flash she knew what to do. It was time to go home.

CHAPTER NINETEEN

The carriages of the express train whizzed by. Tess' ears rang from the sharp, piercing noise that slowly faded as the train entered the tunnel up ahead. She looked at the board. Her train would be arriving soon, bound for Lorikeet Creek, to visit her parents. She clutched her overnight suitcase and a small bag packed with treats to eat during the train journey — green grapes, apricots, and some sandwiches from the deli. A small bottle of sparkling mineral water with lime, a plastic cup and some books had also been packed hastily that morning. She had cancelled all her Saturday appointments. She had to get away from it all. The phone call to Pamela was quick and apologetic, just letting her know she was going to her parents for a couple of days.

Her heart felt heavy and barren as she watched a fragile sparrow on the steely tracks fluttering in a puddle. She hoped it flew off in time — before it got hurt. It had been a while since she'd seen a sparrow. Watching it brought her out of her misery — the same way watching the ducks around the pond would when she was a teenager.

A few groups of people had congregated on the country express train platform. Someone approached, then decided to sit next to her. Tess fumed inwardly, angered at the fact that her private space had been invaded *again*. There were so many other benches free. *Surely, sitting next to me is not the only option. Doesn't anyone value and appreciate that people need space sometimes?* she thought bitterly, seeing Desiree's face instantly in her mind.

"I haven't seen a sparrow for a while," came a man's voice. "They used to be so common in Sydney, not that I've lived here for long. My mother has, and she says that she scarcely sees a sparrow anymore. They're such sweet birds, slightly vulnerable from predators, but quick on their claws."

She looked over at the casual blue boat shoes and the beige chinos skimming the top of them. Her eyes scanned the veins on his strong, toned arms, and then his chest. He was wearing a light blue shirt. "Stewart?"

"Yes. I thought I'd join you. The rain's stopped. It's a nice day to go on a train trip to the country. I haven't been back for a while."

Tess couldn't find the words. She was so confused by him being there.

A train was on its way, approaching the station. The sparrow flew away in time. Tess looked at the board. It was her train. *Our train?* She looked at his small suitcase. He was serious. He wanted to go back home with her. Her legs managed to lift the shocked rest of her from her seat. He also stood up, and offered to carry her bag. He walked beside her as the train pulled up, and followed her to the door. The old clock on the wall showed that it was 9:30am. She was excited that he was there, but didn't entirely understand what was going on. It was as she had pictured it before — waiting at the station, boarding the express to the country with someone special, like in books or films from long ago.

They sat together and looked out the window. She could see his eyes in the gentle sunlight that had streamed into the small carriage. It was as though they were laughing at her confusion.

"You don't mind that I'm here, do you?" he asked.

"No, of course, I don't mind. But ..."

"But what am I doing here? I can explain. I felt so bad about having to cancel last night. After I saw your friends last night at Vinnie's, I was hoping you'd be coming too, but when you didn't, all I could think about was going to see you. I sent you so many messages this morning, but didn't get a response, so I went over to your apartment. Of course, I thought you'd think I was mad appearing there so early again, but I had to see you. You weren't home, and I wasn't sure what to do. Then I remembered the salon. I headed over there next. Luckily, Pamela was there, and she told me you were headed to Lorikeet Creek, of all places."

"But you …" Tess trailed off. She looked at her phone and realised he had in fact sent her several messages. In her eagerness to leave, she hadn't heard them come through.

"But what, Tess? I know I startled you, appearing out of nowhere, but I was eager to see you last night, and then something came up that I couldn't get out of."

Tess's heart beat with anxiety. *Couldn't get out of? Why couldn't he have gotten out of meeting up with Desiree and Evie, and my friends, for that matter?*

He leaned in closer to her and took her hand. Tess felt a rush shoot through her as quick as an express train speeding along the tracks. His eyes looked like toffee — sweet with concern. "I'm sorry, Tess. It was so rude to cancel on you like that. I should never have listened to her. It was Evie's birthday, and she insisted I go, convincing me she'd be heartbroken if I didn't."

"Who convinced you?" she blurted out, even though she knew the answer.

"Desiree. She insisted Evie would be devastated if I didn't. Apparently I broke her heart all those years ago, and Desiree felt responsible. She was always her best friend. She wanted to make it up to her, so she invited her to Sydney so we could all catch up. Evie lives in Melbourne now."

Tess pulled away from him and sank further into her seat. "Of course, she did!" she muttered softly. She couldn't believe Desiree had dragged Evie all the way to Sydney to celebrate her birthday. It was clear it was all because she had realised Stewart was getting closer to her!

He wasn't having any of it. He pulled her close to him again. His knees touched hers. "I didn't want to see her. I wanted to see *you*, Tess, to discuss the courses, among other things. Something happens to me when you're in my life. I feel inspired, like I want to do great things." He sighed deeply. He brushed a hair away from her face. Her eyes felt like they would tear up if she continued to look into his. As though sensing this, he caressed her face with his smooth hand, his fingers sending electric sensations through her. He leaned in closer, his lips a few seconds away from meeting hers …

A woman screamed!

"Harry! Come here this instant," the woman called after her young son. She gave them an apologetic smile as she rushed past them.

Tess had instantly sat back at the scream, as had he. Now they both had a moment to process what was about to happen. The interruption had left them both in awkward contemplation. *He was about to kiss me!* Her thoughts were dancing wildly. Her face became warmer. She dared to glance at him. She felt like she'd burst if someone didn't say something soon. She met his eyes again. They were now smiling as he watched her fidget with her watch, her bag and anything in front of her. She could feel him observing her awkward mannerisms.

He finally spoke. "Looks like we've got lots to amuse us until we get there." He eyed her partly opened bag, and the books and headphones that peeked out. Tess gave him an affectionate smile. "Do you mind if I have a look?" he asked.

How could I mind? "Of course not!" His shoulder and knee brushed against hers as he leant over to retrieve some of the books. Her nose caught a subtle aroma of aftershave. She looked at the stubble on his neck and his strong arms as his hands flipped through the pages of one of her books, touching each beautiful soft page gently — touching her "windows of hope".

He looked at her sceptically. "What's on your mind?"

"Nothing important," she answered, dismissing her thoughts, trying unsuccessfully to stifle a blush.

"Really?" he asked. "I hope that's not true, because what I'm thinking of is something so beautiful and sweet, so inspiring and meaningful, and *important*," he said, as he turned the pages of Jane Austen's *Emma*.

213

"Yes, Jane Austen's writing does contain all that," she acknowledged.

"Yes, it does, Tess, but so do you," he said, quite serious. "So do you," he repeated as he turned to look at her. She held the stare this time, feeling the noise and movement as the train sped along the tracks, like she was riding wild horses — or wild horses were in her heart.

Something shoved Tess' shoulder, the same woman pushing past, chasing her mischievous child again. She abruptly fell right into Stewart's arms. Her hair brushed his face. He took her hand in his, holding it tightly as she regained her balance. "I've got you," he said, holding her hand with a firm grip. The intensity was painfully beautiful — the way he looked at her, like he was feeling what she was feeling simultaneously, with precision and delicacy. She could feel it in his grip — the pain, the longing, the need, like electricity shooting through her.

"Oh my God! I'm so sorry to interrupt you again," the woman exclaimed, her face warm with embarrassment.

"That's okay," they both chorused with matching grins. Tess felt like they were love-struck teenagers interrupted by one of their parents.

"It's difficult travelling with young children," the woman said before heading back to her seat, her little one running in front of her.

They both gave her a sympathetic smile.

The woman then turned and glanced at them again, as though mesmerised by what she had witnessed between them. Tess sensed the woman too had felt the same sort of chemistry with someone special in her life, the same passion in her veins, and the beginning of something real.

Stewart was still holding her hand. He slowly released it, his eyes refusing to look away from hers. "So, Tess," he then said, studying her expression. "You're a woman, right?"

She was puzzled. "Yes, I'm a woman …"

"Okay, then. Please tell me why so many women I know, and perhaps men as well, are so in love with all these brooding, angry guys in these classic novels?" He looked pointedly at some of the books she had packed. "You've got Heathcliff stomping around in boots on the moors, Mr Rochester brooding and stomping around Thornfield Hall, and Mr Darcy ... I mean is he really all that?" he asked, maintaining his serious tone. "I don't get it. How do these angry, bitter men get all these intelligent, positive, beautiful and inspiring women? It must be true then. All the smart, sweet girls love the bad boys."

"Yes, I guess they do," she responded. "I must say, I'm impressed you know the leading men in these classics so well. It's going to be so much fun discussing them with you, amongst other things."

"Oh, amongst other things? And what things are they?"

Tess smiled at him. "I meant, since we're talking about Heathcliff, we might want to listen to Kate Bush. I have *Wuthering Heights* on my phone, and a lot of her other songs. Those are the *other things* I was referring to."

"Oh!" He smiled. "But you do know that we'll have to share the headphones, since you only have one pair."

"I think we'll be just fine. I don't mind sharing with you at all."

"That's great," he said. "In fact, it sounds perfect. But I hope that doesn't ruin any brooding, dark side I have? I mean, then I run the risk of not getting the intelligent, inspiring and gorgeous woman, if your theory is correct, that is?"

"My theory? Oh, that's not my theory at all. I'd forgo a hundred Mr Darcy types for ... um ..." She paused awkwardly. "I mean, I think you'll be okay with the inspiring women," she said in a lighthearted way, not knowing if he was serious.

"You forgot 'gorgeous'," he said with intent, and then turned to look at the books again. Tess looked at the books too, but more than literature was on her mind; it was reading him, studying his words, and trying to calm the nervous excitement that wouldn't subside deep within her chest.

***

Tess opened her eyes to the piercingly beautiful voice of Kate Bush. The lyrics to *Moving* made her feel like she was floating amongst stars. Her eyes then sleepily swept past the scenery. Blurred trees and hills passed quickly amongst a light blue backdrop. She felt the warmth from his chest as she leaned on it. She could feel the left headphone in her ear. Carefully lifting her head, she saw that he still had the other headphone in his right ear, and his eyes were shut. Her eyes then combed his long, toned arm, and looked at his strong hand holding hers tightly — fingers intertwined. Tess sleepily leaned her head back onto his chest. She could feel his heart beating as she listened to the lyrics. The train moved steadily but bumpily across the tracks. Her heart moved contently and succinctly with the rhythm, and with the soft melody of the music, as she continued to hold his warm, smooth hand firmly.

CHAPTER TWENTY

"This looks great, Mrs Harrington," Stewart said to Tess' mother as they sat at the table in the centre of the stone kitchen. "We've never had this before. My mum never cooked anything like this. Actually, she never really cooked a lot. She hated mess of any kind."

"Oh, that's a shame," Tess' mother said. "I guess she had so many cleaners and cooks. Your house was so big — and I must say, I loved the architecture."

Stewart gave Mrs Harrington a warm smile. "Yes, it was a beautiful house."

"So, what does your mother do now?" she asked. "I remember she helped with the business. Do your parents still live nearby? I remember you all left before you finished high school."

"Mum, enough with the questions, already," Tess said. "Let him eat his lunch!" She'd recalled the last time she'd mentioned his parents, when he'd been uneasy talking about the divorce.

Stewart laughed at her outburst.

"You haven't seen him in years, and it's like he's at an interview. I love you Mum," Tess then added as her mother gave her a faux-offended look.

"That's how we usually talk in this house," her father offered.

"Yes, we scream at each other and then we're all hugs and smiles, singing old rock tunes while dad plays his guitar," Tess said, turning to look at Stewart. He was smiling at her. She was positive the smile carried admiration within it.

"Yes, that's how we usually roll," her dad said as he reached across the huge rectangular wooden table for the salad.

Her mother laughed and turned to face her husband. "Do you remember the time Tess came home from school upset about something, and then she took it out on us, slamming doors and muttering to herself until she heard you playing the guitar? Suddenly you were both performing a duet together," she said, laughing uncontrollably.

"Oh my God!" Tess laughed. "Please don't remind me, although it was quite good, I have to admit. You should have had it recorded." She turned to look at Stewart again. He was also laughing, and had sat back in his seat, as though he was ready to watch a performance. He seemed to be enjoying the laughter and stories they were sharing with him. Tess gave him another warm smile. She sensed his family didn't have such joyful moments.

He smiled and cleared his throat before he turned to look at her mother again. "I don't mind letting you know what happened. I feel like I know all of you ... even if we didn't really hang out together. That's what I was telling your daughter." He grabbed Tess' hand under the table, and held it tight as he talked. "My dad sold the business. Well, that's not really true. The business went into liquidation."

"Oh no!" Tess' family chorused.

"That must have been tough!" her father exclaimed.

"It was, I guess, for a while, but we had to adjust. That's why we left town. The last thing my parents, especially my mother wanted was for everyone to know. Well, of course, most people close to us knew, and those people who followed these sorts of things. My parents were mortified. My dad thought we could try and start over somewhere else with a new business. That's where I came in. I had to learn fast and help out. It was a shame because I actually enjoyed school. I'd always imagined pursuing a career in an academic field. I guess my dad thought that if I wasn't going to be a lawyer or a doctor, that there was no point in continuing school and going on to university. I should have insisted though, now that I look back."

"That *is* a shame," Tess said. He held her hand even tighter, as though he needed to regain strength before he continued.

Tess imagined how devastated he would have been — forced to grow up so soon, to leave everything behind. And she'd thought he'd had it all — that it was easier for him, for all of them.

"Anyway, the new business didn't really take off at all. My mum became restless and ..." He swallowed before continuing. Tess could feel his vulnerability.

"That's okay, Stewart. You don't need to continue if you don't feel comfortable," Tess' mother offered.

"No, I want to tell you all. I feel so relaxed around you all, like I can open up and not be judged. I must say I'm surprised you were so hospitable when I turned up here with your daughter. I'd insisted she warn you that I would be staying at your house."

Tess' father gave him a puzzled look. "What do you mean, warn us? It's not like you're a complete stranger."

"Well, let's just say my parents needed a week's notice before we had anyone over, maybe more," he said with a sad smile that seemed to disguise a lot of pain.

Tess chipped in. "My parents don't care about formalities. They accept people willingly and openly."

"I can see that," he said.

Tess sensed he really wanted to get everything off his chest — that he didn't get many opportunities to do that with other people he knew.

"Ok then, I'll go on," Stewart said. "The business failed, which led to a lot of pain and arguments. My parents couldn't be together anymore. They filed for divorce soon after. I've been drifting from one job to another since then, still not knowing what I really want to do career-wise, even though I do know a lot about running a business."

Tess caressed his hand. He looked at her intently. Realising how intimate the gesture was, she pulled her hand away, slightly embarrassed, but he grabbed it back and held it tightly once more.

They kept chatting over homemade vegetable *lasagna* and red wine. Stewart loved hearing about the rock bands her dad had toured with. Tess watched Stewart smile widely as he listened to all the interesting stories her father told. He was really enjoying himself.

They all decided to have their coffee out on the front porch. Tess volunteered to make it, not wanting to ruin the natural flow of conversation between Stewart and her parents. She walked back inside the house feeling like she was floating, as she heard Stewart launch into a conversation about where he learned to make different types of coffee. Tess admired them as they laughed and conversed, looking on from the kitchen window. She re-joined them a while later, stepping back out with cups of coffee, and some lamingtons her mother had made earlier that morning. Mrs Harrington was discussing the origins of tea, as Stewart listened with interest.

After coffee and cake, they headed out for a tour around the restored cottage. Stewart and Tess held hands as they walked around, observing and commenting on the features of the house. They then went to take a look at the shed, and all her mother's crafts and paintings. Her mother talked about the art studio she'd just opened and how pleased she was to finally be able to share her work with international buyers.

"That's impressive," Stewart said. "This house is also a work of art. It's so beautiful that you've kept its natural form, and restored it to its former glory. I can see where Tess gets her appreciation for the old."

"Yes, as a child she loved sitting here in the shed with me while she did her homework and I worked, both of us sipping tea together. We found lots of old photos and antiques from her great grandparents that adorn the house, as you've no doubt seen as we've been walking around. Tess has some of the mirrors and jewellery boxes in her flat."

Stewart nodded. "Yes, I've seen them. They're very beautiful." He sighed in appreciation. "It's great that you still live here, near the pond. You've never thought of moving?"

"We love it here," she said. "That's all that matters. I don't believe in keeping up with the Joneses and all that. There was a time when we moved around a lot, when Tess was young, and her dad toured. But living here has made us realise that when you find a good thing, hold onto it."

It had been a wonderful day. Now, late in the afternoon, she and Stewart walked casually around the pond. They stood on the little wooden bridge and admired the birdlife and flowers in bloom around them.

"It's so beautiful here," Stewart commented. "We got the huge house, but you got to live next to a pond. It must have been great for you, growing up."

"I always thought it was like *Anne of Green Gables*," she said with a laugh.

"You mean, you never imagined Mr Darcy prancing around on his horse, ready to sweep you off your feet and invite you to a soiree at his manor?" he asked with a playful laugh.

"Well, of course I did," she said. "Especially when we had to read *Pride and Prejudice* for English class. I think many of us imagined that … I mean Mr Darcy, come on. I think we all thought he was "all that" *and more*. Well, back then. Not really now," she finished, looking at the pond and sighing.

"What was that for?" he asked. "You sound like you're carrying all the weight of the world with that sigh."

"Nothing. It's silly," she said.

"I don't think anything about you is silly," he said. "Come on, I told you things about me that I hardly talk about. I want to know what's in that fascinating mind of yours."

Tess looked at him and smiled. "Well, I was just thinking about how I used to stand here and feel the adrenalin of something spectacular happening, like wild horses thundering past. My heart would beat with excitement — like I had this secret yearning." Her face coloured from the revelation. "Ignore me," she said, embarrassed, her gaze turned downwards. "I don't know what I'm saying."

"Is that why you love reading so much? You love feeling that sensation — that anything is possible, that life can be all that and more, that you can have magic, flowers, all the colours of the rainbow?"

Tess looked up at him. He understood exactly how she felt. "How did you know?"

"I know, Tess, because that's exactly how I feel. That's why I'm glad I found you again. You were the only one who ever made me feel I could have all that — 'wild horses', as you say."

"Was it really that bad for you growing up?" she asked as he leaned in close to her. She had to digress. She felt like things were moving too fast. She wanted the wild horses, but when she was faced with them, she feared them.

"It wasn't great," he said, stroking her hair, before backing off slightly, sensing her uneasiness.

They continued walking for a while, out from Tess' parents' property and along the road with a comfortable silence between them. He held her hand and intermittently pulled her closer to his chest, hugging her as they walked. Before they knew it, they were near the high school.

Tess felt all sorts of tangled emotions. She looked at Stewart. He seemed to feel the same. He held her hand tight. "I'm game if you are. What do you think? Do you want to look around?"

Tess sighed heavily. She was with Stewart now and a free young woman, no longer bound by school rules, yet Desiree was still in her life, which meant that school was too.

"What are you thinking about?" he asked.

"I don't know. It's so surreal, being back here again, having you back in my life." Her eyes became teary.

"If it's too difficult for you, we don't have to go inside. I know it can be hard to look back sometimes, especially if the memories are ones you'd rather forget."

"I think it might be good for me ..." Tess began.

Stewart's expression showed Tess he understood what she meant, because he too felt what she felt.

As they walked passed school buildings and the huge cafeteria, they reminisced. Tess looked at the art classrooms situated near one of the landscaped areas. It hadn't changed much. She remembered feeling safe amongst the canvasses and colours.

"Remember when your friend Cathy grabbed Evie's bag and tossed everything out of it?"

Tess laughed at the memory. "Yes, I do! She wanted a reaction, because Evie had pushed Cathy's bag off the bench to make room for her own."

Stewart started laughing. "Evie was shocked and speechless. She came running to me for support. I thought she deserved what she got though. She was always so rude when it came to things like that — like she owned the place and everyone else could go jump. She never approached Cathy again."

"You weren't upset with Cathy?"

"No. I can't stand it when people mistreat others. My dad often treated me like I didn't matter — like my feelings didn't matter when it came to making decisions that affected all of us. I think it made me see different perspectives. It's just who I am. I've seen the damage disrespecting someone can do first-hand …" He trailed off, deep in thought.

"I know that's who you are," she acknowledged, meeting his eyes as he looked up at her. "Why weren't the others you hung out with like that?"

Stewart looked towards the basketball court, then beyond to the school oval. He was sceptical. "I think they didn't want to believe that the people they were hurting were truly victims. Of course, not everyone in the group was in the same boat. Some of my friends were a lot more compassionate and supportive. A lot of it depended on what their parents were like. Some of them shared my plight — of having parents who just didn't care. Evie's parents were hardly around, but that wasn't enough to excuse her rude behaviour. I think I saw the truth about a lot of things, accepted it and learned from it. But maybe the others weren't ready to see how things really were, how they behaved and how that behaviour affected others."

Tess nodded in understanding. "That makes sense." Then she had a sudden realisation. "But what about Evie? Isn't she devastated that you just took off like that? She flew to Sydney for you ..."

"Desiree practically dragged Evie to Sydney. Yeah, she liked me back at school, but we were never really a couple. She just thought I made her look good. It did a lot for her popularity, being with the star of the football team. Besides, it never could have gone anywhere, because my heart had other ideas."

Tess felt her heart flutter. She guessed what he meant, but wasn't quite ready to get into it yet, so bashfully held his hand tighter and guided him towards the oval.

"So what made you get into hairdressing?" Stewart asked, evidently picking up on Tess' feelings.

"Do you remember Cathy's mum, Mel, who owned the salon? Well, the moment I stepped into it and let her colour and cut my hair, I felt this power, like I could be whatever I wanted to be. It gave me the power not to care."

"About what?" Stewart queried.

"About the way I was treated at school," she said, feeling vulnerable and exposed. They had reached the green grass of the oval. They were standing in the same spot where she had tripped, and where Desiree had ridiculed her.

She felt his finger on her chin as he lifted it up to meet his eyes. Her lips trembled as the tears streamed down her face, suddenly released.

"Tess," he said in a soft, soothing voice. "I'm so sorry — for them, for her, for the way they treated you. I should have stuck up for you more. I want to make it up to you," he said, stroking the tears away. "She was also vulnerable. Desiree, I mean. She could be awful, but I had sympathy for her. I could relate to the way her dad treated her. She was quiet as a mouse at home or when she was with her family, because he had her under such strict control."

Tess felt slightly shocked at this revelation about Desiree. She was processing a lot. "It's not your fault. You did stick up for me. And I found a way to not care — to distance myself from them."

"I know you did," he said. "And don't think I'm excusing her behaviour either, because these tears tell me a different story — that you aren't completely over it, and that you still carry some of the pain." He leaned even closer and pulled her to his chest. He kissed her forehead, then her tear-stained cheeks. He looked into her eyes. She felt his warm soft lips press onto hers. As he kissed her, he held her closer, stroking her arms and her waist. He pulled her in, but she started to back away. She couldn't take the intensity. She wanted this, yet also didn't at the same time. Why was that? She had imagined it so many times, but now she was trembling in the face of it actually happening.

"Stewart …" she began.

"It's okay," he reassured her. "I caught you off guard."

After a few moments' silence he finally spoke. "Tell me about him … about Michael."

The ease in Stewart's voice encouraged her to relax and feel at ease. "Well, it was a crazy time. We were so young, and I think I had this image in my mind about how marriage ought to be. We did get along at first, as friends. We shared the same interests, but it all changed. I can't pinpoint how and why exactly," she said, looking at the ground as doubt and uncertainty washed over her. She tried to regain her composure and steady her breathing.

"How did it change?"

"It just did somehow. He started getting caught up in work, and he didn't look at me the same anymore. Suddenly we were this responsible couple who had to act a certain way. I think we were too young, and seeing my parents — how they are, so real and respectful of each other, as equals in the relationship — it showed me what we were lacking."

Stewart nodded. "Your parents definitely seem to have done it right — the marriage thing. They're great role models."

"Yes they are. Is that too much to ask for?"

"No, it's definitely not too much to ask for. You want the wild horses." He smiled broadly.

"Yes — and the sprinkles and the sunsets, the storms and the rain. My parents told me I could have all that, and that I shouldn't shy away from it."

He laughed. He suddenly twirled her around, and repeated what she said, like he was acting out a scene: "*The sprinkles and the sunsets, the storms and the rain*. You're not a romantic at all, are you?"

Tess looked at him, and realised that he may have never been told he could have that too. Desiree probably hadn't been told that either. Their parents didn't show them that side of life — of love!

"Well, maybe it's like your mum said back in the shed earlier," he said. "When she showed me some of her artwork, she told me how she mixes colour — that two colours of paint have to blend well before you can use them. Maybe that's why you and Michael didn't blend well — you had different outlooks, expectations about marriage and life. You just need to find someone with the same outlook." He brushed a strand of her wind-blown hair away from her eyes, to meet them with his.

"Maybe I do," she said, weak at the knees.

He didn't attempt to kiss her again, but looked like he wanted to. Tess hoped she hadn't scared him away. Her thoughts were tangled and making her all nervous.

"You know what, Tess?" Stewart continued. "Your parents were wild and free, but they realised that settling down with each other in a place they love is okay too."

Tess gave him a perplexed look.

"What I'm saying is that even wild horses are tamed eventually. They soon come to see that a tamer life has many benefits. If they're not tamed, their wildness becomes too much, and stops being magnificent. There is a beauty to reining it in — cultivating it."

"I guess there is, if you look at it that way." Tess said. She looked over at the school oval, remembering when he had lifted her up from the dirt. The memory didn't bother her anymore. It was now truly precious.

***

The train pulled in at the station at dusk. It was late Sunday evening, and it felt like so much had changed in such a short time. It had been so much fun to go home with Stewart. It was funny how life worked out. She was puzzled by her own behaviour — why she had resisted him. But she felt he understood her hesitations, and would respectfully wait until she was ready to open up to him.

They had spent the night — Tess in her old bedroom and Stewart in the guest room. They had eaten breakfast together with Tess' parents in the stone kitchen, and had visited her mother's studio. It had been a wonderful weekend.

"It's been so great, being with you like this, Tess," he said. They were now outside her apartment building. He leaned in closer and hesitated for a moment, before kissing her gently on the lips. "Was that okay … the kiss?"

"Yes, it's okay," she smiled.

"Just okay?" he asked with a playful smile.

"Well, I guess it's not just okay. It … it was perfect."

They smiled at each other happily.

"I better go," he said, his expression joyful. "You'll have to come see my apartment soon. It really isn't far." He paused momentarily, before saying: "You know, I haven't completely been honest with you."

"You haven't?" Tess asked apprehensively.

"No, I haven't. The truth is, I didn't just run into you by chance. I actually contacted Michael to see if he knew where you lived, after I found out that he had employed Keith, Desiree's husband."

Tess was surprised. "Keith works for Michael? No way. How did that happen?"

"Desiree still had some old contacts from school. She'd read something about Michael's work in investments, and thought he might be able to help them out, after Keith lost his job, so she got in touch, and it turns out he was happy to help. So they decided to move here."

"Talk about coming full circle!" Tess exclaimed. A thought crossed her mind. "Did Keith ever work for his father-in-law, Desiree's father? And what about Desiree? Did she ever work at daddy's ... I mean her dad's company?" she corrected, knowing Stewart's heart was kinder towards Desiree than hers would ever be.

"No, Tess. Neither of them did. Her dad would never hire her anyway, and she's petrified of failing in front of him. He never thought she was smart enough, good enough ..." He trailed off, as though he was troubled by what he'd said. Tess saw compassion in his eyes. "Anyway, his company doesn't exist anymore. It's a long story."

"Oh?" Tess' mother had once mentioned to her that the Marsdens had moved out of the area some years back, but she didn't know the company had closed down completely. "So it isn't operating anymore?"

"Well, actually it is still operating but someone else owns it. Desiree's father nearly lost everything though. It was sad time, and it hit Desiree hard. Tess, like I said, you're stronger than her. Sure, she smiles a lot and tries to appear confident, but she's fragile, like we all are."

Tess still didn't see it. Yes, Desiree had her awkward moments, but she couldn't use her family as an excuse for her behaviour. And Tess couldn't forgive her without her showing some remorse. She was still sabotaging her happiness — she had even brought Evie back when she knew Stewart was getting close to her. But then her heart went to happier thoughts. Stewart had made it his mission to find her! That's all she cared about right at that moment.

"So Michael gave you my address?" she asked. "It wasn't just a coincidence that I ran into you both here? That Desiree rented an apartment here?"

"Actually, it *was* a very strange coincidence. Michael told me the suburb, but seemed reticent to tell me more, so I didn't push it. I got the impression he didn't want to give away too much information. He looked sad when he told me you and he had married and then divorced, and I didn't want to upset him further."

Tess' head was swimming. Desiree had pretended not to know about her marriage to Michael, but evidently she *did* know, if they'd both been talking to him. That's why Stewart had given her a puzzled look the other day. It was yet another of her manipulations. A nagging suspicion made Tess feel that maybe Desiree *did* know where she lived, that she had planned to keep Stewart from living near her. She had a feeling that Desiree may have extracted the needed information from Michael, casting her spell on him as well. *Did Desiree also have a say in deciding which suburb Keith would be working in? She must have heard that Stewart would be moving to the same suburb as me.* It was all too convenient. Tess felt herself growing angry again, but settled her breathing and focused on what was important — the gorgeous man standing by her side.

"So, you decided to move here?" Tess had to know.

"Yes, I'd already been looking at places, but then Keith got the job, and we both ended up moving at around the same time, to the same place. What are the chances? And actually, Desiree beat me to this building. I thought it had a lot of character, but she'd apparently fallen in love with it too. Of course, she didn't know you lived here at the time. We both didn't know. I thought it was you, when you stepped out of Silvio's that Friday night. I couldn't believe my eyes. I followed you discreetly, until I realised that I had frightened you, so I slowed down. I still wasn't completely sure if it was you because it was dark and I hadn't yet seen your face properly. Then I saw you walking into Desiree's apartment building. You were practically running, and I was about to call your name, when you and Desiree came face to face. That's why it was meant to be — running into you like that."

Stewart's expression was one of deep care and passion. It made Tess feel nervous but wonderful at the same time. She would have to put her feelings regarding Desiree aside. Her suspicions were right! Desiree *did* know that she lived in the same building — the one she'd made sure she and Keith moved into, before Stewart did. She had manipulated Michael *and* Stewart. Her plan didn't work though. She couldn't keep them apart. Fate had intervened and even Desiree's charm, or her manipulations couldn't mess with what was destined to be.

"It *was* meant to be ..." Tess mused.

Stewart smiled at her, his eyes full of emotion. His quest to find her had been successful. He looked at his watch. "I better go," he said. "I wish we could talk more about this now, but it will have to wait until next time. I have to pop into work and tell my boss I'll be back at work tomorrow morning." He opened the front door of the building. "It's just a part-time job for now until I get my career back on track. It's good enough for now, though, and Silvio's great."

"Silvio?" Tess asked, confused.

"Yeah, Silvio," Stewart replied. "Didn't I tell you I work part-time at his restaurant?" He looked puzzled. "I mustn't have been clear. That's why I was going to get the food from there the other night — after my shift. I even told your mum about it ... when we were sitting on the front porch? It must've been when you went to make the coffee."

Tess suddenly recalled the phone call from the restaurant. "I thought you were going out to a restaurant to eat," she replied. "I can't believe you work at Silvio's!"

"Yeah, I'm the barista there!" With that he gave her another quick kiss before walking out the door and into the night.

CHAPTER TWENTY-ONE

The barista … The words echoed in her mind, causing her skin to break out into a cold shiver. *He's the barista!* She looked over at Pamela's door.

"I'm going out with the barista. We just started seeing each other." Pamela had said.

Why would this happen, just when things were going so great? Why would Stewart lie to her like that? Pamela's words rang in her ears. It all made sense, how Desiree kept telling her the coffee was better elsewhere, that there were other Italian restaurants besides Silvio's. She was obviously going to great lengths to keep Stewart away from her. And she had become close with Pamela. Was Desiree playing matchmaker to ruin her life? It had her name all over it! She'd taken her best friend away, and now she wanted to take away the love of her life — for that's really what he was. But why would he not tell her? Had she imagined it all — his kindness, his care, the feeling he was someone she could rely on? Maybe he *was* too good to be true. Maybe she had idolised him, like one of the men in the classics. She was so naïve to think love like that could really exist in real life, just like she thought she could build a magical world that no one could destroy.

With heavy steps, Tess walked into her apartment. The little bell jingled gently, echoing the beat of her fragile heart, which felt like a soft shell breaking with ease.

She looked at her suitcase. He had stayed with her at her parents' house, sharing wonderful moments together. She felt like he really cared. But he had also defended Desiree. Why would he, knowing how cruel she could be? It didn't make sense.

Tess was struck down with a terrible thought. Was he in on some cruel plan? Were they all laughing at her? Poor Tess, falling for it — that a man would be so generous with his heart for her, that he would fall for her! Thoughts of deceit, revenge and ridicule were making her hysterical.

She sobbed, shaking all over. All the objects around her appeared fuzzy, and the beautiful colours became one big blurry mess. She walked into her bedroom and sunk into the bed, burying herself under the covers. She didn't want to see anyone. She had always craved her solitude, wanting to hide from the cruel world she had been introduced to in her youth, which she had chosen not to be a part of. She had her peace and her tranquillity and no complications — her wonderful home life — and they had infiltrated it like a disease, and brought about its slow demise. Her whole world was shattered, as was the hope of having someone in her life to complement it.

**

The next few days passed slowly to Tess. She called in sick on Tuesday morning. She wanted to avoid Pamela, as well as most of the people in her life. It seemed to Tess that Pamela was about to say something when she had called, but had refrained. Tess was too weak to find out what it was. Maybe she was ready to fill her in on her new man in her life — *Stewart*, the barista who was the "whole package", as Briana had exclaimed that hot day at the salon.

She did however feel guilty about Helena, and made it her mission to visit her as soon as she felt strong enough. Until then, she wondered what else Desiree had in store for her, and when she would strike next. Tess wondered if she could do any further damage — if there would be any more aftershocks. The hope of finding someone like Stewart had always been in the back of her mind, even if Michael had scared her off believing in happily ever afters. Now, Stewart had cast that belief in stone, not helped by the fact that he hadn't called. This just solidified in Tess' mind that he wasn't who he'd claimed to be.

On Wednesday morning, she'd had enough of moping in her apartment, so she got dressed and decided to visit Helena, who had sent her a couple of messages asking if she was all right. Pamela had also sent another asking the same. She had even knocked on her door, and called out, but Tess had pretended she wasn't in. Images of her with Desiree, and now with Stewart were too much for her to process.

Tess applied her make-up carefully in front of the bathroom mirror. When she was done, she gazed out the small window to the busy street below, feeling the humidity in the air again. The hot weather seemed to be returning. She remembered how carefree she'd been that unbearably hot week, before they walked into her life.

She jolted. She could see Desiree walking down the street, heading towards the shops. She then caught sight of Pamela, walking in the same direction, but several metres behind her. Pamela then crossed the street. Tess was baffled. *One minute they're yoga buddies and then … What on earth is going on?*

Tess decided to head out, knowing she wouldn't run into them in the building. She was fuelled by anger, and walked with haste until, a few minutes later, she found herself walking behind Desiree. Instead of slowing, Tess walked more quickly, instinctively following Desiree. She wondered what her nemesis did with her days — how she spent her time, besides shopping and yoga. She always acted like she was so busy. She imagined her tight, very short school skirt, like a second skin on her as her hips swayed from side to side. Desiree hadn't changed her walk at all since school — in fact, nothing had changed about her. She was superficial as ever.

Suddenly feeling like she was stalking her, Tess slowed down. She saw Desiree turn into the small side street where the grocery store and real estate agency were situated. She stopped abruptly when she realised she was about to pass Silvio's. She couldn't imagine facing Stewart, but she had to go and see Helena, so she would hurry past.

"*Tess!* Hi!"

Oh no! It was Briana, the one person who knew how to attract attention with her rambunctious personality.

"Hi Briana, how are you?" Tess managed, feeling flustered.

At that exact moment she was shoved forward slightly, momentarily losing her balance. She swung around to see who had done such a thing. "Oh, Carter!" Tess exclaimed.

"Tess! So sorry for bumping into you! I hope you're ok. I've got to go — I have a meeting," he explained, walking hastily away with two coffees in his hands.

"I wouldn't mind bumping into *him*," Briana enthused. "He's another hottie in the street. Too bad he's taken."

"Yes, he is taken," Tess thought sceptically. *Let's hope only by Helena,* she found herself thinking.

"Another man who's into blondes," Briana said.

Tess looked at the door of Silvio's, which was opening at that very moment. She had to keep walking.

"Briana, I've got to go. See you at the salon," she called back as she quickened the pace.

"Sure, see you Tess," Briana called out.

Helena was outside of her shop, talking to a woman who was looking at the flowers in the display window. Tess felt ill when she realised it was Jessica. Helena was pointing to some flowers while Jessica nodded enthusiastically. They then went back inside. Tess walked closer to the window to see what was happening, and saw Helena give Jessica a business card and a folder, before shaking her hand. Jessica then hugged Helena, looking very pleased.

After she had left, Tess stepped inside.

"It's not her," Helena said. "I noticed you looking."

"So much for being discrete," Tess replied.

Helena explained that Carter had helped Jessica because her husband had recently lost his job and they couldn't pay the rent. Carter had paid to cover a few months' worth of rent out of his own pocket. For that, Jessica said she would be forever grateful.

"But why was she looking at your shop?" Tess enquired.

"Oh! She was so appreciative about what Carter did that she wanted to thank me as well. She's always wanted to open up a flower shop, and wanted some ideas, so built up the courage to ask me some questions. If Carter is having an affair, it's definitely not with her! I've realised I need to confront him about it. I might do it tonight."

Moments later, Tess walked out of the shop. She noticed Briana waiting at the bus stop further up the road. She recalled what Briana had said. *Another man who's into blondes. Blondes? But Helena's a brunette!*

She hadn't processed Briana's words earlier because she was so focused on avoiding Stewart and Silvio, but now her words rang clear in her ears. She remembered Carter's appointment, him speeding off with two coffees in his hands. And she remembered Desiree walking into the small street where he worked. He had touched Desiree's shoulder so intimately at the real estate agency the other day. Were they having an affair? *No!* She refused to believe it.

She thought of Stewart's words. "You're stronger than her, Tess!" She had seen signs of Desiree's awkwardness and even pathetic desperation, but no evidence of remorse — only revenge. But why? Because Tess had succeeded in creating the life she wanted, and Desiree hadn't? Because Desiree was unhappy in her marriage and Tess had had the courage to leave Michael?

Just when she thought things couldn't possibly get any worse, she saw Pamela up ahead, crossing the road. She knew where she was heading — to Silvio's.

Tess crossed the road. When the coast was clear of Pamela, she practically ran down the street. She needed to see if her suspicions about Carter and Desiree were correct. She walked into the little side street and peered into the window of the real estate agency. She saw Carter standing by his desk. His stylish suit did wonders for his smooth, chiselled face, while her smile poisoned the air between them with betrayal and lies. He had bought two coffees for *them* — for their cosy meeting. Tess looked on in shock, at how unashamedly playful Desiree was being with him — picking up things from his desk, chatting with him, laughing. *There's no denying it*, she thought as she watched Desiree place her arms around Carter, pulling him in for a hug. Carter looked embarrassed. He looked around, seemingly to see if anyone had noticed her gesture.

Tess felt like she was going to be sick. She backed away from the window and slowly walked back down the narrow street, feeling defeated and numb.

She walked without hearing anything but her thoughts, or seeing anything but a blurry vision of Stewart meeting her at the train station. She climbed up the stairs of the apartment building with a heavy heart. She saw colours — red roses amongst full green leaves. A bouquet was sitting on her doorstep to greet her. Her heart beat with nervous anticipation. Part of her wanted it to be from him, but another was happy to run from the complications of relationships.

She picked up the flowers and opened the door. The brass bell jingled sympathetically. "I can always rely on you," she sighed. That's what it had come to — she couldn't trust anyone or anything but her precious objects.

Tess looked for a card as she stepped inside. "How odd," she muttered softly to herself. She noticed that the card attached to the ribbon tied around the bouquet had been torn. All she could make out were the words, *Hi Tess.* "Damn!" she muttered. How would she know who the roses were from now? *Could they be from him? Could they be from Stewart?* They definitely weren't from Helena's shop. Helena never used charcoal tissue paper, and she would never have allowed any of her deliveries to be carried out so carelessly, she thought as she sunk into the couch.

Life seemed to have somehow become even more complicated. *Why would Stewart send me flowers anyway?* Tess felt dizzy. She looked at the red roses. She suddenly remembered what she had seen at the real estate agency. She needed to unwind and gather her thoughts. *Tea always makes things better*. She walked over to the kettle. *How simple life was before all of this happened*. She looked around her empty apartment. It felt quieter than usual, lonely. *She* felt lonely. She had always savoured her solitude, but now she'd had too much of it. Her objects didn't give her the solace she craved. Now, they appeared different. They had been touched and given new life by someone who had admired them. He had touched them, just as he had touched her life, and now she craved the thing she never knew before that she was missing. She yearned for Stewart. He had brought light into her world. Now it looked darker than usual, even as streams of sunlight showered it with warmth. How could she have seen the sun, then go back to the darkness?

CHAPTER TWENTY-TWO

The next morning she was awoken by her phone. It was Millie. The red matte lipsticks had arrived from Paris. She wanted her to be the first to know.

Tess jumped out of bed. She felt like she had a purpose again. She had waited so long for them, and now they were here. The slightest glimmer of hope spurred her on. The familiar feeling of waiting for something to arrive and finally receiving it comforted her. It was like there was hope again for her to experience the excitement she craved. She knew they were merely lipsticks, but the way she had been feeling, she would devour anything positive in her life — no matter how small — with relish.

An hour later, wearing her favourite chartreuse dress, she opened her front door of the building, bound for Millie's. A man holding a bouquet of pale pink roses stepped inside.

"Excuse me, do you know a Tess Harrington?" he enquired.

"Yes, that's me. I'm Tess."

"Well, these are for you."

Tess looked at the beautiful roses. They weren't from Helena's shop either. She took the flowers in her hands. "Do I need to sign for them?"

"Sure, but where do you want me to leave the rest?"

"The rest?"

"Yes, there's a van practically full of them!" he exclaimed.

"What?"

"*Tess!* I can't believe it!" The shock of hearing Desiree's shrill voice nearly made her crush the roses in her hands.

Her nemesis was out the front of the building, with Stewart beside her. Both of them were holding a box with several more bouquets inside.

What was happening? Was this from …

Stewart interrupted her thoughts. "Looks like Michael has gone all out," he said, ending any speculation that the flowers might be from him.

"Michael?" she queried.

"Wouldn't they be?" he asked, looking puzzled.

"I gotta leave these somewhere," the delivery man said, sweat dripping from his forehead. "I've got more deliveries to get through."

Tess felt the humidity in the air as the heat slowly returned. Would she feel its warmth, or would she burn in it? Perhaps the latter, seeing how her life was turning out.

She caught Stewart looking at her intently. "You look great!"

Desiree just looked at her dress, her eyes practically rolling. "I'll help you with all of these, Tess," she chipped in. "I can't believe how many flowers are out there. Whoever they're from, he must mean a lot to you. Isn't it so romantic, Stewart? Looks like Tess may have found the love of her life."

How dare that home-wrecker touch my flowers! Tess thought, anger and confusion consuming her.

Stewart's jaw tightened. Tess could see darkness in his usually cheerful eyes. He looked perplexed, perhaps even angry.

Tess' confusion reached crisis point. It was like a puzzle that could never be solved. Why would he assume they were from Michael? Desiree, on the other hand, didn't seem to have a clue who the flowers were from. One thing Tess *did* know was that they weren't from Stewart.

"Miss …" The delivery man looked impatient. He was perspiring even more profusely now.

"Oh, sorry," she said. "You can follow me up to my apartment." She tried to ignore the look Stewart was giving her. She still couldn't believe he could treat her so cruelly. Both he and Desiree were obviously alike in their ability to break hearts. No wonder he had hung out with her *then*, and still hung out with her *now*, and why he excused her behaviour.

She could feel the footsteps behind her as she climbed the stairs. With trembling hands she opened the door. She turned to look at Stewart as he walked through it, looking at the bell as it jingled. He then met her eyes. *Why do his eyes shine with such sadness?*

Soon, her lounge room was practically covered in pink roses. "I hope you have a lot of vases," the delivery man said, as he handed her a card. She signed for the flowers. "He must be someone special to go to these lengths."

Tess shut the door behind the delivery man as he left, and turned around to see Stewart looking at the vase with the red roses in her kitchen.

"So who are they from?" Desiree queried, indicating towards the many bouquets with a sweep of her hand. "I mean, are they from …" She trailed off as she met Stewart's eyes. He looked serious and puzzled.

Tess opened the note. "They're from Michael," she said, feeling no need to hide it. She didn't want to read the note in front of them, so tucked it away in her handbag. "Well, I'd better get going," Tess said. "I have to be somewhere." She didn't have the time to process the fact that he was in her apartment again — the man dating Pamela when she thought he was falling in love with *her*. "I have to go," she said again with a coldness that surprised her.

"Oh … don't you want to tend to the flowers?" Stewart blurted out. "I mean, he did all this for you." He looked back at the red roses that stood out against the marble bench top and the black and white kitchen tiles. "Did he send you those as well?" he asked. Tess nodded. "Is it strange that he sent you one bouquet of red roses, then so many pink roses so soon after?" He looked at Tess inquiringly, then back to face Desiree, who was fidgeting with her hair.

"He knew I loved pale pink roses," Tess managed, also finding it odd.

"Why does it matter?" Desiree queried, still fidgeting. "He probably wanted to keep the flame alive — keep the surprises coming."

Stewart didn't look satisfied with that answer.

Desiree opened the front door. "We'd better let Tess go," she said, suddenly eager to leave. Stewart followed her with seeming trepidation.

"So you have an appointment?" he enquired, looking back at Tess as they left.

"No, I'm just heading to Millie's," Tess explained, following them out and closing the door behind her.

"Oh, I just *love* that shop," Desiree enthused. "Millie's *such* a sweetheart. Did you know I'm actually helping her with her wedding plans?"

Tess' heart sank. "Yes, of course you are," she muttered. *She even got to Millie,* Tess thought; the knot in her stomach becoming tighter.

"Should you be heading out, then?" Desiree asked. "I mean, it's not like you have an urgent appointment. You should stay home and fix up the flowers. Michael obviously went to a lot of effort. Although, I do understand you wanting to get to Millie's. I just *love* the lipsticks she has there."

Yes, well, maybe you should keep your lipstick away from *my friend's husband's shirt,* she thought bitterly. She wouldn't let her get away with it. She would make her move with Helena when she least expected it.

Stewart was still looking at her. "Why didn't you go to the salon today?"

"I didn't feel well," she blurted out much too quickly.

"Oh." He looked at her with confusion in his eyes.

"Anyway, like I said, I've got to go," Tess managed.

"Say hi to Millie for me," Desiree said. "I might pop over there later, see what else she has at her lovely shop, if there's anything new."

"Bye," Tess said, and sped away before they had the chance to walk alongside her. Her heart still felt for him. She could practically feel his sadness, his confusion. *Why would he look at me like that?* she speculated. *Like he's done nothing wrong?*

***

Tess hurried towards Millie's. It wouldn't be too long until she could finally purchase her beautiful lipsticks. Unanswered questions tortured her brain, but she didn't want to think too much about them. Every time she tried to answer one of them new questions seemed to plague her. But there were so many things she wanted to know. What was happening between Stewart and Pamela? Why did Stewart assume the roses were from Michael when she hadn't even told them who they were from yet? Was it because Michael had mentioned that he regret how things worked out with their marriage? Was Desiree really having an affair with Carter? Did Keith know, or was she hiding it from him? Why would Desiree and Stewart both come back into her life just to ruin it? And why wasn't Pamela talking to Desiree? Her mind ran rife with speculation. As she stopped to cross the road, she thought of a few more questions. *Why did Michael send me the flowers? And why would he send me the red roses as well? Were they even from him? They had to be. I might find the answer to that in the note,* she thought. She sat down on the bench by the nearby bus stop. She took the note out of her bag and opened the envelope.

Dear Tess,

I guess you're surprised that I contacted you. You came up in a conversation recently. To be honest, you come up in different conversations with different people all the time. Suddenly, all the moments we spent together during our marriage came rushing back to me. I was unfair to you, Tess. I wanted to let you know that I'm sorry for my immaturity and my lack of understanding about what's important in a marriage — in life.

I wanted you to know that I did some soul-searching, and have realised that I was afraid when I became your husband — afraid that I would fail personally and financially. I was so afraid of failing and losing you that I pushed you away and lost not only my wife, but one of my best friends. I have grown since then, and have realised you can't live your life through fear, and deprive yourself of what you love. It was the wrong time for us, Tess. I wasn't ready for the responsibility — I guess I choked. Better late than never to realise all of this, right? I can finally see the light.

I wanted to also let you know that I might be moving on with someone else. You'll find out more in due course. Anyway, before this becomes one of those long letters you write to Cathy and she to you, I want to tell you that I think you deserve all the pale pink roses you want. I regret cancelling them on what was supposed to be a special day for both of us. It was really selfish of me. I realise that now.

I hope life is treating you well. I think you will find that someone special very soon.

Lots of love, (Bye Tess)

Michael Peterson

A tear streamed down her cheek and her lips trembled. *Lots of love to you too.* "Bye Michael," she said softly.

Tess had to regroup. Her heart felt so warm from the repressed emotions. It was really a kind and noble thing to do — to apologise, to show her he had "seen the light", and that he was now moving on with someone else. She was confident he would now make that *someone* extremely happy. It hadn't been the right time for the two of them. Their marriage didn't go to waste — he had grown from it. His letter made her realise that love really was possible. It wasn't the right canvas and the right paint, it also needed the right setting, the right leading man and the right leading lady.

Desiree, as usual, entered her mind when she looked over at Helena's shop. She could see the sign faintly from where she was sitting. She could also see the sign out the front of

Silvio's. She scanned the shops across the street. Dante's and Penny's vintage shop was in view further down the road, then further down still was the salon. Her heart ached at how differently she looked at it now. It no longer felt like her second home. She looked at Mr Papas' deli, where she had always felt welcome. She noticed that the door of the indie book shop had now been painted a quirky pink colour. It did look pretty. *Its faults can be seen from across the street, yet it wouldn't be what it was without them*, she contemplated. That colourful door was the perfect entrance to the book shop she adored, and reflected the life inside that shop — life created through stories of love, romance, mystery and adventure. The door gave the whole shop its character and charm.

How she loved this beautiful street. Yet everywhere she looked had been tarnished by Desiree. Even Mr Papas had been under her spell. She then looked over at Millie's. A vision of Desiree came to mind again. She thought about the very first day she had seen the confident woman in the white dress, who wreaked more destruction than the weather had that night. She had first seen her in her white dress, with her beautiful green packages and bags from Millie's … *Oh no!* Tess thought. *Not this time!* Tess raced to the traffic lights. She crossed the road and practically ran to Millie's. She had to get to the lipsticks before Desiree did first.

"Phew!" Tess cried, trying to catch her breath.

"Are you okay? Tess, you didn't have to run. I told you I would save them for you. In fact, I have a few lipsticks packed for you already. You know what? I don't want any money. It's my gift to you, and there are some lipstick holders included as well."

"No, Millie …" Tess protested.

"I want to gift them to you," she insisted, tearing up. "Sorry, I don't know what's come over me. This wedding stuff is making me emotional. Now that I actually have some help, I'm enjoying it. But there seems to be something up with Desiree. You were friends, right? She's been very helpful with the planning, and Pamela seemed to get along with her very well, but I think since that night at Vinnie's — the night you couldn't make it — they've had a falling-out."

"Do you know what was it about?" Tess asked.

"I don't really know. I've been too busy to catch up with anyone. How's Helena, anyway? I've been meaning to talk to her. I hope she managed to get the lipstick stain out!"

"What?" Tess blurted out. "Lipstick stain? What lipstick stain?"

"This is so embarrassing. Would you believe that I ran into Carter … well I actually literally ran into him, you know! I bumped into him on the street and left a big grape-coloured lipstick stain on his white crisp shirt! I was wearing the new grape colour that I was so excited to show you and Pamela … from the new range? I offered to pay for the dry cleaning but he wouldn't have it. You know how kind and generous he is, not to mention sexy." "Yes, so I've heard," Tess said. She looked at the scintillating lipsticks, and smiled at how everything was unfolding. "I better get going. Thanks so much for the lipsticks. I'm so excited to wear them!"

They hugged and agreed to organise a girl's night soon — just the "shop girls", and no one else. According to Millie, they really needed to catch up. She apparently had something to ask all of them.

As she turned to leave the shop, Tess caught sight of a bunch of red roses on the counter. "Hugh again?" she asked. "He really seems to love red roses. Would you believe Michael also sent me some? You remember — my ex?"

"No, they're not from Hugh," Millie replied. "Not this time. They're actually from Desiree."

"What?" Tess jumped.

"Yes. She gave them to me yesterday. She thought the red roses looked amazing when she visited the shop the first time, so she bought me another bunch. It was very thoughtful, don't you think?"

Tess was lost for words.

CHAPTER TWENTY-THREE

Tess rushed out of Millie's. She had a feeling something odd was going on, and Millie had just confirmed it. Did Desiree think she was daft? Didn't she know that Millie would tell her everything? She hadn't covered her steps, and she was definitely no genius mastermind.

Tess was fuming by the time she reached her apartment, and flew up the stairs in a rage. Tess opened the door, raced to the kitchen, grabbed the red roses out of the vase, shook the excess water into the sink, slammed the door with vigour, and headed for Desiree's apartment, where she would tell her *exactly* what she could do with her roses!

Tess reached the apartment, only to realise the door was slightly ajar. She could hear her voice. She was pleading with Keith. Tess held on to the roses and remained still.

"I'm fed up with your excuses," Keith said.

"What excuses? You know why I bought all these things. They're gifts. Half of them aren't even for me!"

"Well, all I know is that we have to be responsible, and you're not even working. We can't even make the rent. I don't know why you insisted on moving into this building. It's one of the most expensive in the area. You *knew* we couldn't afford it!"

"You don't know what it's been like for me!" she cried. "All my friends have left me. Evie hates me. She's always blamed me for what happened between her and Stewart, and now she blames me for what my dad did. She made that quite clear the other night. I don't know why she even came to Sydney, just so she could tell me off. The only person who has stood by me is Stewart, and now he'll probably leave me too. I used to be so popular — but now everyone runs away from me, like I've got some disease."

"Why do you need all the gifts? You can't buy your friends back with a few expensive lipsticks, or buy new friends," Keith barked.

"They're not for my friends. They're for the women who lost their jobs. I just want to make them feel special. I used to go to the factory and talk with some of them. I'd bet you didn't know that about me. I did it because they listened to me. They didn't want anything from me, and they didn't treat me like I was some sort of idiot, just like you are doing now … like my dad always did. Do you know what it's like to be constantly told to shut up and smile, because apparently I'm too stupid to say anything. I couldn't possibly be useful at doing anything, according to my father. But you know what? I realised I married someone like my dad. You treat me exactly the same!" Desiree sobbed. "I can't lose Stewart as well. He's the only one who saw how he treated me, and he doesn't treat me like I don't matter. He's always been a good friend. I thought if he got back with Evie, that Evie might forgive me. But I saw her true colours. People think I'm like her, but I'm not. I care about the people who lost their jobs because my dad was selfish and corrupt. I mean, he convinced Stewart's dad to invest so much of his money in risky investments that they lost everything. Yet, he still talks to me. He's the only one who didn't give up on me."

Tess backed away as footsteps approached the door.

"I don't care!" Keith yelled. "Enough is enough! No more spending money we don't have on gifts no one wants. You even paid for Evie to come here. I still can't get over that one! And I don't want you chumming up to that real estate agent anymore. He knows so many people in my company, and you make me look like a fool."

"What? How did I chum up to him? I just hugged him. He's so warm and friendly. That woman that owns the flower shop — he's married to her. She's so lucky. I can't believe he'll give us some more time to pay this week's rent. I was just grateful. Sorry for being a warm person …"

Tess could hear Desiree sobbing hysterically while Keith said nothing.

After a minute or so, Keith stated coldly, "I've got some work to do. Just keep the spending to a minimum. Your father has ruined so many opportunities for us — the minute they find out I'm married to you, they run."

"How do you think I feel? No one has ever stood by me. I can't even get a job because I have no qualifications. You know my parents never encouraged me to learn anything. It was like I wasn't good enough to get an education."

"Well, you can't hide behind that excuse all your life. And can you stop crying?" Keith said irritably. "I've got an important phone call to make."

"What? I'm not some robot. I can't just switch off my feelings when you tell me …"

Hearing the footsteps draw closer, Tess ran to the front door of the building and walked out into the front garden. She concealed herself behind a hedge. She could hear Desiree heading for the door, still sobbing. Tess realised some of the red roses had fallen on the paved steps. She clutched the rest to her.

Desiree stormed out of the building. She was a mess, shaking and crying. Tess instantly felt pity for her. She was quivering like a child.

An image of her sitting as timid as a mouse at the town hall dinners entered Tess' mind. She looked at Desiree's perfect, matching outfit. It was so tidy — nothing was out of place. Perhaps her obsession with being so perfect was because she felt so out of place — so left out. It was probably her way of having some control. Since seeing her that first day, Tess had thought Desiree didn't belong in her quirky neighbourhood. There was a stark contrast between her impeccable white dress and the alternative shops with their colour, culture and creativity. She didn't look like she belonged at all. Suddenly Tess realised that Desiree was in *her* world, where everyone knew her, where *she* fit in, while Desiree didn't. But Tess felt that it was more than just that.

As she saw Desiree looking so lost and frightened, her eyes revealing fear and insecurity, she wondered if she ever felt that she belonged — even back in Lorikeet Creek, when she was the popular girl.

"Desolate" was a word that came to mind. Desiree was drifting through life with a desolate heart. Tess' own heart warmed with empathy at the thought. She started to understand what Stewart had tried to tell her. "She's intimidated by you, you're stronger than her." Tess also realised her own love for Stewart at that moment was so strong because of who he was. He could see through the pretences and into someone's heart — seeing their true colours. He was genuine and caring, and she could see she meant the world to him. That's why it was so out-of-character for him to betray her. Something didn't add up, and she would find out what exactly it was.

Tess had a flash of recognition, suddenly seeing a part of herself in Desiree. Although she had a wonderful family and a quiet confidence, Tess too had built walls around her own secure world, making sure that it was never invaded. It was similar to how Desiree had built her own world to protect anyone seeing the truth — that she was not confident, but scared and lonely.

Tears streamed down Tess' cheeks. Her heart ached for Desiree. She was a woman just trying to make sense of the circumstances thrust upon her. Tess watched as she began to walk down the steps, her eyes also puddles of tears. One of her high heels landed on one of the red roses.

Tess jumped out from her hiding spot. "Desiree!" she called out. It was too late. All she could do was watch as Desiree rolled down the steps. She landed in the pink rosebush.

Tess froze. She met Desiree's eyes. Her face was tear-stained, covered with a trace of dirt. The roses looked so pretty around her beautiful but still quivering frame. Desiree held the stare. It wasn't one of her usual looks. Tess saw nothing in it. It was the look of a defeated woman.

She walked over and looked down at Desiree. On one side, the red roses reflected her deceit — but now Tess could understand where it had come from. The roses looked fragile as they lay scattered on the steps — exposed to the elements, stripped of their pride and pomposity. One of the red petals was still stuck on Desiree's heel. She had crushed its colour — *its deceit*. Tess looked at Desiree as she pulled herself up into a seated position in the rawness and realness of the dirt, amongst the gentle and fragile pink petals with their array of pure colour touching her hair, her fragile and vulnerable teary eyes exposed the truth.

Tess reached out her hand to help her. Desiree placed her hand in Tess' and allowed her to lift her up. Desiree said nothing. She walked quietly to the door and finally opened her mouth. "Thanks," she managed, finally.

***

Moments later, after helping Desiree into her apartment, Tess climbed the stairs and made her way to her own. She opened the door and realised the little brass bell was loose. Its jingle seemed lifeless, almost fragile. "Oh no!" she muttered to herself. *It must have happened when I slammed the door.* Normally she would have been devastated — her objects were so precious and dear to her. But as she thought of Desiree's vulnerability, she realised that that's all they truly were — objects. What gave them life was the place in which they resided, and the people within that place who gave them meaning.

CHAPTER TWENTY-FOUR

Tess stepped out later that evening. It had been an eventful day. She vowed to call Pamela and tell her she'd be back at work the next day. She'd dashed out to see Helena after her encounter with Desiree. Helena couldn't believe the turn of events and they had a great laugh over the lipstick incident. Helena had also confronted Carter and he ended up divulging the needed information — that he had been helping people — a tad more than usual. Carter had thought that Helena would be upset with his extreme generosity and had reassured her they would all pay him back — that they were trustworthy. Helena felt so proud of her chivalrous husband, and knew he would never be reckless with their finances. She applauded his generosity, like she always had. She was so relieved he was rescuing people like Desiree from ruin, and that her fears of his deceit were unfounded.

It was a balmy evening. She was about to cross the road to avoid Silvio's, but decided against it. She would stop hiding and lying to herself. Maybe Pamela was unaware of what was happening. There were too many unanswered questions that needed answers, and she had to confront Pamela about Stewart.

As she walked past Silvio's, she peered through the front door and saw Pamela. Tess continued walking, still not brave enough to confront her.

As though right on cue, she heard Pamela calling after her as she ran out of Silvio's. "Tess! Stop! I need to talk to you. Please, wait!" she pleaded. "Can we please stop this nonsense, avoiding each other? I wanna talk to you, get it all out in the open. Enough with these secrets. You're one of my closest friends, and there's the salon …"

"I'm not avoiding you, Pamela. Well, maybe a little."

"I know what you're thinking … that I'm keeping secrets about seeing someone too. It's the stupid pact. What were

253

we thinking? We created fear in our hearts — a belief that we shouldn't ever break it. It's like it encouraged us not to live — not to open our hearts, or take chances. Anyway, what you saw in the restaurant ... I was going to tell you about him."

Tess hadn't seen who Pamela was with as she peered through the windows. She didn't want to see her with Stewart with her own eyes though. It was too soon. "I know, you're seeing St...

Pamela finished her sentence for her. "Silv... What was that? What were you going to say?" Pamela looked puzzled.

"Stewart? Is that what you were trying to say?" Tess queried.

"Silvio. I was trying to say Silv... Wait! Let me get his straight. The barista ... Stewart, that same one. Is that who you thought I was seeing? *Your Stewart?* The one who your backstabbing friend, Desiree, tried to set up with Evie? I definitely saw *her* true col..."

"What? Back up for one minute. You're seeing *Silvio, not Stewart?*"

"Why would I see your boyfriend? I know all about you two. You don't need to hide it. Would you believe he thought you were seeing Michael again? That Desiree was at it again. Silvio and I saw the whole thing. He really put her in her place. He worked it out. She made it look like he was still interested in you, leaving those red roses that were supposedly from Michael at your doorstep, and making sure Stewart saw them. She must have really panicked the next day when Michael *did* end up sending you flowers. Talk about a coincidence!"

"But you said you're seeing the barista, that day at the salon. I heard you!"

"*Oh my God!* That? I was just trying to get my client off my back. She always wants to know who's dating who. I knew so many of the female clients were going on and on about him, so the rest is history. I thought it would be funny, thinking of them all jealously gossiping about me and him, when in fact there was nothing going on between us at all!"

Tess sighed in relief. It all suddenly made sense.

"About that *Desiree*," Pamela continued. "I fell for her charms, but it wasn't long until I was onto her. I knew Stewart was the guy Millie had mentioned that day at the salon, when I thought you were keeping secrets from me. Suddenly Desiree was putting you down and trying to make Stewart get back with Evie, like we were in high school. I let her have it. It was such juvenile behaviour." Pamela smiled at Tess. "And I realised why you would let such a great guy like Silvio go. I know why you didn't want him, Tess. Another good guy was already in your heart. I think you didn't even know it at the time. That's why you were confused and even scared when you let him go. The way you ran into Stewart … It was like it was meant to be."

"I think you may be right, Pamela," she said, wondering why she wasn't jumping for joy at Pamela's revelation. "So, you and Silvio …"

"Yes, me and Silvio. I was going to confide in you, but you seemed to be …"

"Keeping things from you? I guess I'm guilty of that. Things happened so quickly. I didn't have time to process it or talk to you about it."

"Well, things happened quickly between us also. Don't get me wrong. We're at the beginning. Things are just getting started, really. I had to make sure you weren't interested. It all started because he wanted to confide in me about you. He soon found out that your heart was definitely closed to his, and the conversation drifted to other things, until we realised we liked each other's company," she explained. "I think he needed for you to let him go — to allow someone else in. We've known each other for a while, but these past few weeks, we've really gotten to know each other properly."

Tess smiled at her friend warmly. "Pamela, you don't need to explain anything. I can really see you and Silvio as a couple."

Pamela returned the smile. "Thanks Tess. We're very happy. Oh, and just so you know, Stewart will be here later on. He's working today. Why don't you come inside for a coffee, to clear the air, so to speak?"

"Um …"

"What is it, Tess?"

"I don't know. A lot has happened today. This whole week and last week have been really weird … Since that storm, remember? And I'm not sure how things are between Stewart and I right now. It might be too much, to see him today."

Pamela shrugged. "Maybe, but I think you should catch up with him. You should have seen how Stewart let Desiree have it when he worked out what was going on, the way she made it look like you and Michael still had feelings for each other. I can't believe she even showed Stewart a fake card … one that she wrote herself. Of course, she didn't leave the card at your doorstep. I assume she didn't want to leave any evidence … especially since Michael found Keith the job. Yeah … I heard all about that too. She apologised profusely, and he backed down when he saw how upset she was. He's a great guy. It's almost like he knows what's good for her — like a true friend. I think he also really cares about you. He hardly paid any attention to Evie that night at Vinnie's, and she looked like she didn't want to be there at all. Stewart asked me several times if you were joining us at the club. I ran out to explain everything, but then I saw you with …"

"With Silvio."

"Yes. I know he was just comforting you. You were hurting, and he saw that you needed someone. I understand, Tess. I'm sorry for being cold and distant with you lately. I should never have sided with Desiree, either."

"I was hurt that you were spending time with her, and making jokes at my expense. Then you became yoga buddies …"

"Yoga buddies?" Pamela interrupted. "I never went to yoga with her. Oh! You saw me carrying the yoga mat. It was for one of Desiree's friends from the gym, who left it in her car one day. Sorry Tess. You thought I was becoming friends with your enemy."

"That's okay. I jumped to conclusions. But you know what, I realised there was much more going on with Desiree than I could ever have known. She isn't as strong as she wants us to believe. She never knew who she was and she's still lost. I think you're right about one thing — she may have been intimidated by me. I see it now. I stood out. She thought I knew who I was, and she was threatened by it. Maybe she saw a strength in me because I really had it all — my family was so supportive and nurturing. They let me be whoever I wanted to be. On the other hand, she looked like she had everything, but really she had nothing." She looked thoughtfully at Pamela. "I think I reminded her, and even Stewart, about what they didn't have. He wanted to be part of it and accepted that there might be a different way — a better way. But she couldn't handle the realisation that her world was not the real thing. She had to convince herself by putting me down."

"Wow. What have you been reading?" Pamela asked with a cautious smile.

"Actually, I haven't had time to read these last couple of days. I read all of this from real life — by studying everything that's been going on around me. Anyway, Silvio is waiting for you. I'll come in another time. I think I'm exhausted."

"Okay," Pamela said, and gave her a hug. "I'm so glad to have you back in my life." Tess saw tears well up in Pamela's eyes. "Maybe *we* could become yoga buddies? I mean, it would be easy enough going before work in the morning. We could walk together. And we'll rethink your library idea, okay? We're a team! And no more pact," Pamela added, smiling at Tess before she dashed back to Silvio.

***

Tess wandered aimlessly. She didn't know why she felt such a sense of overwhelming anxiety. Surely she should be feeling relieved. It was because it was suddenly all so real. He had been almost a figment of her imagination for so long, but now everything she'd imagined could possibly come true. *What if things don't work out?* she worried. *Do I really know him?* All she knew was that he was sexy, kind, intelligent, caring and a true friend. *I do know him*, she thought. *And I think he knows me.* And that kiss … Why did she back down when he'd tried to kiss her? *What am I afraid of?*

She headed back home, processing it all. She came to realise that he must be so confused and hurt by her behaviour towards him. He didn't know she suspected he was seeing Pamela. In turn, he'd thought she was interested in Michael again, until all was revealed. *He doesn't know why I treated him the way I did*, she thought as she approached her apartment building. She had to gather her thoughts.

Tess heard a familiar female voice. "Hello, old chap. I thought I might bother you for a cup of tea."

"*Cathy!*" Tess screamed as she looked at her friend. Her smooth made-up alabaster face, was illuminated by the outdoor lights on the wall behind her. Her green eyes shone with mischief, and her silky shoulder-length black hair danced in the slight evening breeze, as though it was joining in on the fun.

"It sure is. How are you, my brilliant friend?"

"I'm very well indeed!" Tess answered. This was, in fact, the truth. "What are you doing here?" she asked, as she noticed a new tattoo of a butterfly on Cathy's bare arm.

"I thought I'd surprise you! I popped home to visit Mum and Dad, and couldn't wait to come see you too. I had to find out what on earth was happening with Queen Desiree, after your letter. And of course, *everything* about Stewart!" Cathy grinned at Tess and grabbed her in a bear hug, before pulling back and taking in Tess' expression. "Tess … are you okay? Was this a bad time? You look a million miles away."

"Oh, I just have a lot to think about. Actually, you've arrived just in time, for a cup of tea … and for me to fill you in on *everything*."

CHAPTER TWENTY-FIVE

They both settled in a cosy spot in the kitchen with a fresh pot of Earl Grey tea and some Italian biscotti.

She filled Cathy in on everything, including the argument she'd heard between Desiree and Keith, and the scene in the front garden, amongst the roses. She saw compassion in Cathy's eyes when Tess described Desiree's misery. And she was baffled about Tess' reaction when it came to Stewart.

"Okay, here's my theory," Cathy finally said, after pondering the matter for some time. "You're freaking out because you've had this image of him as this ideal guy, and now you're worried he might not live up to that, especially if you're in a long-term relationship. Plus, there's Michael." Cathy touched Tess' cheek gently. "Maybe you think he'll turn out like him. Could that be right? You're worried because your marriage failed because the two of you just didn't work well together. It had no excitement or passion. But you know what, Tess? It's not a book, and I'm saying this as a friend. In real life, we're not always going to be amongst the action, or constantly swept away romantically. The romance and the adventure are just parts of the whole book. It's the journey, the anticipation, the not knowing that's exciting. You can't stay there forever, in your imagination. Love is like climbing a mountain and reaching the peak. It's exhilarating and exciting for a while, but then we have to head back down to where we came from. Mountain views will seem dull and uninspiring if we stay there too long."

Tess looked at Cathy. She was making sense.

Cathy continued. "Plus, life doesn't just end like a book. The beauty of it is that the book can go on if you want it to — it can be part of your every day, with more stories, memories, adventure and passion as new chapters. You get to find out what happens *after* you meet the guy. After you fall in love. Otherwise it just ends. But you don't need to say goodbye to all the characters you love."

Tess remembered Helena saying something similar — that the book goes on, and that you have to continuously work at it. She nodded. "I guess you're right. I know that life can't be like that all the time. I really don't know why I'm afraid to take the leap, but I think you may have hit the nail on the head. I know I didn't really match with Michael. With someone else he might be better. They might blend — like paint," she said with a smile.

"And what about Stewart?" Cathy asked. "Do you blend like paint with him?" She had a twinkle in her eye.

Tess laughed. "Quite possibly. I just need to get over whatever is holding me back with him. Over the past few days I've found out so much more about him, and I've realised I really do love him. I love him, Cathy. I think I always have."

"Well, that's a great start," her friend said with a smile. "And tell me, did you ever feel the same with Michael?"

Tess thought about it. She hadn't ever felt how she did with Stewart. Her heart melted every time he looked at her, every time she felt like he was reading her mind — her heart. "You know what, Cathy? I can't say I've ever felt the way I do about Stewart. When I think of him, and when I'm with him, I feel excited, but also content. And I know what you mean. You need the peace, the contentment and tranquillity, the comfortable silences as well as the passion and adventure, otherwise you wouldn't enjoy those pinnacle moments — those mountain views. *Oh my God!* What am I doing? I have to tell him how I feel!" she cried, placing her teacup onto the saucer as her hands trembled with anticipation. "He really does understand me," she said as she remembered how fascinated he was with everything in her apartment. "Oh no!" she gasped. "The bell! I didn't hear it when we came in. It was loose the other day. It must have fallen or ..." She ran to the front door. The bell was gone.

"It's gone," Tess said sadly. "Someone took my little brass bell."

"It's okay, Tess. People don't just take other people's *bells*," Cathy said with a gentle smile.

"But where is it?" she cried. "I know it's silly, but I felt comforted by it when I came home. I felt a warmth in my heart every time it jingled. I can't really explain it … I should have taken it off the door, kept it somewhere safe until I could fix it."

"You know what, Tess?"

"What?" she asked as she sat back down next to Cathy.

"You might want to get a cat."

Tess smiled at her suggestion. Although she felt like she'd lost a small piece of her heart, she had to let it go. *They're just objects,* she told herself. *Stewart is back in your life. You lost something to make way for something new.*

As they walked back to the kitchen, Cathy suddenly appeared serious. "You know the part when you said that Michael might be better with someone else, and that you'd be okay with that?"

"Yes?" Tess replied.

"Well, he's moving on," she continued.

"I know," Tess said.

"With *me* … He's moving on with *me*. I'm the new 'someone' Tess."

"*What?* You and Michael? When? How? I mean, how did this happen?"

"He had a business trip in London recently, and he might be transferring there with his company. We're waiting to hear, but it all means he might be moving to London. We've kept in touch this whole time. You don't mind do you, Tess? I've always imagined there was no hope of the two of you ever reuniting."

Tess smiled at her friend supportively. "I'm perfectly fine with it all. I'm just surprised. I've never pictured you together, but I can see it, when I really think about it. I'm sure you won't hesitate to put him in his place if he mistreats or ignores you. I did find it strange that he sent me all these flowers," Tess said, as they both looked around the lounge room, which was sprinkled with pink in all corners. "I had to borrow vases from my neighbours, and buy some as well. Next time, tell him to send vases," she said with a smile.

"I'll remember that," Cathy said. "I did have a go at him for how he treated you during your marriage. I made sure that he realised that it won't do — no woman would put up with that. I think he's changed, though. I honestly think that our differences can, in fact, *blend* nicely together to create the right combination — a match."

"So, did you have anything do with all these pink roses?"

"I may have emphasised what a selfish and inconsiderate thing he did. I think he always felt bad about it. Better late than never."

"Indeed," Tess responded, taking a sip of tea, as she felt the world around her settle back into its old rhythm.

"You and Michael ... Who would have thought?" she, once again, said with a smile on her face.

***

Tess looked around her apartment. She had to plan her next move — to see him again. She thought about the conversation she'd had with Cathy, who'd just left to visit her mum a few suburbs away. Armed with confidence for the future, she mused at all her treasures. She thought about how she'd been living her life thus far. Her heart felt like something needed to change, but she'd been so very fearful — resisting it at every possibility. Why was she scared of being in a stale relationship again when she herself had created a world without much adventure and passion, and too much tranquillity?

She looked around at her furniture and realised *she* was the one that didn't belong with *them* — that *she* didn't match their ethos. They were lived in; they took chances. The people around them were able to restore them with new life.

She hadn't really been living — not the way she wanted to, wholeheartedly, and without trepidation.

She wanted wild horses, yet she was living like a mouse — the same way Michael deprived himself of the things he wanted so much, the same way she loved romance but made a pact to forgo it. It was against what she'd learned. She was depriving herself of the roses, of the sprinkles. She didn't experience life. All the old had already had lives of their own. The messiness of life had left its mark on the objects she found beauty in — they lived and shined and bruised and hurt. They had natural beauty. *A life not truly lived,* she thought, *is like a book not read. It is hurt and fear not healed and acknowledged. We can't hide that pain. It's passion not set free, it's love not realised — not allowed to be felt. A life not lived is a disservice to itself. It doesn't allow itself to shine. Like furniture not being used, its purpose is not realised, like a coat that has not been worn. A person's purpose is to live — to love, to feel, to hurt, and to persevere.*

A knock at the door startled her. *Who could it be?* she wondered. She remembered the bell had gone, and felt a deep sadness. She placed her hand on the glass door knob, and remembered the night he was at her door — how nervous she had been. She opened it. There was silence, except for the murmuring of the kids playing in the apartment a few doors down from her. There was no one there. Her eyes then fell to an envelope she'd nearly stepped on. Her heart rate increased at the sight of it. She picked it up and opened it, and began to read the letter inside.

Dear Tess,

I know how much you like to receive letters, so I thought I'd write to you. These last few weeks have been moments of pure bliss, anticipation and contentment. Seeing your beautiful smile again brought back so many memories, and it brought back hope. I was feeling lost for a while, and seeing you again made me realise that some things were always meant to be. Yes, it does seem clichéd, but I honestly feel that whenever

I look into your eyes, I'm where I should be. This letter will be a short one — as I'm sure that you'll be able to read my feelings the moment my eyes meet yours again. Tess, you are the happiness in my life, and the depth that I have longed for. You are my wild horses, my sunsets, my unusually-coloured sprinkles (yes, I remember the story involving your cat, Winston). You, Tess, are my surging waves, my storm, but you're also my peace, and, to quote Shakespeare, "You are the moon".

With love,

Stewart.

Tess placed the letter on the side table in the hallway. With trembling hands she took out the other piece of paper. It was an *appraisal* — for the *brass bell!* Her eyes scanned the certificate, which proved its authenticity as a genuine antique from the 20s — *the jazz era.* It had belonged to a pub that was famous at the time in none other than Lorikeet Creek! The bistro belonged to a Mr Huxley. It was her great grandfather's pub. A photocopy of a newspaper clipping was also in the envelope, announcing the opening of the venue, and there was a photo of her great grandfather, standing proudly in front of it with the brass bell hanging on the door. Tess felt tears welling up in her eyes. It was such an honour to have this information — to be reading about such a precious moment. Her mother had told her that her great grandfather owned a pub, but she didn't know that it was that popular. It wasn't just *popular* — it was *the* place to be seen. Women adorned in flapper dresses and men in suits posed with her great grandfather next to the pub's front counter in another photo.

Suddenly she heard a familiar and comforting jingle. Stewart was peering through the half-closed door, holding the bell in his hand.

"Missing something?" he asked as he rang the bell.

"Stewart!" she managed, unable to stifle the tears now streaming down her face. "Mum told me all about the pub years ago, but I never knew that was where the bell came from! No wonder I was so attached to it. It's not just a bell after all."

"You're right," Stewart said. "It's not just an object, and you somehow always knew that. Just by looking at the translucency of your tears, I see through you, and you know what I see? What I've always seen? A sentient heart. Tess, I know you, I always have … You have depth, and find meaning in everything, in everyone."

Her skin shivered uncontrollably as she felt his hand on hers.

"How did you do all this so quickly?"

"It wasn't that difficult, especially when I knew I was doing it for you, someone I love," he said as his eyes met hers. "I love you Tess, and there's nothing *anyone* can do about it. They can't keep us apart no matter how hard they try."

His lips felt like warm toffee melting. Her face felt warm as he stroked it with his smooth hand, which then traced the nape of her neck. He ran his fingers through her hair. Both hands then worked their way to her waist, and as he wrapped his arms around her, his lips met hers again. Tess felt like she would faint at the intensity of the kiss.

He was now looking at her, a smile slowly forming on his handsome face. He stroked her lips with his thumb. "Was that okay?"

"It was definitely better than okay," she said, unable to look away from him.

"Great. You'll be receiving a lot more of those," he said, and leaned in again.

After their lips parted, they looked at each other for a while, enjoying the moment.

He finally spoke. "By the way, you'll never guess where I got the appraisal done. Do you know that antique shop near the salon? Well, the owner does appraisals on the side. He's fully qualified."

"You're kidding me," she said. "So all this time I've been meaning to appraise the bell and other things in here, and you just waltz into my life and then waltz over to the shop near my work, and …"

"Exactly. Mind you, I had to do a lot of research on the actual pub at the uni library. You see the initials on it, SP? It was initially called Sam's Pub. Your granddad changed it to Sam's Bar and Bistro, but he kept the original bell with the original initials."

"And we found it in one of the craft scrapyards in the area," Tess added. "It wasn't even in the cottage, but somehow it made its way back to us."

"Things that are meant to be together, always find their way back to each other, I guess," he said, stroking her face.

"This is so exciting! I must say, I'm really impressed with your dedication to the bell. And what's also so amazing is that it's not *just* the bell you had appraised."

"What do you mean, not *just* the bell?"

"Well, it's definitely not *just* a bell now," Tess explained. "It's part of who my great granddad was. His dreams, his hopes, his joy, his hard work — they're all in that bell. Now that I think of it, my family actually had a lot of influence and a huge presence in the town. Who knew? And I thought we didn't belong there all this time. This bell symbolises our place. Stewart, you restored the bell, just like my parents restored the cottage, and by doing that … Well, I guess you restored my heart." Tears streamed down her cheeks as all the years of hurt were set free, evaporating into the air.

He stroked her arm reassuringly. "It was never *just* a brass bell, and you always knew it. It's just like I said — you sense these things, you give meaning to them and give them the attention they deserve. I know that these things bring joy to you and I don't want you to ever be deprived of that, Tess."

Tess leaned forward. She placed her hands around his neck and pulled him closer. She kissed him passionately.

"Wow!' What was that for?" he asked, breathing heavily as she released her hands from the nape of his neck.

"For being who you are."

He looked at her and smiled. "Thank you too, for the very same thing."

They gazed into each other's eyes for a moment, before Tess had a sudden thought — the remainders of her anxiety. "Stewart," she began. "I just want to know something. Should I be jealous? Will there be a problem with all the girls lining up to get their coffee fix from the talented and sexy barista, who I finally had the pleasure of meeting, even though I had met him before?" she asked with a serious look.

"That may be a problem. There are also benefits, though."

"Oh, what benefits would those be?" she asked, unable to stifle a smile.

"You get to have the best coffee in town," he said, holding her close with his strong arms wrapped around her.

***

Tess awoke early the next morning. She couldn't sleep. Her new positive energy had kept her awake for most of the night, but to her surprise, she was more energetic than ever on that gloriously warm Friday morning.

She suddenly felt like cutting hair, colouring it, adding highlights, washing and rinsing, polishing the mirrors — the works. She even felt like treating herself to a cup of coffee. Her new barista boyfriend wouldn't be at work until later, so she'd make one herself at home with fresh coffee beans she felt like grinding. *Maybe I should make a cake*, she thought. She always wanted to learn how to use a pastry bag. *Or maybe I should join the gym?* She felt like doing it all. "Boyfriend." She liked the sound of it, and the way it instantaneously conjured up an image of Stewart in her mind.

Thoughts of the previous night ignited passion in her heart. Stewart had left late, after they'd discussed literature courses and listened to her old records with her lying against his chest, wrapped in his arms. Cathy had come back, and was surprised to find Stewart there. They'd ended up talking about school, Michael, and other things, and had agreed to have a reunion before both she and Michael flew to London together. Michael had just found out he'd gotten the job, so Cathy would be taking him back with her. They had found love and their story was just beginning.

Later that morning, Tess opened the door to the salon, ready to start a new day. She breathed in the atmosphere of her second home, and turned on the air conditioner to cool the small space on another hot summer's day. She put some 80s pop on the stereo. *Spandau Ballet will do for now*, she thought. She smiled as she heard the lyrics to one of her favourite tracks, *True*. She didn't need to sing. Her heart was singing already.

Pamela waltzed in, singing along to the lyrics. Tess laughed, and they both performed melodramatically to each other. "Spandau Ballet ... Good choice!" Pamela exclaimed, "especially since we both seem to have joined the romantics."

"Oh!" cried Tess. "That should be next!" She put on *Talking in Your Sleep*, and they sang and danced.

Tess looked at her friend and smiled. "I'm so glad to be back!"

"What? You've only been gone for a few days."

"Yes, but I felt like I'd left, like I was miles away from this place ... from you. I'm glad to be back. This is my second home, and you're ... Well, you're my family," she said, suddenly teary and emotional.

Pamela tried to control her own tears as she ran over to Tess and gave her a big hug. The track *Freeze Frame* by The J. Geils Band came on, and they both laughed and danced like they were on the most 80s of dance floors.

Tess heard a female voice coming from the entrance to the salon. "Umm ... I'm sorry to interrupt." It was Desiree. Tess thought she looked nervous, embarrassed to approach them.

Pamela and Tess looked at each other. Pamela managed a half-smile. "No … you're not interrupting at all," she told Desiree. "You have an appointment with me. You're my first for the day."

At that moment, Mrs Sanders walked in, looking flustered. "Pamela! Do you mind, dear, if you fit me in for a style? I have my sister visiting and she's bringing a group of women we knew from way back, and my hair's a mess. Is it any trouble?"

Tess looked at Pamela. "I don't have any appointments until later."

"Do you mind doing Desiree's hair?" Pamela asked.

"I don't mind," Desiree said without hesitation. "I mean, if it's alright with you?" she asked Tess.

Tess paused. She looked into Desiree's eyes. "I don't mind either," she found herself saying. "I'd be happy to."

After discussing what she wanted done with her hair, Desiree then asked, "So, you learned how to be a hairdresser from Mel — Cathy's mum?"

"Yeah, I worked there after school. I knew then that's what I wanted to do. I realised I had a knack for it."

"And your parents didn't mind that you didn't go to uni? I remember you got really good grades. Actually, of course they didn't mind. They were nothing like my parents. I mean, they were different, in a good way."

Tess smiled. "Yes, they are."

"It must have been great to know that you were good at something, and that you were encouraged to do whatever you wanted in life."

"It *was* liberating," Tess agreed.

"What about school?"

"What about it?" Tess asked with curiosity.

"Did you ever enjoy school?"

"Um … I don't know. It was challenging," Tess replied, meeting Desiree's eyes in the mirror.

"I hated it," she said, sighing heavily. Her face appeared less severe somehow — lighter. It was as though she was relieved that everything had finally come to a head; that her deceit and trickery had been caught out, and she was somehow freed from the pretences she had been so desperately clinging to. "It wasn't always bad for you though, was it? You had friends that understood you … real friends."

"Yes, that part was great, but I always felt … I don't know … small, I guess … like I didn't ever fit in with the rest of the girls, like the ones in your group," Tess said, treading carefully but wanting her to understand her meaning.

Desiree looked down at her lap. "Well, you didn't miss out on much, if it's any consolation. All we did was giggle at every idiot thing the boys said. Maybe I should have joined your group. I might have had a career by now."

"Well, I hear you're doing great with Millie's wedding arrangements. She told me that you've been really helpful," Tess offered.

Desiree's eyes instantly lit up. "Really? She told you that?"

"Why don't you think about starting a career in the wedding industry? You seem to have a knack for it."

"I couldn't possibly. I mean … I'm no expert. I just have some ideas."

"That's how most great things start — with an idea. My dad always said not to let anyone dim the light inside you, and that we each have our own compass in life to guide us. If you truly love doing it …"

"Do you think it would be a good move?"

"Why not?" she said. "Just give me a minute — I'll go and mix the colour for you."

"Um, Tess. Before you go. I just wondered, why did you leave Michael? I'm curious. It's not as if he's a mean guy or anything."

"No, he isn't. I just felt like we couldn't give each other the life we wanted." She could see that Desiree was trying to process her words. "Though, I think you need to know what you want out of life first — before you can make any informed decisions. Your partner needs to know who you really are too. He'll see it in your eyes once you know, I suppose," she added, before heading to the back of the salon to mix the colour.

Two hours later, Tess guided Desiree to the salon door. Desiree was beaming after seeing her freshly coloured hair — golden highlights blended nicely with soft caramel brown.

"You know, I don't think you would have felt left out among the kids I hung out with," Desiree said.

Tess gave her a puzzled look.

"Stewart — he was always your friend."

Tess found herself smiling warmly at her.

"And one more thing," Desiree said. "I should have said this a while ago, because I kept thinking it."

"What is that?" Tess asked.

"Your mum — she's really talented. You must be really proud of her," she said with her own proud smile, before walking out into the sun-drenched morning. "Bye Pamela," she called out as she left.

"Bye Desiree," Pamela called from the basins.

"Bye Desiree," Tess said softly. She looked at Desiree's back as she walked down the street. She seemed more confident than she had been when she'd entered the salon just two hours ago. Tess' heart began to beat quickly. She had an idea.

A few hours later, Tess walked with a spring in her step, feeling the sun burning the footpath under the thin soles of her sandals. She had just visited Millie, and she had suggested she officially hire Desiree as a wedding planner. Millie was taken by the idea, as she wanted the whole wedding to be steered by someone other than her or Hugh. She made her way to her apartment building enjoying the feeling of hot air on her skin. Summer was definitely casting its intense heat on the quaint street again. Tess felt like her heart was on fire every time she thought of him.

She crossed the road and walked to her apartment building. She would see Stewart later that evening, after he finished his shift, where they would have a late dinner with Pamela and Silvio.

As she walked through the landscaped front garden, she admired the orchids draping from the windowsills. She entered the rich, grey-walled foyer, and sped up the stairs. She had to shower and get ready before she made herself a fresh pot of tea. She had just purchased the tangerine tea from the deli. She smiled at what Mr Papas had told her.

"You can't hide it from me, Tess," he'd said.

"What's that, Mr Papas?" she'd asked.

"That your heart is not only smiling — it's singing. So, who's the lucky guy?"

Tess smiled. "Oh, you know! I'm actually reading *Pride and Prejudice* again. It's such a romantic novel. You know the leading man, Mr Darcy? I'm sure you heard of him. He's all that and more — handsome, intelligent."

"I'll find out soon enough!" he laughed. "We all know each other's business in this street!"

She took her key out of her bag and unlocked the door. The brass bell jingled. A warm feeling enveloped her as she listened to the friendly greeting. Tess was truly home!

EPILOGUE

"Okay," Helena began. "So, Tess, remember when I told you and Pamela that your pact would be a thing of the past in a few months, that we'd be sitting here and you would both have men in your lives? Well, here we are after two months, and you have two gorgeous men in your lives!"

"Yes, we know, we know," Pamela laughed. "It was a silly pact. We've already admitted to that. You really can't predict what will happen in life. That pact was like putting a lid on something important ..."

"Or like telling a plant not to grow, to shun light and air — to not thrive," Tess said, feeling proud of her analogy, until she looked at Helena, Pamela, Millie and Penny. They were all trying to control their laughter.

"Sorry Tess. One thing's for sure, we can always count on your analogies, symbolisms, metaphors ..."

"Okay, sorry, but I can't help myself!" Tess exclaimed. "My parents had a fondness for making up their own proverbs and quotes, or tweaking ones they already knew, and I do the same!" She took a sip of her martini. She felt mellow as she listened to the music playing over the speakers. Peggy Lee's sultry voice lulled the air as they sipped their drinks. One of the modern jazz bands doing so well in many of the more contemporary venues around the city would headline there that night.

Tess loved being at Vinnie's on their night out. She also couldn't wait to see Stewart later that evening.

"Okay ladies," Millie said. "Part of the reason I planned this Friday night soirée is to discuss dresses."

"Dresses?" Tess asked, her excitement growing.

"Yes — the bridesmaids' dresses all of you will get to wear, since you all agreed to be my bridesmaids."

"Okay," Tess said, jovially as she looked at Penny. She was sure Penny had similar ideas in mind. She then noticed

Pamela and Helena looking at each other. They seemed to have their own ideas.

"We'll have to come to a consensus on the style of the dress. Once we all agree, Desiree will get them ordered for us. She should be here any second …"

Right on cue, Desiree strode towards them with confidence, gracefully weaving between the many cosy round tables. "Hello girls. Thanks for inviting me," she said. "What a great venue to discuss dresses! Okay, so what are you all drinking? I'm working, so just one for me, but I'll buy a round of whatever you like," she said, beaming with pride. "I'm just so happy I have such a fun job to keep busy with, for such a wonderful person." She smiled at Millie, who returned the look warmly.

"So, did you enrol in that small business course?" Tess asked her.

"I sure did," she replied, tying her hair in a ponytail, ready for business. "Now, about the dresses. You need something that represents who you all are — who you are to each other and to the bride. I think you all have something unique about you — so we need to work with someone who is so talented they can learn about you and create the dress that suits you perfectly. So I was thinking," she said, turning to face Tess, "why don't we hire your mother?"

"My mother?" Tess asked, not sure if she'd heard correctly.

"That's a great idea!" Penny exclaimed.

"What do you think, Tess?" Desiree asked, looking at her inquiringly.

Tess couldn't find the words. *Desiree* was telling her they should hire her mother to make the dresses for Millie's wedding? How did they even get here? She suddenly felt tipsy from the music, the martinis, and the compassion that she was seeing in Desiree's beautiful blue eyes. *She really is pretty,* Tess found herself thinking. She'd never looked at her that way before. Her compassion seemed to bring out her natural beauty. *How sweet is life right now?* She felt a tear stream down her face. Desiree's family had looked down at them for so many years, and now …

"Tess, is something wrong?" Desiree asked, concerned.

Tess wiped the tear away and smiled. "No, not at all. I think it's a wonderful idea!"

"Fantastic!" Desiree cried. "I was thinking, we should all go to Lorikeet Creek and visit. We can have a pre-wedding party there. It will be so much fun!" She looked simply jubilant.

Tess couldn't believe how excited Desiree was. It was almost like she'd finally found the friends she'd always wanted to have — or, perhaps, even the family she'd always wanted to be part of.

"We can all head up, and everyone can bring their partners too!" Desiree announced happily. "Just think of it. Tess' parents won't mind — they were always having big parties for their arty friends when we were growing up. We could hear the music blaring from our houses."

Tess laughed as she wiped the tear away. She put her hand on Desiree's shoulder and gave her an appreciative smile. "I think it's a great idea," she told her, leaning over to hug her.

"Oh!" Desiree said, looking embarrassed. "Thanks. I'm glad you like the idea." Desiree smiled and turned towards Millie, who was also smiling at the idea.

Desiree went into business mode, like the affection was too much for her. "Millie, it's your call," she said. "We'll only do it if it's what you really want."

"Are you kidding?" Millie replied. "Of course I want Tess' mum to make the dresses. She's so talented. It's a really great idea, Desiree. You're really coming through for me with the whole wedding. It's becoming quite fun!"

Desiree tossed her hair awkwardly, and brushed the compliment aside. "Oh, it's nothing," she began to say, before correcting herself. "Actually, that's not right at all. It's rather impressive — what I've got planned. I'm really loving organising it. I'm going to make sure you have the best wedding ever — on a budget, of course."

Pamela chimed in. "Speaking of budgets, you won't have to worry about the hair at all — we've got it covered!" Pamela laughed and looked over at Tess, who smiled and nodded in agreement.

"And make-up," Millie added. "I've got that covered — although we do need an expert make-up stylist."

"Don't forget the flowers," Helena said.

Tess instantly thought of Michael. He and Cathy were doing great together in London. She was very happy for them.

The band began to play. Smooth, modern jazz melodies filled the room. They all sat back in their seats to enjoy the mood. Tess looked around the table. Pamela gave her a warm smile. Penny, sitting next to her, hugged her, and said, "This is great. I'm so glad I had a chance to join you all."

Helena shook her hair rather seductively as she caught someone's attention. Tess looked over and saw Jacob, Keith's colleague. Tess awkwardly waved to him. Desiree did the same. "He's such a flirt," Helena said.

Tess gave Helena a questioning look. "What was that?" she shouted over the music.

"He came to buy some flowers the other day, and yeah, so we flirted a bit. Why should I let Carter get all the attention?" she said with a laugh. "Actually, Carter has been really romantic lately. He found a great holiday house by the beach for us to buy, right in our price range. We'll be going there every chance we get. Just the two of us ... away from it all."

"Oh, that sounds great!" Desiree commented, hearing the conversation. "It'll be a while before Keith and I are able to buy any property," she said earnestly. "But things couldn't be better between us. He's even joined the gym and he's looking so suave lately. He said I've inspired him in many ways, and he can't stop telling all his work colleagues about my career plans."

The music became louder, and a female singer walked onto the small stage.

The women fell quiet, and allowed themselves to surrender to the music.

***

Later that evening, the little brass bell jingled. *Stewart's home*, Tess thought with warmth in her heart. She walked over to him as he entered the lounge room. "*Stewart!* You shouldn't have bought all this! *Tiramisu*, and what else have you got for us?" She looked inside the white paper bag.

"I thought you might be in the mood for some *pana cotta* as well. I'm sure the desserts at Vinnie's aren't that good," he said with a smile, wrapping his arms around her waist. "That's what Silvio keeps telling Pamela. I saw her at the restaurant a few minutes ago. You girls obviously had a great night."

"We actually did, and Desiree was there too. Who knew that would ever happen?"

"Thanks to my compassionate girlfriend. You've set us all in the right direction."

"I don't know. You may have helped me a bit! You've introduced me to feelings I've only ever read about."

"Well, those feelings were always there, waiting to be set free by someone." He gently pulled her closer and began to kiss her. "How about we try some of this?" he asked, as he took one of the plastic spoons in his hand and dug into the *tiramisu*. "How does this taste?" he asked seductively.

"Mmm, it's delectable."

"Speaking of delectable," he said, pulling her closer. He stroked her hair, and began to kiss her with urgency.

His mobile chimed.

"Who could that be?" she asked.

"Oh, it's my mother. She said tomorrow around 2 o'clock is okay for lunch. You have no clients then, right?"

"That's right. I can't believe she agreed to have lunch … *with me … again.*"

"What was that? I can't believe what I'm hearing. *With you?* I think *she* should be asking that question, considering how conceited she and my dad were around you and your family. The truth was, though, she secretly liked all of you. She blames Desiree's mother for keeping her from meeting more "interesting people", as she called your family. I think living in the city has definitely opened her eyes."

"It's great that she's seeing your dad again."

"Well, they're taking it slow. I think they're enjoying dating and feeling young again, like how it was before the business began to get in the way all those years ago. Plus one of their properties has really appreciated and they've come to realise they're a lot better off than a lot of people. Oh, and for the record — she said that she can't wait to see you again. She loves hearing about all your finds, and your granddad's bistro, and your mother's studio. She's starting to really appreciate art — not just pretend to, like her friends. And she wants to know what colour your hair is. 'I'd love to have lunch with that sweet girl. She's the best girlfriend you've ever had', was how she put it. She can't wait to discuss antiques and look around some of the boutiques with you."

Tess smiled. "You can tell her the colour in my hair is rose-golden brown, but I'm thinking of changing it."

"It doesn't matter what colour your hair is, my pretty Tess. You have the ability to add colour to the dullest setting."

She smiled and kissed him, tasting the *tiramisu* on his lips. "By the way — what book are you up to now? I'll read the same one and we can have a discussion about it," she suggested, her heart beating with excitement at the thought of it. Ever since he'd started his English literature studies, Tess was having the time of her life discussing books with him. Stewart had decided he would love to teach English at school or uni one day, and was happy about his career prospects. "I'm re-reading *A Street Car Named Desire*, since you're doing that next," she said. "But tonight I think I'm in the mood for Fitzgerald. That's also in your course." Tess suddenly frowned.

"What is it?"

"I just realised I have to wake up early tomorrow. I have an early appointment at the salon."

"Oh, that's all right. You've got the best barista in town. I've got the strongest and most intense coffee beans. I think they should do the trick."

"I need to be careful though. I can't have too much of a good thing — too much intensity, strength and depth." She caressed his toned arms and looked into his eyes.

"You can have too much coffee, or even too much dessert. But I think it would be okay if we have quite a bit of this," he said as his full, soft lips met hers.

"Well, now that you've officially moved in, I think we may be able to accommodate it," she said between kisses, "but I must say, we do need more shelves for all your books, and your records."

"I think I might be able to work something out. Maybe another bookshelf in the bedroom?"

"Why in the bedroom?" Tess asked.

"I figured we'll be spending a lot of time in there, my dear lady … with all your unbridled passion."

Tess messed his hair playfully before he pulled her in his arms, kissing her hair as he hugged her, moving her close to his heart.

**

Moments later, Tess heard the kettle whistling. Stewart was finishing an assignment about plot and writing techniques. She thought it was cosy having him in the next room, knowing that he was near her, but also relishing the time she had on her own to read.

After handing him his cup of tea and receiving some kisses in exchange, Tess walked back to her chesterfield armchair, and sunk back into it. The fragrance of the tea made her heart feel warm. She looked around the room, at all the beautiful things. Her eyes landed on her mother's abstract painting. She found herself focusing all her attention on it — admiring the true beauty of its colour.

Tess froze. She couldn't believe she hadn't noticed it before. *Could it be? Surely not!* She walked over to the painting. Why was she just seeing this now? Her eyes had noticed it when her mind and heart were free, ready to see things as they were. She saw it clearly now — the hidden, shaded image of a horse. It wasn't running, but was standing still, contently resting amongst the chaos of the many untamed and wild strokes of robust colour. The image was faint, and intentionally hidden.

She felt a serene calmness. Her mother saw the truth. Stewart had alluded to it as well when they had returned to the school oval. Her mother had painted it on the canvas that hot summer's day as Tess had watched her work — as she'd sat on a bench that had been painted, restored and brought back to life. It was that afternoon her mother had painted the image of the horse — a horse tired of running. Tess had told her mother of the image she kept seeing in her mind — of the wild horses that made her yearn for something more. Her mother had gazed over in her direction. She hadn't responded to her question or her comment. She had seen it in her eyes when Tess herself hadn't. Remembering how she worked with a new lease of energy, Tess now knew she'd been inspired by what she had seen. Tess saw it too now, as she looked at the image of the shaded horse blending in with the wild, colourful waves of paint around it. As she looked at the hidden image, which was suddenly very clear, she felt like the canvas had turned into a mirror, one that reflected what her eyes revealed, what they hadn't wanted to reveal until now. She saw her own true colours.

ACKNOWLEDGEMENTS

Writing *True Colours* was like a taking a stroll in a quirky, cosy street; the type I used to frequently visit as a young adult in the trendy streets of Sydney's unique and interesting suburbs. I still tend to wander through them occasionally and have a cup of coffee, or buy a book from one of the many bookstores. While writing this novel, I wanted to capture the essence of such streets; where locals know each other, and where there is a feeling of magic in the air.

Thanks, once again, to my family for being so supportive while writing *True Colours*. I greatly appreciate my husband's support and his help in all things IT, and I am thankful for my children's encouragement and interest.

I'd like to send out a special thanks to my editor Nikki Savvides of The Expert Editor, for all her suggestions.

I'd also like to thank my friends and extended family for their continuous support and encouragement. Thanks to my parents for their wisdom and advice over the years, and also to my mum for making all those beautiful dresses when I was young, and for all the amazing cakes we baked together in the kitchen.

Thanks also to you, the reader, for taking the time to read this book. I hope it was an enjoyable reading experience and that the story touched your heart in some way. I would sincerely appreciate it if you would share your thoughts in a review. Reviews can inspire an author immensely and they mean everything to an author.

Thanks, once again, for reading this book. You can find out more about me and my writing on my website: **antheasyrokou.com** where you can follow me on social media and also subscribe to my newsletter.

Also by

ANTHEA SYROKOU

Eventually Julie (Julie & Friends, Book 1)

Julie has had enough! At 27, she feels overwhelmed with the "shoulds" her family pile on her, and an office job that she detests. It doesn't help that she's carrying her "baggage of unfinished business" with her, weighing her down even more ... making it impossible to see clearly and dig herself out of the rut her life has become.

When she finally decides to take action, a chance encounter presents her with an opportunity to deal with her messy past, so she sets off to Paris to find the answers that can set her free, and live a life full of meaning and passion. Julie loses herself in the sights and smells, and in the beauty of travelling in one of the most romantic cities in the world. She opens her heart to love, and begins to be true to herself ... until she discovers a secret that sets her right back to where she began; uncertain about life — about love!

When Julie arrives back home to Sydney, she needs to make some serious decisions, or risk missing out on true love ... and finally having the career she always wanted.

Join Julie and her delightful and witty friends on a journey of fun, adventure, and passion. Set in and around Sydney, as well as London and Paris, Eventually Julie is a "finding yourself" romance that deals with being stuck in a rut and eventually finding the right ingredients to live a life that is true.

The Greek Tapestry (Julie & Friends, Book 2)

Maria and her older sister, Nicki, were childhood friends with Dimity, the girl who lived across the street. Growing up in Sydney, they even came first in an art project with a tapestry they made by hand, which depicted island life in Greece. They believed nothing would separate them - but would sadly find that nothing was a tall order. When Nicki and Maria's parents uproot them to move to Greece, leaving Dimity behind, they discover that even the strongest friendships can disintegrate.

Now, almost twenty years later, each of them has their own life. Dimity lives in a designer house with her sexy husband, an industrial designer named Malcolm, and their two daughters. She loves Malcolm, but is tired of playing the accommodating wife and daughter-in-law. In need of change and inspiration, she sets off to Greece.

Maria has both the career and the family, but still feels the need to prove herself to her mother. After her mother hides invitations to her cousin's wedding in Greece from her, Maria is spurred into action. She is sick of her mother's interference and heads to Greece in search of answers.

Nicki also has a successful career, but she and her husband, Marco, are unable to have what they really want - a child. Needing a change in life, she follows her sister to Greece, and stays in a peaceful, historic village outside the town of Ioannina.

As Maria, Nicki, and Dimity each try to untangle their complex lives, will they find their way home and weave their own beautiful reality?

Fasten your seatbelts and get ready to join the fun in magical Greece!

ANTHEA SYROKOU is an author who grew up and resides in Sydney, Australia.

Anthea's love for writing was planted at a young age when she studied Greek mythology. Her love for literature continued well into her teenage years when she enjoyed reading novels by many of the great English writers.

As a young adult, she immersed herself in reading women's contemporary fiction and writing about topics, that many could relate to, in a witty, light-hearted way, which became a passion — one that she takes very seriously.

Anthea has a BA degree, majoring in psychology and industrial relations, and a diploma in counselling. She also studied Greek literature at university and has worked in direct marketing, and insurance and investments.

As well as writing fiction, Anthea also writes articles and posts on everyday issues; often adding her dash of humour.

When she isn't writing or reading, Anthea enjoys spending time with her family, travelling, yoga, and escaping to the vineyards. A quiet house with some jazz playing in the background, surrounded by a few lit scented candles is her idea of relaxation. Anthea lives with her husband and their two sons.

For more information, please visit **antheasyrokou.com**